HOMELAND

What Reviewers Say About
Kristin Keppler & Allisa Bahney's Work

Wasteland

"*Wasteland* is the gritty kind of dystopian novel, with the tenacious, imperfect, and badass kind of heroines that melt me faster than a popsicle at noon in Death Valley. Floods, fires, climate change, pandemics, and nuclear bombs. ...Grab a glass of water before you start reading this dystopian gem because if the description of the barren wastelands doesn't make you want to chug it down, you might need it to splash it on your face to calm yourself. The world building is eerily vivid, the characters are complex and compelling and there is oodles of action. If tales of redemption and enemies to lovers in dangerous times is your jam, well, this series is just what you are looking for."—*Lesbian Review*

Outland

"Breaking out of the gates at a hell for leather pace, *Outland* is an action packed, full throttle sequel to the authors' debut novel, *Wasteland*. ...As *Outland* draws to a dramatic close, the authors leave no doubt that this is just the beginning of the ultimate war between the Resistance and the NAF, and with emotions already running high, book three is sure to begin with a bang!" —*Queer Lit Loft*

By the Authors

Wasteland

Outland

Homeland

HOMELAND

by

Kristin Keppler & Allisa Bahney

2023

HOMELAND
© 2023 By Kristin Keppler & Allisa Bahney. All Rights Reserved.

ISBN 13: 978-1-63679-405-1

This Trade Paperback Original Is Published By
Bold Strokes Books, Inc.
P.O. Box 249
Valley Falls, NY 12185

First Edition: June 2023

Credits
Editor: Barbara Ann Wright
Production Design: Susan Ramundo
Cover Design By Jeanine Henning

Acknowledgments

From both of us:

This series was six years in the making. But it takes more than just the authors to bring stories to life.

We want to thank the hardworking team at Bold Strokes Books. To Sandy, Ruth, Cindy, Susan, and Stacia for always answering our endless questions. Thanks to Jeanine for bringing our vision to life with not one, but three amazing covers. We are in awe of your talent.

To Barbara Ann Wright. Words can't express how much we appreciate your thoughtfulness, guidance, and encouragement. You are more than just our colleague and editor, but also our mentor and we would not be worldbuilders without you.

And saving the most important for last, thank you to every single person who has supported us. Whether you've been there for all six years or you're a new reader who is just now discovering Dani and Kate, we appreciate you more than we can ever express. Your encouragement and support is what keeps us writing. You inspire our creativity. Thank you endlessly.

From Kristin: To Brad. There aren't enough words to tell you how much your support means to me. I love you. And as always, to my sons. You make me want to be better in every way. I love you all the time.

And to Shiela, my Hawaiian Sunshine. You are always the first to read anything I've written. I forever look forward to your reviews, thoughts, comments, and concerns. I will never take your insight and excitement for granted!

From Allisa: To Courtney. Without you I would be so lost in this life. Thank you for always being my confidant, my number one supporter, and my greatest love. Our kids are the best because you're the best.

Dedication

Kristin: For Allisa.
We wouldn't be on this adventure without your
determination. And what an adventure it has been!

Allisa: For Kristin.
You are the heart and soul of this story.
Cheers, my dear friend.

CHAPTER ONE: THE CABIN

KATE

W hat do you think it's doing? It's been hovering in the same spot for a while."

"Not sure. Taking pictures or scanning the area?" I pull the binoculars down and squint at the drone floating high in the distance. "It's too small to be carrying any kind of missiles. Must be out on recon."

Mike smacks the gum he's been chewing all afternoon and continues to peer through the scope of his large rifle. "Think Darby would want it?"

"I think Darby would be ecstatic to get a new toy."

He lowers his gun. I take in his sly, plotting smile. "Your flowery bar of soap," he barters.

"Oh, come on," I retort, irritated. He knows that's my most prized possession.

He arches a brow, daring me to accept his challenge.

"Fine, but if you miss, I get first dibs at your food stash." I know for a fact he has a bag of sweets he refuses to share.

"Deal." We grab each other's forearms and shake on it.

He removes his gloves and blows hot air into his hands before rubbing them together. While he gets ready, I bring the binoculars back to my eyes. The drone moves a bit to the left and then stops. There's definitely something round secured to its underbelly. It has to be a camera.

Mike adjusts the rifle on the bipod and lines up his shot, smacking his gum once again. The drone moves slightly more to the left.

A cold gust of wind makes me shiver. I'll take it if it means it'll aid in him missing, but the sun is getting a little low, and I know we're losing daylight. I'd rather not turn into a block of ice while I wait for him to pull the trigger.

"Are you planning on taking your shot, or are you waiting for us both to freeze to death?" I ask, shifting my body in the few inches of snow.

Mike doesn't answer. Instead, I hear him take a deep breath, hold it, and then a sharp crack echoes through the air. Less than a few seconds later, the drone appears to explode and falls from the sky.

Well, shit.

"Yahoo!" Mike cheers and pumps his fist into the air. I roll my eyes, but inside, I'm thrilled he put it down so efficiently.

"Songbird to Oracle," I say into the radio. "Come in, Oracle."

"Read you loud and clear," Jess says on the other line.

"Downed a bird. Engaging in retrieval and heading back. Over."

"Ten four."

I shove the radio into my shoulder bag and stand, stretching my frozen limbs.

"What a shot," Mike says, grinning while slipping his gloves back on and folding down the bipod.

"Yeah, yeah. Let's just grab the thing and get out of here."

Mike follows me to the truck parked not too far away. I look forward to cranking the heat as high as it will allow. "It was at least three thousand meters."

I laugh at his incredibly ridiculous bragging. "It was not. It was more like a thousand. *Maybe* fifteen hundred. Tops."

Mike opens the passenger door and grins at me from atop the truck cabin. "Either way, I nailed it and expect that bar of soap the second we get back."

I groan. "You're the worst." I start the truck and reach for the heat knob. Once she's purring, I glance at Mike, still giddy beside me, and bump his shoulder. "Good shot."

His smile grows.

It takes us longer than I'd like to find the drone. Mike uses a set of thermal binoculars to keep an eye for any NAF ground pilots who may be in the area. It isn't until the sun begins to set and snow flurries begin to fall that we finally find what we're looking for.

We've seen this kind of drone before. At least, I think we have. Right now, it just looks like an exploded mess. "Well," I say, pulling the scarf higher over my nose and mouth. "You definitely got it."

"It's still salvageable, right?" he asks, staring at what I think is supposed to be the drone's body. Or maybe it's a wing?

I glance around, noting pieces and fragments along a pretty wide radius. "Do you see the camera?"

"I think that's what those little pieces are." Mike points to a splattering of splintered parts.

"We need to get you a less powerful gun. A .50 cal might be a little intense for these recon drones." I scan the area, knowing that we don't have long before someone comes looking for this thing. And I really don't want to be here when that happens. "Come on. Collect what you can, and let's get out of here. We still need to cover our tracks."

He sighs and picks up an empty piece of casing, his mood souring. "Darby's gonna be pissed."

By the time we get back to the cabin, the flurries have picked up just slightly, and the sun has completely set. We head inside and are greeted by Roscoe. "Yes, yes, we're back." I take off my gloves and pat my chest. He jumps up so I can scratch behind his ears. "Sorry you couldn't come this time, boy."

"Finally," Elise says and walks in from the kitchen. "Roscoe's been whining for you all day."

Mike drops the bag with the drone parts and kisses his wife. "Would you rather be lying in snow and losing feeling in every single extremity or listening to a dog whine?"

Elise eyes him suspiciously. "*Every* single extremity?"

"Gross, you guys," I say and pretend to gag.

"Jess, they're back," Elise shouts to the kitchen after a suggestive wink. "You just missed Dani," she tells me regrettably. I unzip my jacket, unable to mask my disappointment. "But she said to tell you that she swears she'll be here tomorrow."

Jess comes in from the kitchen, George and Wyatt directly behind her. "Don't bother unpacking. We have to move again. You know the drill. We downed a drone, we gotta go."

"So much for our cozy little cabin," Mike says. He takes off his winter gear and shoves the bag to the side along with his rifle.

Elise sighs. "Just when I was beginning to like the place."

Dinner follows shortly after. We eat the fish that George caught earlier in the morning. Wyatt does a great job preparing it, but supplies are running low. The snow, thankfully, has stopped falling, but the clouds that cover the moon concern me that more is on the way.

Mike insists on stealing my soap right after we eat so he can take a bath, and after a day in the cold, I can't blame him. A hot bath sounds wonderful, but I can't seem to muster the energy to heat up buckets of water tonight, so I opt for a quick wipe down instead.

Saying good night to the others, I walk the narrow hallway to the last door on the right and place the lantern on the nightstand. I turn on the space heater to get the room a little warm, change into sleep clothes, and collapse into the small bed.

The clicking of a door locking across the hall tells me that Elise and Mike have also turned in for the night. Looking out the small window, I see nothing but darkness. Even the sky is black, with no sign of stars. I like to think Dani is out there doing the same thing, despite the moon being barely visible through the thick clouds. Unfortunately, it seems like more snow is on the way.

With a long sigh, I pull the covers up to my chin. I miss her the most when everything is quiet and still. The whispered conversations. The leaning into one another. Her comfort and warmth.

The light from the lantern flickers and casts shadows on the wall. I watch them dance and wonder if there will ever be a time where I don't worry about Dani when she's not with me.

A four-day supply run has turned into seven, and I hate that I'm not there with her. It's been three months of coming and going, and I'm not sure how much longer my emotions can handle the separation. I'm desperate for something more permanent.

I hope whatever is keeping her out there for another night is worth it.

❖

Sure enough, the next day brings more snow.

It's overcast and windy, the fat flakes swirling and pushing sideways as they fall. If Dani and the others don't get back soon, the weather may strand them somewhere for another night.

I glance away from the chessboard to the radio on the table beside Jess, who lounges on the sofa listening to Dani's music player in one earbud with the other attached to the radio. I can't stop staring at the walkie-talkie, hoping that it'll crackle to life, and we can get some kind of update from Dani.

"Are you just going to sit there and sigh, or are you going to make your move?"

Ignoring the taunt, I focus on the little black and white pieces scattered on the board. Mike groans, exasperated while I take my time deciding how I want to move.

We've been at it all morning, distracting ourselves while we wait for the others to get back. I'm in it for the long haul, stretching out the time to take my turn. This game has gone on for days, much to Mike's annoyance, but it helps keep my mind off the lack of updates from Dani and the others.

I scratch my chin dramatically, as if I'm considering my strategy. Something I know that gets under his skin.

"Kate!" He throws his hands up, and I finally move my piece.

"How are you a sharpshooter? You have the patience of a gnat," I quip.

"'Are you planning on taking your shot, I'm cold,'" he says in a whiney voice, mimicking me from the day before.

Elise inhales deeply and sits up, blinking the sleep from her eyes and looks around. "What's happening?" Roscoe, who has been asleep at her feet, stretches and yawns.

"Enjoy your nap?" I ask while Mike grumbles about where I place my piece.

She yawns through her response. "It wasn't long enough. Are they back?"

Mike shakes his head. "Not yet."

Jess pulls both earbuds out and places them beside her before disconnecting the cord from the top of the walkie.

"Anything?" I ask, hopeful that Dani has at least checked in.

She sighs. "No. Is the snow still coming down?"

"It's coming down thick," Elise tells her, looking back out the window. "I wish they had taken the pickup. It handles better in the snow than those damn buggies."

I exchange a worried glance with Mike. He clears his throat and moves his piece. "It's easier to be disguised in an NAF buggy. They're less likely to cause suspicion down all those blockaded roads. Besides, it's not even lunch. They'll be back before it gets bad." He almost sounds convincing.

"It's still nice when they check in," Elise says, and I agree.

No one bothers to talk for a while. Wyatt and George are in the kitchen preparing the trout for lunch. My stomach rumbles excitedly, not caring that we've had fish for five straight days. The rest of us are spread out by the fire in the main room.

"Anything new from the NAF?" I ask and clear my throat. I always try to sound casual when bringing up my former alliance. Breaking away from the National Armed Forces and leaving my friends and family behind to join the Resistance was the hardest decision I've ever made. I don't regret it, but I do miss some of the people.

Especially Ryan.

Jess shakes her head. "Only that the general is holding position. There are new rumors she wants to take Bismarck."

"I see." I keep my expression and tone stoic, trying to not reveal any underlying emotion when speaking about my mother. Jess is kind enough to always call her the general and not my mom. I'm grateful for it.

Sometimes, when it's quiet and I'm alone, my mind wanders to what my mother must think of me now. I wonder if she's looking for me or if she even cares that I left. A part of me hopes that she misses me, but I wouldn't be surprised if she doesn't. My absence may be a relief to her for a lot of reasons.

I hate that I care so much.

Mike meets my gaze and as if reading my mind, smiles softly and reassuringly. He and I have become close the past few months. His friendship brings me comfort when Dani isn't around. It's something I didn't know I so desperately needed until it was given.

"They're back," Elise says and stands at the same time Roscoe lifts his head.

Mike and I rush to the window like excited children. Jess calls to Wyatt and George that they're back, and she stands; clearly, none of us able to sit still at their return.

Rocking on my heels, I wait for them to pull the buggy to the side of the cabin. It takes an insane amount of willpower not to run outside and greet them. Instead, I watch as they swing their bags over their shoulders and head for the cabin.

A gust of cold air and a swirl of snow whooshes through the door as they enter. Lucas comes first, throwing back his fur-lined hood and shivering. Darby is next, followed closely by Jack, and finally, Dani. My stomach somersaults when she pulls the knit cap from her head and shakes the snow from the bottom of her hair. I stare, eager and relieved to see her. Seven days apart felt like an eternity.

As they crowd around the rugs near the door, they kick the snow from their boots and shake it from their coats. Everyone appears to be physically fine, just exhausted, and it makes me wonder what exactly made them detour and if they were able to rest.

Roscoe barrels forward and jumps on Jack, his tail wagging so fast, it looks like a furry blur. Jack smiles and accepts the dog into his arms, scratching him and holding him close while Roscoe licks his beard. Greeting Roscoe is the only time he smiles since losing Rhiannon.

"Are you all okay?" Elise asks, wrapping Dani in a tight hug.

"A sandstorm like they've never seen before," Lucas says seriously, if not somewhat dramatically. It makes me smile. I missed his sense of humor.

"Issue forty," Darby says.

"Fourteen," Dani and I say at the same time. Her eyes meet mine, and she smiles. Instinctively, I take a step closer. Even though the better part of the room is still between us, my hands are restless, and I'm aching to wrap her in an embrace. I want so badly to bury my face in her dark hair and kiss her jaw and lips. I probably would, too, but we've done our best to not be overly affectionate in front of Jack. His loneliness is so thick that it fills any room he enters.

Darby glares at us both. Lucas claps, pulling my attention back to him. He's proud and beaming at my newfound *Major Maelstrom* interest.

"Either way," Darby mutters, "Lucas is right. I'm over snowstorms."

"Don't be so dramatic," Dani says. "It's just a squall. It'll be over soon." She leans in close to Jess and touches her arm. "Hey, kiddo," she says as she kisses her cheek.

Darby pushes past, and Lucas steps out of the way so she can get closer to the fire. "Whatever it is, it sucks," she says and stretches out her hands to warm them from the flames. "All I want is a hot bath, something warm to eat, and a car that we don't have to push in the snow."

Dani scoffs and removes her scarf and gloves. "You didn't even help us push it. You stayed inside and steered."

"It was stressful. I couldn't see anything," Darby argues and blows hot air into her hands and rubs them together. "Besides, I was the lightest. It only made sense for me to be the one to steer."

"Yeah, steered us right into a ditch," Dani fires back. Lucas laughs, but Dani doesn't seem amused in the slightest.

Darby rolls her eyes and turns her attention back to the fire. "I don't know how to drive."

"Then why did you insist on steering?" Dani asks, exasperated. "And why the hell did I let you drive my Jeep a few months ago?"

Darby continues to complain while George and Wyatt join in the mix, and the entire gang is back together, squeezed into one room, and for the first time in a week, I feel a bit of happiness course through me.

I missed the banter. I missed my new family.

Unable to remain in place any longer, I leave my perch near the window and close the distance between us. Dani watches me approach with a smile. "You're late," I scold her half-heartedly, noticing her red nose and pink cheeks.

"I'm sorry," she says, and initiates contact by reaching out to put her hands on my waist. She pulls me close. "I had to push the car."

Recognizing that she obviously doesn't care who's in the room right now, I take advantage and cradle her cold cheeks, leaning in to kiss her. "Are you okay?"

She nods. "Happy to be back."

I lean in and kiss her again. Her grip on my waist tightens. I can tell she wants to be more intimate, but knowing this isn't the time or place, she pulls back and takes a deep breath.

"What took you all so long?" Mike asks, pulling our attention away from each other. He pats Jack on the shoulder.

Jack releases Roscoe and puts his hand over top of Mike's, then slips out of his coat. "Weather, mostly."

"And we had to run a last-minute errand," Darby says, still by the fire.

I don't miss the annoyed expression that crosses Dani's features. I give her a questioning look, but if she was going to say something, it's interrupted by Mike. "Speaking of errands." He grabs the bag that was tucked away by the door. "Kate and I nabbed a drone."

Jack stares at me and removes his wool hat. His mohawk is gone, replaced with short curls covering his head. I meet his gaze for only a second and look away, unable to handle the grief that's still consuming him and the blame he still projects onto me.

Darby hurries over and snatches the bag eagerly. I think this may be the only thing besides food that could drag her away from the warmth of the fire. Mike crosses his fingers while she places the bag on the ground and unzips it. Everyone is silent and eager to get a look.

"What the hell did you do to it?" she shrieks, and Mike and I both cringe. Jack snorts and shakes his head. He looks at me as if I'm the one who took the fatal shot. Darby stands and holds up a piece of the shattered frame. "What were you trying to do? Vaporize it?"

Mike glances at me, his eyes wide with panic. If he wants help, he's not getting it from me. The consequences of winning the bet. I smile sweetly at him. "Um, shoot it out of the sky?"

Darby shakes the bag at him. "What am I supposed to do with this? There's nothing left."

"I'm sure there are a few pieces in there you can use," he protests weakly.

I listen to them argue, amused. No amount of flower-scented soap is worth getting lectured by an angry tech expert.

Dani pulls out her dirty clothes from the duffel bag on the full-size bed in the middle of the room. I close the door behind me and shiver. I miss the warmth of the main room but wouldn't trade being alone with Dani for all the warmth in the world.

The snow still swirls outside, and I wonder how much accumulation we'll get and if we'll be stuck here a little longer. Now that Dani and the others are back, I wouldn't mind staying, despite knowing we can't.

"How was having your own room for a week?"

"Cold," I answer honestly.

"I'm sorry we were gone so long." She sits on the bed and pulls her boots and socks off, discarding them close to the door with the rest of her dirty clothes that need washing. I take the last bucket of hot water into the small attached bathroom. "We got a lead on some gas that, of course, turned into this whole thing about them needing tech that we didn't have. We had to set up an exchange..." She sighs and appears in the bathroom doorway. "I'm sorry."

I pour the water into the tub and stand back, examining the water level as a blanket of steam rises. "I get it," I tell her honestly.

"Have you beaten Mike in that game of chess, yet?"

I test the water and pull my hand back. It's way too hot, but Dani likes scalding baths. Hopefully, her skin doesn't melt off. "Nope," I say and glance over my shoulder.

She's leaning against the doorway, her arms crossed, and a small smile on her lips. Her wavy brown hair is draped over one shoulder, and her gray eyes sparkle in the light of the lantern. She looks absolutely beautiful.

Dani pulls the lightweight sweatshirt over her head along with the plain T-shirt underneath and tosses the clothes to the growing pile by the door. "You're like a cat toying with a mouse," she says, teasing me about Mike.

I shrug. "I have to get my entertainment somehow."

She chuckles and peels away the rest of her clothes. I do a quick scan of her body, mainly looking for any new injuries, even though the view itself is rather distracting. Seeing that she appears fine, I enjoy the way she struts to the tub, obviously making a show of it. "Now who's the cat and who's the mouse?" I click my tongue at her and play into it.

"I have to get my entertainment somehow." She tests the water with her toe, then sinks her foot in, slowly stepping inside. I grab her a clean towel and what's left of our sorry excuse for a bar of soap after losing my good one to Mike and hand it to her, along with a washcloth.

"Oh, that's...hot." She hisses a bit before easing her body lower and sighing. I wonder how she's able to tolerate the excessive heat. Leaning her head back against the lip of the tub, she closes her eyes and takes several deep breaths. My gaze trails down her neck to the tops of her shoulders and back to her face. She peeks at me with a knowing smirk. "Care to join me?"

I snort. "And wade in your filth? No thanks." She chuckles and closes her eyes again, relaxing. "Any run-ins with the NAF?"

"No." She sounds disappointed. "We saw a few drones, though. Weren't as lucky as you, shooting one down."

Leaning against the sink, I cross my arms and watch her dunk her head under the water, the steam rising from her hair when she resurfaces. "Yeah, well, I don't know how much is left of ours, and it cost us our humble little abode and my good bar of soap." If there's a touch of bitterness in my tone, she doesn't say anything.

She holds up the small, unscented beige rectangle and examines it. "That would explain this. Here I was thinking you were taking luxurious baths without me."

I scoff. "Hardly." I think about asking her to keep an eye out for a new one when she's out there, but I know she isn't scavenging for little luxuries. She's making trade deals and securing necessities and helping towns set up defenses to keep the NAF from completely taking over. "What else did you find out?" I ask instead.

"Nothing really. Just a few new NAF base locations. They've been pulling soldiers this way from all over." She's quiet for a minute, and I know there's more to what she's going to say by the way she clenches her jaw. "Another town was burned down. We couldn't get there in time." Her eyes meet mine, and she holds my gaze long enough for me to understand without explaining the gruesome details. She doesn't need to. The story has been the same with every attack these past few months.

Simon.

There is no pattern to his destruction and no indication of where he'll go next. He's dangerous and reckless and out of control. Sometimes, he leaves taunting notes, and other times, he doesn't even bother showing up, just sends a team on his behalf. He's arrogant and getting worse with each passing day. I know it's killing Dani not to go after him.

"Where?"

"North. Early this morning. Near Bismarck."

I exhale, devastated that he was able to get to another town. "Jess said Bismarck might be a target."

"They're in the area, so she might be right," Dani confesses. She submerges so that only her nose and eyes are above the surface. She stares at me like a crocodile assessing its prey. Her gaze is sharp and angry, but I know the anger isn't directed at me.

"We'll get him," I say.

She closes her eyes and disappears back beneath the water. I sigh and wait for her to resurface. When she does, she takes a deep breath and wipes her face before settling back against the tub. Her hands dance along the surface of the water, creating ripples. Then her shoulders slump, and she frowns, unconvinced.

"Hey." I crouch next to the tub until our faces are level, and she looks at me. "We'll get him," I tell her again. When she tries to look away, I gently turn her head back to me. "We'll get him."

Finally, she nods and leans into my touch. I stroke her cheek with my thumb, trying to ease away her pain. "I hate just running errands. I want to be out there, doing something. Anything but just waiting around."

"How much thought did you give on going to Bismarck to help them prepare instead of coming back?" Knowing with absolute certainty that the idea crossed her mind.

"About two seconds before I remembered Darby would have to come with me." She looks at me very seriously. "I'm not joking. If I had to sit in a car with her for one more day…"

I chuckle. "Oh, come on. You love her."

"I tolerate her," she corrects with a pointed gaze. I hum, not believing for one second that Dani doesn't love her, even if she pretends that she doesn't.

"This waiting is what's keeping everyone safe," I remind her quietly. "Your time to fight will come. But in the meantime, can we not rush into life-threatening situations and just be glad that we're relatively safe?"

She sighs exaggeratedly. "I suppose." I kiss her nose, happy to have her concede for the time being. She juts her chin toward the bathroom door. "Hey, go check my bag." Her tone has shifted from serious to playful.

Looking at her skeptically, I sit back on my heels. "Why? What's in there?" She shrugs casually and grabs the washcloth and the bland bar of soap off the ledge of the tub.

Curiosity getting the better of me, I stand and practically run to unzip her bag on the bed. Pushing aside explosive equipment and ammunition, I find two small burlap sacks and bring them back into the bathroom before opening the first and peering inside. I gasp, and Dani turns in the tub to face me. "Is this…" I look at her, excited and bring the bag to my nose to inhale deeply. "You brought me coffee beans?" The smell of them alone seems to give me a boost of energy, and Dani smiles at my reaction. "You found coffee beans?"

"Open the other one."

Still overjoyed with the idea of having real coffee, I untie the knot on the second bag and look inside. Quickly, I press it to my chest, so happy I could cry. Her smile grows and I pull out the bar of soap and take a deep breath in. "Lavender." I smell it again.

"It is," she confirms.

I take the large block of soap out and inhale the wonderful scent a third time, so excited with the pleasant aroma. Carefully, I place my treasures aside and begin undressing, anxious to try the soap. "Looks like I won the bet, after all."

Dani looks at me pointedly. "Could you please try not to gamble this one away?"

I don't answer. Instead, I lower myself into the scalding water and ignore the slosh that spills over the side.

"What happened to not wanting to wade in my filth?"

Scooting closer, I wrap my legs around her waist and drape my arms over her shoulders. She pulls me closer, seemingly not at all upset with my intrusion. I lean in and kiss her. "Thank you," I say, my lips still pressed to hers.

"If I had known coffee and soap would get you this hot and bothered—"

"Shut up," I say and kiss her again.

"You're welcome," she says while smiling against my mouth. She attempts another kiss, but I pull away abruptly and shove the bar of soap into her hands.

I turn and put some space between us. "Wash my back?"

"Really?" she asks. I glance over my shoulder, and she's staring at me in disbelief. "I thought you were going to thank me."

"You can't bring a girl fancy soap and not let her use it."

She sighs and works the soap into the washcloth. She leans in and rubs the cloth along the back of my neck and down my shoulders. "It's an honor to wade in your filth," she whispers in my ear, and a laugh bursts from my lips.

Jess scans the radio frequencies by the fire, George sitting close to take notes. The volume is low, but I can tell that most of the channels are either silent or static. Darby is off to the side, tinkering with her project and muttering under her breath about the shattered drone.

The snow has finally stopped, and Elise and I sit in the two armchairs by the window. I have a blanket pulled up to my chin, trying desperately to keep away the chill that seeps in from the panes. Elise, on the other hand, is leaning back with her sweatshirt sleeves pushed up like she's sitting in a sauna.

"How is Dani really?" she asks, fanning herself and reaching for a glass of water.

I tighten the blanket around my shoulders and sigh, unsure how to answer. The truth is that I pretend to sleep at night when I feel her tossing and turning, lost in her own mind. I know she's processing. She doesn't talk about it, but her restlessness is practically screaming. My hope was that she'd start talking to me when she was ready, but the more time that passes, I've come to realize that I may have to prod her to open up. "Grief is..." I hesitate and finally meet Elise's gaze. "Complicated."

It's a non-answer, and we both know it. She nods, understanding. "Yeah, Dani's not the 'sharing is caring' type." She smiles sadly. "Rhiannon was always good about getting her to talk."

I nod back, knowing Rhiannon was special to all of them in that caregiver role. The shadow she cast is daunting, despite knowing I'm not expected to be her replacement.

"She hasn't really been around much, I guess," Elise says, her brows knitted with worry. "To talk to any of us about it. I'm not sure I've even seen her cry since…since the day we…" She doesn't finish her thought and reaches for her water again.

I notice the mistiness in her eyes. She takes a large gulp, clears her throat, and looks away. My own words replay in my mind: *grief is complicated.* At one point or another, we have all swallowed that lump in an attempt to avoid what we know we *need* to feel in order to heal. I'm not sure Dani should be forced to speak any sooner than the rest of us, but I also know she's hurting, and I ache to be the one to comfort her.

"I'll try to talk to her," I offer, glancing at the door leading to the kitchen where Dani stayed to help Wyatt clean up after dinner. "I think she likes being able to help people, but I know she's itching to jump back in and fight."

Elise's frown deepens. Roscoe, as if sensing her worry, trots over and puts his head on her thigh. She scratches his head and leans forward, lowering her voice. "After her father died," she starts and hesitates. "She didn't…" She stops again, and I look away, not needing the reminder. The entire NAF knows what she did and how many people she took out along the way.

I know what she's saying. She's waiting for Dani to hit her breaking point, to snap and lash out. Despite knowing that Dani acts impulsively, especially when it affects those she cares about, and though the thought of her snapping has crossed my mind a few times in the past three months, the need to defend her is strong. "I think that's why she's trying to stay busy with other things. Focus her energy on something productive."

Elise is quiet for a stretch, appearing to really consider her next words carefully. She finally leans forward and kisses Roscoe on the head. "You may be right, but I worry about how long she can maintain that. Her past has shown that she hasn't always channeled her grief in the healthiest of ways." Elise sits back and sighs. She glances at the kitchen door and shakes her head. "I just worry about her," she repeats.

The kitchen door opens, and Dani walks out, wiping her hands on her pants. She smiles in my direction, and I try to sincerely smile back, but if her questioning look is anything to go by, I know I failed.

She walks over and pats Roscoe on the head. "Everything okay?"

"Yeah." This time, my smile must be more convincing because she leans over and kisses my cheek.

"Has Jack come in yet?" she asks and falls on the sofa beside Jess.

"Not yet. Mike and Lucas are with him. They're making sure the buggies are good to go to leave in the morning and that the snow isn't too deep," Elise answers and goes back to fanning herself.

Jess sighs. "Guess that means I should start packing."

"Jess, has anything come through?" Dani asks.

"A message for you from William." We all stop at the mention of that name. We rarely hear from him. Sharing a look with Elise, I hope this isn't anything to be concerned about.

Jess hands Dani a notepad, and she scans the message quickly.

"What does it say?" Elise asks.

"Coordinates for where he wants us to go," Dani confesses, and she seems to deflate. "Did he say anything else?"

"No," Jess says. "He gave me the coordinates, made me repeat them, and disconnected. He sounded like he was in a rush. Otherwise, I would've called you in."

The room is silent except for the pops and crackle of the fire. Dani crumples the paper and tosses it onto the flames. "We'll head out at sunrise." She gently touches Jess's arm. "Thank you."

I watch her slip on her jacket. There's definitely something going on that she's not telling us. I don't know whether to be offended or concerned.

❖

It's late by the time Dani comes into our room. The clouds have moved on, and the moon shines brightly outside, casting a white glow through the opening in the curtains. Our bags are mostly packed, except for the small heater and some clean clothes, leaving nothing left to do until morning.

I watch from the bed as Dani changes and tosses her clothes into a duffel and slips on her sleepwear. She extinguishes the single lantern on the nightstand and slides into bed, pulling the covers to her chin and snuggling deep under the thick blankets with a deep sigh.

"Good to go?" I ask and scoot closer.

"Yeah." She shivers and wraps an arm around my waist. I settle and press my feet against her legs. She jumps away with a shriek. "How are your feet so cold through your socks?"

I try pulling her back against me. "I'm not used to this kind of weather. I'm perpetually freezing."

She keeps her distance. "I don't know if I want to snuggle with an ice cube." I can tell by her tone she's kidding, and I grab her shirt. This time, she allows herself to be pulled. I wrap myself around her, desperately seeking her warmth.

"How are the buggies? Are we going to be able to get out tomorrow?" I ask.

She shivers when I put my feet back on her legs. "We should be able to get out, but if it starts up again overnight, we might be stuck. Those NAF buggies aren't made for that kind of weather. Even with the larger tires we put on them. Dammit, Kate." She recoils from my touch when I slip my hands under her shirt and rest them on her skin. "Maybe we should have Elise check your circulation."

I press my face against her neck, nestle under her chin, and smile. It's my favorite spot. She returns the favor and slides her hands under my shirt. They surprisingly aren't freezing but are cold enough to make me shudder. "I miss the warm weather."

She kisses the top of my head. "But then, we wouldn't get to warm each other up."

"Under the circumstances, I'd be okay with that." She laughs a bit and holds me closer. "I'm glad you're back," I confess.

"Me too," she says quietly.

She rubs my back slowly. It's comforting and makes me sleepy, but my mind won't let me ease into slumber. Instead, it replays my conversation with Elise over and over again. "Elise is worried about you," I say softly, treading carefully.

Her hands stop moving for a second. "I know."

I'm not surprised at her response. Dani is one of the most perceptive people I've ever met. Yet, now that we're alone and I've opened the door for conversation, I'm not sure what to say next.

Slowly, I peel away and look at her. The glow from the moon casts just enough light for me to see the worried expression etched across her face. I reach to smooth her furrowed brow, but she gently catches my hand.

She hesitates, her eyes meeting mine. My stomach flips, having a sinking feeling we aren't going to be addressing mine or Elise's concerns. She licks her lips and takes a deep breath. "Kate, there's something I need to tell you."

"Okay…"

She holds my gaze, but I can tell she's struggling to do so. I wait for whatever it is she wants to confess, my anxiety ramping up with each passing second. What could possibly make her this nervous? What is it that she's dreading to tell me?

"William got ahold of me when I was gone. He thinks there's a traitor within the Resistance. A traitor who has access to high-level intel."

The pointed look she gives me isn't needed. I know who she means. I pull away, not quite offended but not amused either. "He thinks *I'm* that traitor?"

Dani sits up and twists so she's facing me. "Look, Kate, I need you to know that I don't think that. No one here thinks you're still actively with the NAF."

"Jack does."

She makes a sound as if she's going to protest but thinks better of it. "Jack's hurting. He doesn't know what to do with his anger, so he throws it at you. It's not fair, but deep down, he knows you're not against us."

I ignore her excuse. Jack hates me, and I'm not sure anything will ever change that. He still sees me as the person responsible for White River being destroyed and the reason Rhiannon was killed in the bombing of Rapid City. I'm not surprised he views me as a traitor, but it still stings to hear it aloud. "William also thinks I'm playing sides, doesn't he?"

Her hesitation is long enough for me to know the answer. I look away, angry that this is clearly a trend among the Resistance: men who hate me. "William's just trying to remain cautious. With everything and everyone. This is the first time in months he's made any effort to see me. And he went out of his way to make sure we were alone. That's why he hasn't sent much information over the radio. And by limiting information, he can—"

"Weed out the spy?" I supply.

"There probably isn't one," she rushes to say.

"Wow. You do not sound convincing at all."

There's another pause. At first, I think she's going to try to reassure me about the others and promise me that Jack and William are the only ones, but she shifts uncomfortably instead. When she doesn't reach for me, I know her assurances aren't coming. "Kate. There's something else."

"Something worse than a traitor?" I try to make it sound like a joke, but it falls flat, and I just sound scared. I don't like the silence that follows. "Dani, what is it?"

"There's rumors that she has a UCAV ready and is planning on using it." Her expression is a mix of nervousness and anger. "Bismarck would be just the beginning. What she did in Rapid City is nothing compared to what she's planning next."

My mother said she wanted the entire wasteland to fall before the end of winter, so this shouldn't be surprising, but hearing it out loud still rattles me. "It's only December," I whisper, not sure what else to say.

"The NAF has been one step ahead of us for months. It's like they know where we're going before we get there."

My stomach bottoms out, and I recoil. "That's why they think it's me. Who else would have access to what the Resistance is doing and also have a direct line to the general?" She doesn't look at me. "Dani." My voice cracks. "Do you…" I can't bring myself to finish the question.

Her eyes meet mine, and she shakes her head, scooting close and pulling me to her. I try to wiggle away, but she won't let me. "No, Kate, no." She grabs my face and waits until I look at her. When I don't, she dips her head to catch my gaze. "I know it's not you, but William thinks there's a very real possibility that it's someone in our group, and unfortunately, he might be right."

I do a mental inventory of all my games of chess with Mike and all the fireside heart-to-hearts with Elise. I refuse to believe either one of them is capable of a betrayal this deep. We're a small group; who could it possibly be? I do my best to run through each of the faces of the people I've grown to love: Jess, Wyatt, George, Jack, Lucas, Darby. Finally, I look at her. "What are you going to do?"

"Nothing. I'm not convinced that there is one here," she says casually, hesitating slightly. "But watch what you say until I can prove it's not one of us."

She waits until I nod, agreeing, though I still don't quite understand it all. She pulls me back on top of her and gently runs her fingers up and down my back. My mind races. If there is a traitor with highly classified information, then I'm not sure the wasteland will make it until the end of the month, let alone the end of winter.

CHAPTER TWO: THE SETTLEMENT

DANI

The trip to our new location was supposed to take about four hours, but with the snow on the ground and the possibility of drones looming above, we're already pushing five. Woodlake is apparently a last resort Resistance hideout, which means I'm not expecting much in the way of a warm welcome. William stressed that they would be accommodating, but I know taking us in puts a bull's-eye on the place. Especially since William thinks there may be a traitor in the group. And that alone makes me nervous.

I glance at Kate in the passenger seat as she leans forward to squint out the front window, bringing her hand up to block the harsh morning sun. She's looking for drones. Taking a quick peek, I see nothing but blue sky.

"At least there's no snow today," she murmurs. "But no cloud cover, either."

"Makes for an easier drive," I say, not really good at small talk. I look in the rearview. Neither Darby nor Lucas seems to be paying attention, but I know better than to bring up last night in front of them. Even if they do know about the entire situation. The thought of someone I love selling us out, well, I'm trying not to think about it.

"Have you ever been to Woodlake before?" Kate asks, her eyes leaving the sky for only a second to glance in my direction.

"No. I don't know much about it," I say. "William's been there. He said it's nice, considering it's in the middle of nowhere."

"Will he be there, too?"

"No. Just mentioned he'd have a message waiting."

She nods and looks back to the sky. The awkward tension inside this buggy is so palpable, I feel like I could bite into it. The silence stretches on, the only sound coming from Darby messing with her recent project in the back. It's the rare time I actually wish she would fill the quiet with a sarcastic remark or mindless question, but in typical Darby fashion, she does the exact opposite of what I hope she'll do.

The rest of the trip remains that way. No one says anything except for the sporadic directions given by Kate, who studies the map. Lucas glances at me in the rearview a few times, and I know with absolute certainty that he knows something else is going on and is wisely choosing to stay out of it.

"Turn right on the next turnoff," Kate instructs.

I have to squint to see it, and once I get to the turn, I wonder if this is right. There is no road. No path. If there was once a street here, it's overgrown and covered in snow. I hope the buggy can make it through the couple inches that coat the ground. The thought of pushing it again sours my mood.

"Wait a minute," Kate says, bringing the map closer to her face before looking out the window.

Expecting trouble, I slam on the breaks and lean forward to glance at the sky. "What's wrong? What do you see?"

Barely jolted by the sudden stop, she continues to scan the area. "I've been here before."

"What? *Here?* How can you even tell?" All I see is a long stretch of snow-covered nothingness on either side.

"No, not *here*, here. The town. These coordinates..." She points to the circled spot on the map. "I came from the northeast, but I know this place. I've stayed here."

I stare at her, not following. This is a town I've never even heard of until recently, and Kate is telling me she's been here? "I don't understand."

"Is everything okay?" Mike's voice chimes over the radio. "Why'd you stop?"

Jack's voice is next: "Are we lost?"

"No, just hang on a second." I say back. My eyes stay on Kate. "What are you talking about? When have you stayed here?"

She hesitates. "On my way to see you," she finally explains. "That one time." She doesn't elaborate, and I'm not sure what time she's talking about. "You know. The time we..." She trails off and chances a glance at the back seat, clearly not wanting to say anything in front of an audience.

"When you snuck out for two days to have sex," Darby supplies without looking up.

Kate blushes and clears her throat.

"That time." I smile a little, having very fond memories of our rendezvous in the Resistance safe house in the middle of nowhere. We were still on opposite sides of the war. Simon had burned White River to the ground, and I had just taken out an NAF convoy. It was only a few months ago but feels like a lifetime.

"Archie sent me to this place first. For supplies," Kate continues.

My smile fades a little at the name. I still haven't heard what happened to the Resistance spy. He was the NAF's best cartographer, altering maps and removing towns to keep the gray coats off our backs. We could really use him right now. I hope he made it out.

I look at Kate, wanting to get her out of the open expanse. I don't even want to think about what the NAF would do to *her* if she was ever found.

Her expression changes, and she looks very anxious. I wonder if she's thinking the same thing. "Come on." She smacks the dashboard anxiously. "We're close, let's go."

"We're moving out," I say into the radio. Slowly, I accelerate, waiting for my next set of directions from Kate, who is now bouncing slightly in her seat. Anxious may not be the right word to describe her. More like, excited.

It's a welcome change from the uncomfortable tension and awkward chitchat, and it's the first time Kate's smiled all day. Maybe Woodlake is just what we need.

❖

There's a crude fence surrounding the small town. It wouldn't withstand a heavy pistol attack, let alone Simon and his tanks. The sorry excuse for a watchtower looks more like a hunting perch, and the initial reaction is that I can't believe this is where William sent us.

It's even further perplexing that Kate, with all her military experience, appears content with these weak defenses.

"Are you sure this is the place?" Jack asks through the radio.

Kate leans forward. "This perimeter wasn't here before."

"Yeah, well, I guess everyone's trying to beef up security now," I say, attempting to keep the sarcasm out of my voice because *that* is not security. A man with a rifle slides down from the lookout. He points it to the ground but keeps his finger on the trigger. "If you can even call it that," I mutter, unable to help it, and pick up the radio. "Just stay in your cars and stay close."

The two vehicles behind me slow to a stop, and we wait in a line while the makeshift metal gate slides open. Three men with hunting rifles step through and close the door behind them. They stand side by side as if they're the town's last defense. Except, they don't point their guns at us, either. I shake my head.

An older woman climbs up the ladder and sits on the ledge, taking their place as lookout. At least she has the wits to point her rifle at us. A middle-aged man with long graying hair raps his knuckles on the glass. I glance at Kate and roll down the window a crack. "State your business," he orders.

"Resistance Delta One," I tell him. He stares at me for a long time and swiftly glances at the others in the car. I push the sunglasses on top of my head. "You should be expecting us."

He stares for another moment, then slowly nods. "Yup. I reckon we are." Leaning back, he looks at the other two vehicles and back at me. "Raiders are starting to cause problems around here. Can't be too careful."

"When have you ever seen raiders drive cars?" Darby mumbles from the back.

"We might be able to help with that," I say quickly, keeping the attention on me.

He stares at Darby for longer than I'm comfortable with. I think about reaching for the pistol I keep in the armrest compartment. Instead, I lift my eyes to the rearview. Darby looks mildly concerned, her eyes flicking between me and the man. Lucas doesn't appear bothered, but I can tell by his tense posture that he's on high alert.

Kate leans across the center console and catches the man's full attention. I start to push her back, but she brushes my hand away. "Can you please let Marium know we're here and that we'll need some rooms if she can spare them? We have a few trade items for her trouble."

The man looks at Kate and removes his finger from the trigger. He waves to the men by the gate, and they push it open to allow us entry. "I suppose you know where you're going?"

"Yes, sir," Kate answers and smiles.

"Go on in." He juts his chin at Kate. "My wife made that hat you're wearing." He walks away before any of us can respond.

I arch an eyebrow at Kate.

"That was weird," Darby mumbles.

Kate pats the white puff on the top of her navy blue hat affectionately. "I love this hat."

Slowly, I steer the buggy past the gates and park where Kate instructs. She seems genuinely excited to be back here, and I find that somewhat curious. "Now what?" I ask.

"Now, we go see Marium." She exits first.

"That's right," I say. "Marium."

The rest of us get out and stretch, and I take my first real look around. There aren't a lot of people walking by, but the handful who do give us curious glances. I'm tempted to offer a little wave.

There are a few rows of buildings, more spaced out than White River was, and about a quarter of the size. Most of the buildings are small and wooden, but there are a few that are larger and made of brick. It's clear, even at first glance, that this is a fishing town and not at all a Resistance fighter camp. Maybe that's why William sent us here.

"This is it?" Jack asks as he strides up next to me. Even though he's wearing large sunglasses, I can sense his skepticism. "Doesn't look like much."

"Not really a threat." I put my hands on my hips. "Not worth capturing, either."

He grunts in what I can only assume is agreement. "I'm going to walk Roscoe."

"Jess, George, and Wyatt, stay out here with Jack until we can figure out what's going on." George glances at the door to Marium's building, but none of them protest. I can feel Kate's eyes on me, but I ignore her and reach the door, holding it open for the rest of the group to enter.

A bell rings overhead in the decent-sized, brick, two-story building. Kate kicks the bit of snow off her boots and shoves her gloves in her jacket pocket to wash her hands at the door. The rest of us do the same, and we cram into the main room.

"Cute place," Darby comments from over my shoulder.

I have to agree. There are a few tables and chairs for eating, and on the opposite end is a counter with several stools. Behind it sits a large shelf with what appears to be trade items.

An elderly woman walks through the back door, wiping her hands on a brown apron, her white hair twisted atop her head. "There you are. We've been expecting you." Her gaze lands on Kate. "Oh my goodness. I don't believe it." She smiles wide and bright and hurries over.

This must be Marium.

I watch curiously as she takes Kate's hands and looks her over as if they're long-lost friends. "Thank you so much for having us," Kate says, smiling.

Mike leans over my shoulder. "What's happening?" he whispers.

I shrug. "Wish I could tell you."

"It looks like you found what you were looking for," Marium says, her gaze landing on me. She winks at Kate, and I feel a strange sort of pride when it makes Kate blush, despite finding the entire exchange extremely weird. Marium shuffles back behind the counter. "That voltage regulator really saved us out here, you know. Not to mention your friends."

Kate bounces on her heels. "They made it?" She looks back over her shoulder at the door, looking for whoever the hell she's talking about.

"Are *we* the friends?" Mike asks.

"I don't think so," I whisper.

Marium rummages behind the counter. "Oh yes. A few months ago. I believe they're reinforcing the back fence, but they'll show up for lunch, don't you worry. They never miss a meal."

I lean in closer to Kate. "Friends?"

She removes her hat and responds with a half shrug but doesn't say anything further. She's definitely hiding something. Something big by the sound of it.

Marium places a few keys on the counter and fixes me with a look that has me straightening. "Danielle Clark."

Kate glances at me, and I can feel everyone else do the same. "Yes, ma'am. You must be Marium." She continues to stare. Clearing my throat, I look around. "This is your place?"

"Lodgings, trade, an occasional meal." She finally releases me from her intimidating stare. Her features soften, and her dark blue eyes sparkle. She smiles at the rest of the group crowded behind me. "I was told you needed a few rooms for a couple of days."

"It would be greatly appreciated," I say.

She rests her palms on the counter and leans forward. "The NAF has been spreading quickly. We aren't fighters, but we do support the Resistance's cause. I can spare four rooms, but in return, we'll need your help with a few things for the duration of your stay."

Kate nods. "Of course, we'll do all we can."

I want to tell her to hang on a minute and not make any promises before we know the terms, but Marium beats me to it. "There's a raider camp about twenty kilometers west of here. They've been causing all sorts of trouble of late."

That's the second mention of raiders in the area. I think I know where this is going.

"You want us to take them out?" Kate asks, thinking the same thing.

Marium nods. "Would be mighty helpful."

Kate looks at me, and I bite my tongue, having a feeling that's not all she wants from us. "Anything else?" Kate asks.

Marium watches us and reaches for something in a box behind her. "The NAF is getting close. A trader came through a couple of days ago and warned us. Closing roads, cutting off trade, watching from the sky. Only a matter of time before one of their drones spots our little town."

"And you want us to take care of them, too," I guess.

Marium says nothing, just waits for our answer. I share another look with Kate, annoyed at the high cost for a few rooms for a couple of nights. Kate nods very subtly and glances at the others. Marium stares at us for another beat. There's something in her gaze that's unsettling, but I can't quite figure out what. I wonder briefly if she's changed her mind and is debating kicking us out, even though she's clearly getting the better end of this arrangement, but she pushes the room keys across the counter like she knows we have no other choice. "Lunch is almost ready. We're having bison." There are a few excited murmurs behind me at the mention of something other than fish. I guess the deal is done. Marium motions to the steps. "Go on, and take your bags up."

The door opens, and the bell jingles behind us.

"Right on time," Marium murmurs.

Kate grins so wide, it's a wonder her face doesn't split in two. I turn to see who has her so excited. Two men, one slightly taller, come into the establishment. The first is young, maybe even a teenager, with a short and stubby mustache and beard. The other is a little stocky, with black bushy hair and dark eyes.

"Miguel, Anthony," Kate greets them as she steps forward. It dawns on me as Elise gasps from somewhere in the room. They were two of the prisoners in White River.

"Lieutenant Colonel?" Miguel says to Kate. His tone is questioning and surprised, and he stands at attention. The entire room is silent, everyone watching the exchange with similar expressions of confusion.

Kate rushes past me and throws her arms around Miguel's shoulders. "I told you to call me Kate," she says and pulls him into a tight hug.

Miguel hesitates for a second before he returns her embrace.

When they separate, Kate reaches out to touch Anthony's arm. "Look at you. Look at you both."

"What are you doing here? Why are you..." Miguel takes in the entire group, and his eyes widen. "So it's true? You've joined the Resistance?"

Kate steps back and glances at me, her eyes sparkling, happy. "Yes, and it looks like you have, too."

"Not officially," Anthony says.

"It's not like they give out buttons, Miller," Miguel quips. He looks at me. "Do they?"

"Just tattoos," I answer.

"Mainly, they just eat," Marium says, cutting into the conversation, but her tone is filled with affection. "I'll let you all catch up, but take your reunion outside. I'm trying to run a business here." She makes a shooing gesture, and the others head for the door. "Danielle, a word?"

I meet Kate's eyes. "I'll meet you out there." She glances at Marium and nods, following the group outside.

Slowly, I approach the counter. A sinking feeling that I'm going to be scolded for something overwhelms me. Instead, Marium hands me a sealed piece of paper. The letter from William. She waits as I scan the neatly curved letters. It's a specified time and frequency number to check in. "Is this it?"

"That's it."

I slip the paper in my pocket, frustrated. Three months of getting nothing but locations, times, and radio frequencies. I don't know why, but I thought maybe this time, there'd be something more. Something that indicates a change in the war.

Marium must see something in my expression. "I don't know what you two are up to out this way, but I have a town to look out for, and if I'm going to be honest, I didn't want any of you staying here. It was risky enough letting those two defectors stay. Yes, we needed the help, but their presence isn't without risk. And with NAF setting up camp nearby and rumors about the general having informants all over the place, folks are starting to get nervous."

I'm grateful for her honesty and don't blame her hesitance at all. It's rather unsettling, however, that news of people betraying the Resistance has traveled all the way down to people in towns like Woodlake.

"Keep an eye on your people, and I'll keep an eye on mine," I tell her and try to keep the defensiveness from my voice. "Don't talk to anyone other than me or Kate. Especially with sensitive information. You're right. We don't know who we can trust."

She stares at me long and hard. "Still," she says through a sigh, "seeing the Daughter of the Resistance walk through the streets also has its advantages. You're an icon, and we could use the morale boost."

I wince. It's been a long time since I've enjoyed strutting down streets to cheers and pats on the back. I think of all the damage I've caused over the years and the lives I've taken and the ones I've risked. I no longer see the glory in it.

Her steel blue eyes pierce right through me as if she can read my intentions and sense my feelings. I refuse to look away. Her eyes narrow until finally, she sighs. "Go on. I need to finish making lunch."

I tip my head, a polite nod, and join the others outside. That woman has nerves of steel, I'll give her that. No wonder Kate likes her.

Just outside the door, there's a nice little reunion happening. Elise is checking over Anthony, who allows the inspection with a smile, while Miguel and Mike watch in amusement. Kate looks at me and grins. She seems lighter somehow, the sun catching her hazel eyes and giving them a golden sparkle. The sight of her makes my breath catch. Jack leans against the truck with his arms crossed. It's obvious he's not interested in Miguel or Anthony.

"What's going on?" Jess asks.

"Two of the NAF soldiers we took prisoner in White River apparently live here now," Darby answers way louder than necessary.

"That sounds...awkward," Jess mumbles.

"You seem healed, but it's hard to tell under all those layers," Elise says and pats Anthony on the arm. "Are you feeling okay?"

"Yes, thanks to you," Anthony says and takes Elise's hand. "Thank you. Everything you did...thank you."

Elise smiles. "You're welcome."

Tension seeps into the moment, and I wonder if everyone else is thinking about how not that long ago, they were our prisoners. Now, in a strange turn of events, we appear to be on the same side.

Kate holds up the keys, breaking the spell. "There're four rooms and ten of us. How do we want to do this?"

"Any of you are welcome to stay with us. We have a spare bed," Miguel says, scanning the group. His expression is sincere, but I'm not sure if anyone is willing to take him up on the offer. And I'm not sure I want anyone to. It's bad enough that their presence here could potentially be leaked to the wrong people.

"I'll stay with you," Kate says. Okay, I should've seen that coming. She looks at me, hopeful. "Dani?"

I was hoping we could have our own room and a bit of privacy. Being away from her this past week has me aching to be alone with her, but she looks so hopeful that I'm unable to refuse. Even if that means staying in a house full of ex-NAF soldiers who are all wanted for high treason. "That would be great," I say and attempt a smile. My heart beats a little faster at the look of relief and excitement Kate gives me. "If that's okay with you, Anthony?"

He looks about as skeptical as I feel, but the same kind of encouraging expression from Miguel has him nodding. "Of course. We would be honored." He looks past my shoulder and straightens a little just as someone grabs my arm.

"Can I talk to you for a minute?" Jack pulls me away from the group. We're barely out of earshot before he starts: "What the hell are you thinking?"

"Care to be a little more specific? I'm thinking about a lot of things." I try to keep my voice even, and I give the hand wrapped around my bicep a pointed look.

Jack gets the message and lets me go. "Where are we exactly? A hideout for the Resistance or the NAF? Are you really going to live with them?" It's clear by his clipped tone that he's angry.

"I'm not going to *live with them*, Jack." I'm too annoyed to point out how dramatic he's being.

He glances at the group and steps closer, lowering his voice. "You think they're going to roll out the welcome mat after everything you did to them? Knowing you're the most wanted person in the country?"

"Everything *I* did to them?" I repeat, not appreciating the accusation. "First of all, *we* let them live and released them. Secondly, they left the NAF. They're wanted men now, Jack. They want to be caught by the NAF about as much as we do."

He scoffs. "They'd be stupid not to turn you in."

"Turn *me* in?" I narrow my eyes. "Sounds a bit like you want them to."

He leans away from me and opens his mouth to respond but shuts it just as quickly. Even with his sunglasses over his eyes, I can tell my words hurt.

I take a deep, steadying breath. "Look, I know you're angry. I know you're itching to be out there doing something bigger. I know you are because I am, too, but now is not the time." He shakes his head and turns to walk away. "Listen to me." I step back in front of him, making sure I have his attention. "You have to be patient. You have to trust me."

He meets my eyes as his jaw clenches. "I used to, and look where that's gotten us." He pushes past me. I watch his retreating form, feeling as though I was sucker punched. I want to go after him, but I hear Kate gently calling for me.

"I can show you to the house if you'd like to unload your things?" Miguel is asking when I rejoin the others.

I glance once more at Jack's retreating form and nod.

Kate hands out keys to the others, and we agree to meet a little later, after we've put all our bags in our rooms and had a chance to rest a bit after the drive.

"How have you been settling in?" Kate asks as Miguel and Anthony lead us through the quaint little town. The houses are fairly well spaced, and the dirt roads aren't exactly buzzing, but it still somehow feels alive and lived in.

It makes me ache for my life back in White River.

Miguel nods at a man walking by with a basket of milk bottles. The man doesn't return the gesture. Instead, he's focused on me. When I nod, however, he does it back. Miguel takes the slight in stride. "Fairly well. Took a bit of convincing for the people here to see us as useful instead of threatening, but Marium encouraged them to give us a chance."

"Most everyone," Anthony says.

"Most everyone," Miguel agrees and glances over his shoulder at the man still watching us.

We stop in front of a modest two-story home. It's clear that at one point, there was a front porch, but it has long since collapsed and been cleared. The white paint is chipped, and the curtains in the two front windows that flank the door are a bit tattered. The roof is in fairly good shape, as is the structure.

Miguel opens the door and motions for us to enter. "It's not much, but there's a spare room, and it's all yours for as long as you're here."

I follow Kate inside. There's barely any furniture and nothing personal besides a few books stacked on a small table in the corner.

"This is lovely," Kate says with a smile. She drops her bags inside the entrance and washes her hands in the bowl of water. Once I've done the same, Anthony excuses himself, and Miguel motions for us to follow him up the stairs and to a small room on the left.

"We did a lot of repairs when we got here. Replaced some of the flooring and half the roof," he says almost bashfully.

Kate gently squeezes his arm. "It's wonderful."

He seems relieved. "I'll get you some spare linens."

I drop my bags to the floor and look around. There's a double bed pressed against the wall in the center of the room and a chair in the corner. That's it. No fireplace, no heater, no table. I put my hands on my hips. "There's only one pillow."

Kate places her bags at the foot of the bed. "It was kind of them to offer." I'm not sure if she meant to have any sort of bite to her tone, but it's there, and I'm not sure why.

"I didn't say it wasn't," I say carefully. Kate just removes her hat and jacket before throwing them on top of the bags. "Hey." I take her arm and spin her so she's facing me. "Did I do something to upset you?"

She bristles a little and deflates. "No. No, of course not. It's just...I know you must think they have something to do with the information leak."

"I wasn't thinking that at all. Was I surprised to see them here? Yes. Does it make me uneasy? Also, yes. But I don't think you've been in cahoots with them or whatever it is you're implying."

Kate looks on the verge of tears. "I'm sorry, I'm just overwhelmed and I—"

"Come here." I pull her against me and wrap my arms around her protectively. "Sometimes, I forget how much you've been through these past couple of months. I'm sorry I haven't been around more."

She buries her face against my neck, and I tighten my hold. I hear a muffled grunt, and I kiss the top of her head. She clutches the back of my jacket and takes a deep breath. "Are you going to ask me why they're here?"

"Miguel and Anthony?"

She nods against my shoulder.

"It's pretty easy to guess. You sent them here."

She nods again.

"Honestly, I'm more curious about lunch."

She snorts a laugh, and the sound makes me smile.

Miguel clears his throat from the doorway. Kate pulls away from me slowly and peers at him. "Sorry to interrupt." He extends a stack of blankets. "Please let me know if you need more. Anthony is looking for a heater."

"Thank you." I take the blankets, and Miguel slowly closes the door behind him, giving us privacy.

I discard the bedding and turn to Kate with every intention of continuing our conversation, but she's already reaching for the top sheet, no trace of playfulness in her expression. It's clear the moment is over.

"Did you get William's message?" she asks as she spreads the sheet out over the mattress.

"I did." I grab one of the corners and stretch it out, carefully tucking it under one corner of the mattress. It barely fits. "Just another date, time, and frequency."

She doesn't say anything as she unfolds the thick blankets to cover the sheet. Seeing the bed makes me realize just how tired I am. I wish I could crawl under the covers and sleep until the war is over.

My stomach grumbles, and Kate cracks a smile. "Come on." She grabs her hat and jacket. "Let's get you fed."

The fireplace crackles and illuminates the room, the sky outside dark, the sun long set. Kate sips from her glass. Miguel swears it's mead, but it's so dry and bitter that I doubt very seriously there's enough honey involved to call it such. Kate doesn't seem to mind. In fact, she looks so relaxed that I wonder if she may have had too much.

"I can't believe that after everything, it was a bison that almost took us out," Miguel says and shakes his head.

"To be fair," Anthony continues, "we never had to hunt for food in the NAF. It was always provided."

"Bison are one of the deadliest animals you can encounter out here. They're five times more deadly than bears," I say quietly, unaware that the trio is paying me any attention.

I stand corrected when they all turn to look at me, and after a beat, start laughing.

"Maybe you should've gone after a bear," Kate suggests.

Anthony cringes. "We'll keep that in mind for next time."

A small lull in the conversation follows. It's a comfortable silence, and it blankets the room. Then, Kate's smile falls a bit, and the cozy atmosphere seems to slip with it.

Miguel watches her carefully, his expression shifting to concern. "We heard about you leaving the NAF. It was all over the radio here." His voice is soft, hesitant, like he doesn't want to startle her. "A few of the locals like to keep up with the Resistance chatter. Word spreads quickly."

"Earl?" Kate asks and tries to smile.

"Earl," Miguel confirms.

Kate twists the glass in her hand and stares at it thoughtfully. I hold my breath, ready to pull attention away from her if need be. Her shoulders slump. She's been carrying so much emotional weight these past few months, and sometimes, in moments like this, the defeat shows.

She takes a deep breath and knocks back the last of her drink, wincing as it goes down. "I left the same day you did, actually."

"I'm sorry," Miguel says quietly. "That must've been hard for you."

She places her glass on the hearth by the fireplace. "Not as hard as you'd think." When she looks up, she's smiling, but it doesn't reach her eyes.

Again, the room goes silent. The confession feels heavy.

I want to reassure her somehow, but I hold perfectly still, feeling as though I'm interrupting a private moment between friends. Kate, Miguel, Anthony...all of them gave up everything to start a new life. I know a little bit of what that's like. It isn't easy. My failure to stay out of the war is proof enough of that. It can feel constricting and lonely.

Anthony pours more of his homemade hooch and offers it to Kate, who gladly accepts. "So what brings you to Woodlake?" He shifts the conversation slightly, and I'm grateful for it, despite being skeptical of him asking. I don't like seeing Kate so unsteady.

She jumps on the opportunity to answer, her voice regaining some vibrato. "We've been dodging drones and trying to distribute supplies since the NAF took out Rapid City. Just constantly on the move, trying to stay out of sight and help towns who might need it."

"We heard about Rapid City." Miguel shakes his head, disgusted. "It was horrible. Were you close when it happened?"

"We were in it," I say quickly. Admitting it out loud puts a bad taste in my mouth, knowing my carelessness was the reason they were targeted. Bringing that NAF tracker inside the walls was the reason they knew exactly where to drop those bombs.

Miguel and Anthony both turn to look at me, surprised. "In that case, I'm *really* happy to see you all here and alive."

My grip on my glass tightens, and my chest constricts as flashes of digging Rhiannon's lifeless body from a pile of rubble come to the forefront of my memory. "Not all of us."

Kate reaches for my arm and squeezes. It's meant to be supportive, but it doesn't ease my guilt.

"I am so sorry, I didn't..." Miguel trails off, and I take small, shallow breaths to control the sudden burst of anger and despair that courses through me. "I've been meaning to mention that, um..." he says almost apprehensively. "I'm sorry to hear what happened to your home. To White River. What they did...It was one of the reasons I left the NAF."

"Why we both left," Anthony amends.

I'm not sure how to respond to that. Kate squeezes again, and I take a deep breath, focusing on the air that expands my lungs and releasing it, over and over. I try to block out images of White River burning. Of Rhiannon's pyre overlooking the ruins. All I've lost in such a short time.

"Burning down places where I reside seems to be a popular trend with the NAF," I say flatly.

"I was wondering..." Miguel clears his throat. "Will anyone else be joining your group in town?"

I narrow my eyes. What a strange question. "Why do you ask?"

"He means Rhiannon," Anthony specifies. "He talks about her all the time."

Miguel blushes wildly, and I'm transported back to her tavern in White River, watching Miguel shyly attempt to flirt with her. "I wanted to thank her for…" His voice trails off when Kate reaches out and places a hand on my knee. It's the only thing that stops it from rapidly bouncing.

She looks at Miguel and slowly shakes her head. It takes only a moment for the reality of the situation to settle across his features.

"No," he barely whispers. "No, it can't be." Tears almost fill his eyes, and he grabs the cross around his neck.

I stand, unable to sit still. I need to do something, to get out of this room and get some air. I should check in with Jess to make sure she's all set up with her radio or maybe see if Jack has calmed down. Make sure he's eaten since he refused to sit with us at lunch or dinner.

Kate reaches for my hand. "Dani."

There's a firm knock on the door that makes Miguel jump. Kate stands, and I reach for the pistol on my thigh. Anthony gestures for me not to draw my weapon. "Please, we're all neighbors here."

"Better to be safe," I mutter, and place my glass on the windowsill. Miguel quickly goes to answer the door. I don't know this place or any of these people, and I've learned that letting my guard down is the easiest way to get shot. I draw my gun.

"Hello." He blocks whoever's there.

"We've come to see Kate." I know the voice. It's Wyatt.

I holster my pistol, and Miguel steps aside to allow Wyatt inside. His arm is looped through Jess's, and he eases her over the step up.

"I'm sorry for the intrusion, but this is rather urgent," Jess says while Wyatt guides her hands to the water bowl. "Where's Kate?"

"I'm here," Kate says. "What's going on?"

Using her walking stick, Jess carefully steps toward the sound of Kate's voice. "I have a message for you. It was addressed to Songbird. A meeting request. Tomorrow at Rockwood at oh nine hundred in the center square. They said they had important information to pass along."

"Rockwood? Well, you're definitely not going there," I say, leaving no room for negotiation. "Rockwood is right in the middle of Fargo and Bismarck. You'd be way too exposed to troops moving in and out. Especially if the NAF are looking to take Bismarck next."

"Who is this message from?" Kate asks, taking the piece of paper from Jess's hands and completely ignoring me and my selfish demand.

"They signed off using the call sign Lightning Rod."

Kate freezes beside me. "What did you say?"

"Lightning Rod," Jess repeats. "It came in through an encrypted Resistance channel using an old rebel cipher. So whoever it is has Resistance ties."

Kate looks so pale that I'm afraid she's going to pass out. "Does that mean anything to you?" I ask. She swallows but doesn't answer. "And you're sure you decrypted it correctly?" I ask Jess, peering at the sliver of paper in Kate's hand.

"It's basic training for comms specialists," Jess says, and I can hear the annoyance in her tone, like I just insulted her competence. "The real question is, who sent it, and do we believe it's a trap?"

"It's definitely a trap," I mumble and stare at the call sign on the paper.

"Respond that I'll be there," Kate says.

Surprised at how quickly she accepts the invitation and concerned that she's being too rash, I quickly object. "Kate—"

She turns to me with wide eyes and crumples the paper tightly into her palm. "I need you to trust me."

I nod, but it doesn't stop the uneasy feeling in the pit of my stomach.

CHAPTER THREE: THE MEETING

KATE

All the women are crammed in Jess's room. Elise and Darby stretch out on the double bed, and Roscoe nestles happily between them. Jess and I sit at the table, the radio silently resting atop it. Dani leans against the wall, her arms crossed, staring at it as if willing it to turn on.

"Do you know who this contact is?" Elise asks, scratching behind Roscoe's ears.

"Maybe." There's only one person in the world who called me Lightning Rod, and that was my father. "But it can't be because he's dead."

Dani's stare is now focused on me.

"Maybe the message is from a ghost," Darby says. Dani rolls her eyes. Even though it's meant as a joke, her words still sting. "Sorry," she says when I look away.

"Can we trust this message?" Elise asks.

"I don't know," I answer honestly and try desperately to think of what this could be about.

"I think it's a setup," Jess says. "Someone has access to very personal information on you, and they're using it to lure you out."

"You mean like my mother?" I ask, and I try really hard to keep the accusation out of my voice. Jess cringes a little, and I know I must've sounded harsher than I intended. "I've thought about that, too."

Dani nods. "Darby, is your project ready?"

She looks slightly startled to be pulled into the conversation. "Sort of?"

"Sort of?" Dani asks, not quite annoyed but definitely not amused, either.

"I haven't had time to test flight lengths, battery life, max weight, or optimal distance. So yeah," she says defensively. "Sort of."

"Will it work?" Dani cuts her off, her tone shifting to annoyance.

"In theory?" Darby thinks for a moment. "Probably."

Dani sighs. "That'll have to be good enough."

"Good enough for what?" Darby asks.

"The contact said they had information. If it's someone close to Kate, and it has to be because they used her Resistance call sign and nickname, then I think we should see who it is."

I look at Dani, and she stares back, her expression giving away nothing. Knowing her, she has an ulterior motive for allowing this meetup to happen, and I have a feeling I know what it is.

"You hope my mother is behind this." I don't phrase it as a question, and Dani doesn't bother answering. I sit back in my chair, no longer interested in this meetup if that's the case. I have no desire to be the bait for Dani to get to my mother.

"I don't hope anyone is behind this," she says and pushes off the wall. "But I'm curious as hell."

"You know what they say about curiosity," Darby sings. "It caught the cat."

"Killed the cat," Elise corrects. "It's curiosity *killed* the cat."

Darby stares at her. "Well, that's much worse."

"I don't think it's a good idea," Jess says and reaches for her radio. She pulls it close and fiddles with the knobs, a clear nervous tick. "I know you're planning something, and I just want to say, I think it's a terrible idea."

"Rockwood is a neutral site," Dani continues. "If there were NAF soldiers swarming the place, Jess would know about it, and if the general was there, the place would be buzzing."

"I'm confused. Do we think it's Kate's mom or not?" Darby asks.

"Doubtful. If anything, it could just be a test to see if Kate will take the bait," Dani says. "Kate?" She stares at me so hard, I can feel it. When I finally look at her, she shrugs one shoulder. "What do you say?"

"I don't appreciate being used as bait. Not by whoever is behind this call or by you." Dani starts to protest, but I give her a look that clearly has her reevaluate her response.

"But?" she asks hopefully.

I both love and hate that she knows me so well. "But I want to see who's behind this, too. Information or not, I want to know who knew about the name Lightning Rod and how they know about the Resistance code. I just don't want anyone getting hurt. Not on account of me."

The corner of Dani's lip curls up just a little, and her gaze shifts to Darby. "And that's where Darby's new toy comes in."

Darby looks at Dani, her eyes wide. "Wait. Really?"

Dani reaches for the door. "Let's go talk to the guys," she calls over her shoulder.

It's settled, then. We're actually doing this.

I take a deep, steadying breath. Whoever this is must have known my father. Must know me. My head tells me it can only be my mother, but my gut tells me it's not her. Yet, who else would know my childhood nickname? A small part of me desperately hopes it's someone who knew my father and genuinely wants to help.

It's that tiny spark of hope that has me ignoring Jess's sigh of protest and instead following Dani out of the room.

❖

"Are you sure you're up for this?" Dani asks, placing the old metal box carefully in the back seat of the pickup.

"Do I have a choice?" I bend over, tightening my boot and twisting it around to get used to the knife I stashed inside.

"Of course you do," Dani says and stands in front of me. "Hey." I look at her. She seems concerned. "I know we didn't get a chance to talk much last night."

That's an understatement. We spent the entire evening planning out how we were going to handle today with the whole group and then dragged ourselves to bed for a few hours of sleep.

"But we don't have to do this," she continues.

"Yes, we do." I sigh and lean against the truck while we wait for the others. "If it's really someone who has information that could help…" I let my thought trail and shrug. Dani's been desperate for a swing in the Resistance's favor. This could be it.

"About that," Dani says and then hesitates. "I know what you're thinking."

"Do you?" I challenge.

"You're hoping it's someone who knew your dad." I want to tell her she's wrong, that I don't hope it's anyone, but her expression is so open, so concerned, that instead, I shrug and look away. "I don't want you to be disappointed."

"I think that's unavoidable," I confess softly.

Dani starts to say something but is interrupted by Darby. "Chi-Chi is ready to go." She pats the bag holding her Frankenstein-ed drone and beams, positively delighted at the chance to use her new toy.

Lucas and Mike are right behind her, still half-asleep. Jack pushes past, blowing on his hands and rubbing them together. "Let's go kill some gray coats."

Looks like we all think this could be a trap.

Dani gives me an apologetic look, and we all pile in the truck and a buggy and are out of the gates before the town is even awake and before I can have second thoughts.

It's just past sunrise when we arrive at Rockwood. I've never been here before, but Dani said she's been through once or twice as a child. She doesn't remember much, just that it's a small town inside an expansive, walled perimeter that stretches miles outside the city itself. She mentioned that the town isn't much to behold, but the people would throw down in a fight if forced to.

Just like the ride here, we pass rows of run-down and crumbled buildings and a spattering of houses. The structures appear in good enough condition to be lived in, but why would anyone want to live outside the safety of the town barrier? Maybe because I've always lived inside the safety of military-grade walls, but being completely exposed to raiders and shady travelers has absolutely no appeal to me.

It makes it a great spot for a mysterious meeting.

The sky shifts slowly from pink and orange to a brighter yellow when the main concrete perimeter comes into view. We approach a sliding gate, and it suddenly feels like I'm back on base. It's both unnerving and comforting. I try to come up with an exit plan.

"Maelstrom, are you in position?" Dani asks, slowing the truck.

"Affirmative," comes Lucas's reply, and that's good enough for Dani. She turns off the radio and sticks it in the glove box.

We share a brief look as three guards appear, stopping us from getting any closer to the gates. One of them pulls a grenade launcher strapped to his back over his shoulder and aims it right at the truck. Another holds out his hand, motioning for us to stop while the third aims her rifle.

"This is a nice warm welcome," Jack says from the back seat.

Dani stops the truck. "Let me do the talking." She rolls down her window and offers a quick wave to get their attention.

The guard with the rifle ignores her and instead walks toward my side of the car. It's clearly a precaution but unsettling just the same.

"This is definitely a trap." Jack mutters.

"That's why I'm doing the talking." Dani pushes her sunglasses on the top of her head and casually leans out the open window. "G'morning."

The first guard comes close, his finger on the trigger of the rifle strapped to his chest. "State your business." He appears to be in no mood for pleasantries.

The one by my side peers through the window. I've had guard duty enough as a private to know how this goes. I keep my hands in my lap and hold perfectly still. It's what we used to make all visitors do back on base.

"Just passing through, looking to trade," Dani answers easily. "We won't be staying long."

The guard glances inside the truck and takes his time looking at each of us. I can hear Mike shift behind me. My palms feel sweaty, and I resist the urge to rub them on my pants. The guard checks the empty truck bed.

"We have no affiliation here," he says bluntly.

"Folks still gotta trade, right?" Dani smiles innocently.

He doesn't seem charmed. "Step out of the vehicle."

Dani looks at me. She gives a slight nod, and the four of us exit slowly, keeping our hands where the guards can see them. I stand beside Mike, and he gives me a worried look.

"What are you carrying with you?" the guard asks Dani.

"Just what you see."

Across the hood of the truck, both Jack and Dani appear bored, like they are more annoyed at being made to get out in the cold rather than concerned. I think about all the weapons the two of them stashed inside the truck. I hope these guards don't go looking in random places.

"What are you looking to trade?"

"The old metal box you see in the back. It protects radios from EMPs," Dani answers. "Unaffiliated or not, I'm sure you've heard of the NAF cutting radio signals before they attack places that don't wish to be aligned with them." Neither guard responds, but the look they exchange doesn't go unnoticed. "If your town can spare some tech pieces and a little gas, it's yours."

Both guards finish their brief search and, finding nothing but the old metal box, motion for the others to stand down. "You can keep your weapons, and we'll allow the trade, but do anything stupid and you won't be leaving this town alive. We have no desire to be a part of this war. Understood?"

"Loud and clear," Dani says and gets back into the truck, not interested in any more small talk. The rest of us do the same.

He makes a gesture to someone in the closest watchtower, and slowly, the gate slides to the side. Dani shifts the truck into drive, and we slowly push forward. I glance out the side mirror at the female guard watching us enter the town and take a deep breath, relieved that we made it inside.

"That went well," Mike says. The gates begin to close again before we're all the way through.

"Leave them something in plain view, and they won't bother digging too deep," Dani says, no doubt proud that her plan worked. "Plus, everyone is on edge because of the NAF. That box was too good to pass up. Even if they're delusional enough to think they can keep out of this war."

We roll slowly through town, Dani pointing out advantage spots and areas to avoid like darkened alleys. I scan the streets, looking for any signs of a familiar face or an ambush. There aren't many people out this early, and for some reason, it makes me even more nervous.

"Is this where the meetup is happening?" Mike asks as we pass through what I guess is the center of town.

"Looks like it," Dani confirms.

There are streets that run in both directions, leading to a large center portion of town. It's exposed, and buildings surround it on all sides, making it easy to hide sharpshooters and reinforcements.

"Looks like a good place for an ambush or a public duel," Jack says. "Maybe we'll have a 'Petticoat Duel' two-point-oh." He chuckles at his own joke.

I roll my eyes but don't bother to respond. The nerves inside my stomach are starting to get to me, and I don't want to think about having to fight my way out of here.

"Petticoat Duel?" Mike asks.

"You know, where those two women fought naked," Jack says as if that's the only detail that matters.

Dani sighs. "That's not what happened."

"Half-naked, then," Jack corrects.

KRISTIN KEPPLER & ALLISA BAHNEY

"That's not..." Dani grips the steering wheel and turns the truck down an alley to put it in park away from curious gazes. "No one is dueling."

"I'm just saying, if there *was* going to be a duel—"

"After we sweep all these buildings," Dani interrupts, clearly not in the mood, "Mike, you take position behind us. Keep a close eye down the street for anything suspicious." She points to the building she wants him in. "Jack, you take the one there in the center and stay focused on the immediate area. I'll be with Kate. Keep one of the radios in the box in case things go south so we'll have one that still works. And always keep an eye on the sky." She reaches in her pocket and slips an earpiece in her right ear and fumbles inside her jacket sleeve for a bit before bringing it up to her mouth. "Atomic Anomaly to Major Maelstrom." We wait a bit, and Dani meets my gaze. "We're checking the area and heading into position. Stay on standby." Another pause. "Copy that." She lowers her arm. "They're standing by."

"Think Chi-Chi is ready?" Mike asks.

Jack scoffs. "More like, do you think Darby's ready?"

"They're both good to go," Dani says seriously, even if her mouth does kind of twitch in the way that says she's nervous. "Besides, she doesn't have to do much. We just need the drone to scan the area, then hover a bit to prove a point. Until then, let's try and stay inconspicuous."

I lean in a bit and tug on the end of her jacket. "You might not want to speak directly into your sleeve. It's kind of a dead giveaway."

Dani frowns, and I think she's going to say something to protest, but Mike leans in the front and offers me a piece of gum. Even though I decline, I appreciate the gesture.

Jack pulls a M203 grenade launcher strapped underneath Dani's seat into his lap and inspects it. His eyes seem to sparkle in a way I haven't seen them do in months. "You sure we have enough firepower if things go south?"

"No," Dani answers honestly. "But it'll have to do." Once we're out of the car, she removes one of the taillights and slides out the hidden compartment. She hands Mike the large rifle that was tucked inside. The other taillight houses a sawed-off shotgun still in its holster, which she slides on so the gun is strapped to her back.

Next comes the tailgate. She pulls it down and opens the compartment in the truck bed. It's her utility rig with spare grenades. She hands them to Jack.

"Not enough firepower?" I tease.

"You never know." She examines me for a moment.

I follow her line of sight, starting with my pistol on one side and a pair of knives on the other. Her expression turns thoughtful, and I wonder if she's going to pull more weapons out of the truck.

"I have another blade in my boot," I offer. She meets my eyes and sighs. "Dani, we won't need it." I hope she doesn't notice the waver in my voice. Maybe if I can convince her of that, I'll be able to convince myself. "You saw the gates. If the NAF shows up, we'll know. Especially with Darby watching from the sky, we can get out before any conflict begins." I keep the *in theory* part to myself.

"Let's hope you're right." She grabs the radios and hands one to Mike and one to Jack. "Go sweep the buildings and get in position. Keep an eye out for anything weird and stay hidden."

"Be careful," I tell them both. "We may be able to see if they're coming, but if this really is an ambush, they'd already be here." Mike nods, and Jack gives me a look. It startles me when our eyes meet since he usually refuses to even glance in my direction. I wonder if he's going to say something, but he pulls the scarf over his face and slings the grenade launcher over his shoulder and walks away. Slightly disappointed, I just watch him leave.

Dani pulls on my jacket and pats my sides and chest. "Is it tight enough? Does it feel okay?"

"It's fine," I say but let her inspect that Lucas's Kevlar vest does, in fact, fit properly. "Jack is good with this? With having my back?"

"Jack needs to stay distracted, and any chance to potentially enact revenge, he's all in." Dani stops her inspection to make sure her own vest is secure and then slips on her winter coat, zipping it up.

"That's what worries me," I confess.

"He won't shoot unless given the order," she assures me, and even if I trust her, I'm not sure I trust Jack's state of mind. Ever since he lost Rhiannon, he's been a loose cannon. I wouldn't be surprised if the tiniest of twitches was to set him off.

"And if *he's* the traitor?" I ask softly.

She gives me a look that would strike me dead if it were able. "Jack is *not* a traitor."

"I know, I just..." I shake my head, my nerves ramping up. "If there is one and this is a trap..." I don't finish that those things combined are insanely dangerous. Not to mention how this would be the perfect cover to take me out.

"Nothing's going to happen to you, okay?" Her expression softens, and she gently squeezes my arm. "Kate, are you sure you're ready for this?"

I swallow the lump in my throat. "Not at all."

"They're late." Dani stretches her shoulders back and pops her neck back and forth. After sweeping the town, her anxiety seems to have eased just a bit, so we settled at an empty picnic table near the town square.

I tap my foot; my own anxiety is only worsening. "I'm not sure what you want me to do about it."

"The others are complaining in my ear," she mumbles and pokes at the earpiece.

"Not sure what you want me to do about that, either," I say.

She sighs and glances around as if someone is going to magically appear. Her frustration is contagious, and I'm finding it more difficult to sit still.

More people are awake now and walking up and down the street. No one is paying much attention to us, but it still feels as though we are being watched by more than just Mike and Jack on opposite sides of the street.

I stare at the sky through the branches of the bare trees that surround us, following the path of a singular bird that loops in circles over our heads. No sight of drones, but that doesn't mean we aren't being watched.

Dani abruptly sits up and stares in the direction of the front gate. I look that way but don't see anyone who stands out. "Chi-Chi saw a strange looking car pull up, and they've been stopped by the guards." She presses her ear and listens. I watch her, waiting for an update. It feels like forever. "They were just waved inside." She brings her sleeve to her mouth. "Get ready. It's showtime."

If I thought my nerves were going to implode before, they're really feeling it now. Dani is laser focused on the bend in the road that leads from the front of the gate straight to us. She pulls one of her pistols from the holster and keeps it hidden under the table. I reach for my own and do the same.

A vehicle slowly rounds the corner, and Darby wasn't kidding when she said it was strange. Unlike Dani's Jeep, this is a small, rounder car with a petite truck bed in the back. The yellow paint is faded, and there are two lights secured to the top. Who would have such a vehicle?

The car turns before it reaches us, and I try to catch a glimpse of the driver, but the windows are too dark.

"Did you see who it is?" Dani asks, watching as the car parks in front of a building about thirty meters away. I don't know if she's asking me or Mike.

"No," I answer anyway. My throat feels dry.

Dani and I hold perfectly still, guns drawn, while we wait. For a moment, I wonder if this is another suicide bomber or a distraction so someone can sneak in from behind, and I start to voice my suspicion when the driver's side door opens.

My heart races. Please don't be my mother.

A petite woman steps out. Even squinting, it takes me a moment to register who it is. "Rodrigues?" I exhale and loosen the grip on my pistol.

"Your assistant?" Dani asks, surprised.

She's wearing large dark sunglasses, a jacket that cuffs at her waist, and tight jeans. Her black, ankle-height boots are tied tightly, and her long dark hair whips around her face as she makes her way over. It's odd to see her out of uniform. She looks like such a regular person that it throws me.

My gut tells me this isn't a trap. "Hold your fire," I say to Dani.

"Hold your fire, but stay on alert," Dani says to the others. We both stand, and Dani makes a point to keep her hand on one of her pistols.

Once Rodrigues has crossed the street, she lifts her hands to show that she's not holding a weapon. "I'm unarmed," she says.

"Yeah, right," Dani mumbles and shows no sign of holstering her gun.

"I'm surprised you came," she says to me and pushes up her sunglasses. I don't say anything when she reaches the table, her gaze now locked on Dani. "And you brought Danielle Clark. Hi, I'm Jenisis Rodrigues." She stretches out her hand. I swear I catch a hint of excitement in her voice.

Dani looks at the hand, then to me, and back again, clearly confused, and makes no effort to reciprocate the gesture.

Rodrigues doesn't seem to mind. She lowers her arm and smiles. "It's such an honor to meet you," she says.

Dani leans toward me. "What the fuck is going on?"

I'm just as thrown. "Rodrigues," I say, bringing her attention back to me. She extends her hand again. I grab her forearm briefly, still confused.

"There are rumors going around that you were kidnapped by the Resistance. Did you know that?" She appears amused.

"Let me guess, were those rumors started by my mother?"

She nods. "It's not a good look to admit that her daughter left willingly to join the enemy." She glances at Dani. "No offense."

Dani doesn't even blink.

"I don't understand what's happening," I confess. "What are you doing here?"

She motions for us to sit. Dani doesn't budge. Wanting answers more than I want to stand around and try to intimidate her, I sit across from her.

Dani looks around, still clearly on edge but sits beside me so close that our thighs are touching.

"After you left," Rodrigues begins, "I went to see Supply Specialist Talib. He told me about you requesting two bikes, and then Privates Miller and Silva went missing after you changed the guard rotation, so I did a little more digging. No one knew a thing about their supposed new assignment. Then you disappeared, and the bikes were found in Des Moines, but there was no trace of the three of you. It wasn't hard to piece together after that." She smiles slightly, seemingly proud of herself.

I can feel Dani looking at me, but I stay focused on Rodrigues. "And Miguel and Anthony? What are they saying about them?"

Her smile fades. "They're considered defectors and are wanted for treason."

My heart sinks, even though I already knew that would be her answer.

"Why did you contact us? How do you know the old Resistance code?" Dani asks.

Rodrigues straightens, almost as if she's steeling herself to answer. "My parents are Resistance."

"What?" Dani and I ask at the same time.

"They've been deep undercover since before I was born."

"You're Resistance?" I ask, still trying to process this new bit of information. "Then how did you know about Lightning Rod?"

"Like I said, my parents. They worked with your father a long time ago," she adds quietly.

My heart pounds. "They knew my father?"

"They said he used to talk about you all the time," she continues.

"Did he know your parents are Resistance?" Dani asks.

"They were undercover," she says vaguely with a slight shrug, like that's the end of that.

Now I'm just annoyed. "Is that why you wanted to be my assistant? To get close to me so you could report back to your parents?"

For the first time since arriving, Rodrigues shifts, showing discomfort. "Sort of."

"Sort of?" It's clear Dani doesn't like that answer when she places her pistol on the table. Rodrigues sits back a little, eyeing the weapon carefully. I place a hand on Dani's arm, stopping her from making any more threats. I want to hear Rodrigues out.

She looks back to me, a nervous expression on her face. "Being assigned to you wasn't some great setup. In fact, my parents weren't happy about it. But the order came from above. Major E. J. Allen. It was the first and only time I'd ever been contacted directly."

E. J. Allen. The name sounds familiar, but I can't quite place it.

"Major E. J. Allen?" Dani asks, and I bet she's itching for her father's journals.

Rodrigues doesn't elaborate. "The assignment was simple. Become your assistant and send any intel or advancements or breakthroughs through encrypted messages to a specific channel." She looks at me, her wide eyes pleading. "I wasn't lying when I said I've looked up to your father my entire life. His work had such a profound impact on my childhood. He was the *one* person within the NAF who my parents spoke highly of. When the opportunity came from the top to work alongside you, I was excited. If you were anything like your father…" She waves her hands a bit, like she can pull the words she's looking for out of the air. "I just wanted to put all the pieces of the puzzle together, I guess. It wasn't about betraying you."

"Wait, I'm confused. Is E. J. Allen NAF or Resistance?" Dani asks after a brief silence.

"Resistance," Rodrigues says slowly like she assumed Dani knew that.

"You've never heard of them?" I ask, glancing at her and taking in her concerned expression.

"No." Her jaw tightens, annoyed, and she pins Rodrigues with an accusing stare. "Who is it?"

Rodrigues appears taken aback. "I don't know, either. No one does. Just that they're the Resistance's top spy and has been embedded inside the NAF for years. One of the only ones to climb the ranks and not get caught."

"You don't find that a little suspicious?" Dani presses. "An unknown spy who other spies take orders from and report to without *anyone* knowing who they are or where the information is actually going?"

It does seem a little odd. "I'm with Dani on this one," I say. "How do you know they're really Resistance? How do you know they aren't really NAF using this cover to try to out Resistance spies?"

Rodrigues blushes a little. "I mean, I guess—"

"How do we know you aren't unknowingly collecting intel on us right now to report back to the gray coats?" Dani narrows her eyes. "Did Major E. J. Allen have you request this meeting?"

"No," Rodrigues is quick to assure. "I asked for this meeting on my own. I came across important information that needed to get to you quickly." She looks at Dani. "We need you. We need the Daughter of the Resistance. I don't think you realize how important you are."

I watch the exchange curiously. Dani ignores the compliment and implication of what that confession may mean, and I ignore the fact that there are more spies embedded in the National Armed Forces than I ever realized.

"Why not just ask to meet with me? Why use Kate?" Dani leans forward just enough to be threatening. "And how did you know our frequency?"

To her credit, Rodrigues doesn't pull away. "My parents are Resistance," she repeats as if that answer is still good enough. "I learned all the Resistance frequencies before even signing up for the NAF." She glances at me. "I've tried for the past two months to get ahold of you and got nothing. I was desperate. I needed to get someone's attention and Kate…well…" She gives me an apologetic look.

I meet Dani's eyes. She's not even attempting to hide her annoyances at being played so easily.

"There's something else," Rodrigues says quickly. "There's a spy on your side, too. They're leaking pretty significant information."

Dani and I exchange another look. Looks like William was right, after all.

"You already know," Rodrigues says, her gaze dancing back and forth between us.

"We've heard mumblings," I tell her. "What sort of intel is being leaked?"

"For starters, the general knew about the ambush that was supposed to happen at Sioux Falls. She was ready for it until someone made it public knowledge. Then she had no other choice but to pull back." Her eyes are on Dani. "She knew you were going to attack the convoy to Malmstrom and used the ambush as a distraction to smuggle the drones off base while you were preoccupied." Dani clenches her jaw but says nothing. "She also knew the Clarks were in Rapid City long before she sent her own decoy convoy to Ellsworth to try to trap Danielle, and that William was going to investigate Malmstrom. She hoped to catch him in the blast."

I stare at Rodrigues, shocked at her reveal. I knew I was being left in the dark regarding my mother's movements, but this goes much deeper than I imagined. And it seems pretty clear that whoever this spy is, it's someone close to us.

"Did she know I was in Rapid City, too?" I ask. Rodrigues slowly nods, and my body deflates. My mother knew I was there and bombed it anyway.

"Is there anything she *didn't* know?" Dani asks, her voice ice cold.

"She didn't know that you'd survive everything she threw at you." Rodrigues's voice softens. "And she didn't know you were in White River until you released the Lieutenant Colonel and her team."

I watch as Dani clenches her fists so tightly, her knuckles turn white. "Dani," I say softly, trying to calm her. The air is tense, like nobody wants to move for fear of all hell breaking loose. Dani's breathing is measured, but I can see her jaw clench over and over. "Dani." I say again.

She brings her sleeve to her mouth, not caring at all to keep the microphone hidden inside a secret. "That's enough," she demands, and I can only imagine what the others are saying in her ear.

Rodrigues seems confused by the command. Covert is no longer an option, apparently. I can see the exact moment it registers. "How many people do you have surrounding me right now?" Rodrigues asks, her eyes darting to the buildings on either side of the street.

"Enough," I tell her. "Jenisis, do you know who the NAF spy is? The one who's relaying all this information?"

"No. If I did, I would tell you." She sighs regretfully.

"Then what *do* you know?" Dani asks impatiently.

"Let me show you." She holds up her hands and then dramatically looks around at the buildings. "Would one of you please check my inner right coat pocket?"

I move to stand, but Dani extends her arm and prevents me from doing so. "I'm checking her pocket. Remember your orders."

At least this time, she didn't talk into her sleeve.

Dani points her pistol at Rodrigues as she slowly rounds the table. Rodrigues's brown eyes sparkle as she stares at me. Her lips curve up just the slightest despite looking extremely apprehensive, and I hold my breath, hoping that she is, in fact, Resistance and not planning something stupid.

Carefully, Dani reaches into her pocket and pulls out several folded sheets of paper. I slowly release my breath, relieved.

Dani sits and hands the papers to me. I inspect them carefully, and though I can't understand some of them, I know someone who will. "These are blueprints. You got around the blockers." I move on to the next sheet. "And marching orders. Bismarck is next?"

"Maybe. There's also a lot of weird movement in and out of Rapid City, but no one is mentioning it. I wouldn't ignore it."

"Misdirection," I remind Dani.

She looks at me with a worried expression.

"I tried to write down everything that's going to happen and when," Rodrigues continues. "So much of it is above me, and I can't guarantee it's all going to play out that way, but this is what's circulating around base right now, and I figured this was a starting point."

"Why are you doing this?" I ask. "If you're telling the truth, you're risking your life to be here."

"I know," she says. "Something big is going to happen soon. I don't know where or what, but the Resistance needs to be ready. They need to see Danielle, William, and Thatcher making big moves. Morale is low. We need to know our best players are in the game." The look on her face makes my stomach flip. She's scared, and it's easy to tell.

"And what about Simon?" Dani asks. "What's he up to?"

"No one really knows. It's like he's on this insane covert mission, and he only answers to General Turner." Unfortunately, that's not surprising, and it matches our own intel, but it's still disappointing to hear. She gives Dani a remorseful look. "He's also parading your Jeep around like a trophy."

"He has my Jeep?" She practically growls. "That slimy motherfu—"

"Can you give me a minute with Rodrigues?" I interrupt and touch Dani's arm to bring her attention back to me. She starts to protest, but a gentle squeeze stops her. "Please?"

She stares at me and Rodrigues but eventually gives in. "You have two minutes, but I'm standing right there." She points a few meters away. I agree, knowing it's not worth fighting her over. As she huffs out a final pout, I find myself wishing Rodrigues hadn't shared that bit of information about Dani's beloved vehicle; it only made her crankier.

Rodrigues stands when Dani does and extends her hand. "It really was an absolute honor to meet you."

"Don't screw us over," Dani warns and again ignores the hand.

"Never. With the screwing..." Rodrigues calls out while Dani gives us some space. "Wow, she's...really something in person. Now I understand everything."

I cross my arms. "Jenisis, this isn't some war game or training exercise. What you're doing is incredibly dangerous."

She sighs and shrugs as if it's no big deal. "Yeah, but with you gone, someone has to step up and feed intel to the Resistance. Why not me?"

"For starters, you could be killed."

"So could you," she fires back without missing a beat.

We stare at each other, neither one of us backing down. I can almost hear Dani tell me we only have one more minute.

I break eye contact. "How's Ryan?"

"He was sent into the field not long after you left for an undisclosed mission. I haven't seen him since."

It physically pains me to know that he's out there doing who knows what. It doesn't surprise me that my mother is using him for sensitive assignments. I wish there was something I could do to keep him safe.

Rodrigues looks at me carefully. "Do you want me to try to get him a message?"

"No. No, that won't be necessary." As worried as I am about him, I have to trust Ryan to make smart decisions and stay away from trouble. My mouth feels dry, and I swallow, hoping I can hold back the next question I so desperately want to ask. Rodrigues waits as if she sees my internal debate. I dig my toe into the ground, unable to meet her eyes. "Does my mother care? That I left?" I hate that I'm unable to stop myself from asking, and I positively loathe how my voice cracks when I do.

None of it is worse than the way Rodrigues's expression shifts so easily to sympathy. "I know she does."

"But not for the reasons I want her to," I say aloud. Not because she loves or cares for me as her daughter but because it isn't convenient for her or her image. It doesn't fit her grand plan.

This time, Rodrigues doesn't respond, and I'm grateful for her silence.

"How did you manage to get off base?" I ask, wanting desperately to redirect attention away from myself.

"Shore leave," she answers easily. "My parents are visiting my grandpa nearby, so I was allowed a day to visit all of them. I even managed to get Talib to get me a car without a tracker." She motions to the weird vehicle she arrived in.

Dani clears her throat, and we both look over. She taps her wrist to signify that time is up.

Rodrigues looks surprised. "She wasn't kidding about the two minutes."

"She doesn't trust you."

"I don't blame her." Our eyes meet, and she offers a small smile. "From the moment I met you, I knew. I knew you were going to help end this war one way or another. I was loyal to you then, and I'm loyal to you now. You have my word."

Dani takes a step forward. "Kate." Her tone is serious, and I know it's a warning.

I hold up a finger to Dani, telling her to give me one more minute. "I better go before she has Darby release Chi-Chi."

"I don't know what that means."

"Please be careful," I plead, not bothering to explain. "My mother...she doesn't go easy on traitors." I know if either of us is caught, death will be something we wish for. I've seen it firsthand, the inhumane way she allows prisoners to be treated.

It sends a chill down my spine.

"Take care of yourself, Lieutenant." Rodrigues turns and slowly makes her way back to her car, offering a small wave at Dani as she does.

"I don't trust her," Dani says when I make my way over.

"She's a good person," I say, watching Rodrigues glance around the buildings for any sign of our friends.

"She's lying about how she knows your childhood nickname."

I watch her get in her car and slowly drive back to the front gate. I take a deep breath and frown. "I know."

CHAPTER FOUR: THE UPDATE

DANI

The entire interaction with Rodrigues leaves me unsettled. She's hiding something, and my gut tells me it's something big.

"I can't believe you didn't let me shoot her," Jack says, breaking the silence.

"What kind of information did she give you?" Mike asks. "It was hard to hear what she was saying."

"She's hiding something. We shouldn't trust her," Jack continues as if reading my thoughts.

Mike playfully pushes Kate's shoulder from the back seat. "So that's your assistant."

"Was," Kate corrects. "Was my assistant."

"She's cute," Mike teases. "What exactly did she *assist* you with?"

"Hey," I warn, not at all amused with his implication and further aggravated by Kate's small smile in response. Even if it is followed by an eye roll. "Jack, to your point, I don't trust her, either. None of us should," I glance at Kate, who avoids looking at me. "It goes without saying, but do not repeat anything that happened today to anyone. Got it? In fact, don't talk about *anything* regarding the Resistance outside of the group until we know what the hell is going on."

Glancing through my rearview, I notice expressions of worry etched across their faces. I can't say I blame them. To have an active member of the NAF confirming there are people within the Resistance playing both sides is troubling.

"Are we going to have to move again?" Mike asks.

I sigh and shake my head. "Not yet. Let's just keep our heads down in the meantime."

"Business as usual," Jack mutters.

After hearing Rodrigues begging us to make a big move, I can't help but think that even if she wasn't being fully forthcoming or honest, she definitely isn't wrong, either.

Jess and Elise are sitting at a corner table inside Marium's place when we get back to Woodlake. Roscoe pops his head up from his spot by their feet before I even manage to get the door all the way open.

"They're back," Elise announces. "How did your meeting go?"

I pull out a chair beside her and slip my coat over the back. "Not here," I tell them both. Despite the place being empty, I'd rather not talk about it all in the open.

"Wyatt is making lunch," Jess says, not pressing for any more information and no doubt understanding the sensitive nature of it all.

"Thank goodness," Kate says while washing her hands and removing her coat. "I'm starving."

It's only then that I pick up on the savory smell of fried fish, making my stomach rumble with anticipation. Mike walks in and reaches to wash his hands, but Elise makes a noise to stop him. "Go tell the others that it's lunch." His smile fades, and he walks right back out in search of the remainder of the group.

It doesn't take long for everyone to trickle in at the prospect of food. Mike and George drag away chairs from the other tables, and we push them together, making one large rectangular space. It's a tight fit, but no one seems to mind. We're not often together like this these days. It's nice to all be in one place and enjoy a meal together again.

The room is warm from the woodstove, and the orange glow from lanterns is a nice contrast to the overcast sky outside the windows. It almost feels cozy. Marium helps Wyatt serve the food, bragging about the fresh catch George and Wyatt helped some folks around town catch this morning before disappearing back into the kitchen, leaving us alone. The group is buzzing, excited for a hot meal. Everyone thanks Wyatt once he sits, and my mouth waters over the golden, panfried fillet and sliced potatoes before me.

The first bite practically melts in my mouth, and it only takes a moment for me to place the flavor. My chewing slows as my stomach flips, and a deep nostalgia washes over me, one that I would've once welcomed but now wish would disappear forever.

I all but push my plate away.

"I thought you were hungry," Kate whispers, leaning into me. She glances at the others, her brows knitting in confusion when she notices Mike, Elise, and Jack have all stopped eating. "What am I missing?" she asks, looking at her plate.

"Do you not like walleye?" George asks, seemingly picking up on the tension filling the room. "We've been eating so much trout that I thought this would be a nice change."

I glance at Jack, worried about how he's going to handle this. He holds perfectly still, staring at his plate and clenching his jaw.

"We like walleye. Right?" I prompt.

Everyone is quick to assure him that they do. Everyone except Jack, who takes a deep, steadying breath. The others avoid looking at him, but I continue to stare, waiting for an explosion that I have no doubt will happen.

Kate glances warily at Jack. "What's going on?" she asks.

He continues to stare at his plate. His hands ball into fists on the table.

"Jack," I say softly.

"Is it undercooked?" Wyatt asks, his voice quiet and unsure.

"No," Elise is quick to say. "Really, Wyatt, it's done beautifully."

"What's happening? Is no one eating?" Jess asks.

I swallow the lump in my throat, hating the way it constricts but unable to stop it. "It was Rhiannon's recipe. Her favorite."

Reality seems to come crashing down. It hurts to voice it aloud and even more that my voice still shakes when I say her name.

Wyatt licks his lips nervously and shifts in his seat. "I found it in her cookbook. I thought it might be nice to…" He glances around the table, and his shoulders slouch in defeat as if he realizes he may have made a big mistake.

Jack pushes away from the table so violently, it makes us all jump. He stomps out without a word, leaving his food untouched. I let him go, knowing that urging him to stay would do more damage than good.

Wyatt looks as though he may cry, and it makes me feel even worse. "I shouldn't have." He clears his throat. "I'm sorry."

The bell chimes as Jack leaves. "No," I say softly and smile at Wyatt, tears stinging my eyes. "Don't apologize. You nailed it. Rhiannon…" I stop and clear my throat, determined to say her name without my voice wavering. "Rhiannon would've loved this. She would have been really proud." And I mean it. She would've been so overjoyed that she was able to pass on one of her favorite recipes to someone who shared her passion for cooking.

I can almost hear her telling us to stop being dramatic and just enjoy the damn food. Taking a shaky breath, I do what I know she would want us to do and take a large bite.

"It really is delicious, Wyatt," Elise says and smiles.

Everyone agrees, and Jess reaches out to squeeze Wyatt's arm. He nods and accepts the compliments, but it's too late to resuscitate the moment.

It's the best meal we've had in months, and yet, it's plagued with grief.

❖

After we eat, I find Jack at the edge of the river. His knees are tucked to his chest, and he's hunched over them, staring at the horizon. His large frame looks shockingly small.

Sitting beside him, I hand over a sandwich that Marium made after we finished eating. He takes it and murmurs a quiet thank-you, but he doesn't bother taking a bite.

About a month ago, Darby, of all people, started this new tradition in our group that when moments of grief over losing Rhiannon get too heavy, she starts recalling the funny memories, and it never takes long before everyone jumps in with either details or small smiles. There are still tears, but it's a different kind of cry. It's almost healing.

"Do you remember that time," I start and look at the sun reflecting off the icy water, hoping that I'm not pushing him too far by attempting a Rhiannon story between just the two of us. "We went fishing in that boat we spent weeks building?"

Jack makes a sound like a small snort.

Emboldened by his response, I continue, "And Rhiannon didn't want us to go because she insisted that we didn't know what we were doing. We got, like, a hundred meters out before it started leaking." I look at Jack and see a small smile pulling at the sides of his mouth. "She was shrieking so loud from the shore that I swear people could hear her from town."

He actually laughs. "Her arms were waving all over the place. We scooped the water out as fast as we could, but it was no use."

I laugh, too, picturing us on that boat, water up to our knees, knowing we were in for an earful from Rhiannon. Pretty sure both of us wanted to be swallowed by the lake rather than suffer her wrath.

"She said she wasn't going to let us eat at the tavern for a week because we could've drowned." His smile fades, and he swallows hard. "I miss her," he whispers.

The admission brings the tears faster than I can wipe them away. "Me too," I say through a sob that I wasn't expecting. "Sometimes it hits me so hard…" I swipe at my nose and choke back a laugh. "Like right now."

He wipes his cheeks on his shoulders. "Or when someone cooks a fish."

We sit perfectly still for a moment, just listening to the wind howl as the sun starts its descent on the horizon. I can already feel the temperature dropping as the afternoon fades into evening. "I really miss her."

He sucks in a deep, shaky breath. "Remember the time she fell face-first into the trash can?"

A laugh bursts from deep within my chest, and my eyes well up again, but somehow, crying through these wonderful memories lightens the ache in my chest.

❖

When I get back to the room that I share with Kate, I expect her to be asleep, but she's not. The moon shines through the window, and she turns in bed, her eyes large and worried. I step out of my boots and toss my jacket on the chair. She pulls back the covers and opens her arms. I thought I was all cried out and had no tears left, but the gesture brings more to my eyes, making my vision blurry.

I fall into her arms and bury my face against her neck. She rubs my back as she holds me tight and whispers words I can't quite make out. Her voice is soothing, and her warm breath is comforting. There's so much we need to talk about, so much we need to figure out about Rodrigues and the possibility of a spy, but I just can't bring myself to focus on any of it.

Instead, inside the comfort of Kate's arms, I cry myself to sleep.

❖

The smell of coffee wakes me. The bed dips, and I open my eyes. Kate sits on the edge with the largest mug I have ever seen, steam steadily coming off the top. "Hey," I say and sit up.

"Good morning." She extends the mug. "I thought you could use some caffeine before your call with William."

I rub my eyes and groan. I had forgotten about the call with William. Taking the cup, I notice that it's only half-full. "Did you spill some of it?" I ask, amused.

"It smelled really good. Miguel swears it comes from across the border to the States." Her eyes are wide and innocent and just a little bit guilty.

"So you just had to try it," I guess. She blushes. Any kind of trading from across the border is practically unheard of. Still, it smells fresh, and I take a sip, savoring the rich flavor. "Across the border, you say? What did you have to trade for it?"

"He heard about what happened last night. The fish recipe. He wanted to do something nice."

I don't bother asking who he heard it from. Taking a few more sips, I give the rest to Kate and push off the covers, wanting to wash up and get ready for my call. After pulling on some clean clothes, I take back the mug only to find it empty.

"Are you sure you brought that for me?" I ask, smiling.

"Mostly," she admits and wraps her arms around my neck, leaning in for a gentle kiss. "Are you okay?"

"Keep kissing me, and I'll be better than ever." She sighs, my deflection not working. "I'm okay," I finally admit. "Sad and tired but I'm okay."

She frowns and tightens her hold. "Do you want me to go with you when you call William?"

I shake my head. "No, but I appreciate the offer."

Gently cupping my face, she kisses me again. "We will get back to kissing when you've finished."

"Just kissing?" I tease. She winks, and I pull her into a tight hug. "Thank you." There are very few people who I feel safe enough to break down in front of.

"For what?" she asks.

"For last night. For the coffee." I squeeze a little harder. "For being you."

She squeezes back, and I sigh, knowing quite certainty that if I didn't have Kate to help me through all of this, I would most likely be headed down a very familiar path of darkness.

❖

The door to Jess's room is open slightly, and I knock lightly, but no one answers. "Jess?" I ask and knock again.

I peek inside just as Wyatt stands from the table. "Dani, hi." He looks nervous and then tries a smile, walking from around the table and motioning for me to come in. "Good morning. Jess said you would be by. She's just washing up."

I glance first at the closed bathroom door across the hall and then at the radio, notepad, and set of headphones in the center of the table. Wyatt follows my line of sight and back to me, shifting nervously. He reaches for the notepad and pulls it toward him, ripping off the top page and stuffing it inside his pocket. His face is red, and he looks like he's going to be sick.

"Everything okay?" I ask and step farther into the room, my eyes never leaving his.

He brushes his shaggy hair from his face and avoids looking at me. "I, uh, was just waiting for Jess to finish up, and then I was going to go help Marium with breakfast."

"I see." My gaze goes to the hand still stuffed in his pocket. "Anything come through on the radio while Jess was indisposed?"

"The radio?" He squeaks and clears his throat. "No. Nothing through the radio."

"Dani, is that you?" Jess asks and pushes the door open before I can ask anything else.

Stepping to the side, I let her in. "Yeah," I answer, still staring at Wyatt. "It's me."

"I'm running a bit late this morning. I'm sorry." She extends her hands, reaching for the table, and brushes her wet red hair from her face and ties it behind her. "Wyatt, are you still here?"

"I'm here." He continues to avoid my eyes. "Let me put on my shoes, and then we can give Dani her privacy."

She turns in my direction. "How's Jack?"

I watch Wyatt scramble around the room for a bit. "He's okay. Considering."

"He's just so angry all the time, and then yesterday, with the fish…" She sighs, ever the emotional caretaker. "I'm just worried about him."

"Can you blame him?" Typically, I'd commend her kind heart, but I can't seem to keep from following Wyatt and his erratic behavior.

He scurries to Jess's side. "Your sweater," he says and holds it up behind her.

She smiles and holds out her arms for him to help her slip it on. "Thank you." She turns back to me. "The radio is all yours. Take your time, but please lock up when you leave. We'll be downstairs if you need anything."

Wyatt hands me the key to their room and continues to avoid my gaze. "I shouldn't be too long," I tell her as she reaches for Wyatt.

Once they leave and their footsteps disappear down the hall, I take a quick note of the current channel and switch to the frequency per William's instructions on the long-range handheld. "Atomic Anomaly checking in," I say while my gaze lingers on the notepad Wyatt was writing on when I came in.

"I'm here," William responds. "You're late. Over."

"I had a rough night. Over," I tell him, leaning back in the chair and rubbing my face, still exhausted.

"I take it you got there all right?" He skips the "over," knowing I'll answer a question without the prompt. We have been at this a long time. He and Dad taught me how to do these calls when I was eight. Etiquette isn't high on my list.

"More or less." I stare at the ceiling. "What's happening back east?"

"We're on schedule. Reinforcements should be here in a month or so."

A month or so. I scratch the back of my neck. That's not going to cut it if Rodrigues was being honest with her intel. "Might want to get them to speed it up. The NAF is planning something soon."

There's a slight pause on the other end. "Who told you that?"

"Just a rumor floating around." I don't even entertain telling him about the meeting with Rodrigues. Not yet anyway. I can't even imagine how fast his head would explode if I told him I managed to pick up another secret NAF contact. He's still having a hard time knowing Kate's around.

"I'll see what I can do." There's another long pause. He must be gearing up for something serious. "What we talked about last time. Regarding the…" He lets go of the button. I can tell by the soft click.

"I got it," I snap, saving him from trying to hint at what he wants to talk about: whoever is leaking Resistance information to the enemy.

"Any leads?"

"No," I say and glance at the notepad again and try my damndest not to jump to any conclusions. "I don't know how many times I have to tell you, it isn't anyone on my end."

"And I told you that it makes sense that they would be, given the timeline."

"Drop it. I'll worry about my people, you worry about yours." I am over him insinuating that it's Kate or one of my friends. I don't need the constant reminder that the information leaks started happening around the same time Kate and the others landed on my doorstep.

"I'm just saying, be careful. Stay vigilant."

"Yeah," I say, no longer interested if this is what he called to talk about. "What do you know about a Major E. J. Allen?" I ask, changing the subject.

"Where did you hear that name?" His tone is clipped, surprised.

"Not important. It's not a name I remember seeing in Dad's journals." I sit up straight, now very interested in this conversation. "What do you know about them, and what aren't you telling me?"

"I've never heard the name before," he says quickly. He's lying. I can tell even without seeing his expression. I'm getting really tired of people lying to me. "Look, I'm sorry, I don't have a lot of time. Over."

I debate telling him I don't care. He's being weird, and I want to know why, even if it means giving sensitive information over the radio. "What's the assignment?" I ask instead, filing away to come back to this mystery spy the next time I see him. I'm expecting another trade drop or supply run. That's all I've been allowed to do since Rapid City. It's getting old, and I'm itching to get back into it. My patience for sitting on the sidelines is wearing thin.

"There's a pop-up camp near your location. They just received a large and apparently very valuable shipment of supplies. We need you to take it out."

Excitement bubbles, and I sit up straight, very intrigued. Finally, some real action. "Is this a shipment for them or for somewhere else?"

"They're coming out of Warren."

"Warren?" I frown. "That's over eight hundred kilometers away. Why wouldn't the supplies come out of Grand Forks?"

"My guess is that it has to do with aircraft since their aerial division was sent there after Malmstrom blew."

"How do we know we're not being set up for another trap?" I ask, thinking about how we were lured to the convoy headed to Malmstrom, only to be used as a diversion for the general to smuggle drones off the base while we were distracted.

"We don't," William says regretfully.

I pinch the bridge of my nose, already annoyed that we could be attacking a camp for no other reason than it's a diversion from the real action elsewhere. Always fun playing this mind game with the NAF. "Numbers?"

"Unknown but manageable. We think they have supplies that are going to be used to attack Bismarck."

That bit of information has my undivided attention. "You hear anything about Rapid City?" I ask, heeding Rodrigues's warning about not ignoring the movement in and out.

"Silent on that end," he dismisses. "The camp we need you to go after is settled just west of Dickinson, about two hours northwest of your location. You need to make sure the supplies don't make it out of the camp."

"Hit and run," I say to the empty room while he keeps giving instructions. My specialty.

"They are probably already equipped with drones. It's essential that you take those out as well as the incoming supplies," he says, emphasizing each word. "After you succeed, you will need to move locations."

"We're going to run out of safe houses at this rate," I mutter to myself.

"Don't tell me where you're going," he continues. "I'll keep this frequency open for emergencies."

"Soon we'll be seeing more than just drones," I tell him, thinking about how they got around the blockers.

"I heard that, too."

I catch the beginning of a heavy sigh before his line goes silent. It's clear that he's doing his best not to lose hope, but I have a feeling we're running low on time. I need to get him the information from Rodrigues.

"I have some intel I want to get to you."

There's a long pause. "Can we trust the source of this intel?"

"No." I hesitate a moment before deciding that's all I want to say for now.

It takes William a bit to respond. "I'll try to send a secure contact."

"I need to put the intel in *your* hands." I've had one too many drops where I expected him to be there, and he wasn't. No more secure contacts. I need him to know that this time, *he* needs to be the one to show.

"Understood. I'll make it work." He doesn't let go of the button on his end and takes a deep breath. "You okay?"

"I'm fine." My response is automatic. I'm not looking into sharing my inner turmoil over long-distance radio.

"Be careful," he says quietly. It almost makes me regret pushing away his concern. Almost. "You'll hear from me soon. Over and out."

The connection ends, and I switch back to Jess's main frequency. Indentations on the notepad from earlier catch my eye in the light streaming through the window. Pulling it closer, I stare at the page as the thrill of an upcoming fight swiftly dwindles. Wyatt was writing something, but with such poor lighting, I can't make out the words. I shove the notepad in my pocket and place the pencil behind my ear. I hope there's a simple explanation for his weird behavior.

Otherwise, we may have a very serious problem.

❖

When I walk into the house, there's laughter coming from the kitchen. I wash my hands and slip off my coat. Kate leans back in a chair and looks at me from down the short hallway. "Hey, how did it go?"

"Fine," I tell her, purposely vague on the details. She puckers her lips for a kiss, and I happily oblige.

Miguel smiles and offers a good morning.

A brief silence hangs over us, and I clear my throat, hating how awkward I feel knowing that he probably heard me crying. "Thanks for the coffee."

"It was my pleasure," he says and waves my thanks aside. He motions to Kate. "We were just swapping memories."

I'm grateful for the topic change. "Yeah? Like what?"

"Miguel had just been assigned to my unit. He had the most stubborn horse that did *not* want to follow his commands," Kate says, smiling. "What was his name?"

"Meatball," Miguel says and cringes.

Kate giggles. "That's right. Meatball. We were on assignment, and it was raining. I mean, a torrential downpour, and Meatball bucked him right into the mud."

"I swear, that horse hated Catholics," Miguel grumbles.

Kate bursts into laughter. "Miguel called him Judas after that."

Her laugh is infectious, and I smile, unable to prevent it.

When they stop giggling, Kate wipes her eyes and sighs happily. "That story always makes me laugh."

"Me too," Miguel agrees.

The silence that follows is no longer awkward, but I can't help but feel like I'm intruding. I start to excuse myself, but Miguel looks from Kate to me and stands. "I'll let you two talk. I promised Earl I'd help patch his boat." He clears the table and gives a satisfied nod. "I'll see you both later."

We wait until he has collected his things and leaves before Kate turns, peering at me curiously over her mug.

I lean against the counter and cross my arms. "You seem happy."

She shrugs and puts her mug on the table. "Tell me about the call."

"There's an NAF camp not far from here. William wants us to take them out before they can get supplies to Bismarck."

Her smile fades to a frown. I hate being the bearer of bad news. "So Bismarck *is* the next target? Are you sure?"

"No," I tell her honestly. "But either way, the Resistance wants that camp and the supplies they received shut down." She looks away but not before I notice her panicked look. "You don't have to come, Kate. I'm not asking you to."

She says nothing, only nods.

"I found Wyatt on Jess's radio while she was out of the room," I say, changing the subject.

Her gaze snaps back to me. "What?"

"He was really nervous about it. It looked like he was taking notes. He was quick to shove them in his pocket."

"Did you see what he was writing?"

"No, but I grabbed this." I pull the notepad out of my back pocket and toss it on the table. Kate makes no move to touch it. Instead, she stares at it like it may jump up and bite her at any moment.

"Dani, you can't possibly think—"

"I don't know, Kate. I can't think of anyone else who would be so close to constant, sensitive information. He's always been a bit nervous. And these leaks seemed to start happening a few months ago."

Kate eyes me warily. "Jess trusts him."

"Maybe she shouldn't."

"Dani."

"I'm just saying. There was an EMP in Rapid City from the inside. He managed to get Jess and George into the tunnels *before* the attack."

Kate narrows her eyes. "Didn't Jess say he ran to get Thatcher *after* the radios went dead?"

I groan and pull out the chair beside her and rub my face, hating how paranoid I'm becoming. In all honesty, that entire day is a huge blur. I take the pencil out from where I tucked it behind my ear and pull the pad toward me. Slowly and carefully, I lightly fill the page with the flat side of the lead. Part of me hopes he didn't write hard enough to make an impression.

"What are you doing?" Kate asks, leaning forward for a better look.

"Attempting to figure out what he was so keen on keeping me from seeing." She doesn't say anything. The only sound is the light scratching on the paper. Once I've filled the page, I bring it closer and tilt it to the sunlight, squinting to make out the words. My stomach flips. "Shit."

"What?" Kate quickly stands and peers over my shoulder. "What is it? What does it say?"

"It's a poem." I wrinkle my nose in disgust.

Kate snatches the pad of paper and reads the exposed words aloud. "'The way my heart beats, when you smile it lights the room, forever I choose you.'" Kate clutches the paper to her chest and practically melts. "Aw, that's so sweet. He wrote Jess a love poem."

"Now I know why he was embarrassed. I wouldn't want anyone to see that gibberish, either." I slouch in my chair, equal parts relieved and embarrassed.

Kate laughs. "Dani."

"It's weird."

"It's not weird. It's romantic."

I snort, unable to accept that poetry is anything but a strange way to show affection. I take a deep breath, beyond grateful that it's not intel or coordinates or some type of secret NAF code. I'm also glad I was wrong about the boy. Again. I'm starting to realize all of my misconceptions about him and that he really is just a decent and kind human being. I feel a lot lighter knowing I can cross his name off my list of possible traitors. For now.

Though, his poetry could use some work.

"So you like that kind of stuff?" I ask, watching as she rereads the page.

She blushes slightly and puts the pad on the table. "I don't know. Maybe. No one has ever written me poetry before. It seems nice."

Slowly, I stand. "The sun is hot," I say, walking around the chair to her. She rolls her eyes. "The sky is blue." Grabbing her by the waist, I pull her close. "I really like your ass and the way you shake it, too."

She pushes at my chest, groaning, and I pull her back, kissing her through our smiles. It doesn't take long for her to slip her arms around my neck and press against me.

"Let me show you how romantic I can be in other ways."

"Well, it can't be worse than your poem," she smiles against my lips.

I hoist her up, and her legs circle my hips. I carry her only a few steps and set her on the kitchen table, ready to prove that actions are definitely more romantic than words.

Chapter Five: The Raid

Kate

"You have the worst poker face." Anthony laughs, and honestly, it's the first time I've seen him so happy in the short time that I've known him. It looks good on him.

Miguel's eyes are wide. "What? No, I don't."

Anthony laughs again. "Yes, you do."

"You really do," Elise agrees.

George chuckles a little across the table. "Your eye twitches when you're bluffing."

"You're a horrible liar," Anthony continues.

I laugh at the absolute appalled expression on Miguel's face.

"I am not." He looks around the table. Everyone is smiling and doing their best not to burst into laughter at his horrified expression. Finally, he sinks into his chair, defeated. "Is that the worst thing in the world? To be bad at lying?"

"It is when you're playing for pastries," Anthony points out.

"And on that note," Elise lays down her cards and sits back in her chair, proud and arrogant.

The rest of us groan. She slides the plate of Wyatt's freshly baked plum pastries in front of her and adds them to her collection from the last two rounds.

"Nothing gets me motivated to win like perfectly preserved jam and a good tart," she continues to taunt. Roscoe pops his head up and places his chin on the table. "Don't worry, I'll give you a bite." She pats his head and then splits one and lets him take it from her open palm.

"Who knew you were so competitive?" I say, amused. I fold on my hand. It's nice to see this playful side of Elise.

"You're going to share with the rest of us, though. Aren't you?" Anthony asks, licking his lips and eyeing the plate.

Elise laughs and puts a few tarts back on the plate and pushes it to the middle of the table. "Go on, then."

The teakettle sings from the stove, and Miguel stands to refill our mugs. The lanterns scattered around the small kitchen gives the space an orange glow, and I take a moment to look around the square table. Elise and Wyatt sit close together, with me on their left and Miguel and Anthony on their right. George is across from them, smoking a pipe and leaning back in his chair. Everyone seems happy.

"Do you think they ate dinner?" Elise asks, biting into another tart. She doesn't have to say who she means.

Half our group is missing, burning the midnight oil and trying to figure out how to take out the NAF camp. At first, I was offended by not being invited to join in the planning, but being sidelined and gambling for baked goods has its perks.

"Marium said she'd make sure to send something up." Wyatt stretches his hands high above his head and yawns. "How much longer do you think they're going to be?"

"Tired already?" I tease, pulling in the cards and shuffling them.

"Hey, you try spending all day in the kitchen learning recipes. Marium is a tough mentor. Not like..." His voice trails off, and the room goes quiet. "Not like Rhiannon," he finishes softly.

Miguel pours more hot water into our mugs and offers fresh bags of tea. "I hope this war ends soon."

"Me too," I say and toss the deck to the side, getting the impression no one wants to play another round.

"Why aren't you up there planning whatever it is they're up to?" George asks, taking another puff. Smoke billows around his head, his bright eyes catching the glow of the light and staring right at me.

Sighing, I lean back. "I wasn't asked to be."

"So they're going after the NAF, then," he says, his eyes curious. I shrug, heeding Dani's warning before she went to meet with the rest of the group about sharing information. "That seems mighty dangerous. Planning an attack with only a night to prepare."

"They're leaving in the morning?" Wyatt asks.

"That's the impression I got," I tell them. "But Dani didn't tell me much."

Elise finally pushes her winnings aside in exchange for some tea. "Why so secretive?"

"I don't think she wants the town worrying about military or Resistance affairs. The less people who know what's going on, the less chance of rumors."

Elise hums, accepting my answer.

George stares at me and puffs more smoke. "Any chance of William coming to town?"

I meet his eyes. "Not that I'm aware of."

He puffs some more and slowly nods. I tilt my head curiously. "William and I—"

Before he can finish his thought, there's shouting from outside. We all turn to look at each other, surprised. Simultaneously, everyone leaps to their feet. Miguel races into the other room, and Anthony grabs the rifle propped near the back door. Roscoe barks and growls, his tail between his legs as he sticks close to Elise.

"Wait here," Anthony instructs. Nobody moves as he and Miguel go outside to investigate.

The shouting continues, and I share concerned looks with Elise, George, and Wyatt. The seconds stretch like hours until Miguel bursts through the front door, startling us. "Raiders!"

The single word jump-starts something inside. I race upstairs in the dark, desperate for weapons. After securing a few knives, a pistol, and a rifle, I grab Dani's ammunition bag and toss it into the main bedroom across the hall facing the front of the house. Sprinting downstairs, I slip on my jacket and notice George doing the same.

I grab Elise's shoulder and usher her to the stairs. "Wyatt, go with Elise and barricade the door in the main bedroom upstairs. Dani's bag of weapons and spare ammo are in there. Watch for raiders from the window, and shoot anyone who comes close to the house or tries to get into the bedroom. Do you understand?"

"Yes," he says, but his expression shows utter terror. "But Jess—"

"I'll get her," George says behind me.

Wyatt seems to relax slightly with that answer and after a shove in the direction I need him to go, follows Elise up the stairs, Roscoe already waiting for them at the top.

I wait until I hear the door close and then hand George the rifle. "You good?" I ask.

He grips the gun tightly and slips some ammo into his jacket pocket. "Let's go."

He's out the door first, but I'm close behind. It's dark despite the clear night. The moon illuminates just enough to create shadows within the darkened town, adding to the chaos. The shouts are louder out here, and sporadic gunfire fills the air. Townspeople race to the gate carrying torches, no doubt trying to secure the area.

George and I follow the crowd. It isn't until we get closer that I notice the town has already been breached. "Holy shit," I say, coming to a sudden halt. Raiders spill over the walls like an infestation. Dozens of them.

George pulls me behind a building. "This isn't good."

"We need to stop more of them from getting inside," I say, peeking around the side of the house. I glance behind me, looking for the back perimeter, but I can't see it. "If they're coming in from all sides like this, we won't last long."

"These people aren't fighters," George adds. "If they get overrun…"

"This is bad," Miguel's voice breaks into our conversation as he appears from the darkness.

"Do you have a read on the situation?" I ask.

"The back is clear so far. Anthony went to the front to try to help. The guard in the watchtower was killed. People are locking themselves inside. It's utter chaos," he relays regrettably.

"This town isn't built like a base," I mutter, but that's incredibly obvious. "How many fighters do they actually have?" A raider runs past us, and I take him out with two bullets to the back.

Miguel stares at the fallen raider with wide eyes and then looks at me. "Not enough."

"Yeah, well, now they have us." I glance toward the front gate and then to the men beside me. "George, get to Jess's room. Dani and the others are going to be out here fighting, so keep your granddaughter safe. Miguel, you and I will go through the back gate and try to figure out how these guys were able to scale the walls and hopefully, put a stop to it."

No one questions my orders, and a shot of adrenaline rushes through my veins at taking command of a battle once again. I didn't realize how much I missed it.

George slips off into the darkness, and I follow Miguel to the back of town. An older couple rushes past us and are ushered inside a building by a teenage girl who slams the door behind them.

"This way." Miguel motions me to the left. We slip through two small buildings and then a smattering of trees. The tall wooden fence comes into view, and Miguel leads us to the latch on a narrow gate. Unlocking it, I go through first, holding my pistol in both hands to keep it steady while I look for any type of threat. It's dark enough to keep anyone within the tree line fifty meters away hidden but bright enough that I don't trip with each step I take.

Miguel closes the door behind us, and we press against the fence to try to make ourselves small. Quickly, we move along the perimeter. When we're close enough to peer around the side of the fence at the front of town, I notice the raiders' numbers have dwindled. There are very few raider bodies on the ground, which tells me the guards were overpowered quickly.

There are a handful of raiders along the fence, helping each other up and pushing them high enough that they can pull themselves over. I glance at the watchtower again. From what I can tell, it's still empty. "We could really use a deadeye in the tower," I whisper.

Miguel presses his back against the fence and reaches for the rosary around his neck.

"How are you on ammo?" I ask, pressing flat beside him.

He finishes his prayer and checks. The look he gives me isn't comforting. "Let's just say, I better not miss."

"Yeah, me too." I check that my pistol is good to go and glance at the raiders once more. "I'll take high."

Miguel kisses his rosary and tucks it safely back in his shirt and nods. "I'll go low."

I close my eyes and suck in a shallow breath. Upon release, I think about Dani. Wherever she is, I hope she's not doing something stupid like taking on a dozen raiders with limited ammo. Touching my knives and making sure they are exactly where I want them, I take another steadying breath.

I push off the wall and round the corner firing, hitting high and dropping the raiders trying to climb over and preventing them from entering Woodlake. I down three more, and Miguel takes out another two almost instantly. We've gained the attention of the rest of them, and a large raider fires on us. Instantly, we retreat around the corner for cover. "Great. They have guns." Not having the time to dwell, I quickly regroup. "Get ready."

The words are barely past my lips when three raiders appear in front of us, crude instruments of death clenched tightly in their hands. Miguel shoots one, and I go after the other, both of us spending the remainder of our ammo.

Grabbing one of my throwing knives, I hurl it at the third, hitting him in the neck. He goes rigid, then drops to his knees.

"Nice hit," Miguel says, out of breath and at my side.

"I was aiming for his head," I say, irritated and clearly out of practice.

We rush to their bodies, and I grab the spiked plank of wood one dropped when he hit the ground and hand it to Miguel. I glance at the brute holding his neck. His body twists as he fights to get the knife out. I pull it for him and wipe it on the snowy ground before sheathing it. I pick up my discarded pistol and slip it inside my jacket pocket. "Get back inside, find someone to take position in that fucking watchtower."

Miguel glances at the fallen raider and back at me. "What are you going to do?"

"I'm going to lure the rest of them away."

Another raider rounds the corner, and Miguel swings the plank, taking care of her before I can react. The impact causes her to fall to her knees. Putting his foot on her shoulder and pushing, he yanks back the board, freeing it from her lifeless body. Our gazes meet, and he looks absolutely sickened by what he just did.

"Would you rather have my knives?" I ask.

Two more raiders charge us, and I motion the way we came.

"Go," I yell and sprint toward the river just beyond the tree line, luring as many as I can away from town.

A gun fires from my six, and I hunch my shoulders, trying to stay small, and zigzag through the trees. This was stupid. Really stupid, but it's too late to stop now. So I keep going, running as fast and as far as I can, keeping within the trees for cover.

The tree line seems endless.

Incredibly stupid.

I glance behind me and see two raiders, but I know there are probably more.

The cold air bites my skin, and I find myself wishing for my hat, of all things. The sound of their footsteps subsides, and I believe I've managed to put a little bit of distance between us. Pulling a knife, I crouch beside a tree and spin, balancing the blade between my fingers and familiarizing myself with the weight. I take a couple deep breaths and bring my arm back. When the first raider comes into view, I flick my wrist forward, releasing the blade.

She fires her gun and hits the tree beside me. A splattering of bark flies through the air just as my knife lands in her chest. I quickly pull another knife, let it fly, and hit her in the head.

Pleased, I take a second to appreciate that maybe I'm not so rusty, after all.

She drops slowly, her pistol falling on the frozen ground alongside her with a gentle thud. The relief is short-lived as the second raider flies past her, not even bothering to stop. Two more come into view through the darkness, and I jump to my feet and try to once again put some distance between us.

I've lost track of how long I've been running, but the burning in my lungs and weakening of my legs tells me it's more than I have in quite some time. I hope Miguel was able to get someone in the watchtower and wonder if swinging the raiders back around toward the town would be the best option.

Seeing a break in the trees and water just beyond, I make the decision to turn back. There may be more raiders waiting, but that's where all the help is, too. Dwindling gunshots ring out in the distance. They're still fighting inside Woodlake.

I make a long turn to head back to the gate and try to maintain my speed, knowing that my adrenaline isn't going to last forever. I shove branches out of the way and wonder if I can even make it back. My knees wobble slightly, and the ache in my chest intensifies. The sound of the raiders closing in has my skin prickling with fear.

Grabbing my combat knife, I hold it tight just as my foot hits something on the ground. All I can do to stay upright is reach to brace myself against a tree. Just as I have myself steadied, something large and broad slams into my side and knocks me to the ground.

My head slams against the forest floor, and the pain that shoots through my body causes me to cry out. Instinct kicks in, and I bring my hands up to push at the large raider on top of me. Miraculously, I've held on to my knife, and I shove the blade up under his ribs. He throws his head back and yells in clear agony.

I pull the knife out and plunge it in again and again until he finally goes slack, and I'm able to push him off me. Gasping for air, I try to regroup before I'm hauled to my feet by another raider. He's smaller but strong. He lifts me off the ground and throws me backward. I land hard, my head once again hitting the frozen ground.

My body goes limp, and my vision blurs. Wincing, I try to get up, but I can't. Everything hurts. I hear the raider walk toward me, and though I can't see what's happening, it sounds like more have arrived. I swallow hard, wondering if this is the end for me. Alone in the woods and at the hands of a bunch of rabid raiders.

Definitely not how I imagined going out.

I stare at the moon peeking through the treetops. It's fuzzy, and the forest around me spins. I will myself to move, to find the blade I keep in my boot and fight back, but my body doesn't listen.

The smaller raider comes into view, standing over me, heaving with anger.

The whole interaction feels painfully slow, like he's giving me time to make peace with my fate. All I can do through my haze is wish.

Wish I had a better plan.

Wish I had made amends with my mother.

Mostly, wish I had more time with Dani.

Closing my eyes as two more ugly faces appear above me, I hope that Dani's promise of an afterlife is true.

A loud *thwack* makes my entire body tense, but I don't feel any pain. I take several slow breaths.

I don't feel anything, but I hear it. A scuffle. Then, several gunshots.

Managing to move, I grab the pistol from my jacket pocket and grip it tightly. Everything is still spinning, but instead of the moon overhead, it's a person. I lift my head and squint to get a better look, but everything is fuzzier than before. I can't make out a face because it's obstructed by a fur-lined hood attached to a thick brown jacket.

I raise my gun, hoping it may frighten the stranger away.

They tilt their head, curious.

Crouching, they gently push the gun away and take it like they know it's empty. I squint again, but everything spins so fast that my stomach lurches, and I feel like I'm going to be sick. "Who are you?" I ask, though my speech is slurred.

I don't hear an answer as everything fades to black.

CHAPTER SIX: THE ATTEMPT

DANI

After bringing Kate's hand to my lips, I lightly kiss her knuckles. Her chest slowly rises and falls with each steady breath, and I stare at her, trying to avoid looking at the bandage wrapped around her head.

I should've spent more time with the town to make sure we weren't vulnerable. I should never have let my guard down here. If I hadn't—

"Dani." A hand on my shoulder pulls my attention and silences my mind. Elise hands me a cup of something warm.

Quickly, I wipe my eyes and take it, grateful for the gesture but not at all thirsty. "Thank you," I say and place the mug of coffee on the nightstand beside the bed. She sits in the chair beside me in the dark room. The single lantern flickers, warping our shadows on the wall. "How long?" My voice is scratchy, so I swallow and try again. "How long until we should be worried?"

Roscoe jumps on the bed and curls into Kate.

"We have time," Elise says quietly. The vagueness of her answer isn't lost on me. It's only been two hours, but I'm not sure I can take another minute.

"I should've been there," I say. "I should have never left any of you. I don't know why I keep leaving. If I had just stayed—"

"Dani," she says gently. "Nobody could've predicted this. It most certainly is not your fault."

Shaking my head, I grip Kate's hand a little tighter. "We knew about the raider camp. We were asked to take care of them. I shouldn't have waited."

"Again," Elise says, this time a little louder. "Not your fault. Raiders are unpredictable. You can only do so much."

"It's not enough," I whisper. The lump in my throat grows. "White River, Rhiannon…" I try swallowing, but my throat is still too dry. I take a sip of coffee, wincing when it burns my tongue. "I don't know how much more I can take."

Elise puts a hand on my arm. "Dani."

Roscoe lifts his head with a whine at the same time Kate stirs. Discarding the mug on the bedside table, I lean forward on the bed and take Kate's hand in both of mine. Her face scrunches as if she's in pain, and then, her eyes slowly open. "Dani?" Her voice is hoarse. Her eyes open wide, and she tries to sit up.

Elise makes it to the other side of the bed before I can even mutter a response. "No, honey. Lie back down," she soothes.

We gently urge her down. "I'm here," I assure her. "You're okay."

"Easy now," Elise says. "You hit your head pretty hard. You need to take it slow."

Kate looks from me to Elise and back again. She brings one hand to the back of her head as if just noticing she has a head injury. Her eyes are still wide while she takes in her surroundings. "Where am I?"

"Miguel's room." I lean over and take her face in my hand, tears blurring my vision while I gently run my thumbs over her cheeks. "You're safe."

"The others?"

"Our group is fine. We're all okay."

She nods, and I sit back, intertwining our hands again and bring them to my lips. I can't seem to resist touching her, assuring myself that she's okay.

She closes her eyes and relaxes slightly. "What happened?"

"You took a pretty nasty fall," Elise tells her. "You have a concussion."

Kate's eyes snap open, and she looks at me, frantic, and tries to sit up again. "The person in the jacket. Did you see who it was? What happened to them?"

Carefully, I push her back down and exchange a worried look with Elise. I frown and turn back to Kate. "Jacket? What?"

"Someone saved me, I think." She closes her eyes, and I can tell she's clearly not feeling well. "I fell, and there was a raider, and he was about to..." She swallows hard. "I thought I was done. I thought they were trying to kill me. I pulled out my gun..." She takes a deep breath, her brows furrowed, confused.

I can feel the contents of my stomach rising to my throat. The thought of Kate lying there, helpless and concussed, with raiders standing over her...it's too much.

"My gun was empty." She puts a hand over her closed eyes and winces. "My head is throbbing."

"We don't have to do this now," Elise says. "You really should rest."

"I'm okay," she assures us. "Help me up."

I help her to a sitting position, going slowly to make sure she's comfortable and surrounded by pillows and staying impossibly close. "What happened?"

She takes a few deep breaths, closing her eyes and opening them again. "We were playing a card game, and there was screaming outside. Miguel and Anthony went to see and said that raiders were inside the gates. I had Elise and Wyatt hide in here. George went to find Jess, and Miguel and I snuck around the back to try to stop the raiders from getting over the fence." I squeeze her hand. "There was no one in the watchtower. Miguel went to try to help up front, and I led some of the raiders away from the gate to keep more from getting inside. They chased me through the woods." She swallows and takes a few deep breaths. "They caught up to me. Tackled me. I hit my head. I took most of them out, but I thought they were going to kill me." She looks at me, her eyes filled with tears. "Someone else was there. They didn't look like a raider, but I don't know who it was."

"Miguel told me you took off toward the woods," I tell her, trying to fill in the missing pieces of her story. "Jack and I found you unconscious and alone. You hit your head *really* hard. Nobody was there with you. Maybe you fought them off and just don't remember?"

"I didn't," she says with finality. "I know what I saw. Someone was there. They had on a thick brown jacket with a fur-lined hood." She moves as if she's going to stand.

Putting my hands on her shoulders, I ease her down again. "Okay, just take it easy."

I look at Elise for help. She pats Kate's leg reassuringly. "I'll go see what I can find out about a thick brown jacket and a fur-lined hood."

"Thank you," Kate says pathetically.

Elise leans forward and kisses her forehead and slips quietly out of the room, giving me a look I can't quite decipher.

After she leaves, Kate seems to settle a bit. "Someone was there, Dani. I know what I saw."

"I believe you," I tell her. "But whoever it was wasn't there when we found you." She looks defeated and disappointed. "If it was someone from town, Elise will find them."

"Maybe," she says, though her tone indicates defeat. "But why would they leave me there like that?"

"I don't know." I brush the hair from her face. "I was really scared," I confess softly. "Seeing you on the ground, unconscious. I thought you…" I can't bring myself to say it. My stomach twists. I don't even want to think about it.

"I'm okay," she whispers and gently touches my face. I lean into her cold hand. "I didn't mean to scare you."

I want to say more. That the idea of not having her in my life, even after only a few short months, is more terrifying than any kind of raider attack. Losing her would break me. I will do everything I can to keep her safe because I don't think my heart would survive if anything happened to her. I pull her close. I hug her tightly and bury my face against the side of her neck. "Don't ever do that again," I whisper against her skin.

She nods and hugs me back, stroking my hair and letting me stay pressed against her for another minute while I attempt to collect myself.

Finally, I pull away but lean in, trying to stay as close as I can.

She reaches for the glass of water by the bed and takes a slow, tentative sip. "The town. Was anyone killed?"

"Eight casualties. About a dozen wounded. Elise has been checking on them." Her eyes fall slightly, but I refuse to let her shoulder the blame for this. "You just worry about yourself right now. Let me take care of the rest."

"Dani?" a voice interrupts.

I look over my shoulder. Jack stands awkwardly in the doorway. He glances at Kate hesitantly and then motions for me to come over. "I'll be right back," I promise and kiss her cheek.

She doesn't protest. Instead, she reaches for Roscoe, urging him closer.

I follow Jack into the hall, and he doesn't wait to get into it. "We have a situation." His voice is low and his expression serious. "Jess got another message from a scout nearby. The NAF camp is loading up to move. We can't wait to hit them in the morning. We need to move now."

"Shit." I rub my tired eyes.

"What do you want to do?" he asks.

"It doesn't matter what I want." Glancing back at Kate on the bed, I take a deep breath. "Get the others ready," I tell him.

After what just happened, my heart screams at me to stay, but I know if we succeed in stopping the supplies from getting to wherever they're going, it'll be considered a huge win for the Resistance. We could really use a win right now.

How was it that just a day ago, I was anxious to get back in the fight, and now I want nothing more than to stay out of it? I sigh, deep and heavy. "I'll meet you outside in twenty."

Jack glances at Kate and nods, disappearing down the hall.

"Are you up for this?" Elise asks from behind me, and it makes me jump.

"Shit, you're stealthy." I rotate my shoulders, trying to get the kink out of my neck and refocus my mind, but it's nearly impossible. I glance at Kate spooning Roscoe and frown. "You'll stay with her?"

Elise's expression softens. "Of course I will."

"I'll see if Miguel and Anthony can stay close just in case." Roscoe closes his eyes, content to be cuddled, while Kate gently rubs his side. "Did you find anything about the person Kate described?"

"Not yet."

"Are hallucinations part of head injuries?"

"They're quite common, actually." She puts her hand on my shoulder. "She'll be fine. I'll stay with her until you get back. I'm sure nothing is going to happen while you're away."

I know she's right. With the raiders no longer a threat, the only other worry nearby is the NAF. Thankfully, I plan on making sure they're taken care of, too.

"Please don't be stupid and get yourself killed."

"Never," I tell her. It's a promise I intend to keep.

"There's a lot of movement down there. What do you think they're packing in those trucks?" Mike asks, peering through the scope of his rifle.

"Drones and weapons, probably." Jack scans the tree line, the night vision binoculars pressed to his face. "Why the tree line and not these buildings?" He gestures to the old hotel behind us.

"Probably because they look like they could collapse any minute," Mike says and looks wearily at the decaying structure.

"Great. So glad to be camped out in front of one," Jack mutters.

"It's probably to have room to release the drones." I look up, though I can't see a thing in the dark sky. "If they do, they'll be coming from that direction."

Jack snorts. "Not that we'd see them."

"Which means we should try to sneak in from over there. How's your line of sight?" I ask Mike, ignoring Jack's pessimistic attitude.

"It's not great. Would be better if I could get some height." He examines the closest tree, probably wondering whether he can climb it. "As long as you stay on this side of the trees."

"If only we had a drone to give us a better idea of what we're up against," Jack says and hands Lucas the binoculars. "You know, like we planned."

"Darby's having issues with the battery," I say for the third time. I don't need constant reminders of how valuable a drone would be right now. "See anything useful?"

Lucas takes a moment to answer, slowly examining the camp from where he's crouched. "I'm afraid we're trapped, Captain," he says and continues to scan the area.

I stare at the camp, unable to see much because of the trees and darkness, but I can spot movement close to the handful of fires blazing within. I'm also certain they have guards on rotation. If Jess's intel is right, I doubt we have time to circle the entire camp and look for weaknesses. It may be time to get a little reckless with our approach.

Jack lifts his grenade launcher. "I still say we launch a few of these. That'll distract them."

"Stealth might not be an option here," I agree, taking a look at our supply. We're running low after that fight with the raiders. "But we don't have any grenades to waste, either. We need to make sure each shot counts."

The sound of a truck purring to life catches our attention. It gives me an idea.

"Maybe we can steal their supply trucks," Mike says offhandedly.

It's like he read my mind. "Let's see how close we can get without getting caught."

"And if that doesn't work?" Jack asks.

I motion to the bag of explosives and shrug. "We stick to the original plan and blow the place."

❖

Jack and I crouch behind an overturned tractor trailer, peeking out from opposite ends of it. We're close enough that I can hear chatter and laughter but far enough away that I can't make out specific words. So far, there haven't been any drones overhead. At least, not that we've noticed.

I want to check in with Jess to get an update on Kate before I have to go radio silent, but it's safer not to risk the noise. Still, I rest my hand on the walkie strapped over my coat, tapping it anxiously.

"Looks like they've finished packing up. We're cutting it close," Jack says, still watching the camp and no doubt able to see a lot better now that we've pushed closer. "Which truck should I steal?"

I sense it before I see it. A shift in the wind, like a distant siren song begging for attention. The sound comes next, fast wheels over frost-covered ground. Then, I see her. My longest relationship, my best companion, my pride and joy: my Granite Crystal Jeep Gladiator Rubicon. She looks as gorgeous as ever speeding right for the camp.

My joy is short-lived when I remember who's likely in the driver's seat.

"Is that your Jeep?" Jack asks.

My heart picks up. The night has just taken a very interesting turn.

Mike's voice comes through the radio. "I could be mistaken but is that…" The volume is down, but it's enough for Jack to look again through the binoculars.

"Yeah. It is," I say through clenched teeth.

"The devil walks among us," Lucas whispers from behind me.

"Do you want me to take a shot?" Mike asks from his position back near the crumbling hotel.

"No. He's mine." I release the button, turn down Mike's barrage of questions, and stand, ready to march in there without a second thought. "I'll get the supplies. You set the charges," I command Lucas and hand my satchel to Jack. "Do you remember how to arm these?"

"Yeah, I remember."

"You go left. Lucas will go right. Once they're set and armed, get out of here. Get back to Mike and the buggy." Jack shakes his head. I grab his jacket and pull him close. "Once you've set the bombs, get back to the buggy. If I don't make it out by the time you're back, blow the place with the secondary trigger in the car."

Jack's lips curl into a snarl. "Like hell I'm leaving you."

"The others need you."

"The others need *you*." We stare at each other. Despite him being more than a head taller than me, I don't back down. "Set the damn charges and get out. I'm not losing anyone else, and this is my fight."

Jack practically snarls. "You don't always get to be the hero."

Lucas gets between us and pushes us apart. "There's no more time," he says firmly.

I can tell Jack wants to argue. He's so tense, I can see the veins in his neck. "It's not about being a hero," I tell him over my brother's shoulder. "We're moving in. Hold fire until we've been spotted," I tell Mike and then shut off the radio completely.

Jack stares at me for another beat and slips the satchel over his shoulder. "This is my fucking fight, too." He crouches low and heads to the camp.

"Godspeed, Atomic Anomaly," Lucas says and pulls me in for a hug.

"If anything happens to me, get back to Kate. Do you understand?" I squeeze him tight. When he doesn't answer, I pull back and look at his face. "Promise me."

"I never leave a man behind."

"Lucas. Promise me."

Finally, he nods. "Yes, sir."

"Keep low and out of sight."

He adjusts his hat and takes off in the opposite direction of Jack, making a wide circle around the camp.

From here, I can hear Simon barking orders, and it only fuels my rage. I pull the scarf from my neck and over my face, then slowly work my way from tree to tree to the edge of the camp, trying to stay out of sight of any guards.

The perimeter consists of a few buggies and two box trucks trying to block off access to the soldiers inside the makeshift circle. When I get close to the first truck, I peer around the side. Several fires illuminate about two dozen or so soldiers warming themselves while a few more take down the tents.

"We have to move now," Simon yells from the very center of camp. "These supplies need to be delivered by dawn, and there're reports of Resistance nearby. I don't care if you're cold. Move!"

The soldiers by the fire reluctantly do as they're told. Lifting my gaze to my Jeep parked just beyond them, I pull my pistol and ready myself. I stare at Simon while he stomps around the camp and kicks at crates. I aim, following his erratic movements, my finger on the trigger. I start to squeeze when he ducks into a tent, out of sight.

The second truck sputters to life. We're dangerously close to losing the supplies, and I know Lucas and Jack haven't been able to set all the charges.

"Shit." I release a long breath through my nose and loosen my fingers.

I scan the area again and notice a large canister of water near the back of the second truck. Lowering my gun, I slip to the next closest truck. If I do this right, I can create a diversion for Jack and Lucas so they're able to finish placing the bombs and cause enough confusion that I can go after Simon.

In a quick motion, I open the door and yank the driver out, slamming him to the ground and striking him across the head, knocking him out. I check behind me and grab the heavy water canister, dragging it to the driver's side.

I use the strap that holds my radio to tie the steering wheel so when the truck moves, it'll push through the edge of camp, hopefully gathering the attention of the gray coats. Hauling the canister inside the truck, I hold it over the accelerator. Checking the wheel to make sure it won't move, I shift the truck into drive, and release the canister. I only have enough time to slam the door and dive behind a tree before the truck rumbles through the camp, narrowly avoiding the first fire.

A handful of soldiers dive out of the way. It isn't long before the entire camp is in instant chaos. Sprinting, I charge in the direction of my Jeep, making a dozen long strides before I'm spotted.

"Hey!" A soldier to my right comes to a shocked halt. I fire at him, and the crack adds to the confusion and frantic scrambling.

"It's Danielle Clark," someone yells.

I keep rushing, firing at anyone in front of me and getting shots off on both sides. I get to my Jeep right as a bullet hits the back door. I slide over the hood and use her for cover, popping up to finish off the few soldiers firing at me and praying she doesn't take any more damage.

I can see Jack in the light of the moon along the edge of camp, setting a charge and glancing in my direction with a disapproving stare. A loud crack fills the air, and I know that Mike has taken the diversion as his cue to enter the fight.

"Forget the truck and focus on Danielle Clark," Simon roars from somewhere off to the side. I can see him marching toward the Jeep, his pistol aimed right at me. "Check the camp. I doubt she came alone."

I press against the front wheel, reload, and use most of my bullets on the soldiers that charge me from behind the tents. Once they're down, I stand and charge at Simon. His smug expression falls, and he grabs a young soldier to use as a living shield. I keep pressing forward, ignoring the terrified person he holds in front of him and staring straight into his panicked eyes.

He tries to back up but trips over a pile of wood and releases the kid, who scrambles hurriedly out of the way. I don't give him the satisfaction of any final words. Instead, I aim for his head and pull the trigger.

Click.

I try again and again.

Click. Click. Click.

Simon grins from his spot on the ground, and I hurl my gun at him. It smacks him right in the face with a satisfying *thwack.* He grabs his nose and howls in pain.

I pull my knife just as he seems to notice the discarded pistol left by the boy. I barely have time to dive out of the way when he grabs the gun and takes his own shot, missing.

A few more soldiers appear, and Simon points at me, blood dripping down his nose. "Don't just stand there," he barks. "Capture her."

Scrambling to regain my bearings and find another gun, I stand and turn, only to have my head cracked open. I fall to my knees and press my hand to my temple, wincing as the ground beneath me spins. I'm unable to steady my focus before someone hauls me to my feet and twists my arms behind my back. I squirm and try to get away, but whoever has a hold on me isn't letting go.

I desperately try to wrench myself free, but my wrists are quickly bound, and I'm forced to my knees. If I could just get to my detonator.

"Keep her restrained. The general wants her alive." Simon watches me with clear disdain and leans forward, spitting blood right in front of me.

I try to lunge at him but am immediately pulled back.

Once he realizes I can't go anywhere, he crouches in front me. "My, how the tables have turned." He wipes his nose again, smearing blood along the sleeve of his uniform. His nose sits crooked, clearly broken, and I delight in knowing I'm the reason.

He presses the barrel of his gun right between my eyes.

I thought my life would flash before me right before I died. Instead, I clench my teeth and try to free myself again. There's no sadness, just deep, seething anger.

There's no honor in this death.

He pushes the barrel into my skin, his teeth clenched so hard, I hope they crack. He pushes my head back and releases a feral yell and yanks his gun away.

I don't have time to be confused before he delivers a sharp backhand across my cheek. My head snaps to the side, and I do my best not to let him know how much it fucking hurt.

"Where's Katelyn?" he asks, his face close to mine. I don't answer. He strikes me again. "Where is she?"

"Go to hell," I tell him. Another blow. This time, I can taste blood. Turning my head, I lick my lower lip, feeling where he split it open.

"Is your brother here, too?" He strikes me again. His eyes shine with delight and annoyance. Just the sight of him fuels my anger. "I'm going to ask you one more time," he warns and raises his hand, the handle of his pistol poised to strike.

A shot rings out, and a soldier a few meters away drops.

Mike.

I wonder if I somehow managed to stay on the right side of the tree line.

Simon looks around, angry but not panicked. "Someone get a fucking drone in the air and find them!" He grabs the front of a soldier's uniform and pulls him in close. "Kill anyone who isn't part of the Forces."

I try to free myself again when there's a loud explosion near the edge of camp, and a plume of fire shoots into the air. Jack and his grenade launcher.

Another soldier races to Simon, her eyes wide and scared. "Sir, we have a situation," she says, out of breath.

"I can see that," he snaps.

"Sir, it's about the motor. It's been lost," she says.

I watch as Simon's expression shifts from annoyed to afraid. He glances at me, and another shot from Mike cracks through the air. Everyone drops to the ground.

"Forget the others. Bring Danielle to base." He points at the new soldier. "You, come with me. Now."

She follows him to the Jeep. I try to get free, but the grip the guards have on me is too tight. Whatever motor the soldier was talking about was enough for him to forget killing me. He looked absolutely petrified. I wonder what it is he just cost the NAF.

"On your feet, you Resistance piece of shit," one of them says, and I'm hauled none too gently off the ground.

I try to twist free again as the soldiers that surround me drop, and the shots are enough to make me fall. I roll to my back, ready to put up a fight despite my hands still being bound.

Lucas holsters his gun. "Maelstrom saved the hostages from certain death," he says and helps me up.

"I hate that issue," I mutter while he frees my hands. He throws around that quote every time he comes to my aid. "We have to get the hell out of here," I tell him, rubbing my wrists. "Where's Jack?"

When Lucas doesn't answer, I turn and find him frozen in place. His eyes are wide, and he slowly lifts his hands. That's when I see the pistol pressed against his temple. Instinctively, I begin to dive for anything I can use as a weapon, but a clicking sound stops me.

"I wouldn't."

I stand frozen. My brother holds perfectly still, watching me with scared eyes.

"Where's Kate?" This soldier asks, staring at me.

It takes a moment to realize why he looks so familiar. "Ryan Matthews." I spit out his name, disgusted and furious that I'd allow myself to be caught first by Simon and then by him, of all people. He looks disheveled. His once clean-shaven face is now covered with stubble, and his cropped hair is longer and flops all over the place. Even his uniform is a tad rumpled.

"My men are safe," Lucas answers, his voice steady.

"Let us go," I demand.

He shakes his head. "I can't do that. I have my orders." I take a tentative step toward my brother. Ryan presses his gun harder, making Lucas wince. "Don't take another step."

I stop moving and slowly lift my hands to show I'm not a threat. At least, not yet. My heart races at the nervous expression on Lucas's face. "We've set charges all around your camp. The whole place is going to explode whether we're in it or not. That means you, too, pretty boy."

"Where's Kate?" he repeats.

"Somewhere safe," I tell him and take another small step. "Is that why you're here? For Kate? Or are you Simon's new lapdog?"

"Don't be stupid," he warns and takes a step backward, bringing Lucas with him.

A soldier drops behind Ryan with another crack from Mike's rifle. Several others hurry to get a drone in the air while anyone left has taken cover. "I say you have about two minutes before we're all blown to bits. There's still time to let us go and hop in a buggy and get out of here."

Ryan glances around the camp as if just noticing the chaos. It gives me just enough time to reach for the detonator strapped to my lower back. By the time he looks again, I am holding it up for him to see, my thumb on the button, ready to press.

"So what's it going to be?" I ask calmly.

He hesitates, probably wondering if he should call my bluff. I've strapped a bomb to him before, and he survived. This time, he won't be so lucky, and by the way he stares at the detonator, he knows it.

"They've set explosives," someone yells frantically. "Get the hell out of here."

Our eyes meet. "Don't be stupid," I repeat back to him.

Another beat passes before Ryan pushes Lucas at me and lowers his pistol. "This isn't about Bismarck," he says. "Tell her I'm sorry."

I dive for a discarded pistol and scoop it in one hand, but Ryan is already sprinting toward a buggy. My finger itches to pull the trigger. Something stops me, though. A guilty feeling tells me I can't murder Kate's best friend. Even if he is on the wrong side.

And even if he's her ex.

Lucas rushes to me with a concerned expression. "I'm all right," I tell him.

Simon must've gotten the memo about the explosives because my Jeep fires up, and he tears out of camp, running over anything and everything in his way. I fire a few shots at the tires, but I miss. All I see is the red glow of taillights.

One of the box trucks is on its side in a charred heap, flames dancing around it. It's pretty evident by what's left that this is what Jack took out with his launcher. The second truck runs idle along the perimeter. "Let's grab that truck and get the hell out of here."

There's a slight whirring sound, and I look up. The drone is finally in the air. It's small, clearly used for recon and not big enough to carry explosives. I unload my magazine and make contact just before it disappears into the darkness. Once again, I'm out of ammo. The drone crashes to the ground, and the remaining soldiers rush in our direction.

We take off for the truck before anyone else can use it as an escape vehicle, and I dive in just as Lucas shifts it into gear and slams on the accelerator. Grabbing the radio from my jacket pocket, I turn up the volume. "Coming in hot with one of the trucks."

"Copy that," Mike says. "Everyone is accounted for. Blast it."

We push past the perimeter, Lucas doing his best not to hit anyone despite them shooting at us. Glancing behind me, I flip the switch to the detonator and slam the button.

"Boom," I say right before the blast shakes the truck. The once satisfying sound of explosives only fills me with anger. I'm pissed that Simon got away, and I actually hope like hell that Ryan made it out.

CHAPTER SEVEN: THE REVEAL

KATE

I stare at the crackling fire, ignoring the looks from Miguel across the room. He hasn't left the house since Dani and the others set off to attack the NAF camp. I appreciate his concern, but the constant checking in with me is only adding to my stress. Sighing, I look out the window instead, wondering when Dani will be back.

It's been hours, and the sun has already peeked over the horizon, casting the town outside with a gentle orange glow. Soft scattered flurries whirl through the air, and I pull the blanket a little tighter over my shoulders.

Elise flips through a book she found at Marium's and idly scratches Roscoe's head while he sleeps soundly between us on the small sofa. I'm jealous that he's able to catch a nap. My head pounds, and my body feels utterly exhausted, but I refuse to sleep. Not until I know that Dani and the others are okay.

"Would you like some more tea?" Elise asks softly.

"That would be wonderful," I tell her.

Miguel shoots to his feet. "I'll get it." He rushes over and grabs my mug before I can finish the last sip. Elise holds out her mug as well, and he takes it with a grateful expression, probably happy to make himself useful, and quickly hurries to the kitchen.

Roscoe opens his eyes and sighs, clearly annoyed with the hustle.

Elise waits until Miguel is in the other room. "Some people don't know how they can help, so giving them tasks usually eases that guilt." She closes her book and puts it aside. "I can go check in with Jess if you'd like. I'm due to make rounds anyway."

"No, no, you don't have to do that. Wyatt said he'd come over if there was any news. No need to bug them." I allow my head to slowly fall back to the top of the sofa, and I close my eyes. The image of the person standing over me flashes over and over again. I know I must sound absolutely crazy by insisting that it actually happened. Elise and Dani most likely passed it off as a head injury, but if it's just my concussion, why can't I stop seeing it? And why does it seem so familiar somehow?

"Still painful?"

Instinctively, I touch the bandage. "A little. The throbbing isn't quite as bad."

I can feel her watching me. "I remember this one time, a house needed to be repaired in White River. A huge sandstorm came through and ripped off most of the roof. Dani and Jack were trying to replace these wooden planks, and somehow, Dani got whacked pretty hard in the head."

"Did she see people who didn't exist, too?" I ask but regret how harsh it sounds.

"No. But for weeks, she was wary of shadows." Elise chuckles. "She threw a hammer at a broken tree, thinking it was a wolf hiding in the darkness." She puts her hand on my leg. "Head injuries are tricky. I believe you saw something."

"Then why hasn't anyone come forward?"

"Your head will clear up. The throbbing will stop, and the spinning after sudden movements won't last forever. Just, in the meantime, maybe don't be like Dani and throw hammers?" Her tone is light and teasing.

I know she's right. She has to be. What bothers me is what really happened. Someone had to have taken out those raiders. Is it possible that I was the one to take them out and just can't remember?

Miguel returns with our tea, and I take it with what I hope is a sincere smile. Maybe I should take Elise up on her offer to check in with Jess.

When the front door opens, it's a surprise to all of us. Miguel pulls a pistol, and Roscoe leaps to his feet, hackles raised. By the time I've turned—slowly, so as not to fall off the sofa—everyone seems relieved as Dani comes through looking exhausted.

She seems to notice Miguel first, and the corners of her lips curl into a slight smile before she winces and then washes up by the door. "Good man," she says, clearly pleased that he's taking guard duty seriously. "Why are you out of bed?" she asks, focusing on me.

"I couldn't sit there any longer." Even in the dark, I can tell that she's banged up, and it makes my stomach twist. "You're hurt."

Elise must notice the same time I do because she hurries over. "Dani," she scolds and cups her chin, turning her head from side to side. "What the hell happened?"

"I'm okay. We're all okay. Just a little banged up." She gently pushes Elise's hand away. "The camp won't be an issue, and the NAF will not be getting their supplies." She steps away and slips off her boots and coat. "Thank you for staying with her."

I can tell Elise wants to keep lecturing, but instead, she sighs and glances at me. "She's a much better patient than you are."

Dani snorts a bit and avoids looking at me. I'm anxious to check on her injuries.

"If you're back, that means I can head out." Elise drops her arms and sighs. "I'm going to welcome my husband back and take the world's longest nap. Put some ice on your face. Got it?"

Dani salutes. "Got it."

Miguel shifts awkwardly. "I'll go get some ice."

Dani looks as though she wants to protest, but I beat her to it. "Thank you, Miguel," I say.

When we're alone in the small house, Dani watches me but makes no attempt to come any closer.

"Wyatt was supposed to give me updates. Either he dropped the ball or…"

"I didn't use the radio much," Dani admits and goes to the fire, holding her hands out to warm them.

There's chatter outside the window, and I see a few people walking by carrying long pieces of lumber. It's barely daybreak. The people here have been working nonstop since the attack. I can only imagine the damage that was done. "How does Woodlake look?"

"It's a mess. They're building pyres down by the river." She adds another log to the fire and pokes at it using the iron poker. It's not lost on me that she's avoiding something. "We commandeered a truck of water and provisions. No weapons, though. Jack blew up that truck." She sighs. "We went through a lot last night and could've used them."

"Food and water are better than nothing." She doesn't say anything to that. "Is there a reason you're avoiding me?"

Her shoulders slump, and she turns with a sigh, finally letting me see her injuries, dark bruises already forming. She sits beside me, and my stomach drops at seeing her so banged-up. Gently, I run my thumb over her split lip. "You're not seriously hurt, though, right?"

"We both should invest in protective headgear," she jokes and winces when I cup her cheek.

Something tells me this was more than just an average fistfight. "What happened?" I ask again.

She leans away from me, her expression darkening. "He was there." She turns to meet my eyes. "Simon."

"What?" I ask breathlessly, quickly realizing this was much more serious than taking out supplies.

"He was *right there*. So close, I could see his fucking nose hair." She puts her head in her hands and runs her fingers through her hair. "I had a clean shot, but my gun was out of ammo. Before I could do anything else, he had me tied up."

"He did this to you?" Anger consumes me, and I grind my teeth so hard, I'm not sure my jaw will ever unclench. "How did you get away?"

"Lucas," she answers simply.

I let out a slow breath, grateful that her brother was there.

"He got away. Again." She clenches her hands into fists and stares into the fire.

I squeeze her leg, knowing this whole thing could've gone a lot worse. "But he didn't kill you, either."

"He said the general wanted me alive." She glances at me. "Why would she want me alive?"

"I don't know." To torture her? Kill her publicly? Lock her up as an example? There are so many different reasons flying through my head, but I don't voice any of them. I don't even want to think about it.

Nervously, Dani licks her lips and looks away. "There's something else." She takes a deep, almost steadying breath. "I saw Ryan."

"What?" Sitting up straighter, I fight the wave of nausea that crashes over me. Whether it's from my injury or the idea of Ryan in the same location as Simon, I'm unsure. "Ryan was at the camp?"

"He held a gun to Lucas's head." Her voice is hard, angry, and I think I may actually throw up on the spot. Is Ryan working alongside Simon? Dani sighs, and her entire body seems to deflate. "He said it wasn't about Bismarck and to tell you that he's sorry. And then he let us both go."

He's sorry for what? For being there with Simon or for our fight before I abandoned him? I release a long shaky breath. Whatever animosity there may still be between us, at least he still appears to still have his morals, and now, because I left, he's stuck dealing with Simon.

My heart aches when I think about Ryan walking away from me and letting me go. Then, I picture him helping Dani and letting *her* go, and it's all just too much.

"Are you okay?" she asks gently.

I shake my head, not knowing exactly how to voice all that I'm feeling. The tears come quickly, and I don't even bother trying to stop them. "I couldn't stop this war from spreading. I walked away from family and my friends. I hurt a lot of people. I'm a liability to you and the others here, and I don't feel like I'm doing anything to help." My gaze lifts to hers, and her expression softens. "You could've died."

She pulls me into her, and I grab the front of her shirt, holding tightly. "But I didn't."

"You could've," I tell her again and pull back to look at her. "I hate this. I hate the fighting, and I hate people getting hurt, and I hate that I can't stop crying about anything since I hit my damn head."

Dani chuckles lightly and wipes the tears from my face. "Yeah, it's a fun side effect of concussions."

"I hate it," I mumble and take a shaky breath, trying to regain some sort of composure.

"Let's go get some sleep, okay?" she says and stands, holding out her hand.

Slowly, she helps me to my feet. "You're supposed to ice your face."

She leads me to the staircase. "I won't tell Elise if you don't." I start to protest, but she gives me a pleading look. "I'm fucking exhausted. Please, just lie with me for a little while."

I relent, my body screaming at me to get some rest.

We get halfway up the steps when I tug her hand, making her stop. Roscoe yawns and stares, clearly ready for us to hurry up so he can nap. Dani gives me a questioning look.

I have so much I want to say. *I'm glad you made it out. Don't ever do that again. You really scared me tonight. Don't leave me.*

But none of that comes out. I shake my head, frustrated.

Dani gently touches the bandage on my head. "I know," she says quietly.

This time, when she tugs on my hand, I follow.

❖

Somehow, Dani and I managed to take a short, albeit fairly decent, nap. After a quick lunch, Dani helps around town for the rest of the afternoon, ignoring Elise's orders to take it easy. I don't like the idea of her doing a lot of heavy lifting, but I get the need to be doing something. While she repairs fences and homes, I help distribute the supplies she brought back from the camp.

By the time night falls, things seem somewhat back to normal.

After dinner, the others head out to meet up with some of the villagers to have a drink. I have a feeling it's both a celebration and moment of mourning. Desperate to take this bandage off my head and get washed up, I excuse myself to head back to Miguel and Anthony's with a promise of joining them later.

The house is dark. I grab a single lantern and take it upstairs to the main bathroom. I stare at my tired reflection in the mirror and notice the bags under my eyes and my completely disheveled appearance.

I look so much like my father.

The pang of hurt that comes with thinking about him is intense. I've been thinking about him more and more. Would he be proud of me for leaving?

I splash some cold water on my face and try not to think about it. Some water gets on my shirt, adding to my haggard appearance, and my mind shifts from my father to my mother. She would have a fit if she could see my untidy hair and mismatched clothes. I scrub my face and pat it dry on the towel by the sink and try not to think about that, either. She's not here. It doesn't matter.

So why does it feel like it does?

Desperately, I unravel the bandage and toss it to the side. My hair sticks out a bit at the bottom, and I try to run my fingers through it to make myself look a little more presentable. My fingers keep getting stuck in the tangles. Annoyed, I try to inspect the back of my head, only to find it matted with a little bit of dried blood standing out in stark contrast with my light hair.

Elise said I don't need stitches, that sometimes, heads just tend to bleed.

I finger the sore spot gently and hiss when I press it a little too hard.

There's a firm knock on the front door.

Confused, I grab the lantern and head back downstairs. I guess fixing my appearance will have to wait.

"Kate? Are you here?"

Marium sticks her head in the house.

"Is everything okay?" I ask in lieu of a proper greeting when I reach the bottom step.

"May I come in?"

I don't bother telling her she's already halfway in and instead open the door wider.

"I hate to bother you unannounced like this, especially when you're recovering." Her eyes linger on my head, and I quickly push my tangled hair from my face. "But I'm afraid this is rather urgent."

"What's going on?"

"Danielle has requested your presence and sent me to fetch you."

I eye her warily. Where she's been nothing but hospitable since I've known her, she isn't the first person Dani would send to escort me somewhere.

The hesitation must show on my face because she smiles. "Don't look so concerned. After all that's happened here lately, I have no energy to kill you."

"Thank you?"

She motions at the hook where my jacket is hanging. "Come on. We don't have much time."

"For what?" I ask.

Her lip twitches into an almost smile. She pulls my hat off the hook and hands it to me. "You have a visitor," she answers vaguely. "Dani didn't want to bother the others."

"Marium," I say with no trace of humor. "What's going on?"

She opens the door and motions for me to follow her.

"Do you not know who this visitor is?" I try again.

She sighs, clearly exasperated. "Kate, just come with me."

Finally, I relent and follow her out the door, grabbing my combat knife as I go. We trudge through the small amount of snow and out of town completely, slipping out the back gate that I went through last night.

I feel like maybe I've made another bad decision. She's leading me toward the river, and a small piece of me starts to question Marium and her loyalty to the Resistance. Did Dani really send for me?

I reach for the knife tucked inside my jacket pocket. "Marium," I say again.

"He just got here," she says before I can ask any more questions. She stops at the tattered wooden door of a large fishing shed and knocks, and just like back at the house, she doesn't wait for anyone to answer. Instead, she opens the door, motioning me inside.

I'm relieved to see Dani just within the doorway. "Dani, what—"

I catch movement behind her, and William Russell appears, stepping into the light of the singular lantern in the middle of the shed. "I'm sorry," Dani says, holding out her hand for me. "The others looked like they were having a good time and not knowing who we can trust..." She kind of shrugs, and I get it.

"What's going on?" I ask, taking her hand and stepping farther inside.

"I asked him to meet me. Told him about some intel that I wanted hand delivered," Dani says.

I'm not sure exactly how long they've been here, but I can tell the conversation has been anything but comfortable. Dani's eyes have that fiery look she gets when she's about to tell someone to fuck right off.

Marium departs, shutting the door behind her and leaving us alone. William stares at me, his expression uneasy. "I really don't think—"

"I know what you think," Dani snaps, interrupting him. "I want her here."

He looks just as deadly as her. He stares at me, his apprehension at having me here on full display. For a moment, I think he's going to turn around and leave, but instead, he paces. "Fine," he relents. "How did the attack go?"

"We took out the camp and the supplies," Dani says simply.

My eyes catch the bruise along her jaw, and I wonder if William can see it in the low light or if he even cares it's there.

"We heard something about a motor being lost," she continues.

"What kind of motor?" he asks, looking very interested.

She just shrugs. "My guess is for an aircraft."

He takes a deep breath, clearly relieved. "Then that's one less we have to worry about. In the meantime," he says and seems to go out of his way to avoid looking at me. "We have a personnel problem. There aren't enough people to defend Bismarck."

"You told me reinforcements would be here in a month," she reminds him. "If this is moving as quickly as it appears to be, that's bad."

He rubs at the back of his neck. "We're working on it."

"And Thatcher?" she asks.

He casts a glance in my direction. "She's finalizing negotiations as we speak and putting the next phase of the plan into place."

Dani leans toward me. "She's been working on writing a new government," she whispers loudly.

"Right," I say, remembering the basic gist of her plan. "A regime change. Will this be happening through a coup?"

"Through coercive diplomacy, if we can help it," William corrects.

"But for that, you would need members of the NAF on board, preferably generals," I say, thinking about E. J. Allen and Rodrigues clueing us in on that piece of intel. "Would E. J. Allen be one of those people?"

William looks from Dani to me. "How do *you* know about E. J. Allen?" His gaze lands back on Dani, and he scoffs. "Of course."

She doesn't seem concerned in the least about the annoyed look he's giving her. "Now that we're off radio frequencies, stop lying and tell me what you know about them."

"I don't know much," he says after a moment's hesitation. "I don't even know who he or she is."

"Tell us what you *do* know," she pushes.

"I know that whoever it is tells us what they want, when they want, and that they're in a position of power." He rests against the far wall of the shed.

"Then why didn't you know about the drones?" I ask. I've come to terms with the fact that it was hidden from me, even if it does still sting, but if this Allen person is so high up and playing both sides, surely, they would've known and told the Resistance.

William sighs and turns away from us. "I don't know. I don't know why they choose to tell us some things and not others. I just know that they've never been wrong, and we're grateful for whatever we get." He rubs at his face and moves to sit on one of the stools. "We think it might be a general."

"Not a major?" Dani asks, confused.

"It's an alias," William explains. "Major E. J. Allen was a Union spy during the first Civil War. His real name was Allen Pinkerton."

It finally clicks. That's where I've heard the name before, in the history books. "He embedded himself into the Confederate Army," I supply.

He nods. "That's right."

"Why did no one mention this Allen before? Why did I have to find out from someone other than you?" Dani shifts her weight, clearly agitated.

He doesn't seem affected. "Because we don't reveal sources," he says coolly. Neither of us miss the pointed look in my direction.

"At least I knew who my source was," she fires back.

"Speaking of," he continues, not at all missing a beat, "you mentioned a new one. What did this *new source* of yours have to say?"

She glares at him for a moment and reaches into her jacket pocket and hands him the papers from Rodrigues.

He brings them close to the lantern resting on the cleaning station and scans them quickly. "They're making movements in and out of Rapid City?" He seems surprised. "I thought Bismarck was their big play?"

I think about Dani telling me what Ryan had said about Bismarck, but I don't voice it, and neither does Dani.

"How confident are you that this is correct?" he asks.

"We aren't," she says. "But the NAF is known for misdirection. We shouldn't ignore this. Do you have anyone you trust to look into it?"

William seems to know what she's implying. Resistance traitors with access to valuable intel. "I don't trust anyone these days." Everyone is so tired. So defeated. "I'll see what I can find. In the meantime, don't mention this to anyone." He shoves the papers in his jacket pocket. "I better get back."

He turns to go, and a sudden rush of panic hits me out of nowhere.

"Tell me about my father," I blurt quickly.

They both freeze. William frowns, and Dani regards me curiously.

"Dani said you were there the night he died. I want you to tell me what happened," I say.

"I don't have time for this." His voice is oddly nervous as he hurries for the door. Dani reaches to stop him, but I move even faster, completely blocking him from leaving.

"Tell me what happened. Please." I hate how desperate I sound, but now that I've asked, I need to know. I think about him all the time, and I need some closure.

He stares at me for what feels like an eternity until finally, his posture shifts from standoffish to regretful. "We weren't always enemies," he starts almost sadly. "Me and Jonathan…Theodore and Judy. We were friends once."

Of all the things I was expecting, that most definitely was *not* it. Friends? My mom and Jonathan Clark?

"What?" Dani asks, her voice hoarse and clearly just as surprised. She moves to stand shoulder to shoulder with me, our arms pressed together. "I don't understand."

"We met back east when we were kids. We lived in the same town," he says as if that explains everything, but it only creates so many more questions.

My stomach knots. "Prove it." I know how I sound. Petulant. Disbelieving. Not once have I heard about this from my parents, and unless William can prove it, I just don't trust him.

He remains silent.

"William," Dani pleads. "Tell us."

He looks at her. *Really* looks at her, and I finally see what Dani has said all along about this man who I could never get myself to like, let alone trust. His eyes soften and show a fondness for her. Maybe he truly does love and care for Lucas and Dani.

He sucks in a steadying breath and moves to sit on a small bench across the room. He drags his hands along his thighs and closes his eyes. He slowly opens them before continuing. "Theodore's father was a butcher, and Theodore hated working for him."

I inhale sharply. My father had told me about Grandpa Joe. I never met him, but I have my own set of memories woven from the stories my father would tell.

"Teddy was always sneaking out and tinkering with whatever tech he could find." William smiles, and I choke back a sob at the use of the nickname. "He would try to build things from scraps that traders left behind. Jonathan and I could never quite understand his obsession, but he was kind and funny and smart. We liked being around him."

I bring my hand to my mouth and shut my eyes. I try to picture him as a kid, skipping out on his chores to mess with generators or radios or anything he could get his hands on. I imagine his sandy colored hair falling into his eyes and his clothes not quite fitting his trim frame.

"Then there was Judy."

His tone shifts slightly, and I open my eyes. He looks at a spot on the wall over our shoulders. "She was witty and preceptive and always managed to talk us out of whatever trouble we had managed to get into. She was such a force to be around. When she moved to town, we were all drawn to her. But Theodore..." He shakes his head and chuckles. "He fell for her, hard." He scratches at the stubble on his cheeks thoughtfully. I wonder if he has tried to forget this part of his life and if talking about it now brings him a nostalgic kind of pain like it does for me.

Dani hasn't said anything and hasn't moved, but her arm is still pressed against mine, so I lean into her.

"None of us were well-off. We struggled for everything we had and worked hard to keep it. The Resistance was on the rise, and people were tired of being pushed around by a law we never truly recognized or adopted. There were hopes of stopping the NAF and changing things back to the way they used to be.

"Jonathan and I wanted to join, but we were only fifteen. They had a hard rule: you had to be sixteen to enlist. Our fathers were carpenters and would never allow us to fall in with the Resistance. 'Keep your heads down, stay out of trouble, and work hard. You'll be just fine.'" William scoffs. "We didn't want to be fine. We wanted to be free.

"But Judy." He laughs humorlessly, "She had a real knack for trouble. So much so that her mother made her enlist when she was seventeen. The NAF had come through with recruiters. We all hated them. Despised how they'd go through and take whatever they wanted and punish people for the most absurd reasons. Judy was pissed until she saw the perks for joining."

"Food, quarter, access to tech," I say, knowing the sales pitch.

William nods. "So when she was assigned farther west and Theodore said he wanted to go, we went, too. Hitched a ride on the NAF's coattails and never looked back."

"You followed my mother?" I ask, trying to wrap my head around it. The story I was told wasn't very different: they met young, she enlisted at seventeen, he followed her to the Midwest.

There was never any mention of Jonathan and William.

"We had a plan. Judy would use the NAF for their resources, and Jonathan and I would use intel she found to get in good with the Resistance. Make a name for ourselves. It started out fine. Judy moved on base, and me and Jonathan and Teddy moved to the town nearby. We did odd jobs and made trades to survive, but the NAF was gaining more and more traction. Judy would tell us things she heard or learned, and we would report back to the Resistance, but the longer it went on, the less Judy would tell us. The war was ramping up, and Theodore tried to get Judy to leave, but she insisted that she could change the NAF from the inside. She was so passionate and so convincing that we couldn't help but believe her." He sucks in a long breath and scratches at the back of his head, glancing at me, then quickly averting his eyes again.

It strikes me just why he distrusts me so much. I must remind him of my mother. Trying to change the NAF from the inside, giving the Resistance intel but wondering if I'm still loyal to the NAF.

"Then what?" Dani asks softly.

His eyes meet hers. "Jonathan met Kaya."

Dani straightens a little, like she's preparing for the obvious shift in the story.

"Judy didn't like her," William says. "By then, it was clear that she had no intention of leaving the NAF. She tried to sway us from the Resistance, told us some...unsavory things about them, and attempted to convince us of the NAF's future and how their vision was necessary to better the country. We started seeing her less and less, but when Jonathan and Kaya got involved, suddenly, she was back, along with all her opinions. She said Kaya wasn't to be trusted because her parents had Resistance ties and that she was too dangerous. The NAF showed up not long after that, questioning Kaya and her entire family. Some people were arrested, others..."

He lets the word linger, but he doesn't have to say it for me to know that my mother's actions got people killed. It makes me sick to my stomach.

"Judy got a quick, and big, promotion. Didn't take much to figure out that she was telling her CO anything and everything that could be beneficial to the NAF cause. She used our initial plan and flipped it."

"And my dad?" I frown. I just can't imagine my dad sitting by and allowing all of this to happen.

"Theodore loved Judy more than anything. He made excuses for her, swore she was just confused, and it was a misunderstanding." He takes a deep, almost steadying breath. "We cut ties with her after that. The rest of Kaya's family moved, and Jonathan and I went with them."

"But you stayed in touch with Theodore," Dani says, phrasing it not as a question but as a fact. "That's why you were there the night he died."

"I tried to stay in touch with him the best I could. Jonathan didn't know about it." William shakes his head and looks at his hands in his lap. "After Katelyn was born, he thought it was best that we didn't communicate at all. He didn't want to risk Judy or anyone else finding out and putting his daughter at risk. A couple years later, Kaya had you." He looks at Dani.

I turn to Dani. She's staring at me, her lips shut tightly. I wish I could read her mind. Our lives have been far more intertwined than either of us ever realized. Our parents went from family to enemies. I can't completely wrap my head around it, and I certainly can't picture William and our parents all sitting around like Dani and I do with the crew from White River.

Maybe we're all more alike than we realize. Maybe family really is that fragile.

I turn back to William. He still hasn't answered my original question. "But what happened at the warehouse the night my dad died? Why were you there?"

He stands and turns away, shaking his head like this is where he draws the line of spilling secrets. "I'm not sure I should be the one to tell you."

"Who else would be able to tell me?" I ask, thrown by his statement.

He turns and stares at me. I refuse to look away until he gives in. "Theodore had a huge breakthrough with the drones he was studying and with getting them in the air. He knew it was only a matter of time before someone discovered his success or before Judy figured it out. He knew Judy would always put the NAF first. He said that if she could stay in the NAF after what happened to Jonathan, then he had truly lost her forever. He panicked and contacted me, begging me to help him." He wrings his hands, clearly nervous.

"Begged you to help him with what?" I ask, fearing the answer isn't something I want to hear.

"I had to say yes," he says, as if I didn't say a word. "This was Theodore. The same boy I grew up with. The one who pieced together small tech to try to automatically latch doors because he was too lazy to get up and lock his father's shop at night."

"So what happened?" I urge, desperate to know the truth.

"When I snuck on base like he asked me to, I saw all these massive aircraft," he continues, gesturing with his hands, his steps quickening. "I just kept thinking about how the Resistance could gain some serious ground and maybe even end the war if we had that kind of tech. I tried to convince him to give them to me. To at least give me his blueprints. Anything to give the Resistance an edge. He refused. Theodore was adamant that this information in the wrong hands would only spread violence and hate, and that was not what he wanted or why he called me."

My father was tenderhearted. His compassion always balanced my mom's cold demeanor. It wasn't out of character for him to have panicked when he realized his work might be used for the wrong reasons.

"Then why did he?" Dani asks.

William rubs his brow. "He needed my help to destroy them. Everything. All of it. The aircraft, his findings, his supplies. All the work he spent his life studying." He stops pacing and runs a hand through his unruly hair. "Theodore was always great with tech, but explosives made him nervous. After a fairly heated debate, I agreed to help. Using what we had on hand, I built an explosive to set near the fuel supply to make it look like an accident, but it malfunctioned early and detonated before I had it in position. I was barely out of the way when the charge went off. My memory is spotty after that. A fire broke out, and there was gas all over the floor. There wasn't supposed to be anyone inside, but we heard screams, so Theodore ran in and pulled as many people as he could out of the building. The fire reached the fuel supply, and the place blew."

Bitterness courses through me. "So that's it? My dad made a breakthrough and asked you to help him destroy it and instead managed to get himself killed by your faulty device? Is that what you're telling me?" This whole story was leading up to the fact that my dad died accidentally while trying to hide his own work from my mother.

"Even if he didn't like handling explosives, he could've set the fuel source on fire himself. Why did he need you?" Dani asks, clearly just as confused.

"He wanted me to help him..." He trails off and pauses a moment, as if trying to calculate how to say the next part. "He wanted..." He shakes his head and won't look at us, agitated. "He wasn't supposed to go back into that warehouse, but he did."

"But why—"

"I have to go." William cuts me off. It's clear he's done answering questions.

"William," Dani tries and makes a move to stop him from leaving.

"There's nothing left to say," he snaps, giving Dani such a hard look that it makes her take a step away. He glances at me and back at her and quickly disappears out of the shed.

Watching the door close, I'm left feeling drained, confused, and annoyed. My simple question turned into something much more complex.

"What the hell just happened?" I asked, standing stunned in the middle of the freezing shed.

CHAPTER EIGHT: THE STRUGGLE

DANI

I'm struggling to wrap my head around everything William just revealed. My dad and Judy were friends? I'm simultaneously questioning William's sanity and wondering if he's testing me. Or in some sick and twisted way, testing Kate.

In my entire life, not *once* was this mentioned or indicated in any way. Not from Dad, Mom, William, or anyone else. Dad's journals never gave any indications that Judy had ever been anything other than his greatest enemy.

They despised each other.

Except, clearly, they didn't.

I stare at Kate as the lantern flickers and creates shadows across her face. I can't read her expression, but I'm pretty sure she's just as thrown as I am.

"I just don't understand," she finally says. "Why would they keep this a secret? Why not tell us the truth?"

"I don't know. To save face?" I'm starting to wonder if there ever was a logical reason. Grabbing the lantern, I open the door and motion to leave. "Let's go get warm."

Miguel and Anthony are sitting by the fire, rose-cheeked and clearly a little toasted, when we get back to the house. Miguel smiles when he sees us. "We missed you at the…" He glances at Anthony. "Celebration? Funeral? What was that?"

"Celebration of life?" Anthony guesses with a shrug.

"We missed you," Miguel finally settles on.

Kate tries to smile, but it appears more like a grimace. "Sorry. We had some business to tend to."

They look between us. "Is everything okay?" Anthony asks slowly. He must notice Kate's uncomfortable expression.

"Yeah," I answer instead. "What did we miss?"

"Besides some fairly strong drinks and a few off-key songs?" Miguel asks. "Jess checked in. Wanted to give you a few updates. She said to go see her when you can."

"Thanks for relaying the message." I quickly wash my hands once Kate finishes, and I put my hand on the small of her back, guiding her to the stairs. "We'll see you both in the morning."

I can tell Miguel wants to protest, but he closes his mouth and nods, clearly deciding otherwise. When we get to our room, the first thing I do is place the lantern by the bed and start the heater. The space is small, so it won't take too long before the chill melts away.

"I don't know what I was expecting William to say." Kate's voice sounds defeated. "I thought he'd be able to tell me something that might make me feel better about my dad's death."

"We got an entire rewrite of their lives," I supply. She nods. "Do you want to talk about it?"

She sits on the edge of the bed and closes her eyes. She rubs at her temples and winces. "Do you think we could take a bath?"

I nod. "I'll warm some water."

It takes me a while without a generator, but it's nothing we haven't gotten used to in the last couple of months. The water is a little cooler than I'd like, but Kate doesn't complain when she slides in.

Squeezing in behind her, I don't offer any playful banter. No teasing or sarcastic remarks about the dirtying water or which bar of soap to use. Instead, I use her new soap to gently wash her hair.

"Have you ever lied to someone you loved?" she asks quietly.

My hands still. I'm surprised by the question. "Yes," I answer honestly. "Little things. Telling my parents I was going to one place but really going to another."

"Is that all?"

"I've lied to Lucas about how dangerous a mission was when I returned. I didn't want to scare him. I know I lied to Rhiannon about that all the time. Once, I told an ex-girlfriend her cooking was great when it was actually really terrible." I carefully try to detangle parts of her hair. The more I talk, the more I think I know where she's going with this. "Sometimes, the lies we tell aren't always out of spite or deceit. Sometimes, we tell them to protect the people we care about."

"Even little lies can hurt the ones you're trying to protect," she counters. "And this one, our parents being friends, isn't a little white lie. It's a big deal. Knowing this could have changed the course of so many decisions that were made. I don't know how to process it."

"It's okay to feel betrayed, Kate."

"Aren't you angry?" she asks and looks at me over her shoulder.

"Oh, I'm livid," I assure her. "I feel like I got sucker punched. The worst part is, I can't ask my dad about it. I can't confront him. I'm furious with him for hiding this from me, and I don't even have the chance to ask for his side of it all."

Kate scoots back and takes my arms, wrapping them around her and hugging them against her stomach. She rests her cheek against my arm. "Do you get the feeling William's hiding something else?" she asks after a beat.

My stomach flips uneasily. "Yeah, I do." If he lied about this, then who knows what else he isn't saying.

"So your dad and William were BFFs with the general?" Darby asks, completely invested. She chews slowly, her eyes wide as she hangs on practically every word I say.

Lucas sits quietly beside her. He hasn't said anything. His brows are furrowed together thoughtfully, and he stares at his uneaten breakfast.

I watch him, worried about how he's processing the new information.

"The shock is evident," he says finally.

"Issue fourteen," Darby guesses.

"Why are you here?" I ask, annoyed.

"Because this is my room, thank you very much." She takes another large bite of her biscuit and then puts her chin in her hand and stares at me.

This is definitely not a conversation I want to have with her. But Lucas deserves to know the truth, and she's his support person, so I don't have a lot of choice. Grinding my teeth, I push past the annoyance and drink the watered-down coffee Marium left for us. Deciding I'm not really all that hungry, I wrap some biscuits with jam in a towel. "I have to meet with Jess. Do you want me to come back so we can talk some more?"

He shakes his head. "The world continues to turn."

"I know this is a lot, and I'm sorry you had to find out this way." I squeeze his shoulder. "I'm here if you want to talk, okay? Whenever you need to."

Lucas puts his hand on top of mine and squeezes back with a nod. Before I go, he shoots up from the small table and rummages through his comics. When he finds the one he wants, he thrusts it in my direction. It's issue sixty-one, where Maelstrom's childhood friend reveals a family secret. Fitting. I smile, knowing my brother is trying to help me the best way he knows how, despite me being the one to try to help him. "Thanks, buddy."

He's so compassionate and selfless, always thinking of everyone else before himself, and I don't know how he does it. The world could use more Lucas and less of everyone else.

"Is that all William said?" Darby asks. She reaches for her drone, putting it on the table and checking the propellers while she eats.

"I'm not sure what else you were expecting. That seems like more than enough to me," I snap.

Lucas gently touches my arm. "How are you holding up, my friend?" His eyes are full of concern.

Shrugging, I try to play it off. Last night, I felt betrayed and sad. Today, I'm just angry. "Like I want to punch William in the face the next time I see him."

"The honorable never punch the defenseless," Lucas says, scolding.

"Oh please," I scoff. "William is the least defenseless person we know. He deserves it for this. So does Dad."

Lucas looks positively offended. I feel only slightly guilty about looping our father in the mix. But I'm angry with him, too.

Darby hums, clearly disinterested in my outburst. "Well, huge family secrets aside, I was hoping William would tell us where we're going next. Not that Woodlake hasn't been interesting."

"Where we go next is our call," I say and look at Lucas. "Things are heating up. You mind trying to find a place we can lie low for a few days?"

Lucas salutes while Darby starts to mutter about going somewhere with generators and hot water. I take that as my cue to leave.

When I get to Jess's room, Wyatt isn't there, but George is. He sits beside her, jotting down what she tells him. He looks incredibly tired. "Good morning."

"Dani," he says and covers a yawn. "Good morning."

"What happened last night? It's not like you to skip out on a meeting. Everything okay?" Jess asks.

"William showed up," I explain and pull a chair to the corner table to join them.

Jess's eyebrows rise to her hairline, and George looks much more awake. "William?" he asks, his eyes wide. "He's here?"

"Not anymore."

Jess looks positively offended. "I didn't know he was coming."

"Jess, don't take it personally. He's been lying low and keeping things off the books."

"He wants to keep things off channel. I get it. I don't like it, but I get it." She cycles through a few frequencies, but I can tell she still feels slighted. "I mean, it would've been nice to say hi, is all."

"Did he come alone?" George asks.

"Yes." I draw the word out.

"I worry about him," George says and sighs. "He's running himself and you all way too hard."

"That's war." I shrug but don't disagree.

Jess turns toward her grandfather. "Do you mind giving us a minute?"

He appears taken aback by the question but quickly recovers and pats her hand. "Of course. I could use a break. I'll be in my room if you need me." His eyes meet mine, he nods once, and he's gone.

The door click shuts, and I lean back, crossing my arms, ready to get down to business. "Okay, Jess, what did I miss?"

"You go first," she says and leans a bit closer. "Anything you can share from William?"

A lot of things, but I don't want to get into that. Not now, at least. "He was here for an intel grab."

"Oh, the information you got from Kate's assistant?" she asks, finally understanding why William didn't announce he was coming. He was collecting information, not giving it. "How did he take the news when you told him where it came from?"

"He took it fine."

"You didn't tell him, did you?"

"Sure didn't."

She smiles and searches for the tea on the desk. "My turn." She finally finds the mug and takes a long sip. "There's a continuous loop for the NAF soldiers to stand by." Reaching for the dial on the radio, she finds the frequency and plays it.

"Stand by for what?" I ask, listening to the message repeat itself.

She turns down the volume. "I'm not sure, but I'm guessing it has something to do with the NAF camps that are popping up from Rapid City all the way up to Bismarck. We have people analyzing if there's a strategy to their placements or if they're just random."

"Nothing with the general is random," I mutter, not thinking for a minute that they aren't stationed strategically.

"I agree."

"If this isn't on an encrypted channel, is there a possibility that we were meant to hear this and think something was going to happen?" I ask, wondering if this is some sort of false flag.

She shrugs. "Possibly. Either that or this channel just reaches a broader audience. Maybe the general's head game is for not everything to be a head game."

I groan. Everything is becoming too complicated.

"Also, you received another message from Lightning Rod."

This catches my attention. "So soon? Did it appear urgent?"

"I can't tell. It was just a series of coordinates and a request to meet." She pulls a piece of paper from her pocket. "Wyatt wrote them down." I glance at the series of numbers and debate going back to Lucas's room for a map. Jess shifts in her chair. "Can I ask you something silly? Not business related?"

I don't think she has deviated from business talk since she was assigned this position several months ago. My curiosity piques. "Sure, what's on your mind?"

"What does Wyatt's handwriting look like?"

Wow. Okay, so that, I wasn't expecting. Frowning, I look at the sliver of paper and black scrawl. It's hard to tell exactly what she wants to know based on the few numbers and even fewer letters before me.

She shifts nervously. "I know it's silly. He writes things for me all the time. He writes things *to* me. I guess I just…"

"Hey." I place my hand on her arm, stilling her. She talks with her hands when she's upset or nervous. I want her to know not to be nervous with me. "I get it." She smiles a little and nods. Looking down at the numbers, I do my best to figure out how to explain it. Then, I think back to the poem, and I try to focus on that. "He writes at a slant. A little to the left. And narrow. Like, pressed close together but not so close that everything looks jumbled. It's neat. Precise, almost. No flourishes or extra curves. Just…efficient."

Her smile grows, and there's a slight coloring on her cheeks, highlighting her freckles across the bridge of her nose. "Thank you," she whispers.

I swallow the lump in my throat. Seeing her get emotional always does a number on me. Guilt creeps steadily through my body. I'm ashamed of how quickly I had assumed Wyatt was a traitor, easily thinking that he betrayed us all when really, he was just writing words of love to the kid I love like a sister.

I'm further embarrassed that Kate knew immediately that Wyatt wouldn't be capable of something so heinous. If Rhiannon was here, she would lecture me about faith and trust. I hate how easily I jumped to conclusions and how skittish I've been around the people I love.

Clearing my throat, I try to ignore the regret. "You're welcome, but if you ask me to describe his dreamy eyes and charming smile, I might throw up."

She laughs and reaches out until she finds my hands. She squeezes and takes a deep breath. "Okay. About this message. How do you want me to reply?"

❖

I can't get the message from Rodrigues out of my head. I don't know what she wants, but it must be something important to risk a second meeting so soon.

I rub my eyes, wanting to sleep. Last night was bad. Restless. I couldn't shut off my mind. I'm able to understand why there's so much resentment and hate regarding Judy and my father and William, but why me? Why focus so much of her time on *me*? Is it because of my mother and her bloodline? Or is it because of feelings of hatred she still has for my father?

My father always preached about how he was fighting for a better world for his children and for future generations, but was part of it just pettiness and revenge toward an old friend who betrayed him?

I'd like to think that isn't the case, but with both my parents gone and William refusing to tell us the whole truth, I'm stuck in a horrendous limbo of what-ifs.

Passing Mike and Elise's room as I leave Jess's, I notice their door is ajar. A quick glance shows them sitting pressed against each other on the bed, hunched over a piece of paper, whispering.

Not bothering to knock, I stick my head in their room. "Hey guys." They jump and separate, Mike quickly sitting on the paper. "What are you up to so early?"

They exchange nervous glances. I look between them, noting how much better Elise is at pretending they weren't doing something secretive. Mike's leg bounces, and Elise puts her hand on it, stilling the movement. I desperately try not to make the same assumption that I did with Wyatt. I hate having to tiptoe around my friends.

"We were just talking," Elise says easily. I pretend to believe her. "How are you? Those bruises are healing nicely."

"They're turning purple," Mike says, grimacing.

Elise sighs. "That means they're healing." She says it as if she's explained this to him a hundred times before.

I want to ask about the paper Mike is sitting on and why they felt the need to be so secretive in their own room. "Okay, I'll leave you to it," I say, already backing away.

Neither of them tries to stop me, and it only adds to my paranoia.

I quietly slip back in our room and find Kate in bed but not sleeping. She's sitting on the edge of the mattress, facing the window and listening to my music player. She only notices me when the bed dips. "I was hoping you'd still be asleep," I say and try to smile when she takes the earbuds out.

"Me too," she jokes. "What did Jess say?"

"More camps are popping up. And a general message on loop for the NAF to stand by." I shift closer until I'm in the center of the bed.

She nods and tucks her legs under her, turning to face me. "The NAF uses a common channel sometimes to catch soldiers stationed in towns not currently run by the military. It's standard procedure. It basically means get ready to move out quickly, but it's not a given that will happen."

I nod but don't respond right away, gauging her emotional state. If the bombshell about her father wasn't enough, I'm sure talking about her mother's war efforts will tip the scales of her stability. She seems steady and meets my eyes while waiting for my response.

"Also." I hand her the piece of paper with Rodrigues's coordinates. "Rodrigues contacted Jess again. Another request to meet."

Kate looks at the series of numbers, her brows furrowed. "Do you know why?"

"No." I jump off the bed and reach for my bag, rummaging for a local map. "Just a place and nothing else." When I finally find it, I spread it out on the bed. We trace the lines until Kate pinpoints it.

"This is really close," she says. "Do you think this is about those pop-up camps? Or maybe she got made and has to lie low."

"I don't know. Could be a trap," I suggest, and Kate rolls her eyes. "What? It could be."

"Not everything is a trap," she says, punctuated with a look.

"Everyone around me is lying. Excuse me for being skeptical," I snap.

She smiles softly, understandingly, and kisses me gently on the lips. "Only one way to find out."

"Whoa, hang on." I grab her wrist to keep her from walking out of the room. "Dramatics aside, I really don't trust this assistant of yours."

"I know you don't, but she's the only one who has inside information." She sounds annoyed but doesn't try to pull herself free. "We're running out of time."

"Running out of time for what?" I ask. She looks away and huffs. I've decided she is, in fact, super annoyed. "Hey." I tug her arm gently until she looks at me. "What's going on?"

"Jenisis said it when we saw her. Something big is happening. Ryan confirmed that when he told you it wasn't about Bismarck. Now, camps are popping up and that thing with Simon almost killing you." I snort. He did not almost kill me. "There's a spy and a mysterious person in the woods." She sighs and closes her eyes, her shoulders dropping. "I'm just tired of all the secrets and misdirection. I want answers. I want to do something besides sit here and dissect every little thing that happens."

"Weren't you the one to tell me to be patient and that our time to fight would come soon enough?" She gives me a scathing look, and I can't help but smile. I slip my hand into hers and thread our fingers together. "If we're going to do this, we're going to need help."

She squeezes my hand, seemingly relieved, and nods. Her hopeful gaze makes me realize I'll do absolutely anything she wants or needs, even if it is a stupid idea. My mind flashes back to the conversation I had with Rhiannon about being in love. It has been happening more and more lately. The words on the tip of my tongue.

Not trusting myself to say anything else, I pull her close and kiss her.

"When are you going to tell us what's going on?" Darby asks as she loads Chi-Chi very carefully into the back seat of the old NAF buggy.

"When we get there," I tell her simply.

"And we're just supposed to trust that you aren't leading us into a death trap?"

"If only I was," I say dreamily.

I don't have to look to know she's glaring. "Wow. I feel so much better."

Lucas pats her shoulder and smiles, loading his own bag into the back seat. "Today is a good day for an adventure."

"Issue seven," I say before Darby can guess.

Jack says nothing. He just tosses his guns inside the buggy, and I wonder what's got him so cranky.

"No one else is coming?" Darby asks and looks around. "It's just us and Kate?"

"Jess knows where we're going and what we're doing. She'll send help if we don't check in."

"By then, we'll probably be dead," Darby mutters. "Our skin used as rugs and our bones turned into wind chimes."

I roll my eyes at how dramatic she always seems to be.

Lucas ushers her into the buggy. "The story will work out in the end," he says gently. I'm not sure if it's directed at me or her.

He shuts the door and turns to me with a questioning look. "I hate not trusting anyone," I admit to him quietly. "It's screwing with my head and keeping me awake at night." Jack brushes past with another huff, and I run my hands down my face. "When did I get like this?"

"War is deceitful," Lucas says. "It's only a matter of time before we all chase shadows that aren't there."

"Haven't heard that quote in a while," I tell him sadly.

I think about the last time I got like this, when I didn't trust anyone. Jess got hurt. A hastily built explosive went off too soon, and she was caught in the blast and lost her sight. All because of rumors involving NAF sympathizers and my need to weed them out.

I shake my head, recalling the sound of her cries. It still makes me sick to my stomach. "I don't want to be that person again," I whisper, desperate to stay out of the darkness of paranoia.

"Find your strength," he says, his gaze both sympathetic and encouraging.

Jack walks by again, and my pity party comes to a quick halt. "Are we leaving or what?"

"Yeah," I tell him. "Let's move." This isn't the time to dwell on internal monsters. It's not like I'd be able to slay them anyway.

❖

"We're here," I say in the radio to the other car. "Remember the plan. Go around back, get the drone in the air, and watch for any kind of movement or sign that this might be an ambush."

"Loud and clear," Jack says, and the buggy breaks off to cover our six.

"Let me know when you're in position. Then, we'll move. Over."

"Copy that."

Pulling over behind the shell of an abandoned tractor, I put the truck in park and let it run idle. "We're officially in old South

Dakota," I tell Kate. In a strange kind of nostalgic way, I'm happy to be back. "We're really far from Omaha." It's an obvious statement. Kate was stationed there; she knows exactly where it is, and she knows that for Rodrigues to be so far from base probably can't be good. "Think she ever made it back there after the first meetup?"

"Doubtful," Kate confesses. "Unless she isn't stationed there anymore."

"Long way from Grand Forks," I say, my sentiment not changing. She sighs. "It's probably a trap."

I lean back in the seat and look out my window, a quip about not everything being a trap on the tip of my tongue. There's nothing but frozen fields and gray skies. A few bison roam a safe distance from us, and I think of my childhood when I watched them graze in the fields and pretended I was brave enough to take them on. "Your adrenaline wearing off?" I ask.

She smiles slightly. "A little." She starts to fidget with her hair, something she does when she's nervous.

The truck is warm. Almost *too* warm. Taking off my gloves, I grab the radio and make sure the volume is up. I try not to yawn as I settle back in, waiting for the others to get into position.

I wish I was in my Jeep.

Kate looks the exact opposite of tired. Her leg bounces anxiously, her eyes darting everywhere but at me. I place my hand on her knee, stilling her movements. "This is stupid," she says. "I'm going to get you all killed."

"No one is going to die," I assure her. "We've handled worse situations than a cryptic call." I draw an invisible circle around my bruised face to make my point. She doesn't find it funny. I glance at the small cabin positioned in the middle of nowhere, a safe distance away. "Although, this place *is* exceptionally creepy."

"What if it's my mother?"

"It's not your mom."

"You don't know that."

"My gut tells me it isn't."

"What's your gut saying, then?"

"Kate." I sigh. "What's with the sudden change of heart?"

"I don't know." She stares at the little cabin. "Now that we're here it feels…weird. Like something isn't right."

"Do you want to turn around?"

She doesn't have time to answer as the radio crackles to life. "We're in position," Jack says, his voice loud and clear. "Chi-Chi's enroute. Over."

"Copy that." I reply and put the radio back on my lap. Kate looks out the window, probably trying to find Darby's drone. "It's your call, Kate. We can turn around now if you want."

She doesn't answer.

Jack's voice slices through the silence. "All she sees is a cabin. It's not too far from an old abandoned town. She says there doesn't seem to be movement in the town itself, but someone is definitely inside the cabin." I meet Kate's eyes. "Says she can see our contact's hideous car out back. Over."

"What's it going to be?" I ask Kate, who turns back to look at the cabin. "Are we going in or hightailing it out of here?"

The truck is quiet except for the sound of the sputtering beat of the engine.

"Let's do it," she finally says.

I press the talk button on the radio. "Keep Chi-Chi up and move in with caution. If you see anything suspicious, let me know. Otherwise, stay out of sight and wait for my signal. Over."

"Copy."

I put the radio back between the seats and shift the truck into drive. "Okay, let's go see who's waiting for us."

When we get near the cabin, I slow, keeping my head on a swivel just in case there is someone or something hidden in the area, but nothing stands out.

"Do you think anyone is hiding in the town?" Kate asks.

"Maybe." I pull the truck as close as I'm willing to get. "If they are, hopefully, the drone will spot them first."

I stare forward, uncertain of how exactly to proceed. Like Darby mentioned, the rear bumper of the weird-looking vehicle Rodrigues drove into town is parked off to the side, and smoke puffs from the chimney.

Kate holds perfectly still, sitting and staring at the cabin as if willing something to happen.

"Should we knock?" I joke.

She visibly relaxes and glances at me with a new expression that appears both annoyed and amused.

The door to the cabin opens, and Rodrigues walks out, shielding the sun with one hand and offering an awkward half wave with the other. Kate visibly deflates with relief.

I grab the gun strapped to my thigh and release the safety. I keep the truck in drive, ready to speed away. "Could still be a trap," I say, not convinced with the unarmed display and definitely not trusting this former assistant.

"Could be," she agrees.

"I think we need to—"

But Kate exits the truck, pistol in hand.

"Cool, great talk," I say to her retreating form, unable to keep up with her sudden shifts in moods. "Kate," I call out. But she doesn't stop. Instead, she shuts the door and presses forward to the cabin. "Shit." I throw the truck in park and grab the radio. "Float Chi-Chi above the house, let her know she's being watched. We're going in."

I toss the radio to the passenger seat and rush after Kate.

"Want to tell us what the hell is going on?" Kate shouts, standing in front of the truck.

Chi-Chi flies overhead at that exact moment, and Rodrigues squints up at it. "This isn't an ambush," she calls. "The NAF isn't here."

Kate pulls back the slide of her pistol and aims at her.

Rodrigues lifts her hands in surrender. "After I left Rockwood, I was made. This is the only safe house I know. I need to talk to you, but what I have to say isn't safe over the radio."

Kate shrugs. "Here I am. Talk."

Rodrigues looks at the drone again, and to her credit, Darby is doing one hell of a job flying it. She's just menacing enough to seem threatening but high enough to make a quick getaway if Rodrigues decides to start shooting. "I'm surrounded, aren't I?"

"You're damn right," I say, aiming my own gun at her.

Rodrigues drops her hands and runs them up and down her own arms. "Can we take this inside? It's cold."

"Out here is fine," Kate answers.

She lifts her hands into the air again. "Let me grab my coat. It's right inside the door."

Kate and I both shout at her to stay where we can see her, but like someone with a death wish, she reaches inside the door anyway and pulls out a heavy brown jacket.

"Drop it, Rodrigues," I yell. "I'm not fucking around. I will shoot you. Last chance, show me your hands!"

"Dani, wait." Kate says, stepping in front of me and lowering her pistol.

I try to step around her, but there's something in her expression that's deeply unsettling. Her gaze is laser focused on Rodrigues, who stands perfectly still, the coat still in her hands. The two stare at each other.

"What's going on?" I ask, managing to step around Kate so I have a clear shot on Rodrigues.

"That jacket," she starts. It's brown. With a fur-lined hood.

I look from Kate back to the jacket. Agitated, I watch them continue to stare at each other. Again, I ask, "What the *hell* is going on?"

Chapter Nine: The Truth

Kate

"What the *hell* is going on?" Dani's voice sounds confused, worried.

"It was you?" I ask Rodrigues, dumbfounded. "You're the one from the woods?"

"Please, will you come inside?" she asks, her voice carrying across the breeze.

My arms fall heavy to my sides, my fingers loosen around the gun. This doesn't make any sense.

Dani steps in front of me, her pistol still aimed at Rodrigues. "I don't know what kind of game you're playing, but you better start talking."

"I'll explain everything," she promises. "Just get your gun out of my face."

Dani takes a threatening step forward.

"Dani," I say gently. "Please, let's hear what she has to say." She hesitates, and I can tell she doesn't want to. "I want to know what's going on."

Finally, Dani lowers her gun. "She's not telling us something."

"So let's go find out what it is."

Dani stares at Rodrigues for another beat and nods, reluctantly following me to the cabin.

There's not much to the interior, just like every other safe house we've visited these past few months. A table, a couple of chairs, and a cot in the corner with a sleeping bag atop it. The standard water bowl by the main door was probably put there solely for us. A fire roars in the small fireplace, a cast-iron skillet off to the side, and a door that leads to what I'm guessing is the bathroom.

Propped just inside the door is a rifle, and Dani grabs it without any hesitation and slings the strap over her shoulder, not making it an option for Rodrigues if things go south. She stands rigid near the door, her pistol still aimed at Rodrigues, while I clean my hands.

I keep my eyes on the closed door and push my chin in its direction. "What's back there?"

"Bathroom," Rodrigues confirms.

Dani makes a move to check for herself.

"Wait. There's something I need to tell you." Rodrigues attempts to block her path.

Dani aims the gun at the door, and I quickly do the same.

Rodrigues steps boldly in front of the door, holding her hands out with a desperate look on her face. "Please, let me finish talking before you start shooting," she says, glancing at Dani and back at me. Neither of us makes that promise. "It isn't what you think."

"I don't know what to think," I snap.

"I'll start shooting whether you're in the way or not," Dani promises.

"I need you to *please* trust me. Please trust that I'm on your side." She's begging, and the longer she talks, the more anxious Dani is getting. "I'm going to open the door, but *please*, don't shoot."

Dani glances at me, and I grip my gun tightly, my stomach twisting, wondering what the hell she's hiding. Carefully and slowly, Rodrigues opens the door, managing to stand between us and whatever it is. Dani tightens her stance, ready to open fire, and I don't for one second doubt that she would shoot through Rodrigues if need be.

The light from the cabin illuminates the room just slightly, and I see a man standing in the middle of the room, his hands in the air.

My heart recognizes him immediately. His hair is longer than I remember, shaggy, as if he cut it himself. His flannel shirt is tucked into his pants, and a light jacket is unzipped over his shoulders. He shifts his weight from one foot to the other, nervously, his eyes on me.

"Dad?" I choke on my own words as I stare at a ghost.

Dani's head snaps in my direction, her eyes wide, but she keeps her gun trained on him. "What?"

"Please, don't shoot," he says, his voice scratchy and timid.

"Who are you really?" Dani asks, ignoring his request and taking a step forward.

Rodrigues stands in front of her. "Put it away, please," she begs.

My eyes settle on a worn spot on the wall over his shoulder, and I remind myself to breathe, even though it feels like my chest is caving in. My breathing is heavy, and I try to speak, but I can't manage any words. I stagger backward and place my gun on the table, forcing a breath through my nose.

"Kate?" Dani's tone is questioning, concerned. "Kate. Talk to me."

I shake my head and stumble farther backward.

"Katie? Can we talk, please?" His voice reaches my ears, but it sounds distorted, muffled.

It's not him. It can't be him. I close my eyes and shake my head. We had a funeral. A memorial. My mother cried. I was broken. This isn't real. That day was real. This is…I don't know what this is. But it's not possible.

"Katelyn?" he asks, his voice sounding small and unsure.

"Don't take another step," Dani instructs.

"Please, lower your gun," Rodrigues pleads desperately.

Against my best efforts, bile has risen to my throat, and I dry swallow to force it back down.

"Not until you start explaining," Dani argues. She sounds closer, like she's standing in front of me. My chest flutters uncomfortably, and I wonder for a brief moment if this is what the beginning of a heart attack feels like. I open my eyes but look away. It can't be him. It's not.

"Dani, please listen. I'm on your side, remember? I'm Resistance—"

"Why should I believe you?"

My ears ring, and their conversation sounds distant, muffled. They're arguing, but I can't really make out anything they're saying. I run my sweaty palms over the front of my legs. Over and over again.

I know I should step in, but my throat feels tight, and I can't speak. My arms and legs feel like they're pulsating from within my veins. I manage to take another few steps backward, but I'm unsteady. Reaching out, I try to regain my balance by holding on to the wall. "Stop," I finally manage, but my voice doesn't sound like my own. It barely comes out as a whisper. I'm shaking, and while I'm aware of the arguing going on around me, I can't focus on it. My breaths come in short puffs.

The muffled voices stop, and Dani is there, blocking my view of anything else. She's talking to me, her face close to mine and her hand on my shoulder. I try to take a deep breath, but I can't seem to get a grip on my lungs.

Staring into her concerned gray eyes, I realize that I'm not listening to her. "I can't stop shaking," I say through a sob I didn't expect to bubble to the surface.

She takes my hand tightly and squeezes, never letting me look away from her. "Look into my eyes," she says, her words clearer. "Focus on me." I do my best to do as she instructs. "Squeeze my hand. Take slow breaths."

She repeats the same four phrases again. And again. I try to squeeze her hand and manage to slow the short, puffy breaths I've been taking.

She guides me to the edge of the bed and sits beside me. Once my breathing evens out, she puts the rifle down and places her hands over my arms, rhythmically running them up and down. "I'm right here."

I nod and close my eyes.

"I'm right here," she repeats.

Finally, the shaking slows and subsides. Only when I've managed to inhale a full, deep breath and open my eyes do I realize the room is silent, and everyone is staring at me.

Slightly embarrassed, I close my eyes again and keep squeezing Dani's hands, using her to ground me. I try to focus on breathing slowly and hope the shaking will finally stop.

"I'm sorry," Rodrigues says, breaking the quiet. "I didn't mean—"

"Kate," Dani says softly, ignoring Rodrigues. "I know this is hard. We can leave right now if you want. It's your call." She watches me, concerned. She presses our joined hands to her chest, and I can feel her heart beating. "I'm with you."

I swallow, desperate for something to drink, to ease the scratchiness in my throat. "Water," I request.

Rodrigues appears at my side almost instantly with her thermos. Taking small sips, I take my time. Somehow, I finally find the courage to look at him. *Really* look at him.

He stares back, his eyes full of concern, not at all unlike Dani's. He looks different than I remember, older, thinner…but it's him. He's definitely my father.

I blink a few times and try to get a grip on the fact that this is real. It's real, and my father is here. He's not dead. An infinite number of questions flood my brain at once, but one screams louder than the rest. "How?"

My father shares a look with Rodrigues and sits in one of the two chairs at the table. "It's complicated," he starts. When he doesn't elaborate, my panic starts to give way to anger.

"It's complicated? That's what you're going to go with?" I ask. "How about you uncomplicate it?"

Dani presses her hand against my back. It's reassuring and giving me strength.

"I'm not sure where to begin," he tries again, shifting uncomfortably.

"Try from the beginning," I say. He looks away, wringing his hands. "You died," I say, unable to wait for him to think of what he wants to say. "You were *dead*. Do you know how devastating that was?" My voice cracks, and tears fill my eyes. "Do you have any fucking idea what I've been through?"

"I followed everything. I always knew where you were and all your promotions—"

"I don't care," I yell, shooting to my feet. The tears run in droves down my cheeks, and Dani is right there, her hand still steadying on the small of my back. "You weren't there. You *left* me. Was this always your plan?"

He stares at me, tears filling his own eyes, but he doesn't answer. Yet somehow, that's answer enough.

"I think I'm going to be sick," I confess.

"I made a breakthrough in my work," he says after a stretch of silence. "A discovery that would change everything. Your mother..." I glance at him at the mention of her. "Your mother was being promoted quickly, pushing me and my work. It wasn't lost on me that the two were closely connected. I knew it wouldn't be long before she used my achievement to advance her career to become general." He smiles sadly. "I was never very good at keeping things from her."

But apparently good at keeping things from me, I want to say.

"So instead of just destroying what you made, instead of trying and *staying*, you decided to call William Russell and fake your death?" I ask, finally having enough of the puzzle pieces to see the bigger picture.

His eyes widen in shock. He looks to Rodrigues, who shakes her head and shrugs, looking just as confused as he does. "He told you?"

"He told us you reached out to him. That he asked you to give *him* your work instead. But, no, he didn't tell us that you were alive or that he helped you fake your death," I tell him. My stomach tightens. "How could you do this to me? How could you leave me thinking you were dead? Who would do that to their *child*?"

"I didn't want to," he says desperately. "I didn't see any other way."

"That's bullshit," Dani says, her tone sharp, unaccepting.

"You don't understand," he says looking at her.

"You're right, I don't," she says back.

"I didn't want anything to happen to you," he says, his attention back on me. "I didn't want them to use you as a threat or a bargaining chip to get to me. I was expected to produce results, and my time was running out. I did the only thing I thought that I could to keep us all safe."

"You don't think Mom would've stopped it?" I ask, trying to make sense of all of this but coming up incredibly short. "Do you really think she would've allowed someone to hurt me or you?"

"Do you think she would?" he asks, flipping my question back at me.

She bombed Rapid City knowing I was there. I look away, not wanting to accept the answer I already know to be true.

Dani brushes the back of her hand against mine.

My dad nods sadly. "When it happened, when I made my breakthrough, your mother wasn't a general yet, but she knew the opportunity was in reach. She had used people before for promotions. At one time, if someone had told me she would do the same to me or you, I would never have believed it, but she…" He shakes his head and at least has the decency to look upset. "She was rapidly becoming someone I no longer recognized."

"Why now?" I ask. "Why, after all this time, would you even show up at all?"

"I've been hearing things. Unsettling things about the progression of this war. That the NAF figured out what I discovered years ago." He leans forward in his chair. "Even with you out of the NAF, with your mother in charge, and with the ability to get drones in the air"—he glances at Rodrigues—"Jenisis convinced me that it was time to tell you the truth."

As if just realizing Rodrigues was somehow a part of this, I turn to her at the fire. She shifts her weight, clearly uncomfortable.

"You lied to me," I whisper. "The whole time we worked together, you knew. The encrypted channel you were sending information through, it was to my father, wasn't it?"

"I'm sorry," she says quickly. "My orders were not to tell you. Under any circumstance."

"Who gave you those orders?" I ask. "E. J. Allen?" A thought occurs to me, and I quickly look back to my father. "Are *you* E. J. Allen?"

"Me?" He shakes his head vigorously. "No."

My head starts to pound, and I press my fingers to my temples massaging them, more confused than ever.

"Let me get this straight," Dani starts slowly and points to Rodrigues. "You and your parents are Resistance. Your parents worked with you"—she points to my dad—"and this E. J. Allen told you"—back to Rodrigues—"to keep an eye on Kate and send intel back to you." She finishes by pointing at my dad.

"Yes," Rodrigues confirms.

"I reached out to Jenisis and told her who I was once Kate left the NAF. I told her I needed her help," my dad says.

"You could've reached out to *me*," I fire back, hurt that he didn't even try. "If you've always known where I was, you could've told me." It kills me that he clearly didn't want to.

"Would you have listened?" he asks gently.

I start to respond but sit on the bed instead and put my head in my hands. I'm so tired of all the secrets. "I don't know." So much has happened these last few days that I'm not sure what's real and what's not. There have been so many lies, so much mistrust, that I don't even know what I'm doing anymore. "Were you really made?" I ask without looking up.

"Yes," Rodrigues answers. "I was on my way back to base when Theodore told me there was a warrant for my arrest. I just didn't go back."

"Jenisis…" I can't help sounding accusatory. "That night in the woods when you saved me, why didn't you tell me who you were?"

"I did," she insists. I meet her eyes, not remembering. "When I got to the town, the raiders were already attacking. I saw you being chased around back, and I took off after you. When I finally caught up, you were on the ground. I took them out, and you asked who I was. I put my hood down and crouched beside you. I told you to hang on while I got help, but a group of raiders came at me. I ran out of ammo and led them away from you, and by the time I got back, you were gone."

"Why didn't you come inside?" Dani asks.

"I panicked," she said with an embarrassed shrug. "I called Theodore, and he told me about this cabin, so I came here."

She called my dad, and he helped her. Just like that. The betrayal and jealously that washes over me is suffocating. "I need some air."

The front door flies open right as I stand, and I fall backward on the bed, startled. Dani grabs her pistol and jumps in front of me, and Rodrigues stands in front of my dad.

Jack stands in the doorway with a grenade launcher pointed at all of us. I breathe a sigh of relief that is quickly replaced by a wave of nausea.

"Dammit, Jack," Dani says and lowers her pistol.

He catches sight of my father and keeps the launcher aimed at him. "Who is this?"

"Come on, get inside," Dani says instead of answering and pushes the launcher down. Lucas peers around Jack's shoulder. "Come on," Dani urges again impatiently.

"We're good," Jack calls, but his eyes haven't left my dad.

Darby forces her way inside, cradling her drone like it's a large mechanical baby, Lucas right behind her. "Well, this is cozy," she says, looking around. "The assistant," she says, spotting Rodrigues. She stops short when she sees my dad pressed against the back wall, still looking terrified. "Who are you?"

"Theodore Turner," he manages.

"Kate's dad," Dani clarifies.

My stomach churns again, and everyone looks at me right as I throw up.

❖

Rodrigues and I sit side by side on the floor, our backs against the wall. Darby and Lucas whisper with their heads bent low at the table, and Jack and Dani sit on the cot, arguing in hushed tones.

I cradle a lukewarm cup of tea, unable to stomach sipping from it. My father sits by the fire, avoiding eye contact with everyone and looking extremely out of place. I can't stop looking at him. Part of me wants to hug him, to know that he's real. The other part of me hopes this is a nightmare, and I'll wake any moment. Because this can't be happening. Surely, a parent is incapable of this kind of deceit, right?

"I'm so sorry," Rodrigues says softly.

"I know you're sorry, Jenisis. But apologizing over and over doesn't make it hurt any less." She nods, but I can tell my words sting. I tick the side of my mug with my nails, my eyes finding my father again. "Just no more lies, okay?"

She nods quickly. "No more lies."

"This doesn't mean I trust you. And we are not on good terms, but…" I sigh, no longer having the energy to stay angry. "That doesn't mean we can't be someday." She tries to smile and rests her head back against the wall. "What are you going to do? Now that you're wanted for treason?"

She cringes. "I don't know. Got any tips for being on the lam?"

I snort. "I've got a lot, and you'll hate them all." She sighs; no doubt the gravity of my words feels heavy. "You can come with us." I say it before I can think about the impact and what that may mean or entail. I've been in her position. Hell, I'm still in her position. Lost in both sides of the war, feeling like I'm drifting among too many people but not fitting in anywhere.

"Wait, what?" Jack says over our quiet and clearly not private conversation. "She's not coming with us."

"Jack," Dani warns.

"No way. We already have too many gray coats." He points at me. "*Her* and the two back in town. You want us to be outnumbered?"

"Rodrigues was never really in the NAF. She was undercover," Darby reminds him. "Weren't you listening when Dani explained it all?"

Jack crosses his arms like a kid having a tantrum. "I don't care. We're not taking her back with us."

I feel Rodrigues tense next to me, and while I'm empathetic to her discomfort in the group, I also wouldn't mind sharing the wrath of Jack with someone else. Misery loving company and all that.

"That's up to Jenisis and Kate," Dani says easily. She continues before Jack can protest. "It's their call."

"Since when?" he fires back. I chance a glance at Rodrigues. "We can barely keep ourselves hidden, warm, and fed. Now you want to add one more person?" He seemingly breaks into my thoughts and looks around the room. "Or...two?" He points nonchalantly at my dad. "Shouldn't this be a group decision? Do we even know where the hell we're going?"

Lucas slumps in his chair. "Maelstrom was defeated. There was no easy solution."

"I have a place," my dad says, speaking up for the first time. "My bunker isn't far from here."

"A bunker? You want us to go *underground*? With you?" Jack snorts. "No, thanks."

"You said you needed a place to go and that you needed help," he says, focusing on me. "This is how I can help."

No one says anything, but I know this is my call. With no other options coming to mind, my eyes meet Dani's. Her expression reads reluctance, but she tips her head a bit, indicating we're on the same page.

"How many people can it hold?" she asks.

Jack storms out of the cabin, and honestly, I don't blame him. In fact, for a moment, I contemplate going with him.

Dani manages to get ahold of Jess and conveys the message to get packed because we're moving out. I'm not sure how the conversation went, and Dani doesn't bother to give me details. She only tells me that two people need to take the vehicles back to help the rest of the gang load up and bring everyone back.

Darby refuses to go, and Jack insists that he does.

"I don't want to leave you," Dani says quietly, her head close to mine.

"I know, but we'll be fine. I'll be with Lucas," I remind her.

She watches him tend to the fire and pulls away from me with a sigh. "As soon as we're back, we'll head out together." She zips up her coat and hesitates. "Are you sure you'll be okay?"

I glance at Rodrigues, hunched over Darby's drone as they quietly discuss options on how to upgrade it. My dad sits off to the side, trying to talk to Lucas about kindling. "I'll be okay," I assure her. "I just wish I could thank Miguel and Anthony. Leaving them without saying good-bye...."

She gives me a sympathetic look.

"Maybe tell them I'll stay in touch?" I ask, not knowing what other kind of message I can give them. Seeing them again, happy and healthy, was a salve I didn't know my heart needed. Leaving so suddenly feels wrong.

Dani nods and pulls me into a tight embrace. "We won't be gone long," she promises right as Jack honks the truck horn. Dani ignores his impatience and gently cradles my face. "If you change your mind about any of this—"

"I know," I say quickly. If I put too much thought into everything right now, I will definitely change my mind and probably regret it. I zip her jacket just a little more under her chin. "Go get our friends."

She glances at my dad and then Rodrigues. "I have my radio," she says to both me and Lucas.

I accept a gentle kiss, and with one last look, Dani slips out of the small cabin.

My dad looks at me, and I consider taking the time to speak with him. But the moment passes, and I sit on the cot instead. Lucas sits beside me, and I do my best to ignore the sad, dejected expression on my father's face. Yesterday, I would've given anything to see him again, to hug him, to talk to him, ask him about why he lied about his past with Jonathan and William. Now he's right here, and I can't even bring myself to look at him.

"I'm going to grab some more wood for the fire," he says, probably as an excuse to get out of the cabin.

He steps out the back, and Rodrigues stands as well. "I'll help." It doesn't go unnoticed that she grabs her pistol off the table. It's like she's his personal bodyguard.

I collapse back on the cot and groan. "So many secrets. I'm starting to wonder if I'm even a part of my own family," I say sadly, quietly.

Lucas takes a deep breath and gently touches my arm. "Because at the heart of it, Maelstrom loved family above all else."

He's right. No matter how much pain, no matter how betrayed I feel, he's still my dad. The same man who used to run around the base with me on his shoulders when I was little, pretending we were flying. The same man who used to let me dance on his feet.

I think that's why it hurts so much.

I try hard to fight back tears. "Why would he do this? Why would he lie? Did he not love me enough?"

Lucas shifts, a sad kind of smile on his face, and lies down beside me. "Things are never that simple. There is no black or white. Just gray. We all live in shades of gray."

"Issue sixteen." Darby's voice startles me from across the room.

I may not be as well versed in *Major Maelstrom* as Lucas or Dani, but I know the first twenty or so issues fairly well. For the first time since I've met her, Darby answers correctly. I sit up and look at her, surprised.

She smiles and winks at me.

Lucas brings his finger to his lips and makes a shushing sound. I glance between the two of them, and it only takes me a moment to realize that Darby has been purposely giving incorrect issue numbers, and Lucas is in on it. The whole thing is so unexpected and so absurd that I can't help the laugh that manages to escape. I think I understand now what Dani meant when she said that some lies are okay.

By the time Dani and the others get back to the cabin several hours later, I can't leave fast enough. It isn't lost on me that we're all just going from one small enclosed space to another, but I didn't realize how much I craved Dani's support until she wasn't there.

I press my head against the window, the cold of the glass a stark contrast to the heat blaring from the truck vents. This has officially felt like the longest day ever.

"Do you wanna talk about it?" Dani asks, her voice soft and soothing.

"You mean about seeing my dad or my reaction to seeing him?"

"Either. Both. Whatever you want." She puts a hand on my thigh, and I take a deep breath, leaning back and staring out the windshield.

"My therapist said it wasn't uncommon for them to happen without warning." I close my eyes and think back to the mandatory sessions I was required to take during officer training, and again after my father died. I remember begging her not to tell my mother about my attacks.

Dani takes my hand. "What do you mean?"

"'Fits of panic or attacking anxiety,'" I say, remembering exactly what my therapist called them. I push out another long breath and look at her. She turns to me, and her eyes are glowing with the dim light of the dashboard. "It happened after my dad died." I scoff at my own words. "Or after I thought he died. Again after a particularly botched assignment. And today." I try not to think of the raiders slaughtering half of my unit or how I was awarded a medal just for surviving. "Has something like that ever happened with you?" I ask after a stretch of quiet,

"Not that I recall, but who knows?" Dani shrugs one shoulder. "I had a lot of emotionally charged moments after I lost my parents. I think your therapist would call mine 'fits of rage.'"

We share a smile, and she squeezes my hand. "Thank you," I say quietly, shades of embarrassment still lingering. "For what you did back there. Calming me down."

"I wish I could do more."

Silence takes over again, but I can't seem to quiet my thoughts.

"I can see the gears turning," she jokes. "What are you thinking about?" Lightly, she brushes her thumb across the back of my hand.

I close my eyes and try to fall into the sensation of her touch. "Do you think this is it?" I ask. "Do you think this is the end?"

She exhales slowly, deeply. It makes me wonder if she's been wondering the same. "The end of the war? I hope so." She brings my hand to her lips and trails kisses down my wrist. "The end of us? Never."

"If we make it out—"

"When," she corrects sternly.

"*When* we make it out," I amend. "What do you see for us? What happens once it's over?"

She bites her lip like she's thinking hard. But her answer comes quickly. "Living together in a small house, just you and me. No more roommates." She looks at me with her nose wrinkled, like she's disgusted by the idea of ever having to share a space with her friends again. "Endless baths and dancing until we collapse with exhaustion."

"But you don't dance," I remind her, already on board with her vision.

She wiggles her eyebrows. "I don't mean that kind of dancing."

Groaning, I pull my hand away. I should've seen that response coming.

Dani laughs and grabs my hand, kissing the back of it again and holding it tight. "I just see you, Kate," she says seriously. "I just see myself, happy, with you."

I smile and hope it doesn't appear sad, wanting nothing more than for her vision to come true. For the war to end and for the two of us to live long, happy lives together in a small house close to our friends.

Our eyes meet, and she sets our joined hands in her lap before turning back to the road. I rest my head against the seat and close my eyes. It's a good dream.

Chapter Ten: The Traitor

Dani

By the time we finally stop, it's dark outside. We park under a grove of trees, hopefully out of sight from drones. Theodore walks at the front of the group with a flashlight but doesn't say a word or even look at any of us. Jack mutters about how horrible of an idea this is, and I don't disagree, but thankfully, he doesn't push the issue.

The thick clouds cover the moon, leaving only the light of a few flashlights to help guide us. We take careful steps in the darkness and push deeper into the woods. I stick close to Kate and keep my head on a swivel, not trusting Theodore or the situation. No one says a word until we arrive at the entrance.

"This is it?" Darby whispers loudly.

The door stands aboveground, in the middle of an arched entryway, hidden within the trees. Behind it sits a large cylinder, the top camouflaged by moss and grass, making it just about impossible to see from the sky. The more I examine it, the stranger it looks. Like a door that leads to nothing.

"This is…weird." Elise peers behind it as if she's missing something.

"There's a bunker field not far from here," Theodore says. "Hundreds of all risk military bunkers that used to belong to the Army."

"And this one?" Elise asks curiously.

"Found by chance and built privately." His answer is vague, not that I would expect anything else. It does little to appease my trepidation.

"Little good they did against the doomsday-ers," Darby mumbles from behind me.

Theodore hands his flashlight to Rodrigues and flips open the cover off to the side of the door and firmly presses a code into a keypad. The door emits a buzzing noise before unlatching. Rodrigues helps by pulling on the heavy metal opening and motions for us to enter.

Kate grips the strap of her duffel so tightly, I bet her knuckles are turning white. The air feels thick. So much so, even Roscoe paces anxiously.

No one moves.

Finally, Theodore steps forward, unhooks a lantern from the top of the stairs, ignites it, and descends, motioning for us to follow.

Kate takes a deep breath and passes through the door.

"Maybe we should let Kate check it out first," Darby suggests, trying to get a look down the darkened stairwell.

Taking the flashlight from Elise, I go next, not blaming their hesitation but not wanting Kate to walk into anything unexpected. I keep my grip on the handle of the pistol strapped to my thigh.

There's arguing from the top of the steps, but the farther down I go, the less I hear. By the time I reach the bottom, Theodore is waiting, shifting nervously and standing just outside of an open door. Light from inside spills in behind him.

"Welcome," he says, hesitating slightly as the others finally file in behind us. "I just want you to know that you'll be safe here."

Jack scoffs from behind me. "We'll see."

Kate squares her shoulders and readjusts her bag. "Let's just get inside." She presses forward, barely giving her father a second glance as she passes.

Theodore's hopeful expression falters.

Following her, I step into the main room and come to a halt. The bunker is brightly lit from a series of overhead lights. The space is large, with furniture throughout and a huge workstation along the far wall cluttered with tech. In one corner is the small kitchen with pristine-looking appliances.

"Is that fire real?" Mike asks, walking past me to the strange-looking fireplace along one of the walls. Theodore picks up a remote and aims it at the fireplace, turning it on. Startled, Mike jumps back. Carefully, he approaches again, holding out his hand. "That fire isn't real, but it's warm in here," he says turning to us with wide eyes.

"He has electricity," Darby exclaims and drops her bag to stand on top of a chair. She attempts to poke at the overhead lights.

"Theodore has his own power grid," Rodrigues explains. "The washroom is over that way if you could all please wash up before touching anything else."

"He has a power grid?" Darby squeaks and looks at Theodore. "How in the world did you manage to stash away enough resources for that?"

"It's solar powered," he says awkwardly, clearly not liking the attention. "There's a working sink in the kitchen, too."

"He has plumbing," Darby announces excitedly.

Taking the hint to wash our hands, we split up, half of us to the washroom and the other half to the kitchen. Wyatt tries desperately to describe the room to Jess, but even seeing it all for myself, it still sounds made up.

Darby continues to squeal, fascinated by the light switch that flicks the overhead bulb on and off inside the washroom. Most places use generators for heating water and for battery chargers. Using it for electricity was never really an option, not with the destruction of the power grids across the country. This is a luxury none of us have ever seen.

As if just realizing that we're in his living quarters, Theodore starts to nervously buzz around the room, picking up random items and placing them in other places as if attempting to organize or clean for guests. "I, ah, I apologize," he says, placing a few dirty dishes in the sink once we've moved out of the kitchen. "I go on supply runs once a month. I am due for another one, so there isn't much to eat. I might be able to manage some soup if you're hungry?"

"I could eat," Darby announces and shamelessly picks through the items on his workbench. "Is this an inductive coupler?"

"About sleeping arrangements," Elise asks when she steps out of the bathroom, interrupting Theodore on his way to the workbench.

"Oh yes," he says, clearly flustered and glances from Elise to Darby and back again. "I have two rooms and several blankets." Theodore halts his movements and nervously watches as everyone continues to explore. "Please, make yourself at home. Just, no weapons. If you could leave them by the door?"

"No chance," Jack says, crossing his arms. "There's only one way in and out of this place, and I'm supposed to give up my gun? Not happening."

He has a valid point. I look at Theodore, who appears to be slightly panicked.

"You'd be suicidal to fire a weapon in an enclosed space like this," Rodrigues says, also crossing her arms and staring at Jack.

He takes a step toward her, his hand going for the shotgun strapped to his back. I grab the back of his jacket and pull.

"There is another way out," Theodore speaks up, getting all of our attention. "There's a hatch in the back."

Rodrigues steps in front of Theodore as if shielding him. "You can keep your weapons, but you won't need them. We'll give you a tour."

Darby pouts. "I thought we were going to eat."

Theodore nods, agreeing. "Yes, I can start that soup if you'd like?"

"I want you to show us the hatch," I tell both Rodrigues and Theodore, hoping my tone leaves no room for argument.

Theodore glances at Kate this time, who continues to keep her distance. She stares back, not jumping in one way or the other. It isn't until her head tilts just slightly that Theodore agrees. "Yes, okay, please follow me."

"I'll go," Kate volunteers. "If you want to get Jess set up?"

I don't want Kate going anywhere alone, and I start to protest, but Mike steps beside her. "I'll go with her."

Kate gives me a reassuring nod, and they follow Theodore to the back of the bunker.

"Go with them," I tell Jack, but he's already falling in step with Kate and Mike, not needing to be told. He pats his leg, and Roscoe trots beside him.

"Theodore, are you sure—"

I take Rodrigues's arm, stopping her from not only following but from whatever it was she was going to ask him. "There's something you're not telling us."

She lifts her chin almost defiantly. "I don't know what you're talking about."

I'm impressed when she doesn't back down. "Whatever you're planning—"

"I'm not planning anything," she snaps.

I stare at her, not able to tell if she's lying. "Where's the radio?"

She pulls her arm free and walks to a table near the workbench. "It's right here."

I find Jess and Wyatt quietly talking near the kitchen. "Jess, are you good to set up comms?" I ask.

"I'm ready," she confirms. "New places make me nervous. I'd like to be around something familiar."

"You won't be able to use your equipment. You'll have to use Theodore's," Rodrigues says.

I point to the large radio. "I'm going to need you to bring that into the spare room."

Rodrigues glances at it and at me. "Are you serious?" I don't answer, instead, I stare at her and wait. Finally, she sighs and starts to unhook everything. "This is ridiculous," she mumbles.

"I'm going to get you set up in the spare room so you have privacy," I tell Jess.

"Yeah, that'll work." Jess allows me to lead her in to the small spare room.

Rodrigues is barely able to carry the equipment, and Lucas hurries over to help. We use the top of a chest instead of a table, and Lucas brings in a chair for Jess to sit by it.

"What do we have?" Jess asks, reaching in front of her to feel for the equipment as Lucas connects it all.

"Well," I start, and glance around. "The room is small. Low ceilings like the rest of the bunker. It's very confined, actually." Jess finds the old ham radio and runs her fingers along the face of it.

"Dani…" Jess chuckles. "I meant the radio."

"It's a pretty standard setup from what I understand," Rodrigues says, fielding the question. "Although Theodore made some modifications. This is the only radio that can call out of the bunker, and the radius to listen in on other channels is insanely far. Only a couple of people have the frequency to drop in on this channel, though."

"A spy's dream," I mutter, thinking about Theodore listening in on both sides of the war but not involving himself in any of it. Not even bothering to reach out to his own daughter. It pisses me off.

"It's go time," Lucas announces. He stands proud, examining his work while Jess turns it on.

She nods and runs her fingers along the radio again, getting to know it. "Lucas, could you please go get my bag? Wyatt knows the one. It has pads of paper and some pencils."

"Yes, sir." Lucas slips out of the room.

I wait, knowing Jess isn't finished with me yet. "How do you know I'm not the one communicating with the NAF?"

I stare at her, startled, and glance at Rodrigues, who appears just as taken aback by the question.

"That's why you put me in this room away from everyone, right? Because we have someone sharing Resistance secrets?"

My shock gives way to awe. "I keep forgetting how incredibly perceptive you are." She smiles. "But to answer your question, too easy."

"So because I'm the most likely suspect, that automatically makes me innocent?"

"Exactly." Rodrigues slips out of the room, pulling the door shut behind her. "Besides, if it *was* you, we'd already be captured, and none of this would matter anymore."

She chuckles. "True. How's Kate?"

"Just managing to keep it together, I think," I confess. It's not every day someone finds out that the person they love the most isn't actually dead.

"And you?"

"Just managing to keep it together," I repeat.

She must sense that I don't want to get into my own feelings because she ties her long red hair back out of her face, her expression serious. "This is a dangerous plan, Dani. It's also a stupid one." Ah, there it is, the lecture I knew was coming. "But if I'm going to be stuck here, the least you can do is bring me something to eat."

"Yes, ma'am," I say and watch her lean into the small speaker, already picking up some chatter. I slip out of the room and let her do her thing just as Lucas reappears. "Let me know if she needs anything. Don't let anyone, and I mean *anyone*, else touch that radio." He nods and sits on the cot with a pencil and a pad of paper, ready to help.

Rodrigues is in the kitchen once I leave. "Anything else I can help with?" She barely glances up when I approach.

I lean against the small counter. "How long have you been coming to visit Theodore in the bunker?"

"I've only been here twice," she answers and rummages through some more cabinets. "As I told you before, I didn't know he was alive until fairly recently. I was stationed in Omaha. Not like I could just pop in for a quick chat." She glances at me and pulls out a large pot for what I'm guessing is the soup. "There are only a handful of glasses and bowls. You'll have to either share or take turns."

"I don't trust you," I say. It comes out calmer than I had expected.

"You've made that clear," she mumbles and fills a teakettle with water, completely unfazed.

"But Kate does." That gives her pause. "At least, she wants to. So if you break that trust or lie to her again, I'll make sure you regret it for the rest of your life. And whatever it is you're hiding, you might want to ask yourself if it's worth it."

She doesn't say anything. Instead, she slowly starts the small stove and pulls a small box of tea bags closer.

"If you want a chance to prove yourself, make sure no one goes in or out of that radio room," I tell her. "Including you." Our eyes meet briefly.

"I'll let you know when the soup is ready," she tells me evenly.

George shuffles into the kitchen and motions for me to follow. He leads me to the opposite side of the bunker and glances around nervously and points to the spare room. "I don't trust this place, and I don't want Jess to be alone in there."

"She's not alone," I counter. "Lucas is with her."

"She's a blind sixteen-year-old, Dani," he reminds me.

My jaw tightens. "I'm aware."

"If something happens..." He shakes his head, clearly frustrated. "If something goes wrong, she can't—"

"Lucas will take care of her," I interrupt, losing my patience. "We will all take care of her."

"You can't promise that." He takes a step closer, and I straighten slightly. "How do we know that the NAF aren't closing in on us right now? Where are we, exactly? What's around us? That soldier says there is only one radio, but we don't know if that's even true. How do we know she won't let someone in when we're all asleep?"

Rodrigues watches the exchange from the kitchen, and I wonder if she can she hear us. Her eyes meet mine briefly, but she doesn't say anything.

I sigh. "George, I'm doing my best. We're all doing our best. Being holed up in a bunker with people who have ties with the NAF is not my first choice, either, but it's the only one we have right now. You need to sit tight until it's time to move again. This..." I motion around me. "Fluttering around like a paranoid old bird isn't helping anything. We'll take turns guarding the doors. We'll all look out for each other, and just like every other time we've had to move, we'll probably be gone in a couple of days."

He looks offended. "By then, it'll be too late," he snaps.

Before I can respond, Elise appears and places a hand on his arm, causing him to jump. "George, why don't you come sit with me for a bit? Maybe we can find those blankets Theodore mentioned and get everyone set up for some sleep."

He hesitates, mumbling about not being able to sleep in a place like this, but Elise gently guides him away. I nod at her, silently thanking her.

I notice Wyatt standing near the door that leads out of the bunker, appearing nervous. "How are you holding up?" I ask, startling him so bad, he jumps.

He glances at me and then back at the door. "I'm not sure what to do." He laughs at himself. "Normally, I'd help Jess or cook. I feel useless." He turns to me, his face pale. "Is it safe to get some fresh air, do you think?"

He's the most anxious I've seen him in the few months we've been stuck together. "What makes this place so different from the others?" I ask.

"The lack of windows?" He phrases it as a question, and I know what he's implying. Wyatt is claustrophobic. He must notice my sympathetic look. "I won't, like, freak out on you or anything. I just need some air."

"I can't help with the windows, but when Jack gets back, maybe he can take you and Roscoe outside for a minute. Would that help?"

"Maybe?" He shakes his head and chuckles nervously. "My mom was always good about making sure I had plenty of light and letting me stay outside." His expression falls.

I share his guilt over leaving his mother behind in Rapid City. I feel guilty about leaving a lot of people there. "We'll find your mom, Wyatt. No one has forgotten about her. We'll take back Rapid City." It's a promise I know I shouldn't make because I'm not sure I can keep it. For the moment, though, it's what he needs to hear. Rhiannon's words about igniting hope in others ring in my ears. We need to keep hope to keep fighting.

He nods, but I'm not sure he believes me.

"He wasn't lying about the back door," Jack announces loudly.

We all watch as they filter in: Theodore next, then Kate and Mike. I meet Kate's eyes and only slightly relax when she looks back at me. "Easy enough access?" I ask Jack.

"Locks from the inside. It's not that far down, but it's a pretty dark and narrow passageway." He glances at Wyatt. "You okay?"

"Yeah, fine," he says, nodding much too fast and too many times.

"Do you mind taking Wyatt up for a bit of air?" I ask and hope Wyatt doesn't start hyperventilating. "He's having a hard time with the lack of windows and doors." I give Jack a look that hopefully screams, please read between the lines.

"Rhiannon didn't like enclosed spaces, either," he says and motions for Wyatt and Roscoe to follow him. "Come on then. Grab the lantern."

Wyatt quickly and obediently follows him up the stairs.

I watch them leave, surprised. It's the first time Jack's mentioned Rhiannon without being emotional.

Mike whispers something in Elise's ear, and she nods.

When I take a step toward them, Theodore stops me, standing directly in my path. "Danielle, I wanted to tell you that I was devastated to hear about your father. And your mother, too, of course. Kaya was—"

"Don't," I warn through clenched teeth.

He winces as if I just slapped him across the face as he clenches and unclenches his hands nervously. It's the same thing Kate does when she's anxious.

"Right. No, no. Of course," he stutters.

I lean in, closing the distance. "You lied to her. You lied about your childhood, about her mother, about dying." He winces and leans away. "I'm only here because of Kate. I'm only tolerating you because of *Kate*." I say, keeping my voice low. "Members of my family are dead because of you. My father is dead because of *you*. Because you stood by and did *nothing*. The only thing keeping me from returning the favor is Kate. Because for whatever reason, she agreed to your act of generosity, but don't for a second mistake my lack of retaliation as forgiveness."

His face pales, and instead of responding, he merely nods once and steps out of the way as I brush past.

I go straight to Kate, sitting on a stool by the electrical fire.

She attempts a smile. "Hey. Giving my dad the third degree?"

"What? Me? Never." She gives me a look that I promptly ignore. "Does the hatch work?"

"It does," she confirms. "It dumps you out just along the tree line."

I make a mental note to check it out. Watching Kate carefully, my heart sinks. She appears tired and drained. All the emotions battling for control, angry, anxious, betrayed…I can't imagine how Kate is feeling. I've tried to put myself in her position, if it was my dad instead of hers, but what-ifs don't really compare to the real, raw emotions of actually experiencing it.

"This was a bad idea. I don't know if we can trust him," she whispers finally. "He lied to me. Everyone has lied to me my entire life. I don't know what to believe or who to trust anymore."

"I understand," I tell her, thinking about Dad and William hiding their friendship with the general and Theodore. And how there is a most likely a traitor among my friends. Scooting closer, I take one of her hands. "Hey, look at me." I wait until she does. The sadness etched across her features is enough to make my heart break. "You can trust me. You can *always* trust me. I will never lie to you."

"It's funny, isn't it?" She tries to smile. "The one person I was supposed to hate my whole life is the only one who hasn't betrayed me. The only one who makes me feel safe."

I pull her into me, hugging her tightly.

❖

It's late into the night when Lucas gently shakes me awake from our blankets by the electric fire. I startle from a dreamless sleep, sitting straight up, not having any idea where I am. It takes a moment to focus on Lucas's apologetic face. He points to the radio room just as Kate stirs beside me.

"What's going on?" she asks, her eyes barely open, and her voice scratchy from sleep.

"Jess wants to see me," I tell her and kiss her head. "Go back to sleep. I'll be right back." She starts to get up, but I gently nudge her back down. "You need sleep. I promise, I'll be back in a few minutes."

Thankfully, she yawns and tucks herself back under the covers.

Untangling myself from her, I follow my brother to the dimly lit room. The cot pressed to the wall is rumpled, and the sleeping bag on the floor is jumbled. Whatever came through the radio clearly woke them.

"I'm here. What's going on?" I ask an exhausted-looking Jess stationed at the desk.

"I'm sorry to wake you, but I had it preset to William's frequency when I went to sleep, and this message just came through for you." She holds out a piece of paper.

I lean into the light to read her lopsided writing. "Atomic Anomaly urgent. ASAP. Lower level. Alone," I read aloud, scanning the coordinates. Before I can even ask, Lucas puts a map in front of me and points. He turns away, yawning. "That's not too far. Do they know where we are?"

"No, and he didn't ask," Jess says. "I confirmed the message was received, and then it went radio silent."

"It's gotta be serious if he dropped ASAP." I'd be annoyed if I didn't know things were happening at an alarmingly fast rate, but the "alone" clearly means he doesn't want Kate to come. I take a deep breath and run my hands down my face, trying to wake up a little more.

"The situation could be dangerous," Lucas says, looking just as tired as I feel. "You should never go it alone."

"Yeah," I agree. "I'll bring Jack. Kate should probably stay here. As much as I don't like it, she's kind of the glue between our group and Rodrigues and Theodore." I swallow a yawn, wondering if we have any coffee to make before setting out. "And if Theodore and Rodrigues are up to something, I think it'd be harder for them to betray us with Kate involved. Although, with all the lies floating around, I could be wrong." Groaning, I put my face in my hands, wishing I had gotten a few more hours of sleep. "I just don't know how I'm going to convince her to stay. What do I tell her?"

"You don't have to tell her anything," Kate says sleepily from the doorway, making me jump. "You have to go. You *should* go."

After the initial surprise, I deflate. "I won't be gone long," I promise.

She pulls the blanket higher around her shoulders. "I know," she says and smiles. "And I can't come with you because I'm your safety net here."

"I didn't mean—"

"Dani, it's okay."

I pull the blanket even tighter around her shoulders. "I hate leaving you."

She leans forward, her forehead pressing against my shoulder, and I wrap my arms around her, already missing the warm cocoon of our makeshift bed. "I'm not thrilled with the idea of you leaving, either, but I think we've run out of time."

I press my face into her hair and take a deep breath, catching a very faint scent of lavender. She's right. We've run for as long as we can. The war is here, and soon, we'll all have to fight. "Contact me anytime. Got it? For whatever reason. I'll keep in touch with Jess."

"I know the drill," she says and kisses my cheek.

I hold her a bit tighter. I'm more than aware that it's getting harder and harder to let her go.

Jack is positively delighted to leave the bunker. It doesn't take long to get to the rendezvous, but when we get there, it's no longer dark. Pulling into a half-fallen garage at an old gas station, we get out and crouch within the entrance, guns in hand. We both have eyes on the building where I'm supposed to meet William.

"I don't see signs of anyone else," Jack says, looking up and down the rubble lining the streets. "You sure they're here?"

"Only one way to find out." We move out of the garage when a familiar buzzing catches my attention. Jack and I share a quick look before diving back into the garage and behind what's left of a counter.

"Drones," he whispers.

"Definitely." We sit still, our backs pressed against the base of the counter, listening. "Let's hope they don't have thermal technology," I say when things go quiet. "Or this'll be a really short trip."

We give the drone time to pass and peek out from over the counter and carefully make our way back to the garage entrance. Scanning the skies, I wonder if I misjudged this message.

"Maybe we should've brought Darby and Chi-Chi," Jack mumbles, squinting as the sun begins to rise. He's clearly thinking the same thing I am.

"You don't mean that," I joke, though some aerial cover *would* be nice.

"No." He laughs quietly and pulls his shotgun closer, readying it to take a shot. He no doubt knows that it could never knock a drone out of the sky from this distance, but he clutches it like a security blanket. "But maybe Mike."

"Yeah," I agree. "Maybe Mike." When it appears there are no more drones, I hit Jack's shoulder. "Let's go."

We sprint to the building and race to the lower level like we were instructed. I knock on the heavy metal door leading to the basement. Thankfully, we don't have to wait long for it to fly open.

William ushers us in and locks the door behind us. "You're late," he tells us, clearly agitated. "And you were supposed to come alone."

"Kind of hard to be on time when we were dodging drones," I snap. "And I needed someone I trust watching my back." I want to say, *from you.* From all the lies and dodging.

He glances at Jack and must decide that he's a better option than Kate. He motions for us to follow. "Come on. They won't be able to see our heat signatures down here."

They did have thermal technology. Awesome.

Just another thing he didn't tell me.

Using a lantern, he leads us down the stairs. He gets maybe five steps down before my anger becomes unbearable, and I slam him up against the wall. I can hear the whoosh of air leave his lungs, and he stares at me with wide, surprised eyes.

"You lied to me."

"Dani," Jack warns, slipping his shotgun in his back holster and reaching for me. I knock his hands away.

William says nothing.

I press into him a little harder, my face close to his. "Do you want to know where we went when we left Woodlake?" He doesn't answer. "We've been with Theodore Turner. In his bunker." If William's surprised, he does a good job hiding it. And that pisses me off even more. "You knew he was alive this whole time."

"That's enough." The voice is firm, and it comes from my right. When I look, I'm surprised to see Thatcher standing at the bottom of the stairs holding her own lantern. "The lies were necessary, and despite your hurt feelings, this is bigger than you. So let him go, and get your asses down here. We have a situation."

I stare at William for another beat, my hands shaking. I can't remember the last time I was this angry. It takes all my restraint to release him. With one last scathing look to let him know we are nowhere near finished talking about this, I follow Thatcher into the next room with Jack hot on my heels.

"You knew about Theodore, too?" I ask, her words finally sinking in.

"I did, and you can yell at me about that when we've finished here." I'm tempted to walk out, to tell them both where they can shove it and find someone else to be their puppet, but Thatcher keeps going. "I take it you've heard about the NAF camps popping up?"

"Considering we took one out, yeah, we've heard."

Thatcher stops at another door and motions us all inside. My curiosity gets the better of me, and I hate myself for it. I follow her down the dark hallway. "Then, perhaps you've noticed they circle a specific area."

I notice a large figure down the hall, and it isn't until we get a little closer that I realize it's Bruce, Thatcher's personal security detail. He stands outside a room, his arms crossed, looking bored. He steps aside when Thatcher reaches for the latch.

"What's this about?" I ask, no longer having any patience for games.

"I found our leak," William says from behind me.

All the air feels like it's been ripped from my lungs. My anger switches swiftly to shock, and I whirl to look at him. "What? When?"

Thatcher unlocks the door and pushes it open. Inside the dark, windowless room, there's a single lantern on the far wall that barely illuminates the figure tied to the chair in the center of the small space.

Hugo.

His matted hair falls around his face; his pale skin is dirty and bruised. His head hangs forward, his chin touching his collar. He looks absolutely beaten but clearly not broken.

Ericson leans against the wall, his arms crossed and a cigarette dangling from his lips. He glances up as if bored.

"What the fuck is going on?" Jack asks, his voice laced with disbelief.

"How long?" I ask, feeling sick. "How long has he been funneling information?"

William walks in the room, his eyes never leaving Hugo. "He won't tell us. But if I had to guess, it was right before we moved out west."

Various memories come to the forefront: Hugo helping us plan the attack on the convoy. Hugo walking around the streets of Rapid City alone. Hugo casually strolling through Deadwood. Hugo with free access to the NAF under the guise of having a Resistance contact within. Hugo with access to Jess's communication room to plant a bomb inside.

The bomb that killed Rhiannon.

Jack must realize the same thing. "You son of a bitch." He pushes his way, clearly hell-bent on getting to Hugo.

Thatcher steps in and blocks him, managing to keep him from getting farther into the room. "Easy, big guy. After what he did to my city, no one wants him to pay more than I do, but he still has information, and we can't get that information if you kill him."

Jack struggles against Thatcher until Bruce steps inside. Seeing him, Jack finally relents, taking a step back, his hands in the air like he's surrendering. His chest heaves, and I can see the rage clearly etched across his face.

I stare at Hugo, fighting the sick feeling in the pit of my stomach. "Has he told you anything?"

"No," Thatcher says.

I crouch in front of him, absolutely disgusted by the sight of him. There's dried blood in a streak from his nose, and one of his eyes is swollen shut. "How did you know it was him?"

"I fed everyone fake intel about Thatcher's movements. Moved supplies and units around to make it seem legit," William answers from the doorway.

"You used her as bait," I say. "Even with me." It's a statement, not a question. I thought Thatcher was back east. With how quickly she got here, I wonder if that's even true.

"Even with you," William confirms.

Funny enough, I'm not even mad about it.

I turn back to Hugo. "You had a nice little setup going. Cushy position with William. Direct access to the NAF. What were you getting from them in return? Tech? Promises of a life of luxury?" He says nothing. "Were you ever even Resistance?" He doesn't answer. "You must've been beyond thrilled when Lucas and I joined back up. Whatever they promised you, I bet you thought you could get more with us in the picture."

I think about our meeting with Rodrigues, when she confirmed everything the general knew, things I now know she probably found out from Hugo. "The general knew we were going to ambush their convoy at Sioux Falls. She knew about the convoy to Malmstrom. She also knew you were going to poke around Malmstrom for intel, and that's why she rigged the place to blow. She knew we were in Rapid City and toyed with us like a cat does with a mouse. All because of you," I say quietly. "You planted that bomb inside the communications room." My voice steadily gets louder. "Rhiannon is dead because of *you*."

Hugo looks at me, shifting in his seat. His lips twitch in something between a smile and grimace. "Not just me," he whispers.

The room goes perfectly still for just a second, and then everything seems to happen at once:

Jack lunges, pushing me out of the way. Ericson grabs him as he knocks Hugo backward in the chair, and they both crash to the ground. Thatcher and William are on top of Jack and try to help Ericson pry him off. There's shouting, and Jack lands a punch to Hugo's face before his large arms are restrained.

It takes Bruce, William, and Thatcher to drag him to the other side of the room while Ericson hauls Hugo back to a sitting position. Somewhere in the scuffle, Hugo has managed to get his hands free, and he decks Ericson so hard in the mouth, he staggers backward.

Unholstering my gun, I aim just as Hugo pops something in his mouth and bites. Thatcher yells and shoves Ericson out of the way. She grabs the front of Hugo's shirt and pulls him close, screaming questions at him and tries to pry open his mouth. He appears to be out of it, confused. She tries again and again, asking him about contacts and locations. He doesn't answer.

When he starts to groan, she releases him and steps back, her hands on her hips. I watch in horror as he gasps for air over and over until he starts to seize.

No one tries to help.

Eventually, he falls over, out of his chair. Ericson checks his neck for a pulse. He waits, his fingers pressed against Hugo's skin until finally, he shakes his head. Hugo's dead.

Thatcher rounds on Jack faster than he can blink. "What were you thinking?" He takes a step back, his eyes still wide and focused on Hugo's lifeless form. "He had crucial information that would've been beneficial to the Resistance. Information that is now gone."

"He wasn't going to tell you," Jack counters, collecting himself. He stands at full height, staring back at Thatcher. "You said it yourself. He wasn't talking."

"Certainly not now," she yells.

I step between them and push them away from each other. "It's done," I tell them. I'm disappointed that's how it played out. Hugo died like a coward, but there's no point in wasting time arguing about it.

They stare at each other a bit longer, and then Thatcher brushes past us. "Fine. Come with me. There's much to discuss."

William stares at Hugo, a sad look on his face. I don't know how close they were, but I almost feel sorry for the betrayal he must be experiencing. Almost. I want to tell him to join the club.

I also want to lecture Jack, tell him what he did was fucking stupid and selfish, but I can't seem to bring myself to actually do it. "Do you feel any better?" I ask instead.

He stares at Hugo with a blank, emotionless stare and then shakes his head. "No."

Me neither. "Come on," I tell him.

Hugo's whispered words about not acting alone lingers in my mind.

Chapter Eleven: The Reconciliation

Kate

I miss Dani.

The feeling isn't new or unusual, but somehow, it feels more prominent than ever. She's been unwavering through this emotional roller coaster, and with her gone, I feel alone.

Darby makes another delighted sound from the other side of the room, and Rodrigues laughs. I turn away when my father smiles, pleased at the reaction his inventions are causing. It hurts to be so close to him knowing that he's still out of reach.

"I come bearing gifts from Wyatt." Some sort of sandwich appears in my peripheral. Elise smiles when I take the offering. "How's your head?" she asks and sits in the large chair by the fire.

I scoot over on the ottoman to make room for her feet. "Hurts a little. Headaches are mostly gone." Instinctively, I touch the back of my head.

She nods, apparently pleased. "And your heart?"

I roll my eyes. "That was cheesy. Even for you."

She holds up her hands. "Hey, I'm a healer. I'm allowed to ask about *all* vital organs and mental states."

I sigh, knowing she means well.

"No way," Darby shouts, and I can't stop myself from cringing.

"Do you want to talk about it?" Elise asks gently.

Not in the least, but I know she's asking because she cares. I could tell her I'm fine, but I know she'll see right through the lie.

"How does anyone know what time it is in this place?" Mike asks and squeezes in beside me, putting Elise's feet in his lap. "Is it lunchtime? Breakfast? The middle of the night? The whole lack of windows is really throwing off my internal clock." He looks from Elise to me and back again, seeming taken aback by the look on her face. "What?"

Elise gestures to me, and Mike seems to realize he's probably interrupting. "I should go, right? Let you two have a private conversation." He starts to stand, and I reach out to stop him.

"No, you can stay. I'm just avoiding discussing my feelings," I say and attempt a smile.

"Now *that* I understand." He sits back down, and the air shifts from awkward to slightly uncomfortable. "Hey, do you want to play a game of chess?" He asks so suddenly, it makes me jump. "Or a game of checkers. I saw a checkerboard when I was snooping around last night." Elise smacks his shoulder, disapproving. "What? What else was I supposed to do down here?"

"I don't know if I'm up for chess," I confess, not sure I can handle anything mentally taxing on top of everything else swirling around inside my head. "Or checkers."

"Come on," he begs. "I'm bored. It's either chess with you or listening to them talk about tech." He motions to Darby and Rodrigues with my father at his workstation. He has a point. I'm not much up for tech conversations either.

"I guess I can stop my brooding long enough to whup your ass in a quick game," I relent.

He shoots up like a rocket and rushes to retrieve the board.

"Please go easy on him," Elise says. "He's insufferable when he loses."

The game is swift and merciless. I leave Mike scratching his head, wondering how in the world he can lose a new game so quickly after a month-long session.

Feeling a bit better, I head to the kitchen. "Just checking on you," I say to Wyatt, watching while he tends to something on the stove.

"I'm fine as long as I have a distraction. Your dad…" He glances at me and blushes. "I mean, Theodore, said I can use whatever I find to cook. He was really nice about it, but there isn't much left. I think he's due for a supply run." I look away, not necessarily needing to hear that my father's kindness is still intact. Not when I still feel hurt and betrayed. "This setup is incredible. Electrical stove and oven. I would love to have something like this. You know, if we ever settle in one place."

I'm happy that he's able to focus on something to distract him from feeling closed in. "I bet you do."

"Kate."

Turning, I see Jess poking her head out of the door. "I'm here," I call.

"Dani's on the line."

My stomach flips. It's only been a day, but I'm so desperate to hear her voice that I practically run to the room. Rodrigues watches from the workstation, and for a minute, I think she's going to tell me I'm not allowed to go in. She's been taking her guard duty very seriously. Thankfully, she turns back around without a word of protest.

Once inside, I almost trip over Lucas asleep on the cot.

"He was up all night so I could get some sleep," Jess says quietly. "He probably won't wake up through your call. I'll give you some privacy." She closes the door before I can thank her.

I run my hands through my hair, trying to make myself presentable even though I know she can't see me, and take Jess's seat by the radio. "Go ahead, Atomic Anomaly. This is Songbird, over."

"I've missed your voice," she replies. "How are things there?"

My body finally relaxes a bit since the moment she left. "We're all fine," I respond. "Are things all right with you? Over."

"It's tense. A lot of information is coming in. A threat has been neutralized." There's a pause on her end, and I wonder if she's referring to the traitor. I want to ask, but instead, I wait for her to say more. "We'll be back tomorrow morning. I'll fill in the pieces then."

I'm a little disappointed, both with the lack of information and knowing that I'll have to wait another day to see her. "Nothing new here. Just anxiously awaiting your return. Over."

"Me too." Another pause. "Take care until I get back. Keeping this frequency open. Over and out."

"See you soon," I say quietly, but the transmission has ended. I sigh, wishing we could've talked longer, but even our short conversation was a risk. No matter how much security this place may or may not have.

Lucas snores quietly, and I put the radio receiver back on its hook. I try to focus on the fact that I'll see Dani soon. That this trip was clearly worth the separation, even if it does hurt.

Lucas snores again. I stand and pull the blanket higher over his shoulder before slipping out of the room to let him rest. I'm sure this is taking a huge toll on him as well. Maybe I can fill in for him later to give him a break.

Jess is in the kitchen with Wyatt and George. "All done, Jess," I say, leaning on the small counter.

"Any news?" George asks.

I shrug. "Not really. She didn't want to say much over the line."

He nods as if he understands, and I'm grateful he doesn't push.

"Kate, walk me back to the radio room, please," Jess requests. She reaches for Wyatt, who leans forward and kisses her, and then extends her hand in my direction. Looping her arm through mine, I guide her out of the kitchen, though I know she doesn't really need me to. "I just wanted a little private conversation," she tells me a few steps out.

"Am I in trouble?" I joke. The radio room isn't that far from the kitchen.

"Never." Now, I'm intrigued. She waits a few more steps before she continues. "Dani blames herself for a lot, and she's been carrying her guilt for years." I glance at Jess's scarred eyes and think about Rhiannon, White River, the situation we're in now...all of it she blames on herself. "I can't imagine how heavy that must weigh."

I have an idea but don't voice my thoughts aloud.

"I don't know much about your past. I know even less about the relationship you had with your dad." We reach the door, and I stop, tensing at the mention of my father and dreading where this conversation may be going. "I do know that you carry a lot of guilt, too. I can feel it. You and Dani produce the same kind of energy in that way."

A lump forms in my throat. "I don't know what to do," I whisper.

"Maybe talk to him," she gently suggests. "He's hurting, too."

"I'm afraid if he tells me why, it'll make things worse."

"People do things for reasons we can't always understand. The best we can do is ask and try to see things from their perspective. It's impossible to heal or move on until we do." I wipe my eyes and wonder if I even care what my father is feeling. "Maybe if you hear what he has to say, some of that weight that you're carrying around will be lifted. At the very least, you can stop wondering."

"I'm not sure it's as easy as that," I say.

"No, it never is." Jess opens the door. "But with things moving as quickly as they are, how many more chances are you going to get?"

She's right. We've reached a breaking point in this war, and with Dani on her way back, we won't be here in the bunker much longer. It's now or possibly never. "How are you only sixteen?" I ask, sniffling and wiping my nose.

She laughs and touches my arm as she passes, going back into her room.

After a few steadying breaths, I wipe my eyes and nose once more and look around. George and Wyatt are still in the kitchen. Mike and Elise are nowhere to be found, probably back in the main bedroom, and Rodrigues and Darby are huddled close by the workbench.

My father sits alone by the electrical fire, looking tired and old. He's so much older than I remember. It makes me sad seeing him this way, and Jess is right. I don't know what will happen when I leave here. What if I never see him again after this? Somehow, the thought of that being a possibility hurts just as much as his betrayal.

Slowly, I approach him and motion to the footstool before I lose my nerve. "May I sit?"

For a split second, he looks as though he's seen a ghost, and then he straightens. "Yes. Yes, of course, please."

I don't quite face him, but I don't have my back toward him, either. It's only once I'm settled that I realize I have no idea what I want to say. He doesn't push. He just sits perfectly still and tries his best not to stare at me. It feels weird, being this close to him. When I was little, we used to squeeze together in his armchair and read or work on his blueprints. He would tell me what he was working on, and I would, of course, not understand any of it.

I just loved being around him, listening to him. "You're staring at me," I say, using his awkward glances as an opening.

"I can't believe how grown you are. What a beautiful woman you've become," he says, almost as if in awe.

I shove my hands in the front pocket of my sweatshirt and attempt to sink into it. "That's what happens when you pretend to be dead for over fourteen years." His smile falters, and I almost regret saying it. *Almost.*

"I know you don't understand. Most days, I'm not sure I do, either." He shakes his head and stares past me at the fire. "At the time, it felt like my only choice."

"I thought you died a hero." I try, I *really* try, not to let my anger consume me, but it all feels so tight in my chest that I can't help but snap at him. "Instead, you hid and lived in a cave like a coward."

"Katelyn, it's not that simple." He looks pained but doesn't raise his voice.

"Isn't it?" I counter. "You had *years* to tell me the truth, but it took Rodrigues to convince you? *Rodrigues. You* should've made that choice. Not someone who barely knows you or me."

"My work—"

I scoff. "Your work, your research. It's always about your *technological advancements.* Your work has always come first."

"What I have been working on is bigger than me," he says, leaning forward a little, his tone more pleading, like he's begging me to understand.

"And clearly even bigger than your own daughter." I don't understand, and I'm not even sure I care. "Then, once you achieved whatever it was, you blew it up. So now you don't have that either. What was the point?"

"That's not true," he says, his voice finally loud enough to make Darby and Rodrigues stop pretending that they aren't listening. He takes a few breaths and slouches as if he's tired. "I was scared, Katie. Please, you must understand that. *You* have always been my greatest achievement. I have always tried to put you first. I knew if the wrong people discovered what I had, if your mother knew, they would want more. They would *always* want more, and if they couldn't get it from me..."

He lets the implication hang in the dead air between us. "You've explained this already," I tell him sadly. "That's not why I'm angry. You could've told me you were alive. You didn't have to pretend you were dead. Not with me."

He sighs and looks back at the fire, possibly realizing that no excuse will get me to understand. The weight in my chest will always push back against his reasoning.

"You were on the fast track like your mother. Promotions, officer training..." He shakes his head. "I didn't want to pull you in the middle of this. I didn't want to make you choose between us."

"That shouldn't have been up to you," I tell him.

"Of course it was up to me. I would never put you in that position." He closes his eyes, his lips turning upward in a sad sort of smile. "A part of me always hoped you'd take a liking to engineering, but you always preferred strategy. I'm proud of you. You're smart. Compassionate." He opens his eyes and looks at me. "Your mother is proud of you, too. She always hoped you would follow in her footsteps. She pushed you because she saw your potential."

His comment is so absurd, it almost makes me laugh. "I've been nothing but a disappointment to her. Especially now."

"She boasted about you every single day." His words rip the laughter from my throat. That can't possibly be true. "But her need for power, her need for control..." He lets his words linger, his expression sad, vulnerable.

I think about what William said in the fishing cabin in Woodlake. How my mother turned in Kaya's family and how my dad cut off communication with them after I was born because it didn't feel safe. They used to be friends. Dani's parents and my parents. It's still too wild of a concept to wrap my mind around. I've never fully understood my mother's obsession with Jonathan Clark and his family or vice versa, but the story is starting to slowly come together.

"Why didn't you tell me about being friends with Dani's parents? Or William?"

"Your mother told me not to," he answers simply.

"So you just omitted that whole part of your life?" That can't be the entire reason. There has to be something more. "William said Mom hated Kaya and that she reported her family for a promotion."

He bows his head. "Yes." He stays that way for a long time. "Your mother wasn't always like this. She used to be so carefree. So rebellious and full of life."

I wish I could've seen her like that. The thought surprises me. I want to believe it, and I try to picture her, young, happy, full of life, but I'm not convinced that person ever actually existed. All I know of my mother is the cold and calculating person I left behind.

"I don't know what changed," he continues quietly, his voice filled with despair and regret. "I don't know what made her so hateful and vindictive. The need for power, I suppose. I spend a lot of time reflecting. Wondering how I could've missed all the signs."

"Why did you stay with her? Why didn't you just leave instead of doing *this*?" I can't stop the venom that seeps out among my words.

He lifts his head, and there are tears in his eyes. "Because I loved her. I *still* love her."

I think about my feelings for Dani. How I gave up my entire life for her. Followed her wherever she went. How I will continue to just blindly follow her. I refuse to compare our situation with my parents. "She let Jonathan Clark die."

"It's not what you think." He shakes his head, and the gesture makes my blood simmer, all of my thoughts shifting to the pain Dani carries every single day over her father's death.

"She led the charge that killed him and hunted his children. She's *still* after them."

"Because they retaliated after he died," he says, barely letting me finish my question. "William. Dani. Lucas. They all retaliated. It was treason in itself."

"That's it?" I shout and stand. "She's been aggressively attempting to murder the Clarks, murder Dani, the woman I—" I snap my mouth shut. Closing my eyes, I take a deep breath and try to regroup. "She's doing all of this just because they returned fire for the death of their father and friend?"

He shakes his head again. "Your mother doesn't like to be made a fool of. She took Danielle and William's counterattacks personally, and it turned into something different. She lost sight, but believe me, she was just as upset about Jonathan's death." He practically pleads with me to understand, but I look away, not wanting to hear it and refusing to believe it. "It devastated her."

"Clearly," I say sarcastically through clenched teeth. I want to puke thinking that all these years, she's been obsessed with catching William, Dani, and Lucas, all because she wanted to save face. I don't care how much she used to care for Jonathan and William, it doesn't change who she's become.

"You never truly hate the people you once loved." His voice is sad, quiet.

I round on him, my hands clenched into fists. "She never loved them. If she did, she never would've let it come to this. She had a choice. She *chose* to fight her friends. To go after them. To let them die."

"You're right," he says. "Just like Jonathan chose to sacrifice himself for his cause. Just like I chose to fake my death and hide, and just like you chose to leave the NAF to join the Resistance. We all make choices. We all live with the consequences."

I turn away, refusing to let him see me cry. The entire bunker is quiet. I'm sure the others are listening, but I'm too tired to care. I drop back to the footstool and rub my hands over my face, not knowing if I'll ever be able to fully process any of this.

The only thing I do know is this cycle between my mother and Dani and William, between the NAF and the Resistance, will go on and on until none of them are left to fight. That's what all this jealousy and arrogance has come to.

"Does William know where you are?" I ask.

"No. We didn't stay in touch."

"Why not?"

"It was too dangerous."

I try not to scoff. It seems every excuse I've been given is because something was too dangerous. I'm getting tired of hearing it. "Are you Resistance?"

"I'm not anything."

I let out a sound of disbelief. "Your communication with Rodrigues says otherwise." There's a pull inside me. My gut is telling me something different than my head or my heart. My intuition hasn't failed me yet, and right now, it's telling me that my father is the key to stopping this war once and for all.

I can't change the past, but I do have some say in the future, and I'll be damned if I'm going to sit by and let this feud between old friends ruin my future with Dani.

"Dad," I say.

His eyes meet mine, and I don't miss the tiny bit of affection that crosses his features at the term of endearment.

I lean in and lower my voice. "Mom is about to do something really big. Something that will probably win this war and kill my friends, my chosen family, if we don't stop her. If you stay neutral, she *will* win, and I refuse to let that happen."

His expression falls, no doubt knowing that I'm asking him to come out of hiding. To finally stand up to the woman he loves. "Katie, I can't—"

"Please." I reach to take his hands. "There has to be a reason you asked William to help fake your death and not someone else. I know he asked you to give him your work, and you said no. That you didn't want either side to have it, but we need it, Dad. Please. We're running out of time." I swallow and shake my head, frustrated. "I can't lose her."

He stares at me, his eyes wide, searching. I don't pull my hands back, and I don't look away. I meet his gaze, my expression open and vulnerable. I need him to see how desperate I am.

Finally, he squeezes my hands. "Okay, then." He stands and presses on his shirt as if straightening it. "You had better come with me," he says, full of confidence that I had yet to hear from him.

Quickly, I wipe my eyes. "Where are we going?"

"You're right. It's time I pick a side." He starts to go through the door that leads to the back exit and motions to Rodrigues as we pass his workbench. "Jenisis, if you and Darby would please join us. And grab your jackets."

Rodrigues appears surprised, but it quickly turns to excitement, and she puts down whatever she and Darby were working on. The four of us, along with Roscoe trotting happily in front, head down the narrow tunnel.

When we get to the ladder leading to the hatch, he looks at us. "It's outside?" Darby asks warily.

He nods at Rodrigues, and we follow her out of the hatch, leaving behind a very anxious, very whiny Roscoe circling below.

Darby sticks close to me, and I keep my hand on the handle of the knife strapped to my thigh, hating that I don't trust my father. We walk just along the tree line, away from the bunker. The wind picks up, and I kick myself for not bringing my hat. Pulling on my hood, I stay a safe distance behind my dad and Rodrigues as we press farther and farther away.

Just as I'm about to ask where the hell he's taking us, I see it. A large warehouse, half of it caved in and collapsed. It looks like it's in pretty rough condition.

"We're totally going to die," Darby mutters.

"No," Rodrigues says, glancing over her shoulder. "You're gonna love this."

My father stops in front of two large sliding doors and hesitates. I expect him to make some sort of speech or warning before opening them, but he nods like he's definitely come to a decision, unlocks the padlock, and pushes open one of the large doors, slowly revealing the inside.

The moment the light shines in and I see what he's been hiding, my stomach drops.

"Holy fucking shit," Darby says. "You have a plane!"

I stand frozen, my mouth agape, staring at the large aircraft in the center of the room. It's not a warehouse at all. It's a hangar.

"She's not a plane," my father says with a proud kind of smile.

"It's a helicopter," I correct, unable to look away from the tilt-rotors.

"That's right. I modified her from an old Bell V-280 Valor." He puts his hands on his hips and stares at her, his expression awestruck, like this is his first time seeing it. "It's taken me over twelve years to acquire all the parts and pieces to make her fully loaded and operational."

"This is…terrifying," Darby says, slowly approaching. "I want to touch it."

"Go ahead," my father says with a slight chuckle.

Darby hesitantly rests her hand against the side and lets out a low whistle. "You're right. I love this so, so much."

Taking a few steps toward it, I have to agree. She's beautifully frightening. "Does she fly?"

"Yes," he says. "I've gotten her into the air twice." His expression shifts to concern as he rushes to Darby, who is reaching inside one of the guns mounted on the side. "Maybe don't touch *that*."

Rodrigues stands beside me. "What he didn't tell you is, the first time he experienced a brownout, he panicked so much, I thought he was going to crash."

The thought of my dad living out his dream by actually getting into the air, freak-out and all, makes me both overjoyed and regretful. I wish I could've seen it. "You helped him with this?" I ask, hoping the jealousy I feel isn't evident in my voice.

"Yes," she says hesitantly. "But I didn't realize it. Not until very recently."

We watch my dad and Darby circle the helicopter, my father trying desperately to keep Darby from touching things she shouldn't and probably regretting giving her permission to touch it at all.

"This is for you." Rodrigues pulls a key from her pocket. "The last secret." I stare at it, a weird feeling of relief and a bit of disbelief spreading through my body. "It's a key to the hangar," she clarifies.

I take the key and drag my thumb along its ragged edges. When I look back at Rodrigues, her eyes are wide in awe, staring at the helicopter that she helped create. "Thank you," I tell her quietly. "For helping him. And for helping me." I still haven't forgiven her, not completely, but I have a feeling she's going to stick around long enough to prove herself, and in a weird way, I'm glad she's the one my dad reached out to.

"You're welcome. Besides," she says and bumps me lightly with her shoulder, "what are assistants for?"

We share a small smile. Looking back at the helicopter, for the first time in a long while, I feel a little bit hopeful.

A commotion inside the bunker wakes me. I sit and rub my eyes, waiting for them to adjust to the orange glow of the electrical fire. When they finally do, I notice Lucas following Rodrigues to the front entrance with a lantern, Roscoe nudging her forward and nipping at her ankles.

"What's going on?" My voice sounds scratchy from sleep.

"The general is approaching," Lucas whispers loudly into the otherwise dark space.

That wakes me up. "What?" I grab the knife from under my pillow and throw off my blankets, shooting to my feet.

"Not the best quote, Lucas," Jess scolds from the other side of the bunker, her head sticking out from the door to the radio room. "Dani's back."

I let out a long breath and put a hand over my hammering heart. At least Lucas has the decency to appear apologetic. My father sits up in the chair where he fell asleep, and our eyes meet briefly, but he makes no move to follow me.

"Come on," Rodrigues says, attempting to get Lucas to hurry. "We need to get them inside."

I pull on my boots and grab my jacket, slipping it on while I follow them up the stairs to the entrance. When Rodrigues opens the door, the sky is still dark. Snow swirls lightly in the air as Dani and Jack hurry inside, securing the door behind them.

"Did anyone see you?" Rodrigues asks, worried.

"Not that we could tell," Dani says. She sees Lucas first, pulls him into a hug, and then her gaze lands on me. She pats his back a couple of times and rushes over, holding my face in her cold hands. "Are you okay? We came back as soon as we could."

"I'm okay," I assure her. "What's going on?"

"It's starting," Jack answers for her. "The beginning of the end or whatever dramatic way you want to phrase it."

My eyes linger on Dani, and I search her face. Even in the low light, I can see that she's worried. I guess he was right. My mother is about to make her move. Lucas's choice of words wasn't all that inaccurate after all. "What happened?" I ask.

Dani hesitates, glancing around the dark room. "Not here," she says. She puts her hand on Jack's shoulder. "Get some rest. I'll wake you up in a couple hours." He looks like he wants to protest but doesn't. "Stay near—"

"The radio room. Got it." Our eyes meet for a split second, and then he brushes past me without a word.

The air between Dani and Jack isn't tense, but it still feels heavy. It makes me wonder what happened in the time they've been gone.

"Is everyone else asleep?" Dani asks.

Rodrigues glances behind her. "They were. Not sure about now."

Dani nods as if she expected this answer.

"What's going on?" I press.

She motions down the stairs. "Come with me. Lucas, you too."

If Rodrigues is disappointed that she didn't get an invite, she doesn't show it. Instead, she double-checks that the main door is locked while Lucas and I follow Dani through the bunker, ignoring the looks from my father as we pass. She turns on her flashlight and leads us down the narrow hallway, and for a minute, I think she's going to lead us out the back hatch. Instead, she stops and abruptly turns. "Hugo was the traitor," she blurts.

"What?" Startled, I try to decipher how we could've missed that, how *William* could've missed that. I didn't know him well, but it would explain the strange look he gave me the first time we met. It should've been a big red flag. Maybe if I had paid closer attention or tried to ask him about it...

"There's still one more," she says quietly. Her eyes appear angry, guarded, betrayed.

I release a deep breath, and Lucas covers his face, clearly as gutted as I am to learn there's someone else spilling secrets.

"Thatcher's back," she continues. "She's been back for weeks."

My stomach drops. "So it's really happening. We've really come to a precipice."

"The battle has begun," Lucas adds grimly.

We were all born into this war, raised in this fight, but nothing has ever felt this serious, this monumental, or this dire. "So now what?" I ask, fearing the answer.

"They're securing a Resistance base," Dani says. "We're just waiting for the call to arms." Her voice sounds defeated, like we were once again caught unprepared.

"There's something missing," Lucas says, no doubt picking up on Dani's somewhat dejected energy.

She seems to know what he means because she nods. "The general has at least one fully functional combat drone that was just moved from Warren. A large one."

The look she gives me sends shivers down my spine. Rodrigues warned me months ago about two operational UCAVs. I wonder if there's more, and we just don't know about them.

Dani releases a long breath and leans against the wall. I finally notice how exhausted she really looks. "Not only is it operational, but they've shielded it. It'll be able to withstand EMPs. We're going to need to take it out ourselves."

Knowing how close this UCAV is to unleashing hell has me panicked. "Why is this the first we're hearing about this? Did no one see a convoy pulling a large, plane-like object hundreds of kilometers down the road?" I ask in utter disbelief.

"The NAF has control over most trade routes," she says, a bit dejected. "And even if people saw it, it wouldn't have mattered. They probably wanted us to see. It's virtually indestructible."

"Let me break it down for you," Lucas starts, but when he doesn't finish the statement, I glance at Dani, confused.

She smiles a bit. "Or it was broken down in a tractor trailer and was reassembled somewhere else."

Pleased, Lucas nods.

"Do we have any idea where this operational UCAV might be?" I ask, trying to figure out why my mother would move something that large out of Warren.

"We believe it's in Ellsworth."

"But we don't know for sure?" Dani doesn't answer. I take a deep breath, wishing we had more time to confirm everything before we make any kind of move. "What else did you find out?" I ask, hoping desperately for some sort of good news.

"Intel from E. J. Allen suggests the general plans to attack in a matter of days. She has a few targets in mind but hasn't made a formal decision. So who knows which one they're going after first. Unfortunately, by the time we find out, it'll be too late."

Days? Well, this just keeps getting better and better. "How do we know for certain that E. J. Allen is on our side again?"

"Thatcher swears it."

"And that's good enough?" I ask, wondering why we're all going to go charging in on the word of Thatcher Price.

She shrugs. "It has to be."

"This is the end of the world," Lucas says quietly. His words hang in the air, adding a sense of dread to an already dire situation.

"So what's the plan?" I ask, hoping it'll be something better than I fear. With such a quick turnaround, I'm not optimistic the Resistance will be able to pull together something big enough to stay in this fight. And certainly not against an operational UCAV that can carry 1,700 kilograms of explosives and has now been shielded from an electromagnetic pulse.

Dani leans her head back against the wall and closes her eyes. "Try to get behind all the outposts and sneak a team into Ellsworth to blow the hangar housing the UCAV. While simultaneously dodging an array of surveillance and any other attack drones and who knows how many tanks and soldiers."

"Oh, is that all? Sounds easy enough." I don't even attempt to hide my sarcasm at quite possibly the dumbest plan I've ever heard.

"We've run out of options," she confesses. "There's talk of Rapid City becoming the new capital, and Thatcher wants to send a team in there to take back the city." She releases a deep breath. "I don't know if we're going to have the manpower to pull this off. We're going to need some heavy explosives, and we just don't have enough people..." Her voice trails off. "I don't know how we're going to take out something that big."

Lucas and I share a look. His lips turn upward in a knowing smile, and I know instantly that he's thinking the same thing I am.

My father's helicopter.

Dani opens her eyes, her gaze shifting from me to Lucas and back. "Okay, why are you two staring at each other like that?"

"Tell Rodrigues I'm taking Dani to my dad's warehouse." Lucas nods, and I grab Dani's hand, ignoring her questions, and lead her to the ladder. "I'm going to show you my dad's project. What he tried to hide from my mom and what William so desperately wanted."

She doesn't stop asking questions, which I ignore, but thankfully, she follows me up the ladder. "What warehouse? Where are we going?" she asks looking around outside, shining her flashlight along the tree line. "Kate, what aren't you telling me?"

"Can you please just be patient and let me show you?"

She grumbles when I take the flashlight from her, but she stops asking questions and follows me. When we reach the warehouse, or hangar, she stares at it in disbelief. "What the hell?"

Smiling because I know what's inside, I give her back the light and unlock the doors, pulling one open. She takes a hesitant step forward, shining the light inside. But it isn't until I flip on the lights that she drops the flashlight in surprise. "Holy shit." She stares at the helicopter and takes a step closer.

Her wide eyes make me smile. "Cruise speed of over three hundred miles per hour. Combat range of up to fourteen hundred kilometers. Reinforced armor. Added guided weapon systems. 30mm autocannon, Hellfire anti-tank 70mm air-to-ground missile... this is the stealthiest attack chopper that probably ever existed."

"Does it fly?" she asks, touching one of the lowered tilt propellers.

"It does."

She looks to the weapon mounts. "Is there ammunition for it?"

"Yes." I glance at the sparse pile on one of the workbenches. Only two missiles. A decent amount of 30mm and a half a dozen 70mm rockets. "Some," I amend.

"Enough to take out the UCAV?" she asks, her voice growing more excited with each question she asks.

"Dani, I don't know," I say with a small laugh, feeling her excitement, her sudden optimism, and knowing she's already formulating a new plan. "What I *do* know is that maybe we have a chance."

She reaches out and hesitates just before touching it. "So," she says, glancing at me over her shoulder. "Who's gonna fly it?"

Chapter Twelve: The Betrayal

Dani

I wake with a violent start. Images of my friends betraying me, helicopters crashing, explosions, and Kate reaching for me with a blood-covered hand flash behind my eyelids. Sitting up, I rub my face, trying to stop the nightmare from replaying itself.

A soft hand on my back helps bring me back to reality. Kate drapes herself around my back and places a kiss between my shoulder blades.

"I'm sorry if I woke you," I say, pulling her arms tighter around me.

"Nightmares again?"

"Yeah." Turning my head, I try to look back at her in the dark. "How long was I out?"

"It's only been about an hour," she tells me and yawns. "You've been tossing and turning the entire time."

I'm not surprised. Exhaustion has settled into my bones in a way that has me seriously questioning if I'll ever recover. I haven't been this tired since I first arrived at White River, half-dead and fully broken. I rub my eyes again and release a long breath through my nose.

Her fingers trace a long line down my exposed arm, but she doesn't press me to talk about it.

"Tell me how things went with your dad while I was gone," I say.

She places another kiss on my shoulder and rests her cheek on my back. "We talked. I yelled. He apologized. He showed me the helicopter. I don't know. Things still feel weird. Mainly, I'm just trying to repress anything I can."

Her confession makes me smile. Visions of her from my dream flash again, like a premonition and not just a projection of my greatest fear. "It was the one where you're reaching for me and..." I can't even bring myself to say it.

"Ah, that pesky little dream," she says softly.

Going back to sleep doesn't seem like an option. Not after that. There's too much to do before we have to meet with William and Thatcher and before we face off against the NAF. We're running out of time. "I should get to work," I tell her and start to detangle myself from her warm embrace.

"Dani..."

I quickly pull my shirt over my head. I grab a battery-operated lantern and turn it on, searching for the rest of my clothes. Something inside my gut is screaming at me that this is it. There's no coming back from this one. My whole life fighting has led to this moment, and not everyone is going to make it.

I swallow roughly, pushing down the fears of losing anyone else. "I just want to be prepared this time."

Kate grabs her pants. "Then, let's get back to work."

"No," I say and gently push her back down. "I want you to stay here and rest." She looks as though she's going to argue, and I kiss her before she can say anything else. "I just need to clear my head for a bit, and we promised Jess we'd stay by the radio. Do you want to be the one to tell her that her break from this room is over?"

She glares at me and hands me the key to the hangar. "Low blow, Clark," she says.

I smirk, knowing it was, and kiss her head. Reluctantly, she lies back down, and I grab my bag filled with explosive equipment, some given to me by William and Thatcher just a few hours ago. I slip out of the room quietly, not wanting to wake the others scattered around their makeshift beds close to the fire in the main part of the bunker.

When I get to the hangar, the lights are still on, but the main doors are closed, though the lock has been taken off. We definitely didn't leave it like this an hour ago. I push the door slightly and reach for my pistol, but I spot Rodrigues sitting inside the helicopter and Darby at the workbench, pulling apart a large piece of tech. She glances behind her when she hears my footsteps.

"You mind turning the heater up a bit?" She motions to the decent-sized space heater beside her.

I do as she asks, not sure the warm air will cut through the chill of the open space. "You guys couldn't sleep either?" I pull up a stool next to Darby.

"You weren't that quiet when you got back." There's no malice in her tone, so I don't bother to apologize. "Besides, too much to do." She doesn't bother to look up from her tech.

I smile a little, finding a bit of comfort in the fact we're on the same page. That's all we say to each other for the next couple of hours, quietly working on our respective projects. Rodrigues grabs her flight manuals and falls asleep with them on the cot in the corner.

The others start to trickle in after the sun has risen. Lucas, Jack, Kate…and before I know it, almost everyone is working on their own thing, asking questions and wanting to know what they can do to help.

"You look like you're going to fall asleep," Darby mutters from beside me. She's been reading blueprints and documents all morning, and honestly, I don't know how she's still standing. I have to give her credit, though, when she's hell-bent on finishing a project, she's going to damn well finish it.

"I'm exhausted," I admit through a yawn.

"You know, we can function without you for a couple of hours." She glances at me, and I'm surprised to see concern in her expression. "You're no good to us if you're exhausted while handling explosives."

I push the chest piece I'm working on away. Leaning forward, I rub my hands down my face. My eyes feel like sandpaper, and my body aches. "You're right," I tell her.

She gasps and looks around, shocked. "Do you think anyone heard you admit that?"

Her dramatics, surprisingly, make me smile.

"I heard it," Kate says and drapes her arms over my shoulders from behind. She kisses the top of my head. "And I agree. You need sleep."

"I slept." She makes a disbelieving sound. I lean back and instantly relax. "There's way too much to do. We have to have a contingency plan. There just isn't enough ammunition. If we can't get it done—"

"Dani."

The thought of not finishing makes me anxious, but I'm too tired to argue anymore. "Maybe for just an hour."

"Four," Kate counters.

"Two."

"I'll take it." She kisses my cheek and pulls away.

I think about taking the cot in the corner, but it's already occupied by Jack. Not wanting to wake him, I zip up my jacket and flip up my hood. Looks like I'm headed back to the bunker. Walking back in the cold doesn't sound appealing, but the thought of a warm bed in a quiet room outweighs the discomfort of walking in the shallow layer of snow.

After one last look at my own project, I know both Kate and Darby are right. I should definitely finish this when I've gotten some rest.

"Don't worry," Darby says when I start to leave, "I won't let anyone touch your bomb."

"Don't worry," I tell her with a smile. "I'm fairly certain I turned off the timer."

She whips around to look at me in absolute horror. "What?"

Walking away, I lift my hand and give her a casual wave, ignoring the shouted request for me to come back.

❖

When I wake on my own, my body feels slightly rested, but it still takes me a bit to adjust to the grogginess of waking from a deep sleep. No one came to get me, which probably means I slept for longer than the two hours I had planned.

I quickly run my fingers through my hair and make quick work of leaving bed. When I throw open the bedroom door, I nearly run into Theodore and almost fall completely backward while knocking a stack of notebooks from his hands.

"Oh, I'm sorry," he says, and bends to pick up the books. "I wasn't paying attention." He smiles nervously when I help him. I scan the page of one of the open journals about cyclic pitch and hand it back. "Thank you. I didn't wake you, did I? Katelyn said you were sleeping."

I glance around, looking for Kate and am disappointed not to see her. "No, you didn't wake me."

"Good. That's good." He tucks his books under his arm and motions to the hallway that leads to the back of the bunker. "I need to get these to Jenisis." He only gets a few steps before stopping and turning. "Thank you. For taking care of my daughter."

"I'm not doing it for you," I tell him.

"No. Of course not." He smiles a bit sadly before nodding and walking away. He may be Kate's dad, and I really hope they can one day get past the awkwardness and lies, but just the sight of him makes me protective and defensive.

It's only then that I notice Jess and Wyatt are sitting near the fire. "That seemed awkward," Jess says.

"I still want to punch him for what he did," I admit. "Don't tell Kate."

"What is it with you and punching?" Jess asks, her nose wrinkling a bit. "Did you manage to get some sleep?"

"A little," I admit. "How long was I out?"

"Three and a half hours," Wyatt answers.

I groan, thinking of all the time I wasted. "She should've woken me."

"Oh, don't get pissy," Jess says. "You know she does it because she loves you."

A lump forms in my throat. Kate and I haven't said anything about love to each other, but it's clearly there. We're both so preoccupied with everything else, and my nightmares are scaring me into submission behind the walls I've spent years building around my heart.

Wyatt breaks into my thoughts. "You missed lunch. Are you hungry?"

His question catches me off guard, and a sudden pang of sadness hits forcefully. Clearly, I'm a roller coaster of emotions at the moment. It's just such a Rhiannon question to ask. She always used food to break tension or lighten the mood.

Images of her smiling behind the counter at her tavern with a towel thrown over her shoulder flash in my mind, and my stomach twists the way it often does when I think about her. I swallow the previously formed lump. "No, but thank you."

He nods like he expected as much.

I desperately try to change the subject. "Any word from William?"

"Not yet," Jess answers. "But there's a message circulating about checking in."

I think back to the last time I received a check-in message. It was before I left and found myself in White River. They're very vague messages alerting everyone on a Resistance frequency to quite literally check in with whoever is in charge of their unit. If there is no command nearby, they're supposed to go to the nearest outpost for orders. Everyone involved knows that a check-in call usually means a big fight ahead.

"Guess I'll reach out and see where he wants us to go," I say and take a deep breath. The familiar sense of anxiousness before a big fight starts to creep in. "Did I miss anything else?"

"Mike is jittery," Wyatt supplies.

"Jittery?"

"Yeah, jumpy. Like he can't sit still." He seems thoughtful. "Maybe he's just nervous."

Mike has come with me on plenty of assignments and supply runs. He doesn't usually get flustered. It's more than a tad concerning. "I'll check on him," I say and do my best not to let any kind of emotion into my statement.

Jess picks up on it anyway. "Dani," she says softly. "You don't think…"

Thoughts of Hugo indicating someone else was involved with the NAF come rushing back. I can't ignore them anymore. "I don't think anything," I lie and stand, not wanting to talk about it. "Have you guys seen the helicopter yet?"

"We were just talking about going over to check it out." She grabs her walking stick. "Do you mind if we tag along for a few minutes?"

I smile at the hopeful expression on her face. "Of course not. Get your coats."

Wyatt scrambles, no doubt excited to finally be out of the enclosed space, and Jess heads back to the small radio room.

Once Wyatt is out of earshot, I gently touch Jess's arm. "Hey, Jess?" She reaches for the door and waits. There are so many things I want to tell her. That she's amazing. That I'm sorry she's in the middle of this at such a young age. That everything is only going to get worse, but I don't know how we'd be able to manage any of this without her. "You're doing great with all of this," I say instead.

She smiles and pulls a key from her pocket and locks the radio room door. "Maybe I shouldn't leave. If William—"

"It's okay," I tell her. "If whatever news can't wait ten minutes, we're as good as dead anyway."

"You have such a lovely way with words," she says and tucks the key back into her jeans pocket.

"When did you get a key?" I ask curiously.

Wyatt returns and helps her into her coat. "Theodore gave it to me right after I settled in. He made a joke about locking the room every time he leaves, even though there's no one around to lock it from." She zips her jacket and reaches for Wyatt. "I think he's lonely."

I snort. "Of course he's lonely. He lives underground by himself."

"I just mean that I think having Kate here is mending his heart, and he's trying to do right by her and her new family." She pats my arm and allows Wyatt to lead her to the far side of the bunker, leaving me standing outside of the room, speechless. She *would* be the voice of reason.

Without any further mention of Theodore, Wyatt and I help Jess up the ladder and out of the hatch, and we guide her to the hangar. Much to her delight, the entire group is excited to see her out of the small room.

Theodore is the first to offer to walk her around the helicopter. She accepts, and he leans in, describing it to her in detail. Against my better judgment, I feel myself softening toward him.

Kate and Jack are along the far wall, cleaning their guns. It doesn't appear that they're talking, but they aren't fighting either, which I guess counts as progress. She lays her pistol on the bench and smiles when I head over. "Feel any better?" she asks.

"A little." I motion to the helicopter. "Any progress?"

"I think so. They're adding navigation points now," Kate says. She watches her father climb into the cockpit with Rodrigues and Darby and stretch across the seat, his legs poking out. "I really hope they don't hit the wrong button in there and fire all those missiles."

I look at her, worried. "Is that...could that happen?"

"With Darby in there?" Jack snorts. "Yeah, it's possible."

Staring back at the trio fiddling with whatever it is they're doing, I motion to my brother. "You two keep working. I'm going over there, away from where the missiles are pointing." Kate and Jack share a look, something akin to amusement, and I decide, whatever is happening between them, I'm just going to leave it be.

"The beast awakens," Lucas says and grins.

I glare and sit on the stool beside him. "You're so funny." He laughs, clearly agreeing. Looking over his shoulder, I watch as he finishes what I was working on earlier. "How's it coming?"

He uses the pliers to make a few more twists, then leans away from the device. Taking my time to inspect his work, I don't bother trying to hide that I'm impressed. "Not bad, little brother," I admit.

He puffs out his chest, proud.

"I can't believe you found the pieces and explosives to finish this. I thought for sure we'd be struggling for parts," I muse as I give it a second look.

"I am somewhat of an expert in the wielding of blades," he says. I take that as meaning he's just as capable of scavenging and building bombs as I am.

"Yeah, yeah, don't let it go to your head." Grabbing the casing, I slip it over the hole of the device, covering the main components and grab the plastic weld putty.

"Any word on the outsider?" he asks quietly, his face concerned.

"You mean, do I know who the other backstabber who sold us out to the NAF is?" He nods. Clenching my teeth, I try not to rip too much putty from the stick I keep in my personal stash. "I'm still trying not to think about it." He looks around, his eyes sad. If I had to guess, I would bet all I owned that Lucas was holding out hope that there was no traitor outside of Hugo. "But I don't want you to worry about it. I'll take care of it when or if it comes to that, okay?"

I know he wants to argue because he feels like we're all in this together. That's just how my brother operates, loyal until the very end, but I don't want him part of this.

A crash from across the hangar interrupts the moment, and I'm both thankful and nervous when the sound echoes. I look to the helicopter, but Theodore pops his head out and glances around, just as concerned.

It's only then I see Mike scrambling to pick up whatever it was he dropped. No time like the present to confront him about his weird behavior. I pat Lucas's shoulder and make my way to where Mike and Elise are quietly arguing. "What's going on with you?" I ask casually. "You're definitely not your typical self."

He rushes to put what I can now see is an old car muffler back into a crate. He doesn't respond, just sighs.

"Listen, I can't have my best sharpshooter all jittery. I know something's going on with you." I sigh, wishing he would just tell me what it is without me pressing. "Want to tell me what's got you so nervous?"

"I'm not nervous." He puts his hands on his hips, looking completely unnatural.

"Weird, then." I frown at him, hating that he's been so secretive.

"Weird?" He crosses his arms and glances at Elise. "I'm not acting weird." She's strangely silent during this exchange.

I look back and forth between them, seeing they are clearly in this together. "Are you sure there isn't anything going on? It might be a good time to let it out."

He turns white like he's going to be sick. He shakes his head and nervously looks at Elise again. Who, unexpectedly, sighs very dramatically and rolls her eyes. "Just say it," she says.

He still seems unsure, but after another pointed look from his wife, he finally meets my eyes and takes a deep breath. "Elise is pregnant."

"What?" My gaze falls to Elise's stomach. "When? How?"

"Do we really need to go over the *how*?" she asks playfully.

"What did we miss?" Kate asks, coming up from behind me. She approaches slowly, like she's unsure if she should be interrupting.

"They're having a baby," I tell her, unable to wrap my head around it.

"I knew it!" Kate rounds on Elise, who laughs, delighted. "All your sudden food aversions, the naps, and always being hot, I just knew it." She practically launches herself at Elise, wrapping her up in a huge hug, and both of them laugh.

"Wait, you knew this is what they were hiding?" I ask, offended she didn't fill me in.

"Well, yeah." She laughs again and gives me a curious look. "Didn't you?"

"I thought they were planning to leave the group and go somewhere else. Somewhere safer," I admit. "Among other things," I add, giving her a pointed look.

"Wait, what?" Mike asks, offended. "Why would we leave?"

"I mean, I don't know. You've been acting so weird lately—"

"Stop saying that," he says, annoyed.

Kate pushes him and I away and focuses on Elise. "How far along?"

"A couple of months." She pats her stomach and looks lovingly at Mike.

"We're having a baby," he yells and pulls her into him. He is so proud, lighter, and positively beaming with happiness.

It's infectious.

"Why didn't you just tell us?" I ask and pull them both into a hug. "Why would you make us guess?"

"No one was making you guess anything," Elise scolds. "We wanted to be one-hundred-percent sure, but"—she gestures around us—"we're always moving, and then the raiders attacked, and now this. There just didn't seem to be a good time."

My heart sinks a little at that, knowing that they've been sitting on something joyous, something life-changing, and not feeling as though they could tell us because of all the other stuff going on. "I'm so happy for you," I tell her.

"We all are," Kate adds.

By now, the entire gang is surrounding them, so I step out of the way, giving others a chance to say congrats and give hugs.

"This is cause for a celebration," Theodore declares. "I think I have a bottle of something we can open back in the bunker. I'll go get it."

"No, you stay here," George says. "I'll go. I need to use the bathroom anyway."

I watch George slip out of the front doors and see him bypass the outhouse close by. My heart sinks. Leaning in, I ask Jess for the key to the radio room. She gives it to me without question. "Hey, wait up," I call after George, who is already halfway to the bunker.

He falters but recovers easily and smiles. "Dani. You should be in there celebrating with your friends."

I shrug and rest my hand on the grip of my pistol. "Oh, it's okay. Besides, it's dangerous being out in the open alone."

He frowns questioningly but continues to walk. "It feels nice to have some good news for a change."

"It does."

We move slowly and in silence, until the air is too thick, and the tension of what's not said becomes unbearable. "I heard we'll be leaving soon," he says casually as his eyes dart in my direction. "The Resistance sent out a check-in."

"Things are moving fast."

"Yes, they seem to be."

"William caught the traitor," I say without looking at him.

His steps slow until he stops. "Is that right?"

"Yeah. Hugo. Can you believe it?" I finally turn to him and do my best to pierce a hole through him with a single look. For a moment, I wonder how he's going to play this, but he slowly nods as if not surprised by the news in the least.

"What happened to him? Once he was found out?"

I don't break my gaze and keep all emotion out of my tone. "He killed himself. Lethal dose of cyanide."

He looks up, squinting at the light shining through the trees. "That's horrible."

I show George the key. "If you were planning on using the radio, you're going to need this."

He glances at the key, back at me, and starts walking again. "I don't know what you're talking about."

"She loved you," I say quietly, making him stop again. "Rhiannon." It takes every ounce of willpower not to choke on her name. "Why did you do it, George? We're family."

His body tenses, and his gaze snaps to mine, eyes wide. He shakes his head. "I didn't—"

I step forward, causing him to back up. "Don't you lie to me." My breathing is labored as I take short breaths in and out through my nose. I'm trying my damndest not to let my anger get the better of me. "When? When did you start helping the NAF?"

He closes his eyes and bows his head. I have never seen him look so old. For a minute, I think he's going to deny it, but he takes a deep breath. "A few weeks before Jess turned sixteen."

"Why?" I ask, begging him to make this make sense.

"To protect her. To protect you." He looks at me, pleading. "Don't you see? They would've killed her. They would've killed you both."

I scoff, dismissing his reasoning. "The NAF has been trying to kill me for most of my life."

His sad expression starts to dissolve to resoluteness. He stands a little taller and stares back at me. "I didn't want the same thing for Jess. She deserves better than that."

"So you sold us all out."

He shakes his head; the gesture only intensifies my anger. How can he so casually brush aside the severity of his actions?

"What you did got Rhiannon killed. She's dead because of *you*."

He shakes his head again. "No. That wasn't me."

"Then what *was* you, George?" I ask, gripping the pistol strapped to my thigh, needing something to hold on to. "What exactly did you do?"

He maintains his strong stance, but his once kind, sparkling blue eyes are now dull and dim. He doesn't answer, and as he stares, a range of emotions crosses his features before landing on acceptance.

"Answer her." The soft, devastated voice startles us both.

"Jess," George breaths out in a panicked voice, looking past me at his granddaughter.

She stands tall, her arm through Wyatt's. "Tell *me* what you did." Her voice cracks, distraught and clearly devastated.

He seems to crumble. His shoulders fall, and he looks away as if willing this moment to not be true. He takes several deep breaths and faces her. "I was trading in a town just outside of Rapid City a few weeks before you turned sixteen. You had been talking about joining the Resistance for years. I tried so hard to talk you out of it, but you wouldn't listen to me."

She remains frozen in place and doesn't even allow her face to respond to his words.

George steps forward, and Wyatt guides Jess away. Clearly hurt, George stops walking. "A few NAF soldiers spotted me. They knew who I was. They had been assigned to watch the city, infiltrate it, but with recent military movement in the area, Thatcher's security was tight. They only managed to get inside the gates once under the guise of trading."

He turns to me. "One of them heard about new recruits. Somehow, they knew about Jess. He threatened her. Threatened to *kill* her. I tried to get away, to convince them that Jess wouldn't be a threat, but the only way they would let me go was if I made it worth their while."

"What did you give them?" I ask, keeping my voice even.

His gaze hardens, and he doesn't look away. "You." His confession isn't surprising. "I told them if they left Jess alone, I would tell them where you were."

Jess gasps. "Grandfather..."

I don't say anything, and George doesn't look away. "I told them you were in Hot Springs."

Like a dam breaking, a flood of memories hit me at once. George showing up in White River to tell us the NAF had unexpectedly burned Hot Springs to the ground, me accusing Kate of doing it, and Kate insisting she had no knowledge of it. George knew the reason the town had been destroyed for months. For *months* and didn't say a word because he was the reason all those people died.

"I didn't know what else to do. I panicked."

I clench my jaw and grind my teeth, my stomach twisting in disgust. "You killed those people. That entire town is gone because of you."

"I saved your life," he fires back. "And it would've worked if she hadn't shown up at White River." He motions over my shoulder.

I turn to see Kate standing near Jess, watching the exchange in clear shock.

"If you had just killed her and the others—"

"Stop." That's where I absolutely draw the line. "You let an entire town die. You let them burn and blamed the NAF."

"I did it to save my granddaughter. The NAF was always going to attack Rapid City. I had to ensure we weren't a part of that."

"And look what it cost," I tell him quietly.

"You don't understand."

"I understand perfectly. I understand how rash decisions, even ones with good intentions, can have grave consequences."

"The NAF is going to win this war, Dani. I know you see that."

"Then what are you doing here?" I ask.

"Jess would never leave the Resistance," he says sadly and takes a deep breath. "I needed a place to lie low."

"You're hiding?"

He scoffs and looks at me, disgusted. "You did the same thing. You're all doing the same thing."

I shake my head and start to protest, but before I can even get a word in, Jack's voice interrupts: "You killed Rhiannon." He stands in front of Jess, the others fanned around them. Everyone is now outside, watching, all equally horrified. Jack stares at George, his hands clenched into fists, his chest heaving.

For the first time since I confronted him, George looks absolutely petrified. "No. I didn't. I didn't have anything to do with that. I swear."

"You knew about the tunnels," I say, an ache in my chest.

"I didn't tell them. I swear, I didn't. I needed to keep that a secret so I could get Jess out. I never would've told them about that." His voice shakes a bit, but it only makes me angry.

He only kept it a secret to save his own hide.

"And we're supposed to believe you?" Jack asks, his lip curling upward just enough to make him look even more menacing. He takes slow, calculated steps in our direction, and I brace for an impact.

There's only a split second before Jack is close enough, and he lunges. I grab him and use all my strength to pull, to keep him from doing something I know he'll regret.

George takes several steps backward until he's against a tree. "All I did was tell them Dani and Lucas were in Hot Springs," he says desperately. "I didn't tell them anything else!"

Mike helps me pull Jack back, and I step in front of him, blocking his path. "That's enough," I tell him and keep my hands on his chest. "Back off. This isn't helping."

He stares past me, his eyes filled with anger. I keep my knees bent, ready to push him back if he lunges again. Finally, he pushes me away and storms toward the hangar.

"That's all I did," George continues. "In return, they told me Rapid City was next, and when it went silent, I had better clear out. That's it."

I've been used as bait before. I've been used as a decoy. I've been sold out and betrayed, but the casualness of George's confession, especially since he's been family to me pretty much my entire life, feels like a sharp knife in my back. "And you didn't think to tell Thatcher?" I ask. "The city might've stood a chance if you had just said something."

"They would've kept coming after Jess if I did that. They would've come after me." He is begging now, pleading for someone to understand. Unfortunately for him, no one does.

"How could you do this?" Jess asks, and it's very clear by the shake in her voice that she's crying.

"Jess." He tries to take a step toward her, but Wyatt steps in front, making him come to a sudden halt.

"Clear out the bedroom inside the bunker," I tell Lucas and try to ignore the hurt expression on his face.

"You're taking me prisoner?" George asks in disbelief.

"You're lucky that's all she's doing," Wyatt says from beside Jess. It's the first time I've seen him look angry.

I grab George's arm and pull him away, leading him from the group and to the hatch door.

"This isn't right," he calls but doesn't struggle to free himself. "You can't do this. All I did was try to save you. Save my family."

Lucas goes ahead, and I leave George inside the bedroom with nothing but a lantern. He protests again, but I close the door and wedge a chair underneath the handle to keep him from leaving.

When the group is back inside the bunker, the excitement over Elise's pregnancy has sadly dissipated. Most of them hover just inside, no doubt unsure of what to do next. "What are you going to do with him?" Elise finally asks.

"I don't know yet." I sigh. "I'm sorry. We're supposed to be celebrating you."

"Like I said," she says sadly, "never a good time."

"Dani?" Jess reaches out, and I take her hand. "I don't know what to say. I never thought..." She pauses and wipes her eyes. "I should've known, but I didn't even think—"

"None of us did," I assure her.

Kate is beside me and runs her hand down my arm. Her touch is comforting, and I lean into her, craving more of it.

"It doesn't make any sense," Mike says quietly. "Hugo was with William. He was with all of us. He could've turned any of us in whenever he wanted."

"You were more valuable to Judy alive," Theodore interjects. I turn to him, surprised that he would be so forthcoming. "All the intel that was passed on, she wouldn't have gotten it if Dani, Lucas, and William were dead. It's how she so easily climbed the ranks, by presenting information no one else could get."

I think about how she used my parents the same way.

"But the general tried to kill them multiple times," Darby says, still confused. "Malmstrom—"

I share a look with Lucas. Theodore is right. "She was toying with us."

Darby still doesn't seem convinced. "Simon, though."

"He could've killed us at the camp. He said his orders were to bring me in alive, and now, based on what George said, we know the NAF couldn't get into Rapid City. Not with Thatcher having it on lockdown. They were just buying time and collecting information until they attacked."

No one says anything. I'm sure we're all feeling a bit duped, and that does nothing for our confidence level going into this next fight.

"I'll check on Jack," I say softly. "You all should still have that drink." I kiss the side of Kate's head, and she squeezes my arm. We both recognize that we'll unpack this at a later time.

When I get to the hangar, I see Jack sitting with his back against the far wall. His forearms are draped over his knees, and his head is bowed. His entire body is deflated and defeated.

I slide down the wall and sit beside him.

"You should've let me kill him."

"Killing him wouldn't have changed anything. It wouldn't have brought her back," I say sadly. "Trust me. After my dad, I tried to kill every single person in the NAF." I let out a long breath, thinking about the person I was back then and wondering if I'm really all that different today. "I know you want to burn down the world. The anger inside is consuming, and it'll eat away at you until there's nothing left, and one day, you won't recognize yourself anymore."

"How did you do it? How did you stop being so angry all the time?" His voice is quiet, like he's scared of what my answer may cost him.

"I'm still angry," I tell him honestly. "The trick is to learn how to control it." I bump his shoulder. "Clearly, I'm still a work in progress. That's why I have you. And I have Lucas. And Elise. Mike. Kate. Hell, even Darby." He scoffs a little. "All of you remind me every day what's important. What's worth being around for. You're not alone, Jack."

"Part of me wants to kill him. The other part..." He takes a deep breath, letting his thoughts linger. "How could he look any of us in the eyes after what he did?"

I don't answer. Mostly because I don't know what to tell him. Instead, we sit shoulder to shoulder in silence. I know how difficult it is to have conflicting emotions, especially about someone he trusted.

"I keep wondering, what would Rhiannon do? How would she react?" He leans back, resting his head against the wall.

"I think about that a lot," I confess. "She'd be disappointed. Sad. I think she would still try to see the good in him."

"Yeah." After a moment. I hear him sniff. "It's not fair," he says, and I finally look at him to see the tears streaming down his cheeks. "None of this is fair. She should be here. We should be home and not here, dealing with all this."

The pain in his voice is palpable. I try to picture all of us back in White River, around a fire, laughing, happy. Together.

It's an image that will never come again. Not completely. Not without Rhiannon.

A strangled sob escapes Jack's throat, and he cries, really cries for the first time since the day we laid her to rest on the cliff. I pull him to me, guiding his head to my shoulder. I hold him, wishing I had the words to make it hurt less.

Chapter Thirteen: The Quiet

Kate

A re you sure we're far enough away?" Darby asks from just inside the hangar.

"We're about to find out," Dani says, her eyes glued to the helicopter in the clearing just beyond the tree line as the sun sets.

"Not comforting at all," Darby snaps and takes several steps backward.

The side rotors tilt as the helicopter comes to life. My dad stands beside me, his hands stretched in front of him as if he's trying to physically ease the helo into the perfect position.

I watch, awestruck, as the propellers whirl at a speed faster than I could ever imagine and with bated breath, I wait to see if Rodrigues is able to lift the metal beast off the ground.

Ever so slowly, in the soft glow of orange and pink sky, the battle-ready warbird inches upward in a vertical lift, steadily climbing higher and higher until it hovers well over our heads. The chopping sound is deafening compared to the silence of the barren land before us, and it strikes both fear and awe.

"Easy," I hear my dad say as she takes the chopper higher and higher.

My head is tilted all the way back when Rodrigues flips the rotors and takes it for a proper loop around the area while the entire group erupts in cheers. Unable to hide her excitement, Dani grabs my arm and gives me a shake. My dad claps, equally excited at the successful takeoff and test-drive, but I can tell there's sadness there, too.

My own smile slips when I think about how I was supposed to be in command of a fleet of these. It was supposed to be my responsibility to complete my father's life's work and use these aerial vehicles of destruction to put an end to the Resistance. Instead, I am using one to destroy the NAF and subsequently, my mother.

The flight demonstration doesn't last long, but it brings a spark of hope to everyone while we get ready to pack it in and head out to meet William and Thatcher. Rodrigues enjoys the pats on the back and congratulations on a job well done. For someone who hasn't clocked more than a few minutes of airtime, she handled herself and the helo impressively well.

Rodrigues shoves her hands inside her jacket pockets and stands beside me. "Be careful out there."

"You too," I tell her. "Don't go showing off just because you managed to take a couple laps around the bunker."

She shrugs. "I was born to be a hero, Kate," she says through a smirk. "And made to fly."

Her dark eyes sparkle, and her tone is full of arrogance. She reminds me of someone else I know. "You and Dani are so much alike that it's weird." That makes her outright smile and stand tall, accepting the compliment. "Seriously, though, be safe."

She reaches out, and I grab her forearm. "You too," she says. "And Kate? It's been an absolute honor working beside you and your dad."

Not knowing what to say, I nod and leave her standing beside the helicopter. My stomach twists in a way I try to ignore. I refuse to believe this is the last time we'll work together, but reality tells me it may be.

❖

Dani tries very hard not to stare at the door that leads to the room holding George. Jess has been inside with him for a while, and I know it must be killing her not to be in there, too.

"How's it going, do you think?"

She carefully continues packing her bag and glances again at the closed door. "I don't know. Lucas and Wyatt are with her, so I know he won't try anything." Dani shoves a radio in the duffel.

"Did you think he would?" I ask, having a hard time believing George would ever hurt his granddaughter. Especially after everything he did to try to keep her safe.

"No." She sighs. "I just know what it feels like to get the rug pulled out from under you."

I hum in agreement. We've been through a lot of that lately. "What did William say when you told him about it?"

"I didn't talk to him, but Thatcher said she'd be ready for him when we get there." She stands, puts her hands on her hips, closes her eyes, and takes deep breaths.

Only a few months with this group and already, I consider them family. George's betrayal hurts me, too. Then there's William. Where I'm attempting to patch things up with my father, Dani's still so angry at William for all his lies. I didn't ask her, but I think she's projecting her frustrations regarding her father on him.

She takes one more deep calming breath and opens her eyes. "This has been a very long week."

"*So* long," I agree. Glancing behind me, I frown. "Think Jess will be okay?"

Dani stares at the door thoughtfully. "She's strong. She'll do what she needs to do to get through this, but I hate that she has to."

"We'll take care of her."

Her eyes meet mine, and she nods. No matter what happens, it's important that Jess knows we're still all in this together. Her gaze shifts to something over my shoulder, and she picks up her bag. When I turn to look, I see my dad hesitantly approaching. "I'm going to finish getting things ready," she says, either giving us some space or trying desperately to get away from him. Probably both. She places a chaste kiss on my cheek and steps away.

"She looks so much like her father," my dad says, watching as Dani retreats. His gaze is sad, nostalgic.

"That's what I keep hearing." I wish I could've met him.

"I think you should have everything you need," he says and places a small bag at my feet. "I wish I could give you more."

"Thank you for all you *have* given us," I tell him. Food, shelter, a place to hide and regroup, a helicopter. "Don't let Jenisis do anything reckless. If it doesn't seem like it's going to work, don't let her try. I don't want her dying at the risk of trying to prove herself."

"I can't stop Jenisis from doing anything she's determined to do." We share a smile. "I'll stay close to the radio and let you know if I hear anything."

I nod and grab the bag, slinging it over my shoulder.

"Are you sure you won't stay? You'll be safe here," he says quickly before I can walk away. He's staring at me like it's the last time he'll see me.

A small wave of panic rushes through my body. Even though things are complicated and nowhere near what they were before, I don't want to lose him. Not again. "I can't," I say and feel guilty at the way his expression falls. "Maybe when this is over, we can talk some more. Get to know each other again."

He tries to smile. "I'd love that."

We stand facing each other for a moment as Jack and Darby walk by, packed and ready to leave.

"Kate, if you see your mother…" He hesitates, and I know he's struggling to find the words he wants to say. With heartbreak written all over his face and his voice barely above a whisper, he pleads, "Don't let them kill her." It sucks all the air from my lungs. A ball of dread settles in my stomach at the possibility. I don't agree with my mother, but I certainly don't want her dead.

With tears stinging my eyes, I pull my father in and hug him tight. "I'll do my best," I promise, knowing it's the best I can offer while simultaneously aware of it not being enough. The truth is that I don't know what's going to happen, and even if I wanted to stop it, we both know I can't.

❖

Leaving Elise, Jess, and Wyatt behind in the bunker feels harder than walking away from the NAF. We've been through so much together in such a short amount of time that I can't imagine going on to the next phase of this war without them. I've grown to love them as both friends and family, and watching them stand there when we pull away hurts more than I thought it ever would.

On top of that, the ride to our rendezvous point is horrendous. Dani drives the truck with all our equipment secured in the bed, and the silence that stretches between us is increasingly painful with each passing second. The anxiety is high, and I find myself wishing we could be there just so we can do something with all this nervous energy.

George sits rigidly in the back seat, and I blame him for the sour mood. I resent him for what he did, not only to our group but for taking away the few private moments I have left with Dani before we rush back into battle.

I know we're getting closer when Dani picks up the radio to say that two vehicles, one an old pickup and the other a busted yellow sedan, will be approaching from the northeast. We don't have to wait to receive an affirmative.

A few minutes later, Dani slows and pulls up to a wired fence that snakes all the way around what appears to be an old school. There are a bunch of guards standing around the flimsy perimeter, huddled close to a fire with rifles held to their chests. Two of them step in front of Dani's truck, holding out a hand for her to stop, but they don't seem overly concerned.

"Bout time you showed up," one says, his face serious.

"I've got a prisoner in the back," Dani says, skipping the pleasantries.

The man pokes his head inside the truck. "We're ready for him. Pull on through."

Without any more of an exchange, we're waved inside, and Dani takes us as close to the entrance as she can get, where four armed guards are waiting. It seems like George is just realizing how serious this is when the guards make their way over. He sits up straight, and I see out of my peripheral that his head is on a swivel, possibly looking for a way out of the truck before they reach it.

"Dani. Please," he says, his voice fearful when the guards open the back door and pull him from the truck. "I was only protecting my family. You of all people should know that," he calls. Dani watches, her expression blank as two of them all but drag him inside a building.

"What's going to happen to him?" I ask quietly, unable to watch any longer as George calls out desperately. I may be angry with him, but I absolutely hate that this has to happen.

"He'll be locked up until Thatcher or whoever is able to hold a trial." She watches until the building door latches shut. "Unless we all fall to the NAF, then he might be given a medal, who knows?" Dani shifts the truck back into drive and moves to park on the side of the building.

I don't mention that if the NAF wins, we will all face a lot worse than a trial.

Rodrigues's old car pulls up beside us, and without a word, we grab our bags and make our way inside.

A Resistance fighter waits for us to clean our hands. It's procedural yet comforting to be doing something so routine in a time of clear and utter chaos. As we walk through the building, it seems everyone knows Dani and Lucas. They all stop and stare. Some reach out to touch them. Others let out cheers. It's odd to be in the presence of such royalty when to me, they're just the Clarks.

I wonder when that changed.

The farther into the building we walk, the more I realize that there's an impressive number of Resistance fighters scattered around the old elementary school. We're led to a classroom in the center of the second floor, where a familiar guard stands outside. Bruce. He shows no sign that he recognizes us beyond the subtle nod. It's strange, but I'm honestly glad to see him.

He knocks twice and opens the door, revealing Thatcher, William, and Ericson surrounding a table in the back. There are two others I don't recognize and three that I do. Excitement and surprise drape over my entire body when Miguel and Anthony look up as we step inside.

"Oh my God," I say and meet them in the middle of the room, wrapping my arms around both their necks and trying to pull them in for a hug. "What are you two doing here?"

"We couldn't just sit around and do nothing," Miguel says. "When the call to arms came, we knew we couldn't ignore it and hide."

"Marium told us where to go, so here we are," Anthony adds. He looks behind me and reaches out, grasping Dani's forearm.

As surprised as I am to see them, it's the third familiar face that absolutely floors me. Pushing away from the table is Archie, one of the NAFs best cartographers. He looks a little more ragged, his hair longer, a slightly uneven beard donning his youthful face. He smiles and holds out his arms as if to say, "Surprise," and I laugh a little, feeling lighter at being surrounded by people who are, in short, defectors like me.

"How are you here?" I ask and bend to hug him. "What happened?"

"Dani told Thatcher to get me out of Grand Forks." He looks over my shoulder once I pull away, and Dani gives him a nod of recognition. "Then next thing I know, I'm being whisked away to start working with the Resistance directly."

Looking at Thatcher, I wonder just how many spies she has embedded within the NAF. She extends her hand. "Hello, Katelyn." I clasp her forearm, and she smiles. "It's good to see you again."

"Thatcher." She gives my arm a squeeze, and William clears his throat.

The sound is enough to strip away my short burst of happiness.

"What's the plan so far?" Dani asks, glancing at the table, squeezing between Ericson and Miguel, and getting straight to business.

With the pleasantries clearly over, we fill in around the table to get to work. "The plan is, in theory, very simple," Thatcher says. "We have marked all known NAF outposts surrounding Ellsworth. We will send in small teams from different locations to distract them while a larger force presses in on Rapid City."

"Why Rapid City? I thought we were going after the base?" Jack says.

Thatcher turns to him with a smile that says she's glad he's been paying attention. "We believe Rapid City has become their central hub of the Midwest and will eventually become the new capital. If we can reclaim the city, it will swing momentum heavily in our favor."

Mike clears his throat nervously. "And the people who still live there?"

I'm glad he asked because I was thinking about it. Our last interaction with Rapid City was so unpleasant, and so many people were left behind to either fight or die.

Thatcher turns to Mike and answers his question just as calmly as she did Jack's. "From the few reports we've received, not much has changed in their day-to-day life except for traders who now have NAF escorts. Though entering and exiting the city has been extremely limited."

I recognize the tactic. "The NAF is trying to demonstrate that life isn't so bad with them involved, and in a lot of cases, it really isn't."

Jack scoffs. "Yeah, if you like having babysitters go with you every time you take a piss and being a prisoner in your own home."

Thatcher taps the table and brings everyone's attention back to her. "There aren't many soldiers stationed there, beyond what they need to fortify the perimeter and patrol the city."

"Then why are we sending so many fighters?" Darby asks. She points to the pieces on the map indicating positions of personnel and the approximate numbers.

Dani cocks her head and slowly lifts her gaze from the table to Thatcher.

"Resources," I answer instead. "Rapid City holds resources we need."

"And we don't want any coming out," William adds.

I look at Dani again when I hear her release a long breath through her nose. I can't pinpoint the mood that she's in, but currently, she's giving off the image of cool and collected.

Bruce walks in and whispers something to Thatcher. She gives a swift nod before turning back to all of us. "Please excuse me for a moment." Thatcher leaves quickly, and nobody moves for an uncomfortable amount of time.

Then, Dani taps on a spot on the map bare of any markings. "How bad is this area here? Where there are no outposts. Can we drive through it?"

Archie leans forward in his chair and squints. "The area outside of Ellsworth was hit pretty hard during the last war. Half the base is missing due to heavy aerial fire. Right here"—he points to where Dani had indicated—"is a mountain ridge. If that's not bad enough, near the base of it are large craters. A real pain in the ass."

The NAF must have decided that the terrain would be deterrent enough and used their manpower elsewhere. If there's any chance of us crossing it, it'll have been a grave misstep on the NAF's part.

Dani crosses one arm along her stomach and uses it to prop up her other. She rubs her chin thoughtfully, her eyes never leaving the map. "How long would it take to cut through this area by foot?"

I smile, knowing she's thinking the same thing I am.

Archie shrugs. "Hard to tell without getting a good view of it."

"We could use my drone," Darby says casually. All eyes turn to her.

"A drone?" Archie, seemingly a bit baffled, sputters. "Is there a camera installed?"

"Why wouldn't there be a camera?" She frowns at him like it's the dumbest question she's ever heard.

Archie and William exchange a look. "Would you be willing to drive out there right now to scope it out?" William asks.

Darby hesitates, her eyes meeting Dani's. When Dani doesn't answer, she nods. "Yeah, sure."

"Ericson, take Darby to this location to see if we're able to cross on foot." William circles the spot in question on an identical map and hands it to his right-hand man.

Dani and Lucas share a look, and Lucas takes a step closer to Darby. "Let's move out," he says, clearly indicating that he is also going.

Darby deflates with relief. Space opens around the tightly packed table once they're gone, and William cracks his knuckles, something I've never seen him do. To me, it's a tell that he's more anxious about this than he's letting on.

"The last team will infiltrate the base," he says calmly.

"And how are we going to do that?" Jack asks. I'm sure he's genuinely asking, but at the moment, everything he says is coming off as snarky. It seems everyone is on edge.

"I'm going to let you in the back door," a familiar voice answers.

My body tenses. I turn to see a face I never expected, and my stomach bottoms out.

Her eyes meet mine, and she smiles. "Well, so to speak. Hello, Lieutenant Colonel. You seem to be doing well."

"Major General Foley," I say, startled.

Dani watches the exchange closely, and without taking her eyes off the new woman in the room, she stands beside me, hand on the grip of her gun. "What's going on?"

"Meet my mother's assistant," I say, unable to keep the venom out of my tone. I could never stand that woman.

Dani and William draw their guns first, quickly followed by everyone else. Slowly, Foley raises her hands, but her expression is that of amusement. "A pleasure," she drawls.

Thatcher steps in front of her, acting as a human shield. "Please meet my contact. Also known as E. J. Allen."

Dizziness threatens to knock me over as I try to wrap my head around what Thatcher just revealed. It doesn't make sense. It can't make sense. Only, it makes perfect sense. We knew the contact would have to be someone high up and knowledgeable, and there were rumors that it was a general, but I'm still floored.

"Did you know about this?" Dani rounds on William angrily.

"No," He looks so surprised that I'm inclined to believe him. Dani must too because she doesn't press him on it.

"Who the hell is E. J. Allen?" Jack asks, confused but still pointing his gun at Foley.

"The Resistance's greatest informant, who just happens to be an NAF officer," Dani replies dryly.

"Did we send out a memo?" Jack asks, clearly annoyed that another NAF member has crossed the line into Resistance territory.

Thatcher motions again for everyone to lower their weapons, but nobody does. "There are only two people in this room who knew Elisabeth's real identity, and that's me and Bruce."

Bruce stands in the doorway, his arms crossed and not a single expression on his face.

"When?" I ask, unable to look away from my mother's most trusted officer. "When did you turn on the NAF?" I know it's a hypocritical question, but somehow, her betrayal seems worse than mine, and I can't explain why.

Foley arches her brows. "I have never turned my back on the NAF. I love the National Armed Forces. I have devoted my life to the betterment of this country and to the service of the people who wear the uniform."

It's the first time I've heard her speak so honestly and without an edge to her voice. If I wasn't already so incredibly floored by the sight of her, the way she's speaking would be jarring on every level.

"I don't understand," I admit.

She takes stock of all the weapons trained on her. "Lower your weapons and let her explain," Thatcher orders forcefully.

Slowly, everybody complies. I do a quick check on Archie, Miguel, and Anthony behind me. They appear just as shocked as I am. I wonder if they also think Foley may go back to my mother and turn us all in.

"I'm not sure how long ago you noticed a downward trend in the morality of our leadership, Lieutenant Colonel." She's speaking directly to me. "But for me, it's been simmering for quite some time. Ruling with an iron fist and a complete disregard for human life was growing in popularity and is most certainly not what I signed up for. I'm loyal to my country, but I do not condone genocide."

The way she punches the last word sends a sick feeling straight to my stomach. I know she's talking about my mother, and to associate her with such a harsh label, while not untrue, still hurts. I haven't fully accepted a lot of things about my parents, but knowing she's purposefully killed innocent people is the hardest.

"I knew that being direct with General Turner about it wasn't going to work. I've seen it fail time and again. I'd be blacklisted, just as the others have."

Jack scoffs. "Why not put a bullet in her head?"

His comment makes my stomach lurch.

Dani steps forward slightly. "That still doesn't explain how the two of you"—she motions between Thatcher and Foley—"ended up in bed together."

"Elisabeth approached me," Thatcher explains, crossing her arms in a broad stance. "It took quite a bit of time to trust one another, but she was persistent, and I needed an ally to move forward. She's proved herself."

"In order to put the Resistance into a strong position of power, we eventually agreed that the best course of action would be—"

"To blend the leadership between both factions," I interject.

Foley nods and for the first time ever, smiles at me. I don't like it. "We were working on a way to push her in the right direction. You"—she motions to me—"ending up in White River and being taken prisoner by Danielle Clark was the exact piece of the puzzle needed in order to initiate the coup."

"Why were you so awful to me, then?" I can't keep the malice from my voice.

"Operating on both sides is complicated. One wrong move and everything is for nothing."

That is *not* an answer.

"I'm still not buying it," Dani says and trains her gun back on Foley. "Why didn't you just take the general out?"

"Her successor, as it stands, is General Lawrence. He would've been just as detrimental to peace, maybe even more so."

Dani looks at me, and I nod, confirming Foley's claim. General Lawrence is definitely not the man we want in charge any more than we want my mother.

"This is a delicate situation," Foley continues. "It can't be done by a handful of people playing both sides. In order to gain the attention of not just the country but of the NAF, the Resistance needs to put on a show of force and quite literally overthrow the current leadership."

"What are the terms of this arrangement?" William asks, his expression skeptical.

"The NAF needs a complete overhaul, and the Resistance has struck a deal with General Foley in order to make that happen. Foley is not leading this charge. She is simply working with me to ensure success," Thatcher says.

"What kind of deal?" I ask.

"Immunity, for starters," Foley answers.

"And if the NAF prevails?" William asks.

"I do hope that's not the case." Foley sighs and looks at me. "I hope you found the tools necessary to help ensure a victory."

She's talking about the helicopter. I'm angry that somehow, she knew about my father and that she's the reason Rodrigues was sent to me. I hate that a woman I care so little for was so easily able to manipulate my life.

"Unfortunately," Foley continues, seemingly oblivious to my internal disgust. "I have been left out of the loop about confidential information as of late. I fear the general has become so paranoid with who can and cannot be trusted that we're all on a need-to-know basis."

"And she's decided that you don't need to know everything," I say, knowing exactly how much this hurts because my mother did it to me months ago. It's a weird feeling to be so conflicted. On the one hand, I feel sorry for Foley, knowing how much she seems to genuinely love climbing the ranks and being my mother's right hand, and now she's being forced out of her intimate circle of trust.

On the other hand, Foley is just as manipulative as my mother, and I know that whatever game she's playing, she's ensuring that she'll come out on top.

"Any more questions?" Thatcher asks and looks at the group.

As much as I want to poke and pry, something in Thatcher's tone tells me her question is strictly rhetorical.

"Great. Time is dwindling. Back to work."

❖

"That was by far one of the strangest and most uncomfortable meetings I have ever had the displeasure of sitting through," Dani says. "And that's saying a lot."

I don't respond. Mainly because she's not wrong. We walk down the hall, Dani doing her best to dodge the attention of the few people still awake at the late hour.

"Do you trust her?" Dani asks.

I scoff, wondering why she even bothered to ask. "Of course not."

"But?"

"But I think she wants my mother's position, and she's too far down the rung to get it without help." I sigh. "So, no, I don't trust her, but I also don't think she'd sacrifice her best chance at a power grab."

"Nothing like being used as pawns in someone else's game," Dani says sarcastically but with a huge smile. She comes to a stop in front of a room and opens the door. We drop our duffels and sleeping bags inside and take a good look. The space is small, as if it was once a storage closet, but I don't mind. There's a door for privacy and enough room to lie down, and right now, that's all I care about.

"Our own room, huh?" I say playfully, just happy to be far away from Foley and her knowing glances.

Dani places the lantern on the ground and starts to unroll our sleeping bags. "Sleeping with the Daughter of the Resistance has its perks."

"No heater, though," I remind her, shivering.

"Okay, it has *some* perks." She smiles and wraps her arms around me, leaning in to steal a kiss. "Besides, I'll keep you warm."

I smile into the next kiss, but it isn't lost on me that she's clearly trying to distract me with some very welcome attention. After all our briefings, it's clearer than ever that tomorrow could very well decide the fate of the war, our lives, and the lives of those we love. It's been hanging over us like a persistent storm cloud for months, growing heavier with each passing day, and now we've reached the culmination.

Silently, I help her get one of the sleeping bags spread out on the ground. We strip to our shirts and pants and crawl beneath the second sleeping bag, pulling it up to our shoulders. I scoot impossibly close to her, trying to steal her warmth for myself.

Our noses brush, and her eyes meet mine. We stay like that for a long moment as I memorize the way her eyes shine in the soft glow of the lantern and count the spattering of freckles that dance along the bridge of her nose. I drag my thumb across her bottom lip, smiling when she catches it between her teeth and gently bites, following the nibble with a soft kiss.

Cupping her cheek, I caress her jaw with my fingertips and sigh, wishing we could stay like this forever. "Are you scared?" I whisper, finally breaking the silence.

She covers my hand with her own and kisses my wrist. "Anxious. Ready to get it all done. You?"

"I'm terrified," I confess through a shaky breath. She pulls me closer and presses her forehead to mine. "I've put people I've cared about in risky situations before, but this time..." I swallow hard, trying to find the right words. "I can't bear the thought of one of us not coming back. Of *you* not coming back."

Her expression falls. "Hey." She pulls me into a hug, wrapping her arms around me tightly and gently rubbing my back. "You don't have to do this."

"Yes, I do," I tell her and try to swallow the lump that feels stuck in my throat.

"I wish I could be with you," she whispers.

I don't know if she's talking about in the morning or something more. The tears I have fought so hard all day finally break through, and I bury my face against her shoulder, unable to stop them. "You're planning something stupid. I know you are," I say against her shirt.

"I'm not."

I pull back to look at her again. "You swore you would never lie to me." I stare, unable to stomach anything other than the truth. "So don't lie to me."

She strokes my cheeks and pushes my hair out of my face. Wiping away my tears, she looks into my eyes. "I promise you, I will do everything, *everything*, I can to come back to you."

My lip quivers, and the tears keep coming. Desperation to keep her close, to keep her safe, claws its way to the surface. "I don't know what I'll do if something happens to you."

"You won't have to find out," she promises. I so want to believe her. "I love you, Kate."

"I—"

She kisses me, swallowing my response, and rolls us both until she's nestled comfortably on top of me.

My hands sink in her hair, pulling her deeper as I wrap myself around her, trying to steal every single moment I can.

❖

There's a firm knock on our door, a sign that our few hours of rest are up, and we need to get moving. I wrap around Dani and bury my face in her neck, inhaling as deeply as I possibly can, memorizing her smell, her feel, her everything.

"It's time," I whisper and kiss her skin.

"One more minute," she says and squeezes my arms around her.

We hold perfectly still, breathing in sync, my heart hammering. She turns in my arms and kisses me, our chests pressed together, and I can feel her heart pounding as rapidly as my own. If I could stop time, I would live in this moment forever.

"Dani," I say, breathlessly. "If this doesn't work…"

I'm interrupted by a loud banging on the door and Jack's voice. "Let's go, Clark. The NAF isn't going to blow itself up."

Dani smiles sadly and pushes the hair from my face. "I guess our minute's up."

I want to tell her to wait, that I just need a little more time with her, with us, like this. But she kisses me softly and pushes off the covers, standing and holding out her hand to help me up. I swallow the lump in my throat and allow myself to be pulled to my feet.

I refuse to think our minute together is over. Instead, I try to convince myself that it's just another temporary separation.

When Dani opens the door, Jack is waiting for us impatiently, his gear strapped to his back. "About time," he says. My gaze goes to his freshly shaven head with his short, thick hair back into its signature 'do.

"Look at that." Dani says and ruffles his head. "Mohawk is back."

He pulls away and swats at her. "If anybody but you had tried that, they'd lose an arm."

She laughs. "Good thing you love me, then."

My heart clenches at the word love. He shoves Dani, and they both smile. It's good to see the old Jack again.

My nerves start to ramp up as we follow the sleepy and disheveled fighters outside a few minutes later. Thatcher is already there, pointing people in different directions and making sure everyone knows where they need to go and what they should be doing.

I want to reach for Dani, but she turns to Jack instead. "Can I talk to you?"

He gives her a questioning look but agrees. She touches my arm as if to say she'll be right back, and they step off to the side, just out of earshot. I watch their exchange carefully.

She speaks animatedly, putting her hands on his shoulders and ducking her head to keep his focus on her. Finally, he looks at me and nods once, and she wraps him in a tight hug. The exchange is intimate, and I look away, wanting to give them as much privacy as I can.

I notice Foley is nowhere to be found. Honestly, it's a bit of a relief. Besides not being able to stand her, seeing her is just another reminder that I'll be going up against the NAF today. Even though I know I'm not a part of them anymore, a small piece of me is still hesitant. Still sad.

"You okay?" Dani asks as if she can literally see my conflicting thoughts.

"I'm just glad Foley is gone."

Dani winces. "She's not."

I follow her line of sight upward at the building. I can vaguely see Foley in the soft glow of a second-story window. I sigh. "Fantastic."

"Look." She steps in front of me, grips my biceps, and waits until I look at her. "There's still time if you want to stay here."

"Will you stay with me?" I counter. She gives me a look that says it's not an option. "Then stop asking me if I want to." I glance back up at Foley in the window and try to ignore the unsettling feeling when she stares back. "I'm Resistance."

Foley nods and steps away from the window. I wonder if she could read my lips from so far away.

Dani frowns and drops her hands. "I don't like you going in there without me," she admits.

"I'll be with Thatcher, Jack, and Bruce. That's the A-Team," I tell her and try to smile. When she doesn't return the gesture, I take her hand. "I'll be fine. Besides," I say dismissively, "you're the one sneaking on base with explosives. I'm just clearing buildings in the city so Thatcher can regain control. Easy."

She still isn't amused. Darby and Mike appear from the crowd, looking as though they'd rather be anywhere but here. "Where's Lucas?" Dani asks.

Darby motions to the front of the crowd.

"Listen up, people," Thatcher says in a booming voice. Everyone stops what they're doing and pushes closer. Lucas is standing beside her. She gives him a nod, and he jumps on top of the hood of a truck, facing the sea of people who have gathered. He takes a lantern and holds it outward, scanning the faces looking up at him, waiting.

"Here it comes," Dani mutters.

A gentle breeze whips Lucas's hair around his face. I don't think I have ever seen him this intense. "Whether you be built for battle in body or mind, you are a warrior tonight," he starts. "For too long, we have lived under their rule. For too long, we have lived under the weight of their laws. They may be strong, but we are united. Together, we are a force to be reckoned with."

I smile slightly when I recognize the quotes from the *Major Maelstrom* issue where he takes on the military with his eclectic group of misfit heroes. Not unlike this very moment.

"History has written about us with angry, warped lies, but we will not give in, and we will not surrender. Whether you're beaten, broken, or beyond repair, rise, my friends. Rise. Rise like the tide." He pauses to let the moment settle.

I feel a hand take mine and squeeze. I take a step closer, pressing my shoulder to Dani's.

"This is our moment. Our day of victory. This is the day we fight. Our moment to break free of tyranny and rid ourselves of our oppressors. Today is the day we take charge and take back all that was taken from us. Today is the day we prevail!"

The entire crowd erupts into cheers and whistles.

"Now that's a speech," Jack says and tosses his cap into the air and then pulls it down tightly over his head.

Dani rolls her eyes but smiles regardless.

"You heard the man," Thatcher calls. "You all know your assignments. Let's move and take back our land!"

There are more cheers, and everyone starts to pull off into groups.

Lucas works his way through the crowd and smiles at all the pats on his back. "You just had to show me up, didn't you?" Dani teases.

He shrugs.

"Impressive," I tell him and zip his jacket a little tighter. "Please be careful."

He nods and looks at me with his kind brown eyes. I have never known anyone as selfless as Lucas. He hands me his blue mirrored sunglasses, and I take them, my eyes starting to prickle with tears. I pull him into a tight embrace, one he lovingly returns. "Maelstrom's pulse quickened. He was unaccustomed to such beauty in this world," he whispers.

Squeezing my eyes shut, I hug a little tighter and then step away and am immediately pulled into a hug from Darby. Just as quickly as she pulled me in, she releases me, and Mike is next.

"Don't forget to salute any officers you pass," I remind them, wiping my eyes and looking at the NAF uniforms they're wearing. "I'll see you all soon."

Lucas smiles and picks up their bags, taking them to the pickup parked near the gate entrance where Jack is waiting to say his own farewell.

Dani won't look in my eyes. "Hey," I say and cup her face.

She tries to smile but fails spectacularly. "I'm not good with good-byes."

"Then don't. We don't have to say it. We can just say hello instead."

This time, she does manage a smile. Even if it's a small one. "Hello," she whispers and leans in, pressing her lips to mine.

The kiss is definitely not chaste. It's deep and desperate. It's a promise that we'll fight like hell to be together, no matter what's thrown at us. No matter what tries to divide us. It's our one more minute.

"Dani."

She doesn't respond, just leans forward again.

I kiss her back once, twice. On the third swipe of her lips, I grip her back and manage to pull away just far enough to whisper, "I love you." Our eyes meet. "And you better fucking come back to me."

She nods and pulls me closer. "I guess I fucking better."

Chapter Fourteen: The Sacrifice

Dani

With determination to get this thing done and back home to Kate, I fasten the vest around my white, long-sleeve shirt, hidden from view of the others. Once it's secure, I shrug on the thick and uncomfortable uniform jacket, buttoning it with cold fingers.

I sling my backpack over one shoulder and hurry to the truck, knowing our window to hit the road and make it to the base on time is closing. I make it three steps before William pulls me aside.

"Dani, we need to talk."

"Is this really the best time?" I ask, annoyed and anxious to be on the road and get this day over with.

"It's never a good time, but it needs to be said." His expression is serious and hopeful.

I let out a long breath that clouds around us from the cold. Once the condensation clears, I nod and allow him to pull me to the side.

"When your father died—"

I shake my head and start to walk away. Nope. This was a mistake. I won't do this. Not now. Not ever.

"Dani." He grabs my arm and stops me from going any farther. "Please, I need to say this."

"I don't want to hear it," I say through clenched teeth. "All the lies you've told, all the things you kept from me? I just can't anymore."

"I tried my best to do what was right by you and Lucas," he continues, and for some reason, I stop. "But instead, I made things worse. I lost my best friend. My brother. Hell, I lost all my friends. I was sad and angry, and I dove headfirst into the Resistance, and in doing so, I pulled you and your brother with me."

I swallow hard, thinking about going on runs, planning attacks, and carrying them out, all with William. About his bold decisions and lack of supervision when I recklessly went down the same path, but then I think about how he always made sure we had food to eat, a place to stay, and an ear to listen whenever we needed to talk.

"I was old enough to decide for myself," I tell him. Old enough to join the Resistance, old enough to be on my own. Old enough to choose what kind of life I wanted.

"You were a kid. You were both kids and I…" He takes a deep breath. "I led you down that path, and I'm sorry."

When I turn, it startles me to see him look so dejected. So worn down. "I was sad and angry, too," I remind him.

"I should've done a better job helping you deal with that anger in a healthy way. Instead…" He shrugs and sighs. "Instead, I got you caught up in all of this."

"I hate to break it to you, William, but I would've become this person with or without you."

"You're so much like your father."

This time, I'm the one who flinches. I've heard it before, but the way William says it with such fondness hits harder than before.

"You and Lucas, you were his life. His family was his entire world. His vision for this country, to change the rule of law, it was for you. To make this country a better place for his children and maybe one day, grandchildren." He looks away but not before I see that he's crying. "The day he died, that day was supposed to be it. We knew that if we could stop the NAF from taking position and ownership of the Badlands, we would be able to push them back east and have a real shot at winning this war, but you need to know what happened. It's easy to pin it on Judy, but she didn't kill him."

That is the last thing I expect him to say. I want to argue and tell him I know what I saw, but all I can do is shake my head. Instantly, I can see the moment in my mind. The rain, my father slamming his hand on the detonator of the busted device, the NAF closing in on us. He took my shoulders and looked me in the eyes and told me to run. To take care of Lucas. That he would see me in a few minutes.

I didn't want to go, but he had smiled, told me he loved me, and pushed me away to work on the detonator. I remember he turned to run after us just as Judy aimed her gun and shot him right as the bomb went off.

"He could've gotten away. Judy killed him," I say, knowing very clearly what happened.

William looks away. "She was firing at me."

"No," I tell him, taking a step backward. "She shot Dad while he ran."

"She was shooting at me," he repeats, his gaze finally meeting mine. "Because I had her pinned with my rifle. Your dad was just trying to outrun the blast."

I shake my head, not wanting at all to believe it. Not wanting to believe that he blew himself up. "No, no. Judy killed him. That's why he didn't make it."

"Dani—"

"Why are you telling me this?" I ask angrily, taking another step back.

"Because you deserve to know. Because you're so much like your father that I'm terrified you'll do the same thing. Dani…" He steps closer and reaches out, but I don't want him touching me. "I'm sorry."

"For what?" I ask, trying to swallow the lump in my throat. "For lying to me my whole life or for Dad blowing himself up for nothing?"

"It wasn't for nothing," he protests.

"Wasn't it? The outcome of that battle didn't win the war. It didn't even keep the NAF in the east. Nothing changed, it just got worse and I…" A sob escapes despite doing my best to keep it inside. "And I lost my dad." I can't even begin to think of all my misplaced anger and hatred toward Judy for something she apparently never even did.

"I know, kiddo," he says, his expression full of sadness.

This time, when he reaches for me, I let him. He pulls me into a tight embrace, and I fall into it, grabbing the back of his jacket and doing my best not to cry. "I'm so tired of being angry," I say.

"Me too." He squeezes just a little tighter. "I'm sorry I never told you the truth. You and Lucas deserve so much better."

After everything I've done, I'm not sure I agree with that.

"No matter what happens today, whether we stop the NAF or not, I don't want you involved in this anymore," he says softly. "I'll do whatever I can to make sure you stay out of it. You deserve a normal life with the woman you love."

Our plan of a quiet life and growing old together resurfaces. It will never be a reality if the NAF wins. Today, I'm the spark Rhiannon told me to be, and I'm leading the Resistance to victory.

Even if it kills me.

When I pull away, William wipes his own tears and smiles encouragingly. "We better go."

I fix my jacket and nod, drying the tears from my face and taking a deep, steadying breath. My heart feels just a little bit lighter. Giving William a nod, one that hopefully says we're good, at least for now, we head to Ellsworth.

Once we've gone as far as we can manage, we all file out of our buggies, leaving them behind. Gripping the strap of my backpack in one hand, I use my other to keep balanced while I slide down a particularly large, ice-covered drop-off. The air is so cold that it burns my nostrils and lungs.

Once I hit even ground, I pull on my hat and shiver, wishing for my warm and puffy coat.

"You sure this path is clear?" Mike asks once he has slid down the steep decline.

"I'm looking at it right now," Darby snaps a moment later. She shows us the small monitor in the center of her drone controls. "So, yes. I'm sure." She pulls at the high collar of the gray polyester jacket. "Ugh. Why are these uniforms so itchy?"

Lucas and William come next, followed by Miguel and Ericson. I squint at the sky. No sign of surveillance. I glance into the distance but see nothing but rough terrain and the frozen river. According to Darby's recon last night, it'll be a rough walk but decidedly doable, and with no outposts or signs of guards from here to the base, it should be smooth sailing. "Come on. We're almost there."

We walk for a long time, the only light we have coming from Darby's screen and the lowering light of the moon. I think about Kate and how she's probably getting into position to infiltrate Rapid City. I can only hope the city falls quickly and without much of a fight. More than anything, I hope Kate stays safe.

I swallow roughly and push any thoughts of her in danger from my head. I can't think like that. I have to trust that she will keep her promise and do all that she can to make it out of there.

"Are you sure there's going to be a break in the guard?" Mike huffs from behind me, hoisting his large rifle farther up over his shoulder. His constant questions do nothing to settle the nervous atmosphere.

"Foley said there would be," William answers.

"Yeah, but do we trust Foley?" Darby glances up from her screen. "Miguel, do you trust her?"

He appears startled to be brought into the conversation. "I don't know. Yesterday was my first time meeting her. I tend to believe her."

The tall chain-link fence comes into view, and we press a little farther before crouching behind a line of boulders. The moon starts to fade in the sky while the soft glow of dawn signals the start of the day.

After pulling out the binoculars, I watch the guard in the watchtower yawn. "We're about to find out."

Darby starts to disassemble Chi-Chi and put it back in the box she's been carrying strapped to her back, one that will keep her drone safe from the upcoming EMP blast.

"Alpha, Beta, and Charlie in position and standing by for signal, over," I say into the radio strapped to my shoulder.

"Echo standing by and waiting to fly, over," Rodrigues says from the radio in Theodore's bunker.

"Foxtrot moving into position, over," Thatcher says.

The line goes silent after that, and I try not to think of Kate and Thatcher moving in on Rapid City and the armament they'll be facing. A huge part of me wishes she had chosen to stay behind and keep out of the fight.

Anxiously, I watch through the binoculars, waiting for the change in guard. I check the position of the moon and the rising sun, knowing that we just barely managed to make it on time.

The switch doesn't happen.

Holding my breath, I continue to watch, focused on the guard leaning against the watchtower railing. He's more interested in the flowing river several hundred meters away than scanning the area, which is lucky for the seven of us who are crouched behind a spattering of boulders.

I nervously tap my thumb along the bottom of the binoculars. Slowly, the sun starts to brighten the sky, and I wonder if we actually are too late, and we missed the rotation. Just as I'm about to radio Delta back at the school for Foley to get on the line, the new shift appears atop the watchtower with two thermoses. He hands one to the previous guard, and the two men make idle chitchat, laughing and toasting their thermoses before the night shift finally takes his leave.

The new guard appears outside the tower, and with one last look over his shoulder, he flashes a large flashlight three times in quick succession.

"Signal received, proceeding with caution. Stand by for green light, over," I say into the radio.

Quickly, we press forward, going as fast as we can. Part of me is tense while I run, expecting a barrage of bullets from above. When we make it to the perimeter, Ericson gets to work, cutting the fence enough for us to slip through.

"Okay, now that we're in, where do we go?" Darby asks, her eyes wide and scared.

"The hangars are on the other side of the base," Anthony says, checking the layout given to us by Foley.

Darby groans. "Of course they are."

"Are you sure these uniforms are going to work?" Mike wonders, glancing at the gray uniform and straightening it as best he can.

Miguel pulls gray hats out of his bag and passes them out, handing the first to Mike. "There are so many people on base that as long as you look like you belong here, no one should question you."

"Keyword being 'should,'" Darby says and makes a disgusted face before taking off her stocking cap and replacing it with the gray one.

"The building you want is in that direction," Miguel says to me and points to the east.

I double-check my pistol and face him, pointing to Mike and Darby. "Make sure they get into position and keep them safe. We need that EMP to go off in order for this to work. We don't want them to organize once they know we're inside."

William pulls on his cap, and I notice that he's wearing the lowest rank out of all of us. I'd find humor in it if this wasn't such a tense situation. "Once everyone checks in, I'll throw the device, and it'll be radio silence," he says, hoisting his bag over his shoulder.

"Except for the one we have tucked away," Darby says and awkwardly pats the box strapped to her back.

"Except for the one with you," William confirms. "You'll use that to signal to Rodrigues that we're in the clear, and that'll give us approximately fifteen minutes to apprehend the general. Does everyone have their maps?" He waits until we all confirm that we do.

Miguel seems nervous. He's gripping his rosary tightly, his lips moving, uttering words I can't hear. "You sure you're up for this?" I ask.

He hesitates, slightly. "I'm sure."

The answer isn't comforting, and I'm not sure I like the idea of a nervous former NAF soldier going up against people he used to fight alongside. Not for the first time, I wonder if it was a good idea to bring him.

He tucks his necklace back under his shirt. "I've got this," he says, and oddly enough, I believe him.

William and Ericson will place and detonate the EMP, sending the base into radio silence, and make their way to the general, who should still be in her private quarters. Darby will use her drone as surveillance to report back to Rodrigues, and Mike will provide sniper cover with Miguel, watching their backs. A Resistance team will front an attack on the main gates and use that as a distraction so Lucas and I can plant explosives around the back wall to sneak in a secondary Resistance team.

"Keep your eyes open," I tell the group. "Don't do anything stupid. Stick to the plan, and soon enough, we'll all be getting drunk in celebration. Got it?"

Everyone nods, and there's a chorus of agreement. I take a long look at them, the uniforms making us somehow look more ragtag than ever, but I know with absolute certainty there is nobody I trust more to have my back and accomplish the mission.

The rig beneath my uniform jacket feels tight, and it reminds me that no matter what, that drone will be destroyed, and my friends will make it out.

They stare at me, expectancy in their eyes. William gestures for me to continue, but I'm not sure what to say. I want to tell them how important they are, how much they mean to me, and how much I believe in them. Instead, the words get caught in my throat.

"See you on the other side," is what comes out instead. William shakes his head, and I can hear Lucas sigh. Turns out, I'm still not good at rallying the troops.

"You should've let Lucas give the speech," Mike says.

"Can't you just say good luck?" Darby asks, following Miguel in the direction of their position. "'See you on the other side' sounds so ominous."

Lucas pats my back. Whatever. I thought it sounded fine.

"Hey, Mike." He turns, and I toss him a pack of gum that he easily catches. "Eyes sharp," I tell him. He salutes and disappears with the others.

"Strap in, soldier. It's showtime," Lucas says.

Taking a deep breath, I double-check the map and slip it into my pocket. "Let's go."

Lucas and I walk casually through the base, sticking close to buildings as cover and trying to avoid anyone who appears to be headed in our direction. It helps that the sun has just peeked over the horizon, and the majority of the base is still asleep or slowly waking.

The uniforms may give us a bit of cover, but it's the arrogance of us acting as though we're supposed to be here that really seals the deal. I do my best not to roll my eyes when a sleepy private stops to salute my brother, who's wearing the rank of major. He stands tall and salutes back, clearly enjoying it. It seems odd that there doesn't seem to be nearly as many soldiers around as I would've expected.

When we get closer to the hangars, the feeling of something being off rapidly intensifies. Lucas must sense it too because he slows and looks around. "There's a shift in the wind."

"Yeah," I agree. "Something's wrong." I press the talk button to the radio attached to my shoulder. "What's your status? Over."

"Bravo in position, over," William says through the radio.

"Charlie in position, over," Mike responds almost instantly.

"Standby for Alpha, over," I say. Lucas and I reach the back door to the unguarded hangar and share a look. "Does this seem strange to you?"

He nods and pulls his gun, taking a few steps back and pointing it at the door.

After checking the frame for any kind of device, I find nothing, but that doesn't mean it isn't rigged from the inside. With my back against the side of the building, I push on the handle and force it open, bracing for some kind of explosion or assault.

Nothing happens.

Lucas cautiously heads forward and checks inside. After a brief search of the entryway, he leans out of the doorway. "They've gone."

"What do you mean they've gone?" Pulling my own pistol, I step inside the back of the hangar only to find it completely empty. "Where the fuck is the drone? Are you sure this is the right building?"

Lucas nods, and we both look at the map. I look around the large space as if it's going to magically appear. "How the hell do you hide a fucking plane?"

"We've been double-crossed," Lucas says.

I want to disagree, but there's no other explanation for a missing UCAV of the size we're talking about. "The drone's not here," I say into the radio.

"What do you mean it's not there?" William says back, barely more than a whisper.

"I mean, the hangar is empty," I snap.

"Can you check the other hangars?" William asks, desperation evident in his tone.

"Yeah, if you want to wander around the base for another twenty or thirty minutes," I say, already looking to my left and right, wondering which way to start.

"We'll hold the drop and keep communications open. Charlie, can you get eyes in the sky? Over," William says, his voice breathy like he's quickly moving.

"Yeah, I just need to reassemble her," Darby says.

"How much time will that take? Over," William asks, clearly impatient that things are going south.

"About ten minutes."

"You have five, over," William counters.

"Then why did you even ask me how much time I needed? You could've just said, 'you have five minutes.'" Darby sounds annoyed, and I manage to catch a few choice words for William before she releases the talk button.

I think about the line of hangars on either side of us. "Well, Major, right or left?"

The large hangar doors open slowly before he can answer, and we dive out the back door, pressing our backs against the building.

"Come out, come out, wherever you are." The singsong voice makes the hair on the back of my neck stand on end. Lucas stares at me with wide eyes.

Simon.

"I know you're here. Don't make me give the order to launch the UCAV and blow up Rapid City." I can hear the sneer in his voice. "We know the Resistance wants the city back. It would be a shame to take it out before we had a little fun first."

I stare at my brother, my heart racing. They *were* expecting us. Although knowing Simon, he may be bluffing. He wouldn't blow up a city the NAF wants, would he? Plus, there's no way he has the authority to launch that kind of attack. But if there's even the smallest chance he does, I have to keep that thing as far away from Rapid City, as far away from *Kate*, as I possibly can.

I motion for Lucas to stay put, and he shakes his head. I give him my best "trust me" look. His shoulders slouch, and he shakes his head again but doesn't stop me when I peek around the doorway.

Simon walks slowly into the hangar, pistol in one hand and a walkie-talkie in the other. He's flanked by a half dozen soldiers with ballistic shields. I wouldn't be surprised if more were making their way around the building to corner us.

I catch a glimpse of the UCAV on the runway, looking mighty ready for takeoff. I press myself flat against the wall. "Shit." I grab the radio on my shoulder. "Forget the eyes in the sky, the drone is on the runway."

"Aw, come on now, Danielle. I promise, I won't kill you," Simon taunts from inside, his voice echoing. "Not yet, anyway."

Well, that's just fucking great. We need Rodrigues here now, but it isn't safe until William and Miguel activate the EMP and take out the communications and the tanks along the perimeter to clear the area for the frontal assault.

I need to buy us some time to keep Simon from launching the UCAV.

With his footsteps growing louder, I adjust my backpack. There isn't time to come up with another plan, and we can't wait for Rodrigues. We're going to have to blow the UCAV ourselves.

"Drop the EMP and call in aerial. We're going after the drone ourselves. Over and out." Between protests from William to wait, someone with eyes on Foxtrot announces they are going radio silent and moving into Rapid City. I grab a grenade from my belt, knowing my pistols alone aren't going to cut it against those ballistic shields.

"Clear the hangar and take out the guards. Forget about the back perimeter, we have to take out that drone *now*. I'll buy you some time to plant the explosives, then we get the hell out of here," I instruct and toss Lucas the bag of explosives. He catches it just as the soldiers inside the hangar open fire, no doubt seeing the movement through the open door.

We press flat against the building, bullets flying past us. I pull the pin of the grenade and hold down the lever, hoping the blast will be enough to at least knock them off their feet. "Ready?"

Lucas salutes, slips on the backpack, and brings his rifle to his chest, ready for action. I wish like hell I had Jack's grenade launcher.

With a steadying breath and ignoring my regret, I toss the grenade inside the hangar. The boom and William activating the EMP will most certainly alert the entire base that they are under attack. I just hope Rodrigues can get here fast enough to provide some cover.

Someone yells, "Incoming," right before the blast strikes, and once it does, I charge inside, both pistols drawn, firing through the smoke.

My ears ring, but I'm laser focused, shooting anything that moves and hoping like hell Simon is one of them. More soldiers race in from the open hangar door, but it's the sudden appearance of gray coats behind us that pulls my attention.

Lucas and I return fire and slip inside the hangar, slamming the door and trying to find something to block it. There's a metal shelf a few meters away, and Lucas rushes to drag it over while I use all my strength to keep the lever from being pressed down and the door forced open.

Lucas barely gets the shelves in front of the door when I hear Simon screaming in his radio that the base has been infiltrated and to ready the drone for launch. I fire at him as he and another soldier hide behind two discarded ballistic shields.

He shoots, and we do the same, diving for the shields and barely managing to get behind them. Lucas cries out when he drops to a crouch, and I know he's been hit. "Lucas!"

"It's just a flesh wound, boy," he says through gritted teeth, but the gray uniform does little to hide the blood already appearing on his shoulder. He holds the shield up as best he can with his injured arm and uses his free hand to press against the fresh wound, crying out again.

Yelling in frustration, I fire at the two shields, not sure which one Simon is crouched behind.

Click. Click. Click.

I'm out of ammo. As I'm reaching for another magazine, Lucas tosses a grenade behind us just as the back door is breached. The blast knocks us off our feet, and I land hard on my back.

I barely have enough time to get the shield back up to protect me before a second wave of soldiers come in from both the front and the back. "There's too many of them," I tell Lucas, wincing as bullets fly off the shield. He lobs a second grenade at the door. "Lucas needs to take out the drone on the runway," I say into the radio. "He needs cover."

"Copy that," Mike says. If William is pissed that I'm taking his set of eyes, he doesn't say anything.

Lucas tosses his third and last grenade. No more soldiers file through the back after the blast, so I unload another magazine in Simon's direction. I can hear him barking orders from behind his shield. A handful of soldiers sprint in his direction, and I quickly reload to take them out.

Once things go still, I get as close to Lucas as I can and prop the shield against me, tucking myself behind it and slipping off my uniform jacket. I slice it with my knife, cutting the longest strip I can and using the piece of fabric to wrap tightly around his wounded arm. I hope it'll hold until he can get to safety.

Grabbing the back of his neck, I press my forehead to his. "Get to the drone. I'll distract them here. Mike will have your six."

Lucas starts to move, but I grab him, pulling him back, a strange hum buzzing through my entire body. It feels a lot like panic, like I won't ever see him again.

"If things start to go south, get out of there. Forget the drone and just leave." He nods and looks at the rig strapped to my chest. "And don't come back for me. Understand?"

He stares at me with wide eyes, as if he didn't know this was always going to be the contingency plan. "I never leave a man behind," he says firmly.

"Don't come back for me. If I don't make it out...Kate..." I choke on her name. "Just please," I beg. I'm reloading my pistol as more bullets ping against the shield. We don't have any more time. Lucas continues to stare, his eyes glistening. This time, I push him away. "Go." He doesn't move. "Go," I yell, and without giving him the opportunity to stop me, I hoist the shield to the front of me and press forward toward Simon, unloading my magazine.

"Stop him," Simon yells from behind his shield.

Out of bullets, I drop my shield and pull my knife, diving at the closest soldier and wrestling his cover from his grasp to stab him quickly in the neck.

A sharp sting on my thigh drops me to my knees. A bullet slices through the side of my leg. Yelling, I reach for the detonator stuck to my side and hold it high in the air. I flip a switch on the transmitter and press firmly on the red button with my thumb. "I'll blow the whole place," I shout into the hangar. "I lift my finger off this button, and we all die."

"Hold your fire," Simon yells from behind his shield. "Hold your fire."

The place goes oddly quiet, and my ears ring from the gunfire. I try to stand, but my leg throbs, so I remain on my knees, holding the detonator high above my head. "Drop the guns, or I'll do it," I say, out of breath.

"She's bluffing," one of the soldiers calls from Simon's left.

Slowly, Simon stands from behind his shield, his gaze focused on me. "No," he says, probably thinking about the ankle band explosives I strapped to him back when he was a prisoner in White River. "No, I don't think she is."

"Drop your guns," I say again.

Even from about twenty-five meters away, I can see his expression shift from surprised to angry. "Do as she says," he orders through gritted teeth. The remaining soldiers do so, and I take a deep breath, trying to push down the pain in my leg. "Put down the detonator, Danielle."

"You don't want me to do that," I tell him and try hard not to wince.

"Oh, but I do. Otherwise, I'll greenlight the UCAV to bomb Rapid City. The Resistance has probably infiltrated their walls by now. I wonder how many friends of yours I can kill this time," he says, his twisted smile making me sick to my stomach.

My hand shakes, and my thumb eases up for a second before I press it back down. "There are enough explosives strapped to my chest to take out you, me, and all your friends here. I'm ready to die for my cause. Are you?"

His smile falters a bit, then turns into a sneer. "I very seriously doubt that. Tell me, is William here? Or Katelyn? How will you save them if you're dead?" I hate him. More than I have ever hated anyone in my life. He brings a walkie to his lips. "Bomber launch activation Kilo, India, Lima, Sierra."

I stare at him, my hand still shaking and my thumb aching from pressing down so hard. I glance at the UCAV on the runway, watching to see if it ramps up, hoping like hell Lucas has managed to get at least one explosive into place.

I've never seen a drone that size before and sure as hell don't know how they work, but nothing seems to happen. Simon repeats the command. No response. He repeats it a third time, and only then does he seem to realize that his radio is dead.

William's EMP worked. I release a long breath.

Quickly, Simon spins back to face me, and I pull myself to my feet. "Did you really think I'd strap myself to a live bomb?" I ask, tossing the detonator to the side and removing the chest rig, dropping it to the ground.

Quickly pulling the pistols strapped to the small of my back, I open fire. He yanks one of his soldiers in front of him, using him as a human shield. I take out everyone in the hangar, including the soldier in front of him, leaving just me and Simon.

When I'm out of ammo, Simon drops the dead soldier and fumbles for his own gun as I sprint forward, pushing through the pain in my leg. I put all my weight behind my swing and deck him in the face. He stumbles backward, dropping his gun, and I kick it out of the way, push forward, and punch him again. And again. And again.

He grabs his nose, blood pouring out as I shake my hand to regain feeling before I attack, not even close to finished unleashing my anger on his bloody face.

I swing, but he sidesteps and kicks me in the thigh, right on my wound, knocking me over. Fire shoots through my leg and up my back. I cry out in agony and press my hand against my bleeding leg. I try to stand only to fall back down.

"What did you think was going to happen here, Danielle?" He turns his head and spits. He wipes his mouth with the back of his hand and takes several deep breaths. "You'd sneak on base and stop this? That no one would see you coming? You're predictable. Just like General Foley and just like the rest of those Resistance morons."

He slowly walks in my direction and stares at me while unbuttoning his jacket. He slips it off and tosses it to the side. He rotates his shoulders and runs his hands through his greasy hair, pushing it out of his face. "The funny thing is, when I mentioned that you would definitely try and sneak onto the base, no one seemed to care. I was told it was all taken care of."

I barely have time to curl into myself before a kick lands forcefully in my side. It does little to lessen the blow of his boot to my ribs. I gasp and clench my teeth, trying not to call out despite the immense pain that spreads through my chest. He kicks me again, and I can't stop the cry of agony.

"You see," he says and circles me while I lie gasping on the ground. "The general is smarter than you. She knew you'd come here. She knew there were leaks. Traitors to the NAF. She *allowed* it to happen because she knew you'd all fall so neatly into her trap." He crouches next to me and leans in. "That aircraft out there? It's expendable. Just like most of the soldiers here. It's never been about the wasteland. It's always been bigger than that. Bigger than you." He grabs my thigh and squeezes; pain shoots like a red-hot poker all the way up my leg. "Do you want to know a secret?" He puts his mouth to my ear, and I push his face away. He laughs and grabs my head, holding me close. "Thanks to you and our own little spy, we know all about the tunnel to the warehouse in Rapid City. It's proven to be quite the little hideout for our second UCAV." He puts his finger to his lips and gently shushes me.

"You son of a bitch."

Simon laughs. "You and your friends are just an inconvenient distraction." He shoves my head away from him. "Still, I couldn't resist the opportunity to kill you, so I volunteered to stay."

"Get it over with, then," I say, panting through painful breaths. "Even death is better than listening to you blabber on and on."

Simon laughs again. "The problem is, the general still wants you alive. Can you even imagine how demoralizing it'll be to the Resistance to watch their beloved fighter, Danielle Clark, publicly executed?" He looks at me, and I can see the blood smeared on his teeth. "She promised I could be the one to do it. But before I bring you in and collect another promotion, I'm going to kill every single person you love and make you watch." He pats my face and stands, then kicks me in the ribs so hard, I feel a crack.

I coil into myself and try to take shallow breaths, but it's become unbearable to even breathe.

Two soldiers rush into the hangar, and Simon briefly walks away from my broken body. "Find a radio that works. Call Rapid City and tell the general the threat here is neutralized, then locate the rest of the insurgents and bring them to me."

Misdirection. I hear Kate's voice in my head saying the word over and over. Her mother has played us from the beginning, and she's playing us now. How stupid could we be to do this again and again? Even worse, this time it's Kate who's heading straight into the trap.

The general made two mistakes, though. The first was relying on Simon. The second was not counting on my dedication to her daughter.

I press hard into my ribs. My breath quickens, and I grit my teeth, anger and adrenaline pumping through my veins. I absolutely refuse to let this be the way I die. With renewed purpose, I pull myself up and ignore the way my chest feels like it's going to cave in and the fire coursing through my leg. "Misdirection."

"What?" Simon asks, turning just as the two soldiers are dropped the moment they step out of the hangar.

Mike.

Simon ducks on instinct, and I charge at him with a primal yell and slam into him, taking us both to the ground. He tries to throw me off, but I pin him to the ground and fumble for my knife. He shoves his finger into the wound on my leg and flips us.

He sits on my chest, and for a single moment, I think I may die from the weight on my broken ribs. He punches, and I barely manage to block the blow before swinging my hands up to grab the sides of his face and press my thumbs into his eyes.

He latches on to my wrists, and I shove him off and reverse our positions, pinning him once more. This time, I slam my fist into his face, making his head bounce off the cement, and his body goes limp. He lies motionless as I wait, ready to strike again. When he doesn't move, I climb off and press my hand to my ribs, taking deep, agonizing breaths.

I look around for my discarded chest rig. Seeing it just a meter or so away, I limp over and snag it and the detonator from the ground. My head pounds, and my entire body throbs. I can't single out where all the pain is radiating from, but I grit my teeth and slowly make my way back to Simon.

I flip the vest so the back is now in the front and slip it over his arms. Somehow, I manage to get to my knees and get it around his body. With shaking hands, I secure it closed, the explosives strapped to his back.

He groans and shifts, then blinks into focus while I lean over him, tightening the vest. He makes a move like he's going to swing but pauses to look down at the rig. "What are you doing?"

I see the second it registers for him.

He panics and scoots away just as I manage to clip the last of the latches and flip the switch that's now located between his shoulder blades. He pushes me away and starts grabbing at the vest, looking for a way out.

"I wouldn't flail too much," I tell him as I unsteadily get back on my feet.

He stops, raising his hands in the air and looking at me with wide eyes. "You said—"

"I lied." I click my tongue disapprovingly. "You should know better than to think I *wouldn't* strap myself to a live bomb."

His terrified expression shifts to anger, and he slowly climbs to his feet, taking a step toward me. "You fucking bitch."

I hold up the detonator and wag my finger. "Ah, ah, ah. I didn't lie about blowing us both if I have to."

He stops again, his breathing heavy, and he tries to look behind him, no doubt to figure out a way out of the vest. As amusing as it is to watch him struggle, I don't have time to toy with him.

Limping closer, I land a punch on his cheek. "That's for Rhiannon." I knock him off balance. Another hit. "That's for threatening my family." The next swing throws him completely to the ground, unmoving and bleeding. I stand over him, holding my right hand to my chest and savoring the feeling of my undoubtedly broken knuckles. "And that," I practically spit, "is for taking my Jeep, you dick."

After falling to the ground, I attempt to flex my busted hand and stare at him for a moment, exhausted. My head is swimming, and I'm struggling to keep from lying down and closing my eyes. I can hear Mike firing and people yelling in the distance.

The fight still rages.

I have to get a message to Rodrigues. We have to warn Rapid City.

I make a move to stand but fall back again, every inch of my body protesting. Just when I think there's no chance I'm going to be able to walk out of here, I see Lucas sprinting toward me, his hair falling out of the bun atop his head.

He drops to his knees and grabs my face, looking me over with worried eyes. My head is still spinning.

"Easy," I hiss. "I told you not to come back."

"I never leave a man behind," he repeats. He attempts to pull me up, but I push him away.

"Get to the radio. The general isn't here. She's in Rapid City with a second UCAV. It's in the warehouse. Rodrigues needs to go there, *now*." I allow Lucas to help me to my feet, and I take the detonator to the explosives he planted along the drone. "Have Darby raise Chi-Chi along the fence line when you're all far enough away, then I'll blow the place."

"I never leave a man behind," he says, determined.

I want to yell at him. I want to scream that if he doesn't go now, there's going to be worse problems than just losing the Badlands. I want to tell him that if he stays and we're caught, we're as good as dead anyway, but his eyes are glistening, and his lower lip quivers. Grabbing him by the back of the neck, I pull him close, my heart shattering.

"I understand now, Lucas. I understand why Dad did what he did. It wasn't just to protect us. He did it to give us a chance to live." My eyes are blurry, and there's a lump in my throat, but my mind has never been clearer. I have never been more focused on what needs to be done. "He sacrificed himself to save the people he loved. I get it, Lucas. I really *get* it." He starts to cry, and I smile, pressing my forehead to his. "Major Maelstrom loved his country, but it paled in comparison to the love he had for his family."

His head shakes and he squeezes his eyes shut.

A tear rolls down my cheek, and I press my lips against his forehead and step away. "Go save our family and tell Kate..." My words get caught. "Tell Kate that I'm sorry I couldn't keep my promise."

Lucas pulls me in for a tight hug, and I squeeze him back as tight as I am able.

"I love you," I whisper and step out of his embrace. He stares at me for a moment longer, his brows knit together in a thoughtful sort of way. Then, he sprints out of the hangar.

Glancing down at Simon still unconscious on the ground, I consider kicking him awake, but instead, I leave him there and slowly head to the runway. I stumble and barely manage to keep myself upright. My body feels heavy.

Once I'm there, I fall to my knees and look outward. The sun has completely risen above the horizon, and I stare at the orange and pink glow, soaking in its beauty. The cold air feels refreshing on my hot, sweat-coated skin.

I'm surprisingly calm. Calmer than I've been in a long, long time. My mind is finally clear. I picture my friends, my family, all of us sitting around a large table in front of a fire in Rhiannon's tavern.

We're laughing. We're happy. We're together. Somehow, I know they'll be okay, and it makes my heart feel a little lighter.

I close my eyes and think of Kate. Of the kisses that steal the breath straight from my lungs. Of her soft skin and the way her body arches under my fingers. I think of the way her hair smells of lavender and the musical sound of her laugh. How the safest I've ever felt was when I was in her arms.

I hope that that's what the afterlife feels like, the warm embrace of the woman I love.

A slow smile spreads across my face as I slowly open my eyes.

Chi-Chi hovers just beyond the perimeter. I place my thumbs on both detonators, ready for whatever comes next.

There's an unmistakable hum from my left, and I don't even have to look to know it's my Jeep. The sound of her motor purring gets closer and closer, breaking my trance. And just like that, it's so clear to me that despite what everyone keeps saying, I'm not my father. As much as I'd love to end this war, to bring about a better country, I want to be alive to see it. I want to grow old with Kate and slow dance in the home we build together. I want to be with my friends and family and squeeze every drop out of this life that I possibly can.

I hear shouting as I'm yanked upward, far too rough for my broken body, and pulled into the back of my Jeep. As we speed away, I press down on both detonators, and everything goes black.

CHAPTER FIFTEEN: THE SURRENDER

KATE

We drive slowly since Rapid City isn't that far, even with the wide swing detour. Every second that passes feels like an eternity, and I have a sinking feeling that I'm headed into the lion's den.

With all the cities I've entered before, I've never been this nervous, but I've also never been on this side of the fight. With the Resistance instead of against them. It feels different but somehow the same as my mind is pulled in many different directions. I swallow nervously, thinking about how I'm doing this without Dani by my side. I keep wondering if she's reached Ellsworth and if she's okay.

Most of the fighters who came with us flank our buggy, not unlike how the NAF travel, with the officer's car in the middle. This must have been influenced by Foley. Everyone else is either getting into position to attack the city from different angles or closing in on the outposts between here and Ellsworth. We've spread ourselves pretty thin, something the NAF are probably hoping for. With their limited weapons, I wonder if Thatcher and Foley banked on Rodrigues and I being able to convince my father to give up his helicopter.

Either way, it worked, and without Rodrigues in the picture, our chances of winning this would be mighty low.

My jaw tightens when I recall my dad pleading with me not to let anyone kill my mother. I'm both relieved and terrified that she's in Ellsworth and not here, but I'm still not convinced William, or even Dani, will heed Thatcher's orders to extract her alive. It startles me to hope that they are able to. For all the horrible things my mother is, she's still my mother, and the thought of her not making it chokes me.

"Alpha, Beta, and Charlie in position and standing by for signal, over." Dani's voice on the other end of Thatcher's radio makes my heart rate spike. I can picture her, crouched in the rough terrain, anxious and ready to move in.

"Echo standing by and waiting to fly. Over." Rodrigues responds next. The excitement in her voice is palpable.

Thatcher brings the radio to her lips. "Foxtrot moving into position, over."

She motions for us to push up, and my nerves take a back seat to caution as we keep going forward. We're too far away for our weapons, but that doesn't stop me from holding the handle of the dagger strapped to my hip like I'm expecting an ambush.

"You sure you don't want one of the launchers?" Jack asks while Bruce accelerates the NAF buggy.

"I prefer to use my fists." Bruce smiles almost childishly.

Jack grins. "Me too, but I still love blowing shit up."

"You'll have your chance," Thatcher says and looks out the window and into the sky. "Another drone inbound. That makes three."

Jack, Anthony, and I all try to get a look at the small surveillance drone that whizzes overhead. Each one makes me more and more uneasy.

"Want me to take it out?" Jack asks.

"Save your ammo," Thatcher instructs. No one bothers telling Jack a grenade launcher against a drone would be overkill even if he *did* manage to hit the small moving target.

Sighing deeply, Jack sits back. "They have to know we're coming."

"Of course they do," Thatcher responds easily.

"You aren't worried?" he asks.

The car starts to slow as Thatcher leans forward to look out the windshield. "They're just trying to figure us out. I'd be more concerned if they were dropping payloads on us."

"There's still plenty of time for that," I mutter.

The buggy stops at the edge of a nearby hill. A dozen or so Resistance fighters are already there and a row of five NAF soldiers sitting on the ground, their hands bound behind them. Anthony sits between me and Jack in the back seat and runs his palms along the tops of his legs, his posture stiff. I wonder if he's having an episode.

These soldiers were clearly guards who were ambushed by the Resistance fighters who appeared to have snuck in on them by horseback. The scene is reminiscent of when we were held prisoner in White River. It's a wonder I'm not also triggered.

Jack must notice the same thing because he leans across Anthony and grins at me. "Don't go soft on me now, Blondie."

"Signal received, proceeding with caution. Stand by for green light, over." Dani's voice cuts through the radio and pulls my attention away from Jack.

"Turn off the headlights," Thatcher tells Bruce.

There's enough light in the sky and a large campfire, so we can all see, and we file out of the cars. I adjust Dani's bulletproof vest under my clothes and try not to think of the kind of vest she's wearing. Instead, I focus on a young woman with dark hair who approaches us.

"Kimi, how are we looking?" Thatcher asks and grips her forearm in greeting.

"It's good you're here. Your intel was good. They're already lined up," she says and points in the direction of the city. She hands Thatcher a pair of binoculars and stands with her hands on her hips.

"What's your status? Over." Dani's voice says over the radio.

"Bravo in position, over," William responds.

"Charlie in position, over," Mike's voice cuts through next.

"Standby for Alpha, over," Dani says.

Thatcher continues to stare at the perimeter of Rapid City. My fingers itch to take the radio strapped to her belt to check in and tell them to be safe. To remind Dani of her promise.

"They haven't rolled out anything we weren't prepared for," Thatcher says and hands the binoculars back to Kimi. "Which means that so far, E. J. Allen has proved to be right."

The soldiers start pulling large crates from the back of the two trucks that pull up, revealing two RPGs and four rockets. "Is this going to be enough?" Jack asks and looks at the weapons with wonderment.

"It's going to have to be. So don't miss," Thatcher tells Kimi pointedly.

Even in the low light, I can see the confident half-smile Kimi gives. "I never miss."

Bruce appears from behind us holding two black backpacks. He puts one over his large shoulders, securing it around his midsection. I can tell by the tools sticking out of the top that it's a heavy tactical breach kit. It looks like there's a multipry, a bolt cutter, mini battering ram, and a decent-looking ax.

Thatcher takes the other bag. "With all the attention on the front gates, we're going to slip in right over there."

I see nothing but a high perimeter and a lack of guards along the wall. "Where are the guards?"

"Stacked in the front, back, and by the warehouse and tunnels," she says.

The tunnels. I remember how hot and crowded they were as we escaped the city just a few months ago. It would be nice to be able to use it now. We could go through the warehouse and into the middle of town, but since Hugo gave up that intel, underground is no longer an option. "Do we know if they're hiding anything in the tunnels or the warehouse?"

"My guess is yes. I just don't know what." She holds out the backpack. "This is an explosive breach kit. We're going to need it to blow a hole along that wall."

I take the bag and try to keep it away from my body, simultaneously nervous and perplexed at how easily Dani straps explosives to herself.

"I'll take it," Anthony says, and with a nervous smile, he carefully puts it on, clipping the bag in front to secure it. Everything he's dealt with since our last assignment doesn't make this easy for him. I'm sure his demons will only multiply after this fight.

"What's the matter?" Kimi asks me, the slight smile still on her lips. "Don't like things that go boom?"

"That's Dani's department," I say. "I prefer up close and personal." I lift the knife from its sheath just slightly.

Kimi eyes the blade, her smile widening. "Welcome to the team, gray coat."

A radio from another fighter buzzes to life, and all the teams closing in on the outposts report they are in position. There's gunfire somewhere below, and we know that despite not being given the order to charge, the fight has already begun.

"Our time's up," Thatcher says and takes a deep breath.

"I'm surprised it took them this long," Kimi says, walking to the horses and holding out her hands to make sure they don't react to the new noises.

"The drone isn't here." Dani's voice cuts through, bringing everyone's attention to Thatcher, who pulls the radio from her belt to hear it better.

"What do you mean it's not there?" William's voice crackles.

"I mean, the hangar is empty." Dani sounds stressed, slightly panicked, even. My stomach drops.

"Can you check the other hangars?" William says, coming across equally anxious.

"Yeah, if you want to wander around the base for another twenty or thirty minutes," Dani says, clearly irritated.

Thatcher shoves the radio back into her belt, and the rest of the conversation is muffled as she starts giving orders. "We need to get in position now. No time to waste. Foxtrot, grab the horses. They're the quietest and safest way to get down this hill to the perimeter. Kimi, get ready to blast those tanks once we've blown the entrance."

It's been a while since I've been on a horse, so I watch hesitantly as Thatcher, Bruce, Jack, and Anthony are all led to specific ones.

Kimi walks a beautiful white and brown mare in my direction and pats her neck. "This is Yanaba. She will take good care of you."

She helps me up. Once I'm in the saddle with the reins, confidence flows through me.

"Get your radio in the protective box once I give the command, and initiate the attack on the outposts," Thatcher tells Kimi, circling her atop a black stallion. "Then, blow a hole in the front gates to let our troops in. I'll disable their equipment from within."

"Yes, ma'am," she replies right as Thatcher urges her horse in the opposite direction. She looks at me and stands tall. "Fight on, Songbird." Before I can ask how she knows my name, she smacks Yanaba on the behind, and the pinto horse races after the rest of the group.

I pull Dani's maroon scarf over my face, covering everything but my eyes and push Yanaba to go faster. For a few precious moments, I'm flying. I slip away from my worries and fears. I allow myself to focus on nothing but the feel of the winter air that whips around my face and the weightless feeling of being carried forward on my steed.

The moment is lost when I spot a large drone circling overhead a fair distance away. This one is not like the others. This is a combat drone. If we don't hurry, it'll wipe us all out before we even have a chance of attacking.

Bruce is cutting a hole in the chain-link fence that surrounds the concrete wall before I can fully dismount. Once he's finished, Anthony slides through the opening and drops the backpack on the ground. With shaking hands, he quickly rummages inside until he finds what he wants.

Nervously, I watch while Anthony sets up the devices, hoping he'll be able to keep it together long enough to get us through the wall and hating myself for wishing it.

"Get behind those rocks," Jack instructs and grabs the back of my jacket to pull me with him.

"I can walk," I tell him and shove his hand off me.

He doesn't say a word, just pushes me behind him and crouches low behind the boulders, waiting.

Thatcher removes a small metal box strapped to the side of her horse and hooks it to Bruce's backpack, then takes the duffel secured behind the saddle. She calls out a command in a language I don't know and pats the horse's side. The stallion takes off, the others closely behind, and they appear to race back up the hill from where they just came.

Thatcher walks in our direction and pauses only when the walkie-talkie on her hip clicks on. "Forget the eyes in the sky, the drone is on the runway," Dani says.

Thatcher's eyes meet mine. "Anthony, let's wrap this up and get in there," she calls. With Bruce directly behind her, she crouches low to the ground beside us. After one final placement, Anthony takes the spool of wires and carefully starts to unwind them, backing up in our direction.

My heart pounds so viciously that I wonder if others can hear it.

Thatcher calmly locks her radio inside the box clipped to Bruce's bag and looks in the duffel, revealing a large device that I can only guess is the EMP.

"Do not leave me," Jack orders, and it takes me a second to realize he's talking to me. "I want you within arm's reach at all times." If this wasn't such a tense situation, I would have asked who put him in charge and told him to focus on himself.

Anthony tucks in behind the boulder and looks at us. "I'd cover your ears."

"Drop the EMP. We're going after the drone ourselves. Over and out." Dani's voice is the last thing I hear before pressing my palms to my ears as hard as I can and pinning myself against Jack's back, bracing for impact.

The explosion shakes the ground, and my ears ring even through my hands. Jack hauls me to my feet before I really have a chance to find my balance. We rush to the newly blasted wall just as rockets are fired from the hill, and a bomb drops near the front gates from the drone overhead.

Explosions erupt, and I can only assume that Kimi has hit her targets and hope the NAF didn't take out too many Resistance fighters. I pull my knives and grip them until my knuckles hurt. I stick close to Jack while we wait for Bruce to make sure the coast is clear. When he gives the signal, we file through the damaged perimeter.

In theory, the plan is simple: drive away hostile forces and reinstate the original government by putting Thatcher back in her office and back in charge.

In reality, it's utter chaos.

I resecure the scarf around my face as we follow Thatcher through the edge of the city and try to stay undetected. Some buildings lie in broken piles along the streets from the previous drone attack, mounds of brick and wood, with no indication anyone desires to rebuild them. A few civilians and soldiers race through the streets. They're all running in opposite directions. Some are screaming, and others are just seemingly trying desperately to find some sort of cover.

Alarms blast through the city as if the guards were just waiting for the first shot to be fired. It takes me back to when the same deafening alarm rang through the city to warn us about the previous drone attack. My skin prickles at the memory of it all.

Bruce and Thatcher dive behind a building, and Bruce opens fire down an alley. Jack does the same on the opposite side of the wall, Anthony and I close behind him.

So much for lying low.

I try to look around Jack's muscular frame, but he pushes me back, slamming me hard into the brick. I yell at him, but I doubt he can hear me over the sirens. Another explosion shakes the ground, and I reach across Anthony, pinning him against the building to steady him.

The familiar thumping and rumble of a tank gets louder. I can't see it, but I know it's getting closer to the front gates. I look at Anthony and realize that he's not doing well. He clutches the bag to his chest and sits with his back to the wall. His eyes are tightly shut like he's pretending none of this is happening.

"Anthony," I yell. "Anthony, give me the bag!" When he doesn't budge, I try to pry it from his arms. He grips it tighter. "Anthony," I try again. He opens his eyes, wide and fearful. "Let me have the bag."

"We've gotta move," Jack calls when the slow-moving tank has passed. He reloads his shotgun and peeks around the corner.

I pull on the backpack again, and this time, Anthony releases it. His expression morphs from fear to shame. "It's okay," I tell him, even though I'm not sure he can hear me. I strap the bag to my back, pretending that the explosives inside won't blow me into a million little pieces. "Breathe," I tell him and sling my arm through his to help him move.

We press forward to the center of town, and Thatcher, still holding the large EMP, signals something to Bruce. He seems to understand, and rifle in hand, makes himself a human shield, ensuring Thatcher gets farther into the middle of the street.

A few NAF soldiers rush in our direction, and I grip my knives while shielding Anthony, still shell-shocked, behind me. I bring back one of the blades, ready to let it fly when Jack spins and fires off two blasts, knocking both soldiers off their feet.

Another rounds the corner of the building just past me, his eyes locked on Jack. I have just enough time to crouch and whip my arm forward, releasing the blade. It hits the soldier in the lower back and drops him.

Jack aims his shotgun at the downed soldier.

"Stop," I yell and rush over. Crouching, I pull my knife from the man's back. He cries out and then goes limp and silent. I wipe the blade on his pants. "Save your bullets," I remind Jack.

The alarm stops without warning, and the slow rumble of the tank quiets. The hair on my arms stands on end, and the air feels electric. About fifty meters away, something drops out of the sky. A surveillance drone. It lands with a thud and shatters.

Thatcher activated the EMP.

Almost instantly, the silence is pierced by screams and gunfire.

Thatcher and Bruce rush back in our direction. "We need to start clearing the buildings. Kimi's team will secure the front of the city. You two start here and go around the perimeter," Thatcher orders and checks her rifle. "Anthony, Bruce, you're with me."

I know that they're headed to the jail to free any Resistance fighters who were tossed in there when the city fell to the NAF. I check Anthony's expression again. "I don't think he's up for it."

Thatcher looks at him and then back at me, seemingly noticing I'm wearing the backpack now. Her expression is torn, like she knows what she needs to do but isn't sure she can do it.

"I'll go with you instead," I offer.

"Do you know how to mount a breaching charge? Or how to use a premade strip charge?" I open my mouth to tell her that I could probably figure it out, but she silences me with a wave of her hand. "Give me the bag."

She doesn't look angry or even disappointed, but somehow, handing the bag over feels a bit embarrassing, like I've singlehandedly ruined her plan to take back the city. She slips the straps over her shoulders and motions for Bruce to turn. She takes the radio from the box. "This is Foxtrot. We need an extraction on the breached far wall. One of our own, do you copy? Over."

"Copy that, Foxtrot, on our way. Over." It sounds a lot like Kimi, but through the slight static, it's hard to tell.

The siren wails again, and I see more than hear Thatcher curse as her hands go to her ears. "We should take out that hand-crank siren," she calls to no one in particular. "Wait for the extraction team and then get to the buildings."

I don't even have a chance to respond because the moment she's finished yelling, she and Bruce sprint back to the center of town.

"I can do it," Anthony calls. He sounds determined, but he looks absolutely petrified. "Please, I can do it."

He's so young, and he's already dealt with so much. "We need to get you someplace safe," I tell him. His expression is equal parts disappointed and relieved. "You've done great, but we need to get you out of here."

"On your feet," Jack shouts and pulls Anthony by his jacket.

There's movement from our left, so I jump in front of Anthony, knives in hand and ready to protect him. It's three Resistance fighters, rifles pressed to their chests and rushing toward us.

"Is this the extraction?" the tall woman in front asks, motioning at Anthony, who is still protesting that he can help. She doesn't wait for a response and instead tries to go around me.

I grab her arm, stopping her. She tenses and makes it a point to look at my hand wrapped around her bicep and then back to me. "Go easy on him," I shout over the siren.

Her eyes don't leave mine for a beat, and then she nods like she understands. Reluctantly, I let go of her arm, and she ducks so she's face level with Anthony. I can't hear what she says to him, but I'm surprised when he stops protesting and moves to walk with her.

"I'm sorry," he shouts.

The leader motions for the other two to round up, and they form a kind of circle around him. "If you find any civilians, send them this way. We'll get them up the hill," she yells to both me and Jack.

"Affirmative," I tell her and watch them disappear out of the breached hole. I'm disappointed in myself for bringing Anthony, but I don't have time to dwell on it now.

"Let's move," Jack calls.

I spare one final look at Anthony's retreating form before heading straight for the first building to clear. It seems abandoned, but we aren't taking any risks. Carefully, we stand on either side of the door with Jack nearest the handle. I ready myself to be the one to clear first. He uses his free hand to do a soft check. The door is unlocked.

His eyes meet mine, and he swings the door open. I step in with Jack close behind. He takes the left, and I take the right, and we quickly clear the makeshift office building. We take our time around corners, through doors, and at different points up the stairs and through hallways. It's completely empty.

We move to the second building. It's filled with living quarters, and we find a family cowering in the corner of a bedroom with their hands raised, begging for their lives. Jack points to the Resistance tattoo on the side of his neck, and they relax enough to hurry out of the dwelling and in the direction we point.

The third building is barely standing. Half of it is rubble that was clearly bombed in the last attack and never repaired. I pull Jack close. "I have a bad feeling about this one."

He glances at the front door that is somehow still on its hinges. With the siren continuing to blare, my stress level and our communication are both strained. Luckily, we've adapted to understanding each other silently, so I take a turn opening the door.

When Jack steps in, he steps right back out, yelling. I swing my gun to his corner of the room and open fire, taking out two soldiers who were crouched behind an overturned table. Jack recovers quickly, yelling out a truly impressive string of curse words. We finish clearing what's left of the bottom level once he's gathered himself. The staircase upward is caved in, and after determining there's no one left, Jack places his shotgun on the torn-up sofa and starts to lift his shirt.

He doesn't even get his shirt pulled up before there's a blast near the front of the city, and the siren falls silent again. I pull on my ringing ears and rush to check on Jack. "Are you okay?"

"No, it fucking hurts," he snaps. He carefully lifts his shirt, wincing the entire time.

When the wound comes into view I grimace. I'm not a medic, but I know that if he doesn't get this at least wrapped up to stop the bleeding, he may be in trouble.

He inspects his side and turns to give me a better view. "Is the bullet still in there?"

"I don't think so," I tell him, peering closely. "Looks like a graze. As far as gunshot wounds go, I think you got kinda lucky."

"It took out half my side," he argues.

I roll my eyes. Now he's just being dramatic. "Come on, we have to get you wrapped up to stop that bleeding."

"I think my rib is broken." He carefully lowers his shirt and grabs his gun. He walks gingerly behind me, limping like he broke his leg.

"Maybe we can find something in the next building," I tell him and check the area before moving in that direction.

"The medical one is over there," he says, pointing to the next row over, closer to the heaviest fighting.

I watch a few NAF soldiers stationed outside several buildings and keeping civilians from leaving. There doesn't seem to be a Resistance presence there yet.

"Can you shoot?" I ask.

He gives me another look and pumps his shotgun.

We carefully make our way to the medical building, sticking close to cover. There are a few NAF soldiers leaving with bags over their shoulders. We wait to see if anyone else comes out, but after what feels like an eternity and no one does, I motion for Jack to keep going.

We're even more careful entering, knowing there's a good possibility there are still more troops inside. Once the first level is clear, I take a good look around. The place is absolutely ransacked.

The building shakes with an explosion, and debris falls from the upper level. The entire place groans under the weight of the blast. "If they keep lobbing grenades, this building is coming down," Jack says.

Through the sporadic booms, I barely hear someone calling for help. I stand perfectly still and listen. The calls are so muffled that I close my eyes to try to discern a direction. I hear it again and open my eyes. Jack and I exchange a look. "You hear that, right?"

The call comes again, and both of our gazes shoot to the ceiling. "It came from upstairs," he states and carefully approaches the bottom of the staircase.

"Let me go first," I say quietly. He pretends like he doesn't hear me and slowly walks up the stairs, as close to the wall as he can be without actually being pressed up against it.

The building has five stories, so it takes us a lot longer to clear each floor than I would like, considering Jack is dripping blood everywhere, and the grenades just won't stop coming.

Each level appears less pillaged than the one before, and the cries for help grow louder the higher we ascend. It isn't until we've reached the top that we see them. Part of the roof has collapsed, and a support beam has blocked people inside one of the rooms.

"We have to get them out," I say, rushing to the beam. "We're with the Resistance. We're going to get you out of there." I push as hard as I can, but it doesn't budge. Pulling the scarf down around my neck, I take in a deep breath, enjoying the cold air that cools my face.

"Please hurry," a woman yells. "The roof collapsed, and there are children in here!"

Jack tries to lift the beam but stops almost as quickly as he starts with a loud groan.

"Jack, stop."

"You think you can lift that on your own?" he fires back, panting and pressing his hand to his side.

"We need to get you patched up," I tell him and look around, noticing for the first time that this must be where the doctors and their families live. There are no medical supplies nearby, just open doors leading to a hallway full of empty apartments.

"There are supplies on the lower levels," the woman says.

I don't tell her most of the place has been ransacked. "I'll go look," I tell Jack. "You wait here."

He's about to argue, but when he lifts his hand and sees the blood, he relents and leans against the wall for support. His face is noticeably flushed, and he looks terrible.

"Don't move," a voice shouts from behind us near the stairwell.

Jack and I draw our guns. There are three NAF soldiers staring at us from down the narrow hallway at the top of the stairs.

"Drop your weapons," the large man in front orders.

"Like hell," Jack practically spits back at him.

I push the barrel of his shotgun down, keeping him from starting a shoot-out. Carefully, I place my pistol and my knives on the ground in front of me. Slowly, I stand with my hands in front of me where they can see them.

"You too," they direct Jack.

"Jack, just do it," I urge him.

"No fucking way."

"They'll open fire, and there are kids in the room behind us," I remind him. "Just do it."

He curses under his breath and finally puts his shotgun on the ground.

"On your knees and hands behind your head," the same soldier orders. I don't recognize the two in front, and the one behind them has a gaiter covering their face.

"There are kids trapped in that room," I tell them. "At least get them out before this building collapses."

The large one scoffs. "We don't take orders from defectors."

My body tenses. I should've re-covered my face.

The smaller soldier in the front sneers. "Katelyn Turner. What was the reward for bringing her in alive?" he asks the other two.

When they exchange smiles, I pull the knife hidden inside my boot and let it fly, hitting the large one in the chest.

Jack and I both dive for our guns, but by the time we raise them to shoot, the third soldier wearing the gaiter has smacked the smaller soldier in the back of the head with the butt of their rifle, dropping him almost immediately.

Jack braces to take a shot just as the third soldier pulls down the face covering. My heart skips when I recognize familiar brown eyes staring back at me.

Ryan.

"Jack, wait," I call desperately and shove his gun to the side, preventing him from firing a shot.

Ryan aims his rifle at Jack, but I stand between them, making it so they would have to shoot through me to get to the other. I hold my hands out in either direction like I'm taming wild animals. "Ryan, please," I beg.

He stares at Jack for a moment, then looks at me, his expression softening. Slowly, he lowers his rifle.

"Jack," I say, looking back at him.

The building makes a creaking sound, and for a brief moment, I'm certain that it's going to collapse around us. Finally lowering his shotgun, Jack hurries back to the beam blocking the family inside, ignoring the need to patch himself up.

Without a word, I follow him to help. After one failed attempt, then another, Ryan appears next to me. "On three," he instructs without looking at either Jack or me. "One, two, three."

All of us grunt as we finally manage to get the beam to budge just enough that the people inside are able to open the door and slip through.

"Thank you," the woman says and bows her head in gratitude.

"Just go," Jack urges, clearly struggling to hold the beam away.

The woman and her two small children hurry down the hall, and we let go, the heavy support crashing back down.

"I'm going to look for supplies," Jack says to me, hand pressed against his side, his breathing labored. "I'll be close by." He finishes off the last statement with a glare in Ryan's direction; it's a clear warning. I can't decide if I want to snap at him for his sudden concern for my well-being or tell him to sit and save his energy. This is a side of Jack that I thought was only reserved for Dani.

Ryan keeps his eyes trained on me while Jack enters the apartment across the hall, leaving the door wide open. "Are you hurt?" His tone is soft and caring.

I want to throw my arms around his neck and hug my lost friend, but we're not on the same side anymore. We aren't partners, and I'm not sure we're even still friends. I take a step back instead.

"No, I'm fine." I glance at where Jack is tossing things out of a drawer with one hand, his other pressed to his side. "Why are you in Rapid City?"

My question seems to snap Ryan back to business. His eyes go wide as if just realizing he'd forgotten we're enemies now. "You shouldn't be here. If the general sees you—"

"Sees me? She's..." I stop, recognizing something unsettling in Ryan's frantic words. "*Sees* me? What do you mean?"

"I mean, if she knows you're here or if *anyone* knows you're here and brings you to her—"

"But she's in Ellsworth."

"She's not in Ellsworth. She's *here*, Kate." He gives me a look. The same one he used to give me when we'd go over tactics, and he disagreed with my assessments. "She arrived yesterday to personally oversee the drone test."

My stomach bottoms out. "What drone test?"

"The UCAV," he says slowly, like that would make me understand anything coming out of his mouth.

"The one at Ellsworth?"

He frowns. "What? No, that's out of commission. They lost the motor." His expression shifts. "You didn't know she was here?"

"No. Foley said—"

"General Foley?" His brows knit in confusion. "Why would General Foley be telling you anything?"

"Clearly, neither of us knows anything." I walk back to where I put my knives and scoop them up, more anxious now than ever to get back to my assignment.

"Is General Foley leaking information to the Resistance?" Ryan asks.

I don't answer.

"Kate." He follows me and reaches to take my arm.

Before I can blink, Jack is there shoving Ryan back. "Don't touch her," he warns, flexing beneath this jacket.

"I'm trying to warn her. To warn you both," Ryan says desperately but doesn't attempt to move any closer.

"It's okay," I tell Jack and pat his shoulder, not at all used to this new display of protectiveness and unsure of how to calm him down. The building groans again, and I know we are just wasting time.

Jack stares at Ryan. "Look," Ryan starts again, sounding desperate, "your mom switched everything up at the last minute. She dismissed most of her confidants and reassigned personnel, one of them being General Foley. Only a select few were privy to the details, Simon included."

My eyes fall to the new rank on Ryan's uniform, and for some reason, it feels like a betrayal. "Looks like you got that promotion after all."

He scoffs. "I didn't have much of a choice." The building sways when a strong blast goes off nearby. "It isn't safe for you to be here."

"No shit." I say, even though I know it's petty.

He reaches inside his satchel and tosses Jack a sealed roll of sterilized bandage. "We need to move."

I stare at Ryan for a beat and then help Jack wrap the bandage tightly around his side.

"Where's the UCAV now?" I ask Ryan once Jack is patched up. He hesitates, and I step into his personal space. "Where is it?" I ask again, leaving no room for him to misinterpret my anger.

He straightens his shoulders and doesn't take his eyes off mine. I step closer and square up to him. I see the exact moment his eyes shift, and he chooses me over the NAF. "The warehouse outside the gates."

"And the general?" I press.

He clenches his jaw. "Probably trying to get the UCAV into the sky."

Jack and I share a look. "The tunnels," I say. He nods and readies his shotgun.

With the radios down and no communication available, there's no one to tell about this. Looks like I'm going after my mother myself.

Ryan grabs my arm and drops it when Jack takes a step closer. "Kate, it's suicide. The tunnels are heavily guarded. Maybe even more than the front gates."

"He's lying," Jack says, lifting his chin.

"No. He's not." I try to recall everything I can about how to get into the tunnel that leads out of the city. It was in a building near the Alex Johnson Hotel. From what I remember, the back entrance was barricaded, so the only way in was through the single front entrance and then down to the tunnel systems. The two of us alone wouldn't be able to force our way through. "How many grenades do you have?" I ask Jack.

"Two."

"That'll have to do." I walk to the stairwell and retrieve my knife from the dead body. I wipe it off on the soldier's coat. I snag their rifles and sidearms, giving one of each to Jack.

"I'll create a diversion so you can get there," Ryan offers, following us down the narrow stairs. "This building is a hot spot for both sides."

"Ryan—" I start to protest, but I'm cut short as he shoots past me on the stairs and interrupts.

"Let's go," he commands.

Outside, a firefight is under way, and it looks as though the NAF is losing. If Ryan walks out there in his uniform, they'll kill him. My eyes meet his. Clearly thinking the same as me, he hands me his guns and takes off his uniform jacket. "When I get their attention, you slip out the side window and make a run for it."

"Ryan," I say desperately. He's planning on surrendering without knowing whether the Resistance will capture or kill him. I want to tell him not to do this. To not risk his life for me, but the look in his eyes is enough for me to know that he's determined. "Know you have served your land well."

His resolve slips only slightly. Without another word, he slowly walks out of the building, his jacket raised high above him in surrender. "We surrender!" He looks to the several NAF soldiers crouched behind cover nearby, clearly pinned. "It's not worth dying for," he tells them. "We surrender."

There appears to be a protest from the soldiers, and everyone starts yelling. Ryan gets on his knees, his hands still high in the air. I don't have time to see what happens after that because Jack yanks me to the window and all but pushes me out, away from the diversion.

I secure the scarf around my face once again before we weave through the chaos, bypassing all the buildings that Jack and I are supposed to be clearing. Glancing behind, I know I won't see Ryan, but I look anyway, desperately hoping he is okay. I squint through the smoke of a burning building, my throat tight, and do my best to push aside my sadness and focus on getting to the tunnels.

Despite the extra firepower, we save our bullets, dodging any kind of confrontation as best we can. Most of the action seems to be along the perimeter, the NAF doing what they can to keep anyone from entering or leaving. Dozens of civilians have seemingly decided to join the Resistance, using what they can as weapons and choosing to fight for their city. Without their tanks or drones, the NAF are struggling to stay in control, which means we have a chance.

When we close in on the building that houses the tunnel to the warehouse, we spot a standoff between a line of NAF soldiers and Resistance fighters hunkered behind anything they can find. There are, surprisingly, more Resistance fighters than I expected, but none of them have the firepower to penetrate the NAF's line of defense.

Crouching low behind a large pile of rubble, I try to assess the situation. A long line of NAF soldiers are taking cover behind a concrete barrier that wraps around the entire building. The

Resistance fighters across from them are firing desperately, but their bullets aren't doing much against the wall.

"Now what?" Jack asks.

"We throw the grenades behind the line, and in the confusion, we run like hell to the front door and hope we can get inside." It's nothing fancy; it's not even smart, but it's the only plan we have right now.

"That's it?" Jack snorts. "You've definitely been spending too much time with Dani."

The comment sends a pang through my chest. I hope like hell she's okay. "We don't have a lot of options here." I hold out my hand expectantly and wiggle my fingers.

Understanding, he hands me one of the grenades.

"Want to see who can throw the farthest?" I offer a pathetic smile. We may die today. I need to find something to lighten that realization.

He blinks at me with a blank expression until he finally cracks a tiny smile. "What does the winner get?"

"Bragging rights?"

It seems to be enough of an incentive. He pulls the pin and squeezes the lever. "Count of three."

I pull my own pin and count. "One, two, three!" We hurl the grenades as far as we can. I hear him groan in pain with the movement. I'm not sure how much more fighting his body can handle.

Without waiting to see who the winner is, I crouch, covering my head with my arms and pushing my hands against my ears just as the grenades explode. Once the shock wave of the blast is over, I race forward, grabbing my knives and gripping them tightly. Jack regroups and is right on my heels.

We use the disorder to our advantage and sprint to the front of the building. Resistance fighters do the same, and in the blink of an eye, instinct takes over. This is what I specialized in, close combat. My body knows what to do before my mind can catch up, and within seconds, I'm dancing. Spinning and ducking, throwing my arms out to block attacks and cutting my way into the building.

Once we're in, Jack blasts the few soldiers in front of the entrance to the tunnels. A few Resistance soldiers manage to get inside, and a woman orders them to clear out the area. "Good thing you showed up. Our grenades were duds." She watches the fighters take off up the stairs and glances at us. "I only have a dozen fighters left. Any word on reinforcements?"

"No," I tell her and look at the rug that I know is covering the entrance to the tunnel system. "I need you to focus on clearing this building and keeping it under Resistance control." I hand her my spare guns.

She takes them and frowns questioningly. Not bothering to explain, I throw back the rug and pull on the door underneath as hard as I can, revealing the staircase.

"When reinforcements arrive, send them after us. Until then, don't let anyone down this tunnel. Got it?" I ask, wiping my blades on my pants and readying myself for more action.

"Who are you?" the woman asks.

"She's the one saving your asses. Do as she says and close the door behind us," Jack orders and pushes me out of the way to go descend the darkened staircase.

There's gunfire within the building that briefly pulls the woman's attention away from him. She turns back to me with a quick nod, appearing to make up her mind. "Fight like hell," she says.

I step down and follow Jack. She quickly closes the trapdoor and casts us into darkness.

"I don't suppose you have a flashlight, do you?" he asks when I run into his back.

"Clearly not," I say, irritated. I can feel him move forward, so I do the same, reaching to put my hand on the rough wall to steady my movements. It's unsettling to move in complete darkness. If one of us gets taken out because we slip and break an ankle, I will be severely pissed.

We continue downward until a faint glow comes into view. Relieved, I pick up my pace just a little until Jack stops me. "Get flat against the wall," he whispers.

I do as he says and stretch my neck out to listen. I can hear quiet voices talking from a distance. He pumps his shotgun, and it echoes down the hall, making me cringe. "Maybe we can be a little stealthier?" I whisper. "Let me go first."

He extends his arm and pushes me back. "Dani made me swear I'd keep you safe so that's what I'm going to do."

I'm so surprised by his confession that I don't push back. The silence that follows is both awkward and tense. "And here I thought it was because you finally started to like me."

"You wish, gray coat." The teasing in his voice doesn't go unnoticed.

Before I realize what's happening, Jack steps in front of me and blasts two soldiers as they come around the corner.

"Now everyone knows we're here," I mutter and push off the wall, ready for another fight.

"Good. I hate all this sneaking around." He reloads, and with time not on our side, we rush to the lit hallway and run as fast as we can. I'm able to move more quickly than Jack with his injury, but he refuses to let me lead, blocking my way the entire time.

There aren't many guards down here, at least not during the first part of our stretch, but once we reach the bunker at the end of the narrow tunnel, there are a dozen soldiers waiting.

Jack fires until he's empty. He holsters the shotgun and pulls his pistols. "I'll take care of them. Just get to the ladder. I'll be right behind you."

I want to argue, tell him to let me go and take care of himself. But he doesn't give me time to respond and charges like a madman, firing at everything that moves. I take a deep breath, hoping like hell he doesn't get himself killed, and tighten the grip on my knives. If memory serves me right, the next doorway will lead to another tunnel and to a ladder that'll take me to the warehouse.

After another breath, I take off. Miraculously, I make it through the door and down the next tunnel, only taking out two guards. I holster my knives and scale the ladder with Jack's gunfire echoing behind me. There is no cover at the surface, but I slow once I reach the top and carefully peek into the warehouse.

My stomach bottoms out when I see my mother standing near the UCAV, ordering it to get in the air, over the city. The others respond with something about blockers and shields and radio transmissions not working, but my mother yells back that she doesn't want to hear it.

A few soldiers push open the doors as the drone buzzes to life.

They're neglecting to guard the ladder, so I use it to my advantage and quietly crawl out. I crouch behind a pile of supply crates and scout the area as they continue to be preoccupied.

From my vantage point, I count ten soldiers, which is shockingly low, considering the general is within. Recalling what Ryan said about cutting ties with people, I realize that my mother has become so nearsighted, maybe even so desperate, that she's doing a poor job covering her own ass.

There's a makeshift control station with someone guiding the large, plane-like drone slowly out of the warehouse. The general hovers over his shoulder, pointing at one of the screens, ordering him to get it back up and running.

I glance at the slow-moving drone, remembering the intel about shielding technology.

My heart hammers in my chest. Part of me wants to wait for Jack, but the urgency in my mother's orders indicates there isn't time for waiting. I take my knives and take out the closest two soldiers before quietly working my way forward. Unfortunately, the third soldier I sneak up on puts up a fight. He flings me forward like a rag doll, and I land hard.

The knives clang to the ground, and all attention is on me.

I reach for one of my pistols, but it gets stuck in the holster. Pulling as hard as I can, I just manage to get it free when the third soldier points his gun at me.

I can't get away before he shoots, and the bullet hits me square in the chest.

Crying out, I realize I'm not dead thanks to Dani's vest, but he may have broken a rib. The adrenaline has me recovering quickly. I fire off a shot and down him. Unloading the rest of my magazine, I take out three more soldiers.

Finally, I'm able to grab my knives and hurl one at a soldier running right at me. He falls, dead before he hits the ground. I use the second blade to finish off another who is frantically reloading behind an officer's buggy. Now it's just me, my mother, and three tech specialists.

I aim my second pistol at my mom, who stands behind the control center desk, her own gun trained on me. The tech specialist at the control center holds perfectly still with his hands in the air. Two more are next to the UCAV that has stopped moving.

Out of breath but with steady hands, I stare at my mother, daring her to take the first shot.

She just stares back, disappointed, then lowers her pistol. "Oh, Katelyn, your combat skills have become so barbaric."

"This has always been my style. You just never approved." I glance at the gun still in her hand and motion for her to drop it. With a heavy sigh, she does. "I'm surprised you didn't pull the trigger."

"Do you really think I'd kill my own daughter?"

"A few months ago, I would've said no. Now…" I shrug, letting the implication float between us. "All of you, on your knees right here and hands where I can see them."

"Did the Resistance send *you* to do their dirty work?" My mother asks while not bothering to move on my command. The three specialists file together and drop to their knees. My mother rolls her eyes. "Lower your gun, Katelyn. Unless you plan on killing me?"

I grip the pistol tightly in both hands, my finger hovering over the trigger. "I don't want to kill you," I confess and hope she didn't catch the waiver in my voice. Where the hell is Jack and the reinforcements?

She watches me curiously. "You have something to say," she guesses.

Not knowing how many bullets I have left, I wonder if I should try to take out the control unit or save them just in case more soldiers come up the ladder instead of Jack. Slowly, I circle my mom and the three specialists so I'm facing the tunnel entrance and still have sight on the front of the warehouse.

"What are you planning on doing?" my mother asks, turning so she can face me. "Whatever it is, can you please just—"

"I want to know why," I say, overcome with an endless number of questions. "Jonathan and William were your friends." Her eye twitches in surprise. "Why would you try to kill them?"

"Why would they try to kill *me*?" she fires back, her expression of impatience turning to anger. She scoffs, her lip curling slightly. "You've been talking to William. He's warped your perspective on the truth."

"Then you tell me. Tell me *your* truth," I say angrily. "Because all I know is that you're killing a hell of a lot of people for some petty revenge against a couple of men who saw things differently than you."

"Is that what you think this is about? You are such a child," she says, her tone condescending.

"I know you're the reason Jonathan is dead. You're the reason all those people in the cities *you* bombed are dead. And if you—"

"I didn't kill Jonathan. He killed himself." Her words hit like a slap in the face. "But I suppose that didn't fit William's narrative. You want to know the truth? Jonathan blew *himself* up, and for what? This?" She points to me, her face scrunched and disgusted. "This so-called Resistance movement? I asked him to stand down. To surrender. But he didn't."

Her eyes are glassy, and it's the most genuine sadness I've seen out of her since Dad's funeral. A small piece of me wants to comfort her. The same piece that knows she'll always be my mother, regardless of her actions. A bigger piece knows better, and I stay silent.

"I loved Jonathan," she continues. "His friendship meant the world to me. I cried for weeks after his death." I almost catch a weakening in her voice, and for a moment, I consider exactly how devastated she would be to discover that Dad faked his death, in part, to escape her rule.

"And then, you hunted his kids," I supply with no sympathy.

"That had nothing to do with Jonathan," she says through clenched teeth. "Danielle Clark made her choice when she took on the NAF after his death. I asked William to reason with her and her brother, but he refused. The Clarks killed countless honorable soldiers. They were a threat to this country, and that had nothing to do with their father. I won't stand for it. I refuse to let Danielle and Lucas Clark embarrass this great military institution any longer. No more games. It ends today."

She makes a move to the control panel. Panicked, I pull the trigger and blast the console open. Sparks fly up in her face. She barely jumps, and when her eyes meet mine, she practically seethes.

I release a long breath through my nose. "I have to bring you in, Mom. You have to be held accountable for what you've done."

"Do you have any idea what you're doing? We have the opportunity to open the borders and reach out to other countries. Be the first to reestablish flight and regain trading and expansion under *our* terms. We have the chance to become the most powerful nation in the world."

I keep my gun on her. "Everyone should have a say in what happens. Not just you and the NAF."

"And go back to what? A democracy? A republic?" She laughs. "Look how well that's worked for us. It's a joke." She tries again for the control panel, and again, I shoot at it, stopping her.

"Mom, please. They'll kill you. Just let me bring you in." She stands perfectly still. "You've already lost. Don't make me shoot you."

"How did you end up being such a disappointment?" she asks softly.

"If this is what it means to be a disappointment," I tell her, realizing her words don't hurt nearly as much as I thought they would, "I'll gladly take it."

Her eyes shift, and I see Jack standing near the entrance to the tunnels with a rifle pointed directly at my mother. He doesn't lower it when a dozen or more Resistance fighters swarm in from the outside of the warehouse and up the ladder, all rushing toward my mom. She finally lifts her hands in surrender, her eyes still locked on me and a small smile donning her lips as someone roughly twists her hands behind her back and forces her on her knees.

"Are you okay?" a voice comes from next to me.

I turn to see Jack slowly lower his gun. I'm redirected by a Resistance fighter, then, and asked to step aside. Watching my own mother get arrested makes me dizzy. She doesn't try to fight it as they secure her hands against the small of her back. Her eyes never leave mine.

"Kate, are you good?" the voice repeats.

Thatcher steps in front of me, blocking my view. She gently pushes the pistol down and away. The noise of the warehouse comes whooshing back.

Thatcher ducks her head to catch my eyes, and I nod that, yes, I'm okay, despite it not being true in the least.

"Echo checking in. Redirected route to Rapid City. Two minutes until contact. Over," Rodrigues's voice breaks through our conversation.

I look at the radio strapped to Thatcher's side, and she grabs my arms. "We have to get out of here, right now."

Jack is there, guiding me to the front seat of a buggy. My mother is shoved into the officer's buggy along with Thatcher, Bruce, and two others.

Four fighters cram into the back seat, and everyone else sprints back to the tunnels, yelling and motioning for everyone to move. It's all a blur, really. The two vehicles accelerate away from the warehouse. The helicopter slowly rises over top of the mountains, and Jack slows, his neck craning to look at it through the windshield as it whizzes over us.

After the car is in park, we spill out to watch in absolute awe as Rodrigues seamlessly flies over and fires a single missile at the warehouse. Jack pulls me into him and acts as a human shield despite being a safe distance away. A large plume of fire skyrockets into the air, and for a moment, everything is still.

It isn't until I hear Thatcher cheer and the others follow suit that I realize I'm still clinging to Jack, and tears are falling freely down my face. "Thank you for not taking the shot," I say.

He pulls me a little tighter. "Rhiannon wouldn't have wanted me to."

I nod against him, but I know that if Jack really wanted to take out my mom, he would have. There's a nagging suspicion tickling the back of my mind that it wasn't Rhiannon he was thinking of when he put down his gun, but instead, he was thinking of *me*.

❖

News of the general being apprehended by the Resistance travels quickly. There's pure jubilation in the streets of Rapid City. It's barely past breakfast, but people are celebrating and drinking. I watch them laugh and cheer, wishing that I was jovial enough to join in.

Instead, I wiggle out of the bulletproof vest and examine the lead wedged inside. I rub at my side, still sore and already bruising and know Dani won't be thrilled that I was shot, even if her vest did save my life.

While watching NAF soldiers be escorted away, I wonder if Ryan is among them somewhere. I'm desperate to know if Dani is okay, and I'm cursing the EMP we released for knocking out just about every single source of communication.

"Are you okay?" Jack asks without looking at me as we sit outside the only medical building still standing.

I sigh. "Everyone keeps asking me that."

"Yeah, me too," he says and presses his hand against his side. "Are you, though?"

My thoughts drift to my mother being whisked away, the clear disappointment probably permanently etched into her features and of my father still hiding in his bunker. I think of Dani, Lucas, and the rest of the White River crew. How over these past couple of months, they've become my family. That even though things with my parents are as complicated as ever, I have them to help me through it. I finally have a support system that believes in me and stands up for me.

A couple children run by in the street, laughing and pretending to be piloting the helicopter, and I take a deep breath. We're progressing. After today, we have to. And that's all I've ever wanted.

"Yeah," I say quietly, glancing at him. "Yeah, I think I will be."

He nods like he gets it, and I have a feeling that he does. "Do you think this is the end of the war?" he asks through a long sigh.

I take my time considering. "I hope so. I'm kind of looking forward to living a normal life and not hiding or fighting."

He nods. "Me too."

"There you are," someone breaks into our conversation. I use my hand to block out the sun despite Lucas's sunglasses, and squint at the figure towering over us. It's Thatcher. She holds out her radio and smiles. "She's asking for you."

For the first time all morning, excitement surges through my exhausted body, and I take the radio. Thatcher's smile grows, and she walks away, accepting a drink from Kimi, who has come down the hill to celebrate.

Jack pats my shoulder and stands, making a strangled kind of noise as he does. "I'm going to go get this checked out and maybe find a bottle of whiskey." He slowly heads to the door of the medical building behind us.

"Jack?" I call, stopping him. He turns. "Thank you." I say it again, hoping he understands that I mean it. His eyes meet mine, and he tips his head forward just slightly before disappearing inside.

I lick my lips and hold the radio in both hands and press the talk button. "Dani?"

"Hi," she says breathlessly.

I close my eyes, relieved to hear her voice, and smile. "Hi."

EPILOGUE

DANI

The sun feels unusually hot today. Sweat trickles down the back of my neck and over my brow. I squint through my sunglasses at Mike, hoping my hands won't slip in these gloves.

"A little to the left," he instructs. Jack and I shift the large heavy sign. "No, no, that's too much, go back." He waves his hands in the direction we just came from. Jack and I share a look and inch the sign back. "Keep going."

"Hey, maybe you want to get off your ass and do it yourself," Jack yells, clearly just as frustrated as I am.

Elise slowly stops next to her husband with a tray of cold drinks. "Language," she chastises.

"The baby can't hear me from inside there," Jack says, annoyed.

"You don't know that." Elise squints up at the sign and holds out the tray. "It looks fine. Get down here and drink something."

Lucas quickly ties my side of the beam, temporarily securing it and then hurries to Jack's side and does the same.

I stand, arching my back and stretching out my shoulders, glad to have a break in this heat. Carefully, I follow Jack and Lucas down the high ladder propped against the side of the newly rebuilt tavern. After pulling off my gloves, I stick them in my back pocket and wipe my brow with the back of my hand.

Elise offers me a cold glass of lemon water, and I take it with a sincere thanks. I turn and look up at the hand-carved sign.

Rhi's Tavern.

The wood was salvaged from her original building, stained, and painted red with hand-carved white lettering.

"It looks great," Elise says, lowering the tray and resting one hand on her large stomach. "She would've loved it."

"Yeah," I agree. "She would've."

"It looks good."

I smile and turn to see Kate walking in our direction, Roscoe trotting happily by her side. Her blue T-shirt matches her blue mirrored sunglasses, and wild strands of hair that have escaped her messy bun stick to the sides of her face. She stops next to me and puts her hands on her hips. She's slightly out of breath and admires the newest addition to the tavern. Sweat glistens on her sun-kissed skin. She completely takes my breath away.

"How's the fence?" I ask, leaning in to steal a brief kiss.

Kate smiles and makes a familiar hum when I pull away. She lifts her shirt away from her body, airing herself out. It's impossible not to stare. "It's getting there. Miguel and Anthony are finishing up."

A low thumping redirects our attention to the sky, and it isn't long before Rodrigues and the helicopter come into view with a large shipment of wooden beams and other building supplies dangling underneath it. Roscoe barks happily and takes off to the front gates. Rodrigues carefully lowers the load outside of the front perimeter.

Kate, Jack and I go to meet her at the entrance, where there are already a few people waiting to help detach the supplies. We stand back in awe as she lands the helicopter once the materials have been cleared. She's been coming every other week for the past six months with items to help us rebuild White River, but the sight of the helicopter overhead never gets old.

Rodrigues pops open her door and greets a few of the people waiting to load the materials into the back of my Jeep. Once her feet touch the ground, she bends to give Roscoe a proper hello. After a few belly rubs, she pats her thigh, and he happily follows her to us. Ever since she was named commander of the new aerial unit, she's had an unmistakable swagger in her step.

It'd be annoying if it didn't look so good on her.

"Beautiful day," she says in greeting and extends her arm to Kate and me. She smiles at Jack, who offers a quick hello before running his hand through his mohawk.

"Where are you coming from?" Kate asks and leads us back inside toward the new tavern, probably to get Rodrigues something to eat and drink.

"Sioux City." She pulls off her fingerless gloves and shoves them in her front pocket.

Kate glances over her shoulder. "She flying okay?"

Rodrigues smiles. "Like a dream." She pulls a folded piece of paper from her back pocket and hands it to Kate. "From your dad."

Kate takes the letter but doesn't open it. Instead, she twists it around in her hands. "Thanks. How is he?"

"Good. Looking forward to seeing you next week."

She hesitates slightly. "And Ryan?" She doesn't always ask about him, but when she does, the answer is always the same.

"Also good."

Kate nods, expecting the response but also looking somewhat disappointed. The last time I asked Kate why she didn't reach out to him herself, she told me he was busy being the advisor to the new general and didn't want to waste his time.

I didn't bother telling her that she could never be a waste of time.

Kate kicks at the dirt a little, not looking at Rodrigues. I know she wants to ask about her mom, too, but she won't, though she keeps up with the news through various couriers and other contacts. Sometimes, she sits with Jess, and they listen to the trial on the radio. I don't ask much about it, but I know she's going to be serving a significant amount of time in jail under the new government.

We reach the tavern, and Rodrigues stops. She puts her hands on her hips and examines the progress we've made since her last visit. "This place is really coming together."

"Hopefully, we'll finish most of it before the really hot months," I say.

"Is everyone back?" she asks, nodding hello to a few people who pass by.

"We got word to most of them that we're rebuilding White River. Everyone who wanted to be here is here," I say with both elation at them returning and regret that some didn't feel like they could.

"You'll be thriving again in no time," she smiles and pats my back. "Especially with Mayor Kate Turner in charge."

She groans. "I'm not mayor."

I smile. "You're kind of the mayor."

"What's the news on the political end?" Kate asks, changing the subject to my very least favorite topic. I groan. Politics. I want absolutely nothing to do with it. Kate shoots me a look. "We need to know what's going on."

"Why? As long as they stay out of my town, I don't care what they do."

Kate laughs. "Because it affects you, too."

I flash her a smile. "And this is why you're the mayor."

A very welcome cool breeze passes through, and Rodrigues pushes the stray wisps of hair from her face. "President Price is making progress. It's a slow process trying to get all of the other generals on board, but with Foley helping, I think it'll be done by winter."

"Is Foley still pissed she didn't get the gig leading the NAF?" Jack asks.

Rodrigues shrugs. "A little but only in private."

"President Thatcher Price," I say with fondness and a touch of amusement. "There's no way I am ever calling her madam president."

"Are we going to stand outside and melt, or can we go inside away from the sun?" Elise asks, closing the distance between us. "Hey, Jenisis."

"Hey, Mama," Rodrigues smiles and accepts a long hug. "How are you feeling?"

"Fat."

"No." Rodrigues shakes her head and smiles, pushing her sunglasses on top of her head to make a show of checking her out. "You look amazing. You're glowing."

"It's sweat," Jack supplies.

Mike smacks the back of his head.

Jack rubs at the spot. "Ow! What?"

Mike wags his finger at him. Jack should know that any teasing of Elise is off-limits for the foreseeable future. Ignoring the comment, Rodrigues keeps her attention on Elise. "Are you sure you won't let me fly you to Rapid City? It won't take long at all."

"No, thank you," Elise dismisses quickly, resting her hands on her belly. "The sky is no place for me."

Rodrigues nods, understanding. "It's just a really long drive for a checkup."

"Well, the midwife is coming to me next time. I'm signing an eviction notice for this kid." Elise stretches her back, sticking her stomach out.

"Jenisis!"

We all turn to see Darby race out of the tavern with a huge smile on her face. Lucas happily bounces out behind her.

"Darbs!" They do this weird secret handshake and end it with a hug.

"Sticking around for a bit this time?" Darby asks, her eyes wide and hopeful.

Rodrigues glances at Jack with a sly smile. "I might be persuaded to stay a little while."

He blushes and looks away, his hand back at his hair. It would be amusing if it wasn't so strange to see him actually look bashful.

Darby, completely missing the social cues, links her arm through Rodrigues's and pulls her in the direction of the tavern. "Oh good. I have this new thing I'm working on. I'll show you after lunch, though, because whatever Wyatt is cooking smells amazing."

Once they're out of earshot, Kate rounds on Jack with a mischievous and knowing smile. "You and Rodrigues, huh?"

He tries to play it off. "What are you talking about?"

"Oh please," Elise says with a scoff. "We all know you're fu—"

"Language," Jack interrupts.

"Isn't she a little young for you?" Kate interjects.

Even through his shades, I can sense his angry glare. "Isn't Dani a little young for *you*?"

Kate appears positively offended. "What?" She glances at me, and I just shrug, enjoying the exchange. "Wait, how old do you think I am?"

We reach the steps to the tavern where Darby and Rodrigues are waiting. Before any of us can enter, Mike turns, holding out his hands to stop us. "Wait. Everybody wait right here for a minute."

The others do so without hesitation as I glance around, confused. "What? Why?"

Lucas puts his hand on my shoulder. "There are times when patience outweighs persistence." His expression is serious, but I don't miss the twinkle in his eyes.

"Issue sixteen," Darby says over her shoulder.

I groan. "Dammit, Darby, it's issue twelve. Can someone please tell me what's going on?" I ask, desperate to get inside and have a strong drink.

Jess opens the door and steps outside, Wyatt directly behind her, followed by William and Ericson.

Startled to see them, I glance at Kate, and back. "When did you get here?" It's been months since I've seen William and only once since he and Lucas pulled me off the runway in Ellsworth.

William doesn't bother answering, but it's the little smile he's trying to hide that concerns me the most. I hate being the center of attention, and they're clearly up to something.

"Dani." Elise stands in front of me and takes a deep breath. "Before you arrived, White River was a humble little town. We didn't have a lot of trade connections or someone who would really stand up and fight for us. Because of you, we gained a champion, resources, and connections to cities we never dreamed we'd be linked to. Sure, we landed on a hard time and lost people we loved..." She stops when her voice cracks.

I look away, knowing that she's thinking about Rhiannon. I swallow the lump in my throat and try to blink away the sting of tears. Kate touches my arm, and it grounds me.

"But if it hadn't been for you," Elise continues, "we wouldn't have won this war. We wouldn't have this second chance at rebuilding our home and coming back stronger. Without you, none of us might be standing here today. And for that, we want to thank you."

Kate nudges me a little, and when I look up, Elise is smiling at me. All of them are smiling. Elise nods, and Wyatt opens the doors to the tavern. I'm confused when Kate leads me inside as though this wasn't the first building we restored all those months ago.

Regardless, stepping over the threshold and leading the group within feels different this time. Like a fresh start. Nobody says anything once we're all inside. Instead, they all gather near the front and watch me. I'm not sure what they're expecting or what they're waiting for. I push my sunglasses on top of my head and look around, wondering who else may pop out of nowhere and surprise me. I frown back at the group and glance at Kate, wondering what I'm missing. She makes a subtle motion with her elbow to the right. Looking in that direction, I see it.

Rhiannon's old jukebox.

My heart jumps to my throat. I thought it was lost in the fire. I whip my head back to the group with wide eyes. "What is this? How?"

Everyone looks at Kate. She offers a slight shrug as if this wasn't the biggest surprise of my life. "We wanted to do something special for you. For this place. Darby had the idea of restoring the jukebox. Rodrigues found one back east when she was on a supply run months ago. She got it to my dad, and he gutted it and worked on the parts we needed."

Darby nods and smiles excitedly. "Then, Jenisis got them all to me, and I installed them and added more songs from your music player. But really, we all—"

I interrupt by pulling Darby into a hug. It catches her by surprise if the *whoosh* of her breath is any indication. She awkwardly pats my back but eventually hugs me back.

I have no words. There's no way I can properly thank them. No way I can actually express how much I love them.

"Go on. Take her out for a spin," Lucas calls, and I finally release Darby.

I clasp arms with Rodrigues, thanking her. She will never fully understand the significance of this moment, but she nods as if she does.

I walk to the old jukebox and run my hands along its charred and roughly patched sides. It reminds me of Rhiannon. She would've been so happy to have this back, to have her tavern up and running with Wyatt at the helm, and to have her friends together all in one place.

My hand shakes as I slowly scroll through the songs. They're all there. Every single one of them. And each one holds a special memory of this place, of my life here. A familiar title catches my eye, and my hand stops, my heart beating wildly in my chest. I smile, selecting the song. Slow and familiar notes play through the tavern, the beautiful melody stirring up the butterflies in my stomach.

"Songbird."

The first notes swim from the speakers, and I turn, my gaze focused on only one person. She recognizes the familiar piano and smiles softly from across the room, still surrounded by our friends. Our family.

When I reach her, I hold out my hand. "I believe I owe you a dance," I say, recalling how I denied her all those months ago in my living room. I was a different person then. "And what good is music if not for dancing?" I ask, repeating the sentiment she had asked me that day.

She blushes and takes my hand, letting me pull her close. I don't think I've ever been this at peace, and it's all because of the woman in my arms. "Aren't you afraid you'll fall madly in love with me?" she teases, asking me the same question that she did before. Her beautiful hazel eyes sparkle in the low light, and my heart soars, confident and complete.

I chuckle and put one hand on the small of her back and with my other, thread my fingers through hers. Leaning forward, I bump our noses and happily sigh. "I'm already madly in love with you."

About the Authors

Allisa Bahney

Allisa grew up in a small town that's buried in the cornfields of Iowa. She works in education and has a master of science degree in effective teaching with minors in creative writing and film studies. Allisa spends her free time coaching middle school volleyball, binge-watching TV shows, writing, playing with her children, and entertaining her wife. She loves to travel and misses her dog literally every minute she's not with her.

Kristin Keppler

Kristin was born and raised in the DC metro area. A lifelong sci-fi and film nerd with a degree in production technology, she owns a small media production company that endeavors to help other small businesses succeed. Kristin spends the majority of her free time helping her husband wrangle their two young sons and their dogs. Any additional free time is devoted to writing, gaming, and cheering on the Virginia Tech Hokies.

Books Available from Bold Strokes Books

A Degree to Die For by Karis Walsh. A murder at the University of Washington's Classics Department brings Professor Antigone Weston and Sergeant Adriana Kent together—first as opposing forces, and then allies as they fight together to protect their campus from a killer. (978-1-63679-365-8)

A Talent Within by Suzanne Lenoir. Evelyne, born into nobility, and Annika, a peasant girl with a deadly secret, struggle to change their destinies in Valmora, a medieval world controlled by religion, magic, and men. (978-1-63679-423-5)

Finders Keepers by Radclyffe. Roman Ashcroft's past, it seems, is not so easily forgotten when fate brings her and Tally Dewilde together—along with an attraction neither welcomes. (978-1-63679-428-0)

Homeland by Kristin Keppler and Allisa Bahney. Dani and Kate have finally found themselves on the same side of the war, but a new threat from the inside jeopardizes the future of the wasteland. (978-1-63679-405-1)

Just One Dance by Jenny Frame. Will Taylor Spark and her new business to make dating special—the Regency Romance Club—bring sparkle back to Jaq Bailey's lonely world? (978-1-63679-457-0)

On My Way There by Jaycie Morrison. As Max traverses the open road, her journey of impossible love, loss, and courage mirrors her voyage of self-discovery leading to the ultimate question: If she can't have the woman of her dreams, will the woman of real life be enough? (978-1-63679-392-4)

Transitioning Home by Heather K O'Malley. An injured soldier realizes they need to transition to really heal. (978-1-63679-424-2)

Truly Enough by JJ Hale. Chasing the spark of creativity may ignite a burning romance or send a friendship up in flames. (978-1-63679-442-6)

Vintage and Vogue by Kelly and Tana Fireside. When tech whiz Sena Abrigo marches into small-town Owen Station, she turns librarian Hazel Butler's life upside down in the most wonderful of ways, setting off an explosive series of events, threatening their chance at love…and their very lives. (978-1-63679-448-8)

Broken Fences by Jo Hemmingwood. Former army sergeant Seneca Twist has difficulty adjusting to civilian life until she meets psychologist Robyn Mason and has a place to call home. (978-1-63679-414-3)

Never Kiss a Cowgirl by Ali Vali. Asher Evans dreams of winning the National Finals Rodeo in Vegas, and Reagan Wilson wants no part of something that brings back the memory of what killed her father. (978-1-63679-106-7)

Pantheon Girls by Jean Copeland. Cassie Burke never anticipated the detour life was about to take when a meeting with a prospective client reunites her with a past love and reignites the star-crossed passion they shared twenty years earlier. (978-1-63679-337-5)

Roux for Two by Aurora Rey. For TV chef Chelsea Boudreaux and hometown boy Bryce Cormier, love proves as tricky as making a good pot of gumbo. (978-1-63679-376-4)

Starting Over by Nance Sparks. Jennifer has no idea if she can mend Sam's broken soul after the sudden loss of her wife, but it's never too late for starting over. (978-1-63679-409-9)

The Accidental Bride by Jane Walsh. Spinsters Miss Grace Linfield and Miss Thea Martin travel to Gretna Green to prevent a wedding, only to discover a scandalous passion—for each other. (978-1-63679-345-0)

Three Wishes by Anne Shade. A magic lamp, a beautiful Jinni, and a cursed princess make for one unbelievable story. (978-1-63679-349-8)

Undiscovered Treasures by MJ Williamz. For Cyl and her friends Luna and Martinique, life's best treasures often appear when you're not looking. (978-1-63679-449-5)

Curse of the Gorgon by Tanai Walker. Cass will do anything to ensure Elle's safety, but is she willing to embrace the curse of the Gorgon? (978-1-63679-395-5)

Dance with Me by Georgia Beers. Scottie Templeton mixes it up on and off the dance floor with sexy salsa instructor Marisa Reyes. But can Scottie get past Marisa's connection to her ex? (978-1-63679-359-7)

Gin and Bear It by Joy Argento. Opposites really can attract, and as Kelly and Logan work together to create a loving home for rescue cat Bear, they just might find one for themselves as well. (978-1-63679-351-1)

Harvest Dreams by Jacqueline Fein-Zachary. Planting the vineyard of their dreams, Kate Bauer and Sydney Barrett must resist their attraction while battling nature and their families, who oppose both the venture and their relationship. (978-1-63679-380-1)

The No Kiss Contract by Nan Campbell. Workaholic Davy believes she can get the top spot at her firm if the senior partners think she's settling down and about to start a family, but she needs the delightful yet dubious Anna to help by pretending to be her fiancée. (978-1-63679-372-6)

Outside the Lines by Melissa Sky. If you had the chance to live forever, would you take it? Amara Rodriguez did, and it sets her on a journey to find her missing mother and unravel the mystery of her own heart. (978-1-63679-403-7)

The Value of Sylver and Gold by Michelle Larkin. When word gets out that former Boston homicide detective Reid Sylver can talk to the dead, the FBI solicits her help on a serial murder case, prompting Reid to assemble forces once again with Detective London Gold. (978-1-63679-093-0)

When It Feels Right by Tagan Shepard. Freshly out of the closet Marlene hasn't been lucky in love, but when it comes to her quirky new roommate Abby, everything just feels right. (978-1-63679-367-2)

Lucky in Lace by Melissa Brayden. Straitlaced stationery store owner Juliette Jennings's predictable life unravels when a sexy lingerie shop and its alluring owner move in next door. (978-1-63679-434-1)

Made for Her by Carsen Taite. Neal Walsh is a newly made member of the Mancuso crime family, but will her undeniable attraction to Anastasia Petrov, the wife of her boss's sworn enemy, be the ultimate test of her loyalty? (978-1-63679-265-1)

Off the Menu by Alaina Erdell. Reality TV sensation Restaurant Redo and its gorgeous host Erin Rasmussen will arrive to film in chef Taylor Mobley's kitchen. As the cameras roll, will they make the jump from enemies to lovers? (978-1-63679-295-8)

Pack of Her Own by Elena Abbott. When things heat up in a small town, steamy secrets are revealed between Alpha werewolf Wren Carne and her human mate, Natalie Donovan. (978-1-63679-370-2)

Return to McCall by Patricia Evans. Lily isn't looking for romance—not until she meets Alex, the gorgeous Cuban dance instructor at La Haven, a newly opened lesbian retreat. (978-1-63679-386-3)

So It Went Like This by C. Spencer. A candid and deeply personal exploration of fate, chosen family, and the vulnerability intrinsic in life's uncertainties. (978-1-63555-971-2)

Stolen Kiss by Spencer Greene. Anna and Louise share a stolen kiss, only to discover that Louise is dating Anna's brother. Surely, one kiss can't change everything…Can it? (978-1-63679-364-1)

The Fall Line by Kelly Wacker. When Jordan Burroughs arrives in the Deep South to paint a local endangered aquatic flower, she doesn't expect to become friends with a mischievous gin-drinking ghost who complicates her budding romance and leads her to an awful discovery and danger. (978-1-63679-205-7)

To Meet Again by Kadyan. When the stark reality of WWII separates cabaret singer Evelyn and Australian doctor Joan in Singapore, they must overcome all odds to find one another again. (978-1-63679-398-6)